A new man . . .

Tex wondered what the crowd would say if he should lean over and pull a royal flush out of Williams' ear, or a full-house from the nephew's nose. They might be surprised if they found out that the cold-eyed gunman at Williams' elbow carried a handful of Colt cartridges in his tight-shut mouth. He had no rabbits to lift out of hats, but that trick was threadbare from being overworked, anyhow. He waved both hands, a smart-Aleck grin sweeping across his face. "I've rode cayuses, punched cows, an' played draw from Texas to Montanny, an' near back ag'in. So far I ain't throwed, rolled under, or cleaned out; an' I'm allus willin' to be agreeable. Where you gents lead I'll foller, like a hungry calf after its ma." His voice had grown loud and boastful and he joined the swiftly forming card group with a swagger as it settled around the table in the barroom, his bovine conceit hiding the silent struggle going on within him.

Tex of the old days was fighting Tex of the new. The smug complacency of the local boss stirred up the desire to break him to his last cent, to make a fool of him in the way others had been broken and made ridiculous; but the new Tex won: As usual he would play Hopalong's game—which was as his opponents played, straight or crooked, as they showed the way. He had no real wish for large winnings, for if he made his expenses as he went along he would be satisfied, and he could do that from his knowledge of psychology, a knowledge gained outside of classrooms. He now had no reputation to defend or maintain, for Tex Jones was not Tex Ewalt, famed throughout cow-country. The name meant nothing. But how pleasant it would be to repeat history in this town, so far as Williams was concerned!

By Clarence Mulford
from Tom Doherty Associates

Clarence E. Mulford

TEX

F
MUL

A TOM DOHERTY ASSOCIATES BOOK
NEW YORK

JH Jon

This is a work of fiction. All the characters and events portrayed in this book are either products of the author's imagination or are used fictitiously.

TEX

A Forge Book
Published by Tom Doherty Associates, Inc.
175 Fifth Avenue
New York, NY 10010

Forge® is a registered trademark of Tom Doherty Associates, Inc.

ISBN: 0-812-56687-4

First Forge edition: February 1999

Printed in the United States of America

0 9 8 7 6 5 4 3 2 1

CONTENTS

CHAPTER I

The Trail Calls

MEMORY'S CURTAIN rises and shows a scene softened by time and blurred by forgetfulness, yet the details slowly emerge like the stars at twilight. There appears a rain-washed, wind-swept range in Montana, a great pasture level in the center, but rising on its sides like a vast, shallow saucer, with here and there a crack of more somber hue where a ravine, or sluggish stream, lead toward the distant river. Green underfoot, deep blue overhead, with a lavender and purple rim under a horizon made ragged and sharp by the not too distant mountains and foothills. An occasional deep blue gash in the rim's darker tones marks where some pass or canyon cuts through the encircling barriers. A closer inspection would reveal a half-dozen earthy hollows, the rutting holes of the once numerous buffalo which paused here on their periodic migrations. In the foreground a white ranchhouse and its flanking red buildings, framed by the gray of corral walls, nestles on the southern slope of a rise and basks in the sunlight. From it three faint trails grow more and more divergent, leading off to Everywhere. Scattered over the vast, green pastures are the grazing units of a great herd, placid and content, moving slowly and jerkily, like spilled water down a gentle, dusty slope. But in the total movement there is one thread with definite directness, even though it constantly turns from side to side in avoiding the grazing cattle. This, as being different and indicating purpose, takes our instant attention.

A rider slowly makes his way among the cattle, by force of habit observing everything without being fully conscious of it. His chaps of soft leather, worn more because of earlier associations than from any urgent need on this northern range, have the look of long service and the comfort coming from such. His hat is a dark gray sombrero, worn in a manner suggesting a cavalier of old. Over an open vest are the careless folds of a blue kerchief, and at his right hip rubs a holster with its waiting, deadly tenant. A nearer approach reveals him to be a man in middle life, lean, scrupulously neat, clean shaven, with lines of deep humor graven about his eyes and mouth, softening a habitual expression which otherwise would have been forbiddingly hard and cynical.

His roving glances reach the purple horizon and are arrested by the cerulean blue of a pass, and he checks his horse with a gesture hopelessly inadequate to express the restlessness, the annoying uncertainty of his mood, a mood fed unceasingly by an inborn yearning to wander, regardless of any aim or other condition. Here is a prospect about him which he knows cannot be improved upon; here are duties light enough practically to make him master of his time, yet heavy enough to be purposeful; his days are spent in the soothing solitudes of clean, refreshing surroundings; his evenings with men who give him perfect fellowship, wordless respect, and repressed friendship, speaking when the mood urges, or silent in that rare, all-explaining silence of strong men in perfect accord. His wants are few and automatically supplied: yet for weeks the longing to leave it all daily had grown stronger—to leave it for what? Certainly for worse: yet leave it he must.

He sat and pondered, retrospective, critical. The activities of his earlier days passed before him, with no hypocritical hiding or blunting of motives. They revealed few redeeming features, for he carelessly had followed the easy trails through the deceptive lowlands of morality, and among men and women worse even than himself in overt acts and shameless planning, yet better because they did not have his intelligence or moral standards. But he slowly rose above them as a diver rises above treacherous, lower currents, and the reason was plain to those who knew him well. First he had a courage sparkling like a jewel, unhesitant, forthright, precipitate; next he had a rare mixture of humor and cynicism which better revealed to him things in their right proportions and values; and last, but hardly least by any means, an intelligence of high order, buttressed by facts, clarified by systematic study, and edged by training. In his youth he had aimed at the practice of medicine, but gave too much attention to more imaginative targets and found, when too late, that he had hit nothing. His fondness for drinking, gambling at cards, and other weedy sowings resulted from, rather than caused, the poor aim. Certain unforgivable episodes, unforgivable because of their notoriety more than because of the things themselves, brewed a paternal tempest, upon which he had turned a scornful back, followed Horace Greeley's famous advice, and sought the healing and the sanctuary of the unasking West.

In his new surroundings he soon made a name for himself, in both meanings, and quickly dominated those whose companionship he either craved or needed. An inherent propensity for sleight of hand provided him an easy living at cards; and his deftness and certainty with a

six-gun gave him a pleasing security. However, all things
have an end. There came a time when he nearly had
reached the lowest depths of moral submersion when
he met and fought a character as strong as his own, but
in few other ways resembling him; and from that time on
he swam on the surface. It would be foolish to say that
the depths ceased to lure him, for they did, and at times
so powerfully that he scarcely could resist them. For this
he had to thank to no small degree one of the bitterest
experiences of his life: his disastrous marriage. Giving
blind love and unquestioning loyalty, he had lost both by
the unclean evidence unexpectedly presented to his
eyes. In that crisis, after the first madness, his actions
had been worthy of a nature softer than his own and he
had gone, by devious ways, back to his West and started
anew with a burning cynicism. But for the steadying influence of his one-time enemy, and the danger and the
interest in the task which Hopalong Cassidy had set before him, the domestic tragedy certainly would have
sent him plunging down to his former level or below it.

Time passed and finally brought him news of the
tragic death of his faithless wife, and he found that it
did not touch him. He had felt neither pity, sorrow, nor
relief. It is doubtful if he ever had given a thought to
the question of his freedom, for with his mental attitude it meant nothing at all to him. He had put among
his belongings the letter from his former employer,
who had known all about the affair and the names and
addresses of several of his western friends, telling him
that he was free; and hardly gave it a second thought.

Turning from his careless scrutiny of the distant pass
he rode on again and soon became aware of the sound
of hoofbeats rapidly nearing him. As he looked up a
rider topped a rise, descried him, and waved a sombrero. The newcomer dashed recklessly down the slope
and drew rein sharply at his side, a cheerful grin wreathing his homely, honest face. Pete was slow-witted, but
his sterling qualities masked this defect even in the eyes

of a man as sharp as his companion, who felt for him a strong, warm friendship.

"Hello, Tex!" said the newcomer. "What's eatin' you? You shore look glum."

Tex thought if it was plain enough for Pete Wilson to notice it, it must be plain, indeed. "Mental worms an' moral cancer, Pete," replied the cynic, smiling in spite of himself at the cogitation started in his friend by the words.

"Whatever that means," replied Pete, cautiously. "However, if it's what I reckon it is, there's just two cures." Pete was dogmatic by nature. "An' that's likker, or a new range."

"Somethin's th' matter with you today, Pete," rejoined Tex. "Yo're as quick as a reflex." He studied a moment, and added: "An' yo're dead right, too."

"There ain't no reflection needed," retorted Pete; "an' there ain't nothin' th' matter with me a-tall. I'm tellin' you common sense; but it's shore a devil of a choice. If it's likker, then *you* lose; if it's driftin' off som'ers, then *we* lose. Tell you what: Go down to Twin River an' clean 'em out at stud, if you can find anybody that ain't played you before," he suggested hopefully. "Mebby there's a stranger in town. You'll shore feel a whole lot better, then." He grinned suddenly. "You might find a travelin' man: they're so cussed smart they don't think anybody can learn 'em anythin'. Go ahead—try it!"

Tex laughed. "Where you goin'?" he abruptly demanded. He could not afford to have any temptations thrown in his way just then.

"Over Cyclone way, for Buck. Comin' along?"

Tex slowly shook his head. "I'm goin' th' other way. Wonder why we haven't got word from Hoppy or Red or Johnny?" he asked, and the question acted like alum in muddy water, clearing away his doubts and waverings, which swiftly precipitated and left the clear fluid of decision.

"Huh!" snorted Pete in frank disgust. "You wait till any of them fellers write an' there'll be a white stone over yore head with nice letterin' on it to tell lies forever. You know 'em. Comin' along with me?" he asked, wheeling, and was answered by an almost imperceptible shake of his friend's head.

"I'll shake hands with you, Pete," said Tex, holding out his deft but sinewy hand. "In case I don't see you again," he explained in answer to his friend's look of surprise. "I'm mebby driftin' before you get back."

"Cuss it!" exploded Pete. "I'm allus talkin' too blamed much. Now I've gone an' done it!"

"You've only hastened it a little," assured Tex, gripping the outstretched hand spasmodically. "Cheer up; I don't aim to stay away forever!" He spurred his mount and shot away up the incline, Pete looking after him and slowly shaking his head.

When the restless puncher stopped again it was at the kitchen door of the white ranchhouse. As he swung from the saddle something stung him where his trousers were tight and he stopped his own jump to grab the horse, which had been stung in turn. A snicker and a quick rustle sounded under the summer kitchen and Tex took the coiled rope from his saddle, deftly unfastening the restraining knot. The rustling sounded again, frantic and sustained, followed by a half-defiant, half-supplicating jeer.

"You can't do it, under here!" said Pickles, reloading the bean-shooter from a bulging cheek. "I can shoot yore liver out before you can whirl it!" Pickles was quite a big boy now, but threatened never to grow dignified; and besides, he had been badly spoiled by everybody on the ranch.

"Whirling livers never appealed to me," rejoined Tex, putting the rope back. "Never," he affirmed decidedly; "but I'm goin' to whirl yourn some of these days, an' you with it!"

"Those he loves, he annoys," said a low, sweet voice,

its timbre stimulating the puncher like a draught of wine. His sombrero sweeping off as he turned, he bowed to the French Rose, wife of the big-hearted half-owner of the ranch. If only he had chosen a woman like this one!

"I seem to remember him annoyin' Dave Owens, at near half a mile, with Hoppy's Sharps," he slowly replied. "Nobody ever told me that he loved Dave a whole lot." At the momentary cloud the name brought to her face he shook his head and growled to himself. "I'm a fool, ma'am, these days," he apologized; "but it strikes me that you ought to smile at that name—it shore played its unwilling part in giving you a good husband; an' Buck a mighty fine wife. Where *is* Buck?"

"Inside the house, walking rings around the table—he seems so, so—" she shrugged her shoulders hopelessly and stepped aside to let Tex enter.

"I don't know what he seems," muttered Tex as he passed in; "but I know what he is—an' that's just a plain, ornery fool." He shook his head at such behavior by any man who was loved by the French Rose.

Buck stopped his pacing and regarded him curiously, motioning toward an easy chair.

"Standin's good enough for me, for I'm itchin' with th' same disease that you imagine is stalkin' you," said Tex, looking at his old friend with level, disapproving gaze. "It don't matter with me, but it's plain criminal with you. I'm free to go; yo're not. An' I'm tellin' you frank that if I had th' picket stake that's holdin' you, all h—l couldn't tempt me. Yo're a plain, d—d fool—an' you know it!"

Buck leaned back against the edge of the table and thoughtfully regarded his companion. "It ain't so much that, as it is Hoppy, an' Red, an' Johnny," he replied, spreading out his hands in an eloquent gesture. "They could write, anyhow, couldn't they?" he demanded.

"Shore," affirmed Tex, grinning. "How long ago was it that you answered their last letters?" He leaned back and laughed outright at the guilty expression on his friend's face. "I thought so! Strong on words, but cussed poor on example."

"I reckon yo're right," muttered Buck. "But that south range shore calls me strong, Tex."

" 'Whither thou goest, I go' was said by a woman," retorted Tex. " 'Yore people are my people; yore God, my God.' I'm sayin' it works both ways. You ought to go down on yore knees for what's come to you. An' you will, one of these days. Think of Hoppy's loss—an' you'll do it before mornin'. But I didn't come in to preach common sense to a lunatic—I come to get my time, an' to say good-bye."

Buck nodded. Vaguely disturbed by some unnamed, intermittent fever, he had been quick to read the symptoms of restlessness in another, especially in one who had been as close to him as Tex had been. He went over to an old desk, slowly opened a drawer and took out a roll of bills and a memorandum.

"Here," he said, holding both out. "Far as I know it's th' same as when you gave it to me. Ought to be seven hundred, even. Count it, to make shore." While Tex took it and shoved it into his pocket uncounted and crumpled the memorandum, Buck also was reaching into a pocket, and counted off several bills from the roll it gave up. These he gravely handed to his companion, smiling to hide the ache of losing another friend.

"I shore haven't earned it all," mused Tex, looking down at the wages in his hand. "I reckon I'm doin' this ranch a favor by leavin', for there ain't no real job up here no more for any man as expensive as I am. You got th' whole country eatin' out of yore hand, an' th' first thing you know th' cows will catch th' habit an' brand an' count 'emselves to save you th' trouble of doin' it."

"You'll be doin' us a bigger favor when you come back, one of these days," grinned Buck. "You shore did yore share in trainin' it to eat out of my hand. For a while it looked like it would eat th' hand—an' it would 'a', too. Aimin' to ride down?"

Tex's eyes twinkled. "How'd you come to figger I'm goin' down?"

Buck smiled.

"No, reckon not," said Tex. "Ridin' as far's th' railroad. I'll leave my cayuse with Smith. When one of th' boys goes down that way he can get it. I'll pay Smith for a month's care." Reading the unspoken question in his friend's eyes, he carelessly answered it. "Don't know where I'm goin'. Reckon I'll get down to th' SV before I stop. That'd be natural, with Red an' Hoppy stayin' with Johnny."

"They might need you, too," suggested Buck, hopefully. If he couldn't be with his distant friends himself, he at least wished as many of them to be together as was possible.

"I'm copperin' that," grunted Tex. His eyes shone momentarily. "Yo're forgettin' that our best three are together. Lord help any misguided fools that prod 'em sharp. Well, I'm dead shore to drift back ag'in some day; but as you say, those south ranges shore do pull a feller's heart." He looked shrewdly at his friend and his face beamed from a sudden thought. "We're a pair of fools," he laughed. "You ain't got th' wander itch! You don't want to go jack-rabbitin' all over th' country, like me! All you want is that southwest country, with yore wife an yore friends on th' same ranch; down in th' cactus country, where th' winters ain't what they are up here. I'm afraid my brain's atrophied, not havin' been used since Dave Owens rolled down from his ambush with Hoppy's slugs in him for ballast."

Buck looked at him with eager, hopeful intentness and his sigh was one of great relief and thankfulness. He need not be ashamed of that longing, now vague and nameless no longer. His head snapped back and he stood erect, and his voice thrilled with pride. Tex had put his finger on the trouble, as Tex always did. "I've been as blind as a rattler in August!" he exclaimed.

"Not takin' th' time to qualify that blind-rattler-in-August phrase, I admits yo're right," beamed Tex. He arose, shoved out his hand for the quick, tight grasp of his friend and wheeled to leave, stopping short as he found himself face to face with Rose Peters. "A happy omen!" he cried. "Th' first thing I see at th' beginnin' of my journey is a rose."

She smiled at both of them as she blocked the door, and the quick catch in her voice did not escape Tex Ewalt.

"I was but in the other room," she said, her face alight. "I could not but hear, for you both speak loud. I am so glad, M'sieu Tex—that now I know why my man is so—so restless. Ruth, she said what I think, always. We are sorry that you mus' go—but we know you will not forget your friends, and will come back again some day."

Buck put his arm around his wife's shoulders and smiled. "An' if he brings th' other boys back with him, we'll find room for 'em all, eh Rose?" He looked at his friend. "We're shore goin' to miss you, Tex. Good luck. We'll expect you when we see you."

Tex bowed to Rose and backed into the curious Pickles, whom he lightly spanked as a fitting farewell; and soon the noise of his departure drummed softer and softer into the south.

CHAPTER II

Refreshed Memories

THE DUSTY, grimy, almost paintless accommodation train, composed of engine, combination smoking-baggage car, and one day coach, rumbled and rattled, jerked and swayed over the uneven roadbed, the clicking at the rail joints sensible both to tactual and auditory nerves, and calling attention to the disrepair into which the whole line had fallen. In the smoking compartment of the baggage car sat Tex Ewalt, sincerely wishing that he had followed his first promptings and chosen the saddle in preference to this swifter method of traveling.

All day he had suffered heat, dust, cinders, and smoke after a night of the same. It had been bad enough on the main line, but after leaving the junction conditions had grown steadily worse. All day he had crossed a yellow gray desolation, flat and unending, under a dirty blue sky and a dust-filled air shimmering with heat waves. He had peered at a drab, distant horizon which seemed hardly to change as it crept eastward past him, at all times barely more than a thin circle about as interesting and colorful as a bleached hoop from some old, weather-beaten barrel. Wherever he had looked, it had been to see sun-burned grass and clouds of imponderable dust, the latter sucked up by the train and sent whirling into every crack and crevice; occasional white spots darting rearward he knew to be the grim, limy skulls of herbiverous animals; arrow-like trails cut deep into the drought-cursed earth, and not too frequently a double line of straggling, dispirited willows, cottonwoods, and box elders, marked the course of some prairie creek, whose characteristic, steep earth banks, often undermined, now enclosed sun-dried mud, curling like heated scales, with here and there pools of noisome water hidden under scabs of scum. Mile after mile of this had dulled him, familiar as he had once been with the sight, and he sat apathetic, dispirited and glum, too miserable to accept the pressing invitation of a traveling cardsharp to sit into a game of draw poker. Gradually the mild, long swells of the prairie had grown shorter, sharper, and higher; gradually the soil had become rockier and the creek beds deeper below the rims of their banks. The track wound more and more as it twisted and turned among the hills, and for some hours he had noticed a constant rising, which now became more and more apparent as the top of the watershed drew nearer.

He dozed fitfully at times and once the sharper had roused him by touching his shoulder to ask him again to take cards in a game. To this invitation Tex had opened his eyes, looked up at the smiling poker devotee and made a slight motion, dozing off again as the surprised gambler moved away from one he now knew to be of the same calling as himself. Towns had followed each other at increasingly long intervals, insensibly changing in their aspect, and the horizon steadily had been narrowing. Here and there along the dried beds of the creeks were rude cabins and shacks, each not far from an abandoned sluice and cradle. Between the hills the pastures grew smaller and smaller, their sides more precipitous, but as they shrunk, the number of cattle on them seemed to increase. Rough buildings of wood or stone began to replace the low sod dugouts of a few hours ago, and he knew that he was rapidly nearing his destination.

Suddenly a ribbon-like scar on the horizon caught his eye. It ran obliquely from a northeastern point of his vista southwesterly across the pastures, hills, and valleys, like a lone spoke in some great wheel, of which the horizon was both felloe and tire. At this he sat up with a show of interest. Judging from its direction, and from what he remembered of it at this section of its length, it would cross the track some miles farther on. He nodded swiftly at this old-time friend of his cattle-driving days—he had been a fool not to have remembered it and the cow-town not far ahead, but the names of all the mushroom towns he had been in during his career in the West had not remained in his memory. Years rolled backward in a flash. He could see the distant, plodding caravans of homesteaders, or the long, disciplined trains of the freighters, winding over the hills and across the flats, their white canvas wagon covers flashing against the sky, the old, dirty covers emphasizing the newness and whiteness of their numerous patches. But on this nearing trail, winding into the southwest there had been a different migration. He almost could see the spread-out herd moving deliberately forward, the idling riders, the point and swing men, and the plodding, bumping chuck wagon with its bumptious cook. This trail, a few hundred yards wide, beaten by countless hoofs, had deepened and deepened as the wind carried away the dust, and if left to itself would be discernible after the passing of many years.

The name of the town ahead and on this old trail brought a smile to his lips, a smile that was pleasantly reminiscent; but with the name of the town came nearly forgotten names of men, and the smile changed into one that was not pleasant to look upon. There was Williams, Gus Williams, often referred to as "Mutton-head." He had been a bully, a sure-thing gambler, herd trimmer, and cattle thief in a small way, but he had been only a petty pilferer of hoofed property, for his streak of caution was well developed. Tex had not seen him, or heard of him, for twenty years, never since he had shot a gun out of Williams' hand and beat him up in a corner of his own saloon.

The rapidly enlarging ribbon drew nearer and more distinct, and soon it crossed the track and ran into the south. He remembered the wide, curving bend it took here: there had been a stampede one rainy night when he was off trick and rolled up in his blanket under the chuck wagon. They had reason to suspect that the cattle were sent off in their mad flight through the dark by human agency. Two days had been spent in combing the rough plain and in rounding up the scattered herd, and there had been a sizable number lost.

A deeper tone leaped into the dull roar of the train and told of a gully passing under the track. It ran off at a slight angle, the dried bed showing more numerous signs of human labors and habitations, and when the train came to a bumping, screeching stop at a ramshackle one-room station he knew that he was at the end of his ride and within three stations from the end of the line, which here turned sharply toward the northwest, baffled by the treacherous sands of the river, whose bank it paralleled for sixty miles. Had he gone on in the train he would have come no closer to his objective and would have to face a harder country for man and horse. Gunsight, where his three friends were located, lay about a hundred miles southwest of the bend in the track; but because of the sharp bend it lay farther from the station beyond. From where he now was, the riding would not be unpleasant and the ford across the river was shallower, the greater width of the stream offset by a more sluggish current. This ford was treacherous in high water and not passable after sudden rises for a day or two, because the force of the swollen current stirred up the unstable sands of the bottom. As a veteran of the old cattle trails he knew what a disturbed river bottom often meant.

The wheezing exhaust and the complaining panting of the all but discarded engine added dismal sounds to a dismal view. He stiffly descended the steps, a bulging gunny sack over his shoulder and a rolled blanket and a sheathed rifle fully utilized his other arm and hand. Dropping his burdens to the ground he paused to look around him.

It was just a frontier town, ugly, patched, sprawling, barely existent, and an eyesore even to the uncritical; and cursed further by Kansas politics which at this time were not as stalwart as they once had been, reminding one of the mediocre sons of famous fathers. In place of the old daring there now were trickery and subtle meannesses; in place of hot hatreds were now smoldering grudges; where once old-time politicians "shot it out" in the middle of the street, there now were furtive crawlings and treacherous shots from the dark. Like all towns it had a name—it will suffice if we know it as Windsor. Being neither in the mining country nor on the cattle range, and being in an out-of-the-way position even on the merging strip between the two, it undoubtedly would have died a natural death except for the fortuitous chance which had led the branch-line railroad to reach its site. The shifting cattle drives and a short-lived townsite speculation had been the causes for the rails coming; then the drives stopped at nearer terminals and the speculation blew up—but the rails remained. This once flamboyantly heralded "artery of commerce" swiftly had atrophied and now was hardly more than a capillary, and its diurnal pulsation

was just sufficient to keep the town about one degree
above coma.

Tex sneered openly, luxuriously, aggressively, and
for all the world to see. He promised himself that he
would not remain here very long. Before him lay the
squalid dirt street with its cans and rubbish, the bloated
body of a dog near the platform, a dead cat farther along.
There were several two-story frame buildings, evidently
built while the townsite game was on. The rest were
one-story shacks, and he remembered most of them.

He picked up his belongings and sauntered into the
station to wait until the agent had finished his business
with the train crew, and that did not take long.

The agent stepped into the dusty, dirty room,
coughed, nodded, and passed into his partitioned office. In a moment he was out again, looked closely at the
puncher and decided to risk a smile and a word: "Is there
anything I can do for you?" he hazarded.

Tex put his sombrero beside him on the bench and
wiped his forehead with a sleeve. He saw that his companion was slight, not too healthy, and appeared to be
friendly and intelligent; but in his eyes lay the shadow
of fear.

"Mebby you can tell me th' best place to eat an'
sleep; an' th' best place to buy a horse," he replied.

"Williams' hotel is the best in town, and I'd ask him
about the horse. You might do better if you didn't say I
recommended him to you."

"Not if you don't want me to," responded Tex, smiling sardonically for some inexplicable reason. "Reckon
he'd eat you because yo're sendin' him trade? Don't
worry; I won't say you told me."

"So far as I am concerned it don't matter. It's you I'm
thinking about."

Tex stretched, crossed his legs, and smiled. "In that
case I'll use my own judgment," he replied. "Been
workin' for th' railroad very long?"

"Little too long, I'm afraid," answered the agent,

coughing again, "but I've been out here only two months." He hesitated, looked a little self-conscious, and continued. "It's my lungs, you know. I got a transfer for my health. If I can stick it out here I have hopes of slowly improving, and perhaps of getting entirely well."

"If you can stick it out? Meanin' yo're findin' it too monotonous an' lonely?' queried Tex.

The agent laughed shortly, the look of fear again coming into his eyes. "Anything but the first; and so far as being lonely is concerned, I find that my sister is company enough."

Tex cogitated and recrossed his legs. "From what I have already seen of this town I'd gamble she is; but a man's allus a little better off if he can herd with his own sex once in a while. So it ain't monotonous? Have many trains a day?" he asked, knowing from his perusal of the time-table that there were but two.

"One in and one out. You passed the other on the siding at Willow, if you've come from beyond there."

"Reckon I remember it. Much business here to keep you busy?"

"Not enough to tire even a—lunger!" He said the word bitterly and defiantly.

"That's a word I never liked," said Tex. "It's too cussed brutal. Some people derive a great deal of satisfaction in calling a spade a spade, and that is quite proper so far as spades are concerned; but why go further? A man can't allus help a thing like tuberculosis—especially if he's makin' a livin' for two. Yo're not very high up here, but I reckon th' air's right. It's th' winter that's goin' to count ag'in' you. You got to watch that. You might do better across th' west boundary. Any doctor in town?"

"There's a man who calls himself a doctor. His favorite prescription is whiskey."

"Yeah? For his patients?"

"For his patients and himself, too."

"Huh," grunted the puncher. He cleared his throat.

"I once read about yore trouble—in a dictionary," he explained, grinning. "It said milk an' aigs, among other things; open air, both capitalized, day *an'* night; plenty of sleep, no worryin', an' no excitement. Have many heavy boxes to rustle?"

"No," answered the agent, looking curiously at his companion. "I had plenty of milk and eggs, but the milk is getting scarce and the eggs are falling off. I—" he stopped abruptly, shrugging his shoulders. "D—n it, man! It isn't so much for myself!"

"No," said Tex, slowly arising. "A man usually feels that way about it. I'm goin' up to th' hotel. May drop around to see you tomorrow if I'm in town."

"I'll be mighty glad to see you; but there's no use for you to make enemies," replied the agent, leading the way outside. He stopped and took hold of a trunk, to roll it into the building.

"Han's off," said Tex smiling and pushing him aside. "You forgot what th' dictionary said. Of course this wouldn't kill you, but I'm stiff from ridin' in yore palatial trains, mile after weary mile." Rolling the trunk through the door and against the wall, he picked up his belongings, gravely saluted and went on his way whistling cheerily.

The agent looked after him wistfully, shook his head and retired into his coop.

Tex rambled down the street and entered Williams' hotel, held a brief conversation with the clerk, took up his key, and followed instructions. The second door on the right-hand side, upstairs, let him into a small room which contained a chair, bed, and washstand. There was a rag rug before the bed, and this touch of high life and affluence received from him a grave and dignified bow. "Charmed, I'm sure," he said, and went over to the window to view the roofs of the shacks below it. He sniffed and decided that somewhere near there was a stable. Putting his belongings in a corner, he took out his shaving kit and went to work with it, after which he walked downstairs, bought a drink and treated its dispenser to a cigar, which he knew later would be replaced and the money taken instead.

"Hot," said Tex as though he had made a discovery. "An' close," he added in an effort not to overlook anything.

"Very," replied the bartender. This made the twenty-third time he had said that word in reply to this undoubted statement of fact since morning. He did not know that his companion had used it because it was colorless and would stamp him, sub-consciously, as being no different from the common human herd in town. "Hottest summer since last year," said the bartender, also for the twenty-third time. He grinned expectantly.

Tex turned the remark over in his mind and laughed suddenly, explosively. "That's a good un! Cussed if it didn't nearly get past me! 'Hottest summer since last year!' Ha-ha-ha! Cuss it, it *is* good!" He was on the proper track to make a friend of the second man he had met. "Have another cigar," he urged. Good-will and admiration shone on his face. "Gosh! Have to spring that un on th' boys! Ha-ha-ha!"

"Better spring it before fall—it might not last through th' winter, though some'r tougher'n others," rejoined the bartender, his grin threatening to inconvenience his ears.

Tex choked and coughed up some of the liquor, the tears starting from his eyes. He had meant it for an imitation choke, but misjudged. Coughing and laughing at once he hung onto the bar by his elbows and writhed from side to side. "Gosh! You oughter—warn a fel—ler!" he reproved. "How'd'y think of 'em like that?"

"Come easy, somehow," chuckled the pleased dispenser of liquor. "Stayin' in town long?" he asked.

"Cussed if I know," frankly answered Tex. He became candid and confidential. "Expectin' a letter, an' I can't leave till it comes. Where's th' post office? Yeah?

Guess I can find it, then. Reckon I'll drift along an' see if there's anythin' come in for me. See you tonight."

Crossing the street he sauntered along it until he came to the building which sheltered the post office, and he stopped, regarded the sign over its door with open approval, and then gravely salaamed.

" 'Williams's Mecca,' " he read. "Sign painters are usually generous with their esses. Wonder why? Must be a secret sign of th' guild. Why are monument works usually called 'monumental'? Huh: Wonder if it is th' same Williams? If it is, where did *he* ever hear of 'Mecca'?" It was a refreshing change from the names so common to stores in towns of this kind and size. "An' cussed if it ain't appropriate, too!" he muttered. "In a place like this what could more deserve that name than the general store and post office, unless it be the saloons, hotels, and gambling houses?" He started for the door, eager to see whom he would meet.

A burly, dark-visaged individual looked up at his entry. He would have been amazed had he known that a score of years had slipped from him and that he was a callow, furtive-eyed man in his early twenties, cringing in a corner with his present visitor standing contemptuously over him and daring him to get up again.

Tex's face remained unchanged, except for a foolish smile which crept over it as he gave greeting. "Though I ain't goin' to pray, I shore am turnin' my face to th' birthplace of th' Prophet," he said. "Yeah, I'm even enterin' its sacred portals." He watched closely for any signs for recognition in the other, but failed to detect any; and he was not surprised.

The heavy face stared at him and a tentative smile tried to change it. The attempt was abortive and the expression shifted to one of alert suspicion, shaded by one of pugnacity. He was not accustomed to levity at his expense. "What you talkin' about?" he slowly asked.

"Why, th' faith of all true believers: *There is but one God, and Mohammed is his Prophet.* May th' blessin's of Allah be on thee. Incidentally I'm askin' if there's a letter for th' pilgrim, Tex Jones?" He cast a careless glance at a cold-eyed individual who lounged in the shadow of a corner, and instantly classified him. Besides the low-slung holster, the man had the face of a cool, paid killer. Tex's interest in him was not to be correctly judged by the careless glance he gave him.

"Then why in h—l didn't you say so in th' first place, 'stead of wastin' my valuable time?" growled the proprietor, reluctantly shuffling toward the mail rack in a corner. He wet his thumb generously, not caring about the color given to it by the tobacco in his mouth, and clumsily ran through the modest packet of mail. Shaking his head he turned. "There ain't nothin'," he grunted.

"It is Allah's will," muttered Tex in pious resignation. He would have fallen over had there been anything for him.

"Look here, stranger," ominously remarked the proprietor, "if yo're aimin' to be smart at *my* expense, look out it don't become yourn. Just what's th' meanin' of all these fool remarks?"

"Why, yore emporium is named 'Mecca,' ain't it?" asked Tex innocently, but realizing that he somehow had got on the wrong trail.

"What's that got to do with it?" demanded Williams, who could talk as mean as he cared to while the quiet, cold man sat in the corner.

"Everythin'. Ain't you th' proprietor, like th' barkeep of th' hotel said? Ain't you Mr. Williams?"

"I am."

Tex scratched his head, frankly puzzled. "Well," he said. "Mohammed came out of Mecca to startle th' world, an'——"

"He didn't do nothin' of th' kind!" interrupted the proprietor. "Mecca was out of Prophet, by Mohammed; an' a cussed good hoss she was, too. Though she didn't startle no world, she was my filly, an' plenty good enough for this part of th' country. Of course, mebby back from where you came from, mebby she wouldn't have amounted to much," he sneered. "Now, if you got any more smart-Aleck remarks to make, you'll be wise if you save 'em till you get outside."

Tex burst out laughing. "It's all my mistake, Mr. Williams. I thought you named yore store after a poem I read once, that's all. No offense on my part, sir. Are you th' Mr. Williams that keeps th' ho-tel?"

"I am: what about it?"

"I'm puttin' up there," answered Tex. "If a letter comes for me, would you mind puttin' it in yore pocket an' bringin' it over when you go there? It'll save me from botherin' you every day. Yore friend at th' station said I'd find you right obligin'. An' he knows a good ho-tel when he sees it. He sent me there."

"That scut!" bellowed Williams, his face growing red. "You'll come after yore own mail, my man; an' you'll do it polite. There ain't no mail here for you. Good day!"

"I'm patient an' I can wait. I didn't hardly expect to get any letter so quick, anyhow. After th' recent experience of reasonin' right from th' wrong premises, however, I'll not be a heap surprised if I get a letter on tomorrow's train. Thank you kindly, sir. I bid you good day."

"An' mind you don't call that cussed agent no friend of mine, th' job stealer!"

"Whatever you say; but, don't forget to bring over that letter when it comes," sweetly replied Tex, and he carefully slammed the door as he went out. Going down the street he grinned expansively and snapped his fingers because of a strange elation.

"Th' old thief!" he muttered. "Heavier, more ill tempered, and downright autocratic—an' how he has prospered! Regular, solid citizen, the bulwark of the commonwealth. An' cussed if he ain't got himself a bodyguard; a regular, no-mistake gunman with as mean an eye as any I ever saw. Of course, his brains have improved with the years, for they couldn't go the other way and keep him out of an asylum. 'Muttonhead' Williams! All right: once a sheep, always a sheep. I'm going to enjoy my stay in Windsor. Good Lord!" he exclaimed as a sudden fancy hit him. "Wouldn't it be funny if the old fool has been working hard and saving hard all these years for his old enemy, Tex Ewalt? He always was crazy to play poker, and I got a notion to make it come true. Gosh, if a man ever was tempted, I'm tempted now! Muttonhead Williams, allus stuck on his poker playing. Get behind me, Satan!"

CHAPTER III

Tempted Anew

A HAND bell, ringing thin and clamorous somewhere below caused Tex to gather up the cards with which for two hours he had been assiduously practicing shuffling, cutting, and dealing. Putting them away he washed his face and hands in the tin basin, combed his hair without slicking it with water, and went down to supper.

He paused momentarily in the doorway to size up the dining-room. The long table was crowded by all sorts and conditions of men. Miners down on their luck and near the end of their resources because of the long drought which had dried up the streams and put an end to placer mining operations, rubbed elbows with more fortunate men of their own calling, who had longer purses. Two cowpunchers from a distant ranch sat next to two cavalrymen on a prized leave from the iron discipline of a remote frontier post, both types dangerous because free from the restraint which had held them down for so long a time. A local tin-horn gambler and the traveling card-sharp were elbow to elbow, and several other men, evidently belonging to the town, nearly filled both sides of the table.

At the head sat Gus Williams, most influential citizen and boss of the town, and he made no attempt to hide his importance. Next to him on the left was a lean, hard-looking, shifty-eyed man who seemed to shine in reflected light, and who showed a deference to the big man which he evidently expected to receive, in turn, from the others. If it was true that there was only one boss, it was also true that he had only one nephew. To the right of the boss was the cold-eyed person whose seat in the general store was well back in the corner. No one moved or spoke except under his critical observance. His cocksure confidence irritated Tex, who was strongly tempted to try the effect of a hot potato against a cold eye. He thought of his friend Johnny Nelson and grinned at how that young man's temper would steam up under such an insolent stare. Moving forward under the gunman's close scrutiny Tex dropped into the only vacant chair, one near the nephew, and fell to eating, his vocal chords idle, but his optic and auditory apparatus making up for it. The conversation, jerky and broken at first, grew more coherent and increased as the appetites of the hungry men yielded to the bolted food. The protracted drought was referred to in grunts, growls, monosyllables, sentences, and profane speeches. It was discussed, rediscussed, and popped up at odd moments for new discussion.

"Never saw it so bad since th' railroad came," said a miner.

"Never saw it so bad since th' first trail herd ended here," affirmed the nephew.

"*I* never saw it so dry, for so long a spell, since th' first trail herd *passed* here," said the uncle, his remark the strongest by coming last; but he was not to enjoy that advantage for long.

"Hum!" said a cattleman, apologetically clearing his

throat. "I never saw it as dry as it is now since I located out here."

The miner frowned, the nephew scowled, and the uncle snorted. The last named looked around belligerently and smote the table with his fist. "I remember, howsomever, that I did see it near as dry, that year I strayed from th' Santa Fe Trail, huntin' buffalers for th' caravan. We passed right through this section an' circled back. I come to remember it because when we crossed th' Walnut I jumped right over it, dry-shod. Them was th' days when men was men, or soon wasn't nothin' a-tall."

"I reckon they wasn't th' kind that would play off sick so they could get another man's job away from him, anyhow," growled the nephew, introducing his pet grievance. "I run that station a cussed sight better than it's bein' run now; an' anybody's likely to make mistakes once in a while."

"A few dollars, one way or another, ain't bustin' no railroad," asserted the uncle. "It was only th' excuse they was a-waitin' for."

"Nobody can tell me no good about no railroad," said the freighter, his fond memory resurrecting a certain lucrative wagon haul which had vanished with the advent of the first train over the line.

"Hosses are good enough for me," said Tex, looking around. "Which remark reminds me that a rider afoot is a helpless hombre. Bein' a rider, without no cayuse, I'm a little anxious to get me a good one. Anybody know where I can do it reasonable?"

All eyes turned to the head of the table, where Williams was washing down his last mouthful of food with a gulp of hot, watery coffee. He cleared his throat and peered closely, but pleasantly, at the stranger. "Why, it's Mr. Jones," he said. "I reckon I have such a hoss, Mr. Jones. Mebby it ain't any too well broken, but that hadn't oughter bother a *rider*."

Tex grinned. "If that's all that's th' matter with it I

reckon it'll suit me; but I can tell better after I ride it, an' learn th' price."

"Want it tonight?" frowned Williams.

"No; I ain't in no hurry. Tomorrow'll be plenty of time, when you ain't got nothin' else to do but show it. Speakin' of railroads like we was, I reckon they ain't done nothin' very much for this town. While I'm new to these parts, I'm betting Windsor was a whole lot better when th' drive trail was alive an' kickin'."

Williams nodded emphatically. "I've seen these plains an' valleys thick with cattle," he said, regretfully. "There was a time when I could see th' dust clouds rollin' up from th' south an' away in th' north, both at once, day after day. This town was a-hummin' every day an' night. Money come easy an' went th' same way. Men dropped in here, lookin' like tramps, almost, who could write good checks for thousands of dollars. Th' buyers bought whole herds on th' seller's say-so, without even seein' a hoof, an' sold 'em ag'in th' same way. Money flowed like water, an' fair-sized fortunes was won an' lost at a single sittin'. I've seen th' faro-bank busted three days hand-runnin'—but, of course, that was very unusual. Mostly it was th' other way 'round. All one summer an' fall it was like that. Then th' winter come, an' that was th' end of it so fur's Windsor was concerned. Th' Kiowa Arroyo branch line was pushed further an' further southwest until th' weather stopped it; but it went on ag'in as soon as spring let it. By th' time th' first herds crossed th' state line, headin' for here, that line of rails was ready for 'em, an' not another big herd went past this town. Of course, there was big herds drivin' north, just th' same, bound for th' Yellowstone region on government contract, an' some was bein' sent out to stock ranges in th' West, but they followed a new trail found by Chisholm, or old McCullough. I've heard lately that Mac is workin' for Twitchell an' Carpenter. But if you'd seen this town then you shore wouldn't know it now. D—n th' railroads, says I!"

Tex frowned honestly at the thought of the passing of this once great cattle trail, for the memories of those old trails lay snug and warm in the hearts of the men who have followed them in saddle. He looked up at Williams, a congratulatory look on his face. "Well, that shore was hard; but not as hard, I reckon, as if you had been a cattleman, an' follered it. It sort of hurts an old-time cowman to think of them trails."

"That's where yo're wrong," spoke up the nephew. "He *is* a cattleman. Th' GW brand is known all over th' state, an' beyond. It was knowed by every puncher that followed that old trail."

"There wasn't no such brand in them days," corrected Williams. He did not think it necessary to say that the GW mark was just starting then, far back in the hills and well removed from the trail; that it grew much faster by the addition of fully grown cattle than it did by natural increase; or that a view of the original brands on the fullgrown cattle would have been a matter of great and burning interest to almost every drive boss who followed a herd along the trail. Later on, when he threw his herd up for a count, the drive boss was likely to have re-added his tally sheet and asked heaven and earth what had happened to him. "Well, them days has gone; but when they went this town come blamed near goin' with 'em. It shore ain't what it once was."

Tex thought that it was just as well, since the town was mean enough and vicious enough as it was; he remembered vividly its high-water period; but he nodded his head.

"It ain't hardly fair to judge it after such a long dry spell," he said. "Th' whole country, south an' west of th' Missouri is fair burnin' up. Th' Big Muddy herself was a-showin' all her bars."

"That's th' curse of this part of Kansas," said the nephew. "That an' job jumpers."

"Yes?" asked Tex. "How's that?"

"Station agent a friend of yourn?"

It became evident to Tex that the uncle and the nephew had been discussing him. Gus Williams was the only man to whom he had mentioned the agent. He shook his head. "Never saw him before I stepped off th' train today," he answered, looking vexed about something. "We up an' had some words, an' I told him I reckoned he might find healthier towns further west, across th' line. I'm a mild man, gents: but I allus speak my mind."

"An' you gave him some cussed good advice," replied the nephew warmly. "This ain't no place for any man as plays off sick an' does low-down tricks to turn another man out of a job. If it wasn't for his sister I'd 'a' buffaloed him *pronto*. Which reminds me, stranger," he warned with an ugly leer. "She's a rip-snortin' fe-male— but I shore saw her first. I'm just tellin' you so you won't get any notions that way. I'm fencin' that range."

"Don't you worry, Hen," consoled a friend. "Yo're able to run herd on her, balky as she is, an' when th' time's ripe you'll put yore brand on her. So fur's th' job's concerned, yore uncle'll get it back for you when he gets ready to move. We ought to ride that Saunders feller out of town, *I* say!"

"There's plenty of time for that," said Williams, as he turned to address another diner. "John, show Mr. Jones that gray when he gits around tomorrow. Aimin' to stay in town long, Mr. Jones?"

Tex shrugged his shoulders. "Got to wait for a letter—don't know what to do; but I shore could be in worse places than this here hotel, so I ain't worryin' a lot. Bein' a stranger, though, I reckon time'll drag a little evenin's."

Various kinds of smiles replied to this, and Williams laughed outright. "I reckon you understand th' innercent game of draw?" he chuckled.

Tex froze: "Sometimes I think I do," he said, and laughed to hide his struggle against the pressure of the old temptation. He fairly burned to turn his poker craft against this blowhard's invitation, to wipe from that self-complacent face its look of omniscience. "An' then, sometimes I reckon I don't," he continued; "but I'm admittin' she's plumb fascinatin'. From th' pious expressions around me I reckon mebby I've shocked somebody."

Williams led in the laughter that followed, his bull voice roaring through the room. "You'd better buy that hoss before you assist in th' evenin's worship," he cried in boisterous good humor, "for I'm sayin' a puncher ain't nowhere near in th' prospector's class when it comes to walkin'; though I reckon th' boys will play you for th' hoss, at that, an' you'd be no better off in th' end. My remarks as how this town has slid back didn't have nothin' to do with our poker playin', Mr. Jones. If you feel like settin' in ag'in' a Kansas cyclone, you can't say I didn't warn you."

Tex wondered what the crowd would say if he should lean over and pull a royal flush out of Williams' ear, or a full-house from the nephew's nose. They might be surprised if they found out that the cold-eyed gunman at Williams' elbow carried a handful of Colt cartridges in his tight-shut mouth. He had no rabbits to lift out of hats, but that trick was threadbare from being overworked, anyhow. He waved both hands, a smart-Aleck grin sweeping across his face. "I've rode cayuses, punched cows, an' played draw from Texas to Montanny, an' near back ag'in. So far I ain't throwed, rolled under, or cleaned out; an' I'm allus willin' to be agreeable. Where you gents lead I'll foller, like a hungry calf after its ma." His voice had grown loud and boastful and he joined the swiftly forming card group with a swagger as it settled around the table in the barroom, his bovine conceit hiding the silent struggle going on within him.

Tex of the old days was fighting Tex of the new. The smug complacency of the local boss stirred up the desire to break him to his last cent, to make a fool of him in the way others had been broken and made ridiculous; but the new Tex won: As usual he would play Hopalong's game—which was as his opponents played, straight or crooked, as they showed the way. He had no real wish for large winnings, for if he made his expenses as he went along he would be satisfied, and he could do that from his knowledge of psychology, a knowledge gained outside of classrooms. He now had no reputation to defend or maintain, for Tex Jones was not Tex Ewalt, famed throughout the cow-country. The new name meant nothing. But how pleasant it would be to repeat history in this town, so far as Williams was concerned!

He always had claimed that he could learn a man's real nature more quickly in a game of poker than in any other way in the same length of time, and he did not mean some one more prominent trait, but the man's nature as a whole; and now he set himself to study his new acquaintances against some future need. The game itself would not engross him to the exclusion of all else, for while he was Tex Jones externally, it would be Tex Ewalt who played the hands, the Tex Ewalt who as a youth had discovered an uncanny ability in sleight of hand and whose freshman and sophomore years had given so much time to developing and perfecting the eye-baffling art that every study had suffered heavily in consequence; the Tex Ewalt who had found that his ability was peculiarly adaptive to cards, and who had given all his attention to that connection when once he had started to travel along the line of least resistance. So well had he succeeded that seasoned gamblers from the Mexican line north to Canada had been forced to admit his mastery.

Before the end of the second deal he had learned the rest of the nephew's more prominent characteristics, but had not bothered to retaliate for the cheating. On the third deal he was forced to out-cheat a miner to keep even with the game. Before the evening's play was over he had renewed his knowledge of Gus Williams, and now knew him as well as that loud-voiced individual knew himself; and he had not incurred the enmity of the boss, because while Tex had won from the others he had lost to him. While not yielding to the temptations rampant in him, he had compromised and left Williams in a ripe condition for a future skinning. At the end of the play only he and Williams had won.

As the others pushed back their chairs to leave the table, Williams ignored them and looked at Tex. "You an' me seem to be th' best," he said loudly. "So there won't be no doubt about it, let's settle it between us."

Tex raised a belated hand too late to hide his yawn, blinked sleepily, and squinted at the clock. "I'm surprised it's so late," he said. "It takes a lot out of a man to play ag'in' this crowd. My head's fair achin'. What you say if we let it go till tomorrow night? I been travelin' for three days an' three nights an' ain't slept much. You'd take it away from me before I could wake up."

Williams laughed sarcastically. "You shore been crossin' a lot of sand since you left th' Big Muddy, but I don't reckon none of it got inter yore system." He paused to let the words sink in, and for a reply, and none being forthcoming he laughed nastily as he arose. "Texas is a sandy state, too. Reckon you was named before anybody knowed very much about you."

Tex paled, fought himself to a standstill and shrugged his shoulders. Out of the corner of his eye he saw Bud Haines, the cold-eyed bodyguard, become suddenly more alert.

"Windsor's got a h—l of a way of welcomin' strangers," he said. "You'll have a different kind of kick to make tomorrow night, for you'll be eatin' sand. I play poker when I feel like it: just now I don't feel like it. I'll say good night,"

"Ha-ha-ha!" shouted Williams. "He don't feel like it, boys! Ha-ha-ha!"

Tex stopped, turned swiftly, pulled out a roll of bills that was a credit to his country and slammed it on the table, reaching for the scattered deck. "Mebby you feel like puttin' up seven hundred dollars ag'in' mine, one cut, th' highest card, to take both piles? Ha-ha-ha!" he mimicked. "Here's action if that's what yo're lookin' for!"

Williams' face turned a deep red and he cursed under his breath. "That's a baby game: I said poker!" he retorted, making no effort to get nearer to the table.

"That's mebby why I picked it," snapped Tex, stuffing the roll back into his pocked. "You can wait till tomorrow night for poker." Turning his back on the wrathful Williams and the open-mouthed audience, he yawned again, muttered something to express his adieus, and clomped heavily and slowly up the stairs, his body shaking with repressed laughter; and when he fell asleep a few minutes later there was a placid smile on his clean-shaven face.

CHAPTER IV

A Crowded Day

AFTER A late breakfast about noon Tex got the gunny sack, threw it over his shoulder and went to the Mecca, nodding to the proprietor in a spirit of good-will and cheerfulness. Bud Haines did not appear to be about.

"I come in to see about that cayuse," he said. "Where'll I find it?"

"Go down to th' stable an' see John," growled Williams. "You'll find it next to Carney's saloon, across th' street. Got rested up yet?" The question was not pleasantly asked.

Tex threw the sack over the other shoulder, hunched it to a more comfortable position, and grinned sheepishly. "Purty near, I reckon; anyhow, I got over my grouch. I was shore peevish last night; but th' railroad's to blame for that. They say they are necessary, an' great blessin's; but I ain't so shore about it. Outside of my personal grudge ag'in' 'em, I'm sore because they've shore played th' devil with th' range. Cut it all up—an' there ain't no more pickin' along th' old trails no more, like there once was. I don't reckon punchers has got any reason to love 'em a whole lot."

Williams flashed him a keen look and slowly nodded. "Yo're right: look at what they've done to this town. We ain't seen no real money since they came."

Tex shifted the sack again. "Everybody had money in them days," he growled. "If a feller went busted along th' trails he allus could pick up a few dollars, if he had a good cayuse an' a little nerve. Why, among them hills—but that ain't concernin' us no more, I reckon." He shook his head sadly. "What's gone is gone. Reckon I'll go look at that cayuse. You ain't got no letter for me yet, have you?"

"Le's see—Johnson?" puzzled the storekeeper, scratching his unshaven chin.

"No; Jones," prompted Tex innocently, hiding his smile.

"Oh, shore!" said his companion, slowly shaking his head. "There ain't nothin' for you so far."

Tex did not think that remarkable not only because there never would be anything for him, but also because there had been no mail since he had asked the day before; but he grunted pessimistically, shifted the sack again, and turned to the door. "See you later," he said, going out.

He easily found the stable, grinned at the bleached, weather-beaten "Williams" painted over the door and going into the smelly, cigar-box office, dumped the sack against the wall and nodded to John Graves. "Come down to look at that cayuse Williams spoke about last night," he said, drawing a sleeve across his wet forehead.

"Shore; come along with me," said Graves, arising and passing out into the main part of the building, Tex at his heels. "Here he is, Mr. Jones—as fine a piece of hossflesh as a man ever straddled. Got brains, youth, an' ginger. Sound as a dollar. Cost you eighty, even. You'll go far before you'll find a better bargain."

Tex looked at the teeth, passed a hypnotic hand

down each leg in turn as he talked to the gray in a soothing voice. Children, horses, and dogs liked him at first look. He frankly admired the animal from a distance, but sadly shook his head.

"Fine cayuse, an' a fair price," he admitted; "but I'm dead set ag'in' grays. Had two of 'em once, one right after th' other—an' come near to dyin' on 'em both. If I didn't get killed, they did, anyhow. It's sort of set me ag'in' grays. Now, there's a roan that strikes me as a hoss I'd consider ownin'. Of course, he ain't as good as th' gray, but he suits me better." He walked over to the magnificent animal, which was far and away superior to the gray and talked to it in a low, caressing voice as he made a quick examination. "Yes, this cayuse suits me if th' price is right. If we can agree on that I'll lead him down th' street an' see how he steps out. Ain't got nothin' else to do, anyhow."

Graves frowned and slowly shook his head. "Rather not part with that one—an' he's a two-hundred-dollar animal, anyhow. It's a sort of pet of th' boss—he's rid it since it was near old enough to walk. That gray's th' best I've got for sale, unless, mebby, it might be that sorrel over there. Now, there's a mighty good hoss, come to think of it."

Tex glanced at the beautiful line of the roan's back and thought of the massive weight of Williams, and of the sway-back bay standing saddled in front of his store. He shook his head. "Two hundred's too high for me, friend," he replied. "As I said, I don't like grays, an' that sorrel has shore got a mean eye. It ain't spirit that's showin', but just plumb treachery. If you got off him out on th' range he'd head for home an' leave you to hoof it after him. I got an even hundred for th' roan. Say th' word an' we trade."

Graves waved his arms and enumerated the roan's good points as only a horse dealer can. The discussion was long and to no result. Tex added twenty-five dollars to the hundred he had offered and the whole thing was gone over again, but to no avail. He picked up the sack, slung it onto his back, and turned to leave.

"I'm shore surprised at th' prices for cayuses in this part of th' country," he said. "Mebby I can make a dicker with somebody else. Of course, I'm admittin' that th' roan ain't got a sand crack like th' sorrel, or a spavin like th' gray—but that's too much money for a saddle hoss for a puncher out of a job. See you tonight, mebby."

Graves waved his arms again. "I'm tellin' you that you won't find no hoss in town like that roan—why, th' color of that animal is worth half th' price. Just look at it!"

"All of which I admits," replied Tex; "but, you see, I'm buyin' me a hoss to ride, not to put on th' parlor table for to admire. Comin' right down to cases, any hoss but a gray, that's sound, an' not too old, is good enough for any puncher. You should 'a' seen some that I've rode, an' been proud of!"

"Seein' that yo're a lover of good hossflesh, I'll take a chance of Gus gettin' peeved, an' let you have th' roan for one-ninety. That's as low as I can drop. Can't shave off another dollar."

"It's too rich for Tex Jones," grumbled the puncher. "See you tonight," and the sack bobbed toward the door just as a sudden brawl sounded in the street. Tex took two quick steps and glanced.

A miner and a cowpuncher were rolling in the dust, biting, hitting, gouging, and wrestling and, as Tex looked he saw the puncher's gun slip out of its open-top sheath. The fighting pair rolled away from it and someone in the closely following crowd picked it up to save it for its owner. The puncher, pounds lighter than his brawny antagonist, rapidly was getting the worst of the rough-and-tumble in which the other's superior weight and strength had full opportunity to make itself felt. Suddenly the miner, thrown from his victim by a tremendous effort, leaped to his feet, snarling like a beast, and knicked at the puncher's head. The heavy, hob-nailed boot crashed sickeningly home and as the writhing man went suddenly limp, the victor aimed another kick at his unconscious enemy. His foot swung back, but it never reached its mark. A forty-pound saddle in a sack shot through the air with all of a strong man's strength behind it and, catching the miner balanced on one foot, it knocked him sprawling through ten feet of dust and débris. Following the sack came Tex, his eyes blazing.

The miner groped in the dust, slowly sat up, moving his head from side to side as he got his bearings. At once his eyes cleared and his hand streaked to the knife in his belt as he half arose. Tex leaped aside as the heavy weapon cut through the air to sink into a near-by wall, where it quivered. The thrower was on his feet now, his face working with rage, and he sprang forward, both arms circling before him. Tex swiftly gripped one outstretched wrist, turned sharply as he pushed his shoulder under the armpit and suddenly bent forward, facing away from his antagonist. The miner left the ground on the surging heave of the puncher's shoulder, shot up into the air, turned over once as Tex, not wishing him to break his neck, pulled down hard on the imprisoned arm, and landed feet first against the wall, squarely under the knife. Bouncing up with remarkable vitality, the miner wrenched at the wicked weapon above him and then cursed as the steel, leaving its point embedded in the wood, flew out of his hand.

Tex shoved the smoking Colt back into his holster and peered through the acrid, gray fog. "If you don't know when yo're licked, you better take my word for it," he warned. "Seein' as how yo're a rubber ball, I'll make shore th' third time!"

A snarl replied and the miner leaped for him, the

hairy hands not so far extended this time. Tex broke ground with two swift steps and then, unexpectedly slipping to one side and forward in two perfectly timed motions, swung a rigid, bent arm as the charging miner went blunderingly past. The bony fist landed fair above the belt buckle and it was nearly half an hour later before the prospector knew where he was, and then he was too sick to care much.

Tex turned and faced the crowd with insolent slowness. His glance passed from face to face, finding some friendliness, much surprise, and a few frank scowls. He stepped up to the man who had retrieved the puncher's gun and, ignoring the crowd altogether, took the weapon from the reluctant fingers which held it and went back to the front of the stable, where Graves had succeeded in bringing the prostrate puncher back to consciousness. Tex ran his fingers over the wobbly man's head and face, grunted, nodded, and smiled.

"Bad bruise, but nothin' is busted. Why there ain't I'm shore *I* don't know. I figgered you was a goner. Here, take your gun, an' let us help you into th' stable."

Once on his feet the puncher pushed free from the sustaining hands and staggered to a box just inside the door, where he carefully seated himself, drew the Colt, and rested it on his knees, his blurred, throbbing eyes watching the street.

Tex grinned. "You can put that up ag'in—he's had all he can digest for a little while. Punchin' for Williams?"

"I'm ridin' for Curtis: C Bar. Over northeast, a couple of hours out. I'm keepin' th' gun where it is: th' miners run this town. Where do you fit in? One of th' GW gang?"

"Nope; I'm all of th' Tex Jones outfit. Stranger here, but shore gettin' acquainted rapid. Got any good cayuses for sale out at yore place? Our mutual friend, here, wants th' Treasury for th' only good animal he's got. Bein' a stranger is a handicap."

Graves leaned forward. "That hoss is worth—" he began in great earnestness.

"—not one red cent to me, now," interrupted Tex, smiling. "Come to think of it, I ain't goin' to buy no hoss a-tall. I've changed my mind."

"We got th' usual run out on th' ranch," said the injured man. "You know 'em, I reckon. Poor on looks, mean as all h—l, with hearts crowded with sand. I'll be leavin' in half an hour if th' miners don't interfere— borry a cayuse an' ride out with me."

"Nope," replied Tex. "I ain't goin' to buy, a-tall, as I just said." He turned. "Good luck to you, friend. Barrin' th' soreness, an' yore looks yo're all right," and he went out, picked up the bulging sack, and passed down the street. Leaving the sack with the bartender in the hotel he went on to the station and smiled at the agent, who was joking with a red-headed Irishman.

"Hello; here he is now," exclaimed the boss of the depot. "Friend, shake hands with Tim Murphy. Tim, this is Mr.—Mr.——"

"Jones," supplied Tex. "Tex Jones, of Montanny, Texas, an' New York."

"Pleased to meet you, Mr. Geography," grinned Murphy. "Th' lad here was a-tellin' me ye gave him a friendly word an' some good advice. From that I was knowin' ye didn't belong around here. I'll shake yer hand if ye don't mind. Th' sack wint like an arrow, th' wrestlin' trick couldn't be bate, I never saw a nicer shot, an' th' finish does ye proud. Ye fair tickled me when ye wint for th' soft spot. 'Tis a rare sight in street fights, an' in th' ring, too, for that matter. Welcome to Windsor!"

Tex laughed heartily and gripped the hairy fist. He liked the feel of the great, calloused hand, and the look on the smiling, tanned face, from which twinkled a pair of blue eyes alight with humor, honesty, and courage. "But did you ever see a man come back as quick as he did?" he asked.

" 'Twas surprisin' for a bully," admitted Murphy, grudgingly.

"That's where yo're wrong: he's no bully," contradicted Tex. "He's a brute, all right, savage as th' devil, an' foul in his fightin'—but he ain't any coward. It fair stuck out of his eyes."

"Trust me to miss anything like that," growled the agent; "and trust Tim not to," he added.

"Hist, now!" warned Murphy, motioning with his thumb held close to his vest. "Here comes th' lass. An' what do ye be thinkin' av th' town now, Mr. Jones?"

"Just what you do," laughed Tex, turning slowly.

"An' how are ye this day, miss?" asked Murphy, his hat in his hand and his red face beaming.

"Very well, indeed, Tim," replied the girl. She glanced at Tex as she turned to her brother, holding out the lunch basket. "Jerry, I couldn't get any decent eggs—and they had no milk for me." There was a poorly hidden note of distress in her voice, and a faint look of anxiety momentarily clouded her face. Neither was lost to the observant puncher.

Tex liked her instantly. Her voice was full and sweet, of resonant timbre—a voice one would not easily tire of. Her figure was slender, and yet full and rounded, promising a wiry strength and great vitality. The sunbonnet she wore hid most of the chestnut-brown hair, but set off the face within it with a bewitching art. Altogether she made a very pretty picture.

"It doesn't matter, Jane," smiled her brother, quick to sense her worry. He pinched the full lips with caressing playfulness. "I'm getting stronger every day, and food isn't as critical a subject as it once was. The credit is all yours—Jane, meet Mr. Jones. I was speaking about him last night."

Tex bowed gravely. "How do you do?" he murmured. "Conscientious care is more than half of the battle. The credit he gave you appears to be well deserved."

Jane Saunders, accustomed to embarrassed self-consciousness or stammering volubility, smiled faintly as she acknowledged the introduction. The man was as impersonal and as sure of himself as any she ever had met. She looked him fairly in the eyes.

"How did you come to advise my brother to go farther west?" she asked, but while her voice was casual, her look challenged him.

"It was given upon certain conditions of the weather this winter, Miss—I do not believe I caught the name."

"No fault of yours," she laughed. "Jerry always ignores it in his introductions. It is Jane Saunders. Then it was only in the nature of a physician's advice?" she persisted, her eyes searching his soul for the truth.

Tex nodded. "My knowledge of his complaint is very sketchy; but like all amateurs I paraded what little I had. I thought that perhaps the winters out here might not be as dry as they are farther west. No doubt it was entirely uncalled for. We will hope so, anyway."

"Are you a physician, Mr. Jones?"

"No, indeed; although I went part way through the course. What little time I had left from more interesting activities, I gave to study."

"Ye was speakin' about th' aigs an' milk, miss," said Murphy, his face alight with eager anticipation. He chuckled. "Ye needn't be askin' no more favors av Williams' black heart. I've a little somethin' to show ye all, if ye'll step down th' track a bit. An' Costigan is goin' to get him a cow. Th' missus said th' word, an' divvil a bit Mike can wiggle out av it. Ye'll have first call on th' milk, so I hear. Mr. Jones, if ye'll be kind enough to escort Jerry, I'll lead th' march with th' lass."

"Oh, well," sighed Tex, gravely offering his arm to the station agent, "I suppose it *is* yore party; but I'm admittin' yo're not overlookin' Number One. Lead on, MacDuff." He caught her quick glance at the abrupt change in his language, and smiled to himself. It never paid to be too well understood by a woman.

"Th' Irish are noted for bein' judges av good whiskey, fine hosses, an' fair wimmin," retorted Murphy. "I'll take no chances of any pearls bein' cast careless."

"I notice you put th' wimmin last," countered Tex. "Grunt, Jerry! Quick, man! Before Miss Saunders looks around!"

"He said pearls, Mr. Jones," said Jane, laughingly. "I'm afraid he intended it all to be plural."

"It was wrongly written in th' first place," complained Tex. "Tim has an uncanny instinct; he only met me about ten minutes ago."

"Ten is a-plenty, sometimes," chuckled Murphy. "But I'll own to havin' a previous sight av ye. Wait now: here we are."

They stopped in front of the toolhouse and watched Murphy walk along one of the two ties spanning the drainage ditch at the edge of the roadbed. He unlocked the doors and flung them wide open as a clamorous cackling broke out in the building. On one end of a hand car was a crate of chickens and leaning against it were several bundles of long stakes. A pile of new lumber could be seen in the back of the shed, while a fat spool of wire rested near the stakes.

Murphy turned, his face red with delight at his surprise. "There ye are, miss," he cried proudly. "A round dozen av them, with their lord an' master. I couldn't let that Mike Costigan go puttin' on his airs over his boss, so now there'll be aigs for aignoggs that I'll have a claim to. For safe-keepin' we'll build th' coop in yore back yard where it will be right handy for ye. Ye can now tell Williams to kape his aigs. If he don't understand yer soft language, I'll be tellin' him in a way he can't mistook."

"You angel!" whispered Jane, tears in her eyes. She was not misled by his remarks about eggnoggs. "Oh, Tim—you shouldn't have done it! Why didn't *I* think of it? And how is it that Mrs. Costigan suddenly needs a cow? If I've heard her aright, she has stalwart, old-fashioned ideas, bless her, about nursing children. And I never knew she was partial to eggnoggs. Jerry, what shall we do to them?"

Jerry blew his nose with energy. "For a cent I'd lick Murphy right now, and Mike immediately afterward," he laughed, sizing up the huge bulk of bone, sinew, and toil-hardened muscle of the section-boss. "Tim, you and your boys are the one redeeming feature of this country. And you redeem it fully. How long have you been plotting this?"

"G'wan with ye, th' pair av ye!" chuckled the section-boss, his face flaming. "If Casey hadn't stopped th' train down by this shed yesterday we couldn't 'a' surprised ye. Ye never saw a consignment handled quicker or more gintly."

"And I was wondering why he did it," confessed Jerry. "The brakeman said he was trying his brakes. Tim, you should be ashamed of yourself!"

"An' I've been that, many a time," retorted Murphy. He turned to Tex. "I'll be leavin' it to ye, Mr. Jones, if a man hasn't certain rights after bein' nursed for three weeks by a brown-haired angel, an' knowin' that th' same angel nursed Mrs. Costigan an' th' twins whin they was all down with th' measles. Patient an' unselfish, she was, with never a cross word, day or night—an' always with a smile on her pretty face, like th' sun on Lake Killarney."

Tex looked gravely and judicially at Jane Saunders. "You haven't a word to say, Miss Saunders. The verdict of the court is for the defendant. Case dismissed, without costs of either party against the other." He turned to the section-boss. "When are we buildin' that coop, Murphy?" he asked.

"Tomorrow, Tex," answered the Irishman. "We'll be after runnin' th' darlin's up there right away, an' come back for th' lumber an' wire. That'll give us an early start. Th' sidin' will let us ride 'em near halfway an' save a lot of flounderin' in th' sand."

"We'd better come back for th' darlin's after th' coop is ready for 'em," said Tex, grinning. "If I know coyotes as well as I reckon I do, th' harem will be a lot safer in this here shed; an' I'm glad it's got a board floor, too. Lend a hand here an' we'll change th' cargo on this meek steed. *Gently, brother, gently pray.* Now for th' lumber." He burst into a chant: "*I once was a bloody pirate bold, an' I sailed on th' Spanish Main, yo-ho! Th' treasure chests were full of gold, which gave us all a pain you know.*" He glanced at one of his hands and grimaced. "Blast th' splinters. An' would you look at that corn? Blessed if th' man hasn't got enough to feed another Custer expedition! Murphy, you certainly do grow on one!"

Murphy paused with a huge armful of lumber, and looked suspicious. "On one what?" he demanded.

"Prickly pear plant, I reckon, in lieu of anything else; or on a mesquite tree, perhaps, for you shore do know beans when th' pod's open. *An' it stopped—short—never to go again, when th' old—man—died,*" hummed Tex. "All aboard. Clang-clang! Clang-clang! I can still hear that bell in my sleep. Yo're th' engineer, Murphy; I'll act in an advisory capacity, at th' same time pushing hard on my very own handle. Ladies first! Miss Saunders, if you please! That's right, for you might as well ride in state. Up you go. From your elevated position you may scan the country roundabout and give us warning of the approach of redskins. *A Book of Verses underneath the Bough, a Jug of Wine, a Loaf of Bread*—and fried eggs—*Oh, Wilderness were Paradise enow!*"

"I see no redskins, Advisory Capacity," called Jane, who thoroughly was enjoying herself; "but hither rides a horseman on a horse."

Tex looked up and saw a recklessly riding puncher coming toward them. He slyly exchanged grins with Murphy and kept on pushing.

The rider, smiling as well as a swollen face and throbbing temples would permit, slid to a stand, removed his sombrero and bowed.

"My name's Tom Watkins," he said. "I just come down to tell you, friend, that I've learned what you done for me, awhile back. I'm——"

Tex interrupted him. "You just came down in time, Thomas, to drop yore useful rope over that bobbin' handle an' head west at a plain, unornamental walk. High-heeled boots was never made for pushin' han' cars over ties an' rocks. An' I suspect Murphy of stealin' a ride every time my head goes down."

"Then I'd be cheatin' myself," retorted Murphy, looking upon the newcomer with strong favor. "Th' car would be after stoppin' every time I rode, like th' little boat with th' big whistle." He turned to the agent. "Jerry, there's no tellin' how fast this car will be goin', for I misdoubt that animal's intentions. Suppose ye run along an' throw th' switch for us. Hadn't ye better get down, miss?"

"Not for the world, Tim!"

The disfigured puncher grinned even wider, dropped his rope over the handle with practiced art and wheeled his horse. "What'll I do when I git to th' end of th' rails?" he asked, mischievous deviltry, unabashed by what had befallen him, shining in his eyes, and there was an eager curiosity revealed by his voice.

"What'll he do, Murphy?" demanded Tex.

"He'll stop, blast him!" emphatically answered the section-boss.

'You'll stop, Thomas," said Tex. "As Hamlet said: 'Go on, I'll follow thee!' "

"But he's not nearly a ghost yet," objected Jane. Her cheeks were flushed, her eyes sparkling from the fun she was having. Many days had passed since she had had so good a time. It was a treat to get away from the ever-lasting "Yes, ma'am" and "No, ma'am" which had been the formula for conversation with everyone to whom she had talked except her brother and Murphy.

"No, ma'am," said the puncher. "Not yet."

Jane shuddered and grimaced at Tex as the rider turned away. "That's all I've heard since I've been out here," she softly called down to him.

"Yes, ma'am," he replied, not daring to look up.

The procession wended onward to the edification of sundry stray dogs, and Costigan's goats, tethered near the toolshed, promptly went into consultation as to what measures to pursue, apparently deciding upon a defensive course of action if the worst came to pass.

The end of the rails reached, the engineer of the motive power stopped, sized up the ground roundabout and then looked hopefully at his companions. "Reckon we can manage th' haul. Totin' them boards afoot shore will be tirin'. Where we drivin' to?"

Jerry pointed out the little house, but shook his head. "We can't make it."

"Cowboy," said Tex, "that ain't no plowhorse. When she feels th' drag of this vehicle in th' sand she'll display her frank an' candid thoughts about it."

"Then blindfold her," suggested Tom Watkins. "She won't know it ain't a steer she's fastened to. You fellers can git behind an' push, too."

" 'Sic transit gloria mundi,' " murmured Jane, preparing to descend to earth.

" 'Sic transit' glorious Monday," repeated Tex, stepping to assist her. "Only it ain't Monday. Take my honest hand, lady, and jump." He turned and looked at the grinning engineer. "Now, you cactus-eatin' burro, try yore handkerchief. If *our* idea works, all right; if *yore* idea don't work, it's Murphy's fault. Commence!"

"I'm thinkin' it would work better if th' car was off th' track," caustically commented Murphy. "I misdoubt if we can climb that buffer; th' flanges on these wheels are deep an' strong an' I'm shore we can't pull th' rails over. If th' engineer will lend a hand here we mebby can clear th' track without unloadin'. I'll take th' off side; ye byes take th' other, which makes it even, for it is a well-known fact that one Irish section-boss is worth two punchers. Are ye ready, now?"

"I've heard they can run faster than two cowpunchers," retorted Tex. "For the ashes of your fathers, *lift*! Try it again—*now*. Inch her over—that's the way. Now then, *lift*! Once more—*lift*! Phew! All right: proceed, cowboy," he grunted.

"Hold yer horses!" shouted Murphy. "What's th' good av a section-boss that can't lay a track?" he demanded, taking up a two-by-four, Tex following his lead. The car was lifted onto the timbers and the procession went on again. "Will they spread, now?" queried Murphy doubtfully, watching them closely. He had just decided they would not when they did. After numerous troubles the little house was reached, the lumber unloaded, and the car sent back without rails.

"Goin' to make any more hauls?" asked the horseman.

"We are not," said Tex with emphasis. "We could 'a' toted this stuff over in half th' time. *Tempus* fidgets, an' I'm catchin' it. Yore ideas are plumb fine till they're put in practice."

"*My* ideas?" queried the disfigured rider, his rising eyebrows pushing wrinkles onto his forehead. "Didn't you tell me to chuck my rope over that bobbin' handle?"

"Do you allus have to do what yo're told?" retorted Tex. "Answer me that! Do you?"

The rider looked down at Jane, who was nearly convulsed, and sighed with deep regret, and because her presence forbade the only appropriate retort, he shook his head sorrowfully and turned to haul the car back to the track.

"Hey!" called Tex. "Sling them spools of barb wire across yore saddle. We might as well get more of that stuff while we have yore good-natured assistance. Just chuck it on any place an' bring it here."

"You just can't chuck a spool of wire on a saddle any place," retorted the puncher. "Was you speakin' about ideas?"

"An while yer about it," said Murphy, "ye might bring back a spade, th' saws, three hammers, that box av nails, an' them staples. Th' staples are in a little keg—th' one without th' handle. I've a mind to start buildin' today. What do ye say, Tex? Good for ye: yer a man after me own heart."

Despite his aches and bruises the puncher's feet left the stirrups and slowly went up until he stood with his shoulder on the saddle. He waved his legs three times and resumed the correct posture for riding. Words were hopelessly inadequate. He looked at Jane, who was shrieking and pointing at the ground under the horse. Thomas craned his neck and looked down. He thereupon dismounted and picked up one Colt's .45, one pocket-knife, one watch which now needed expert attention, various coins, a plug of tobacco, and three horseshoe nails. Murphy stared at him, spat disgustedly, and attacked the pile of lumber.

After the puncher's return the work went on rapidly, and when the roof of the coop was finished, the three perspiring workmen stepped back to admire it.

"We've got to slat them windows," said Tex, thinking of coyotes.

"An' we got thirteen nests to build," said Thomas Watkins.

"Th' saints be praised!" ejaculated Murphy, staring incredulously at the battle-scarred recruit. "Mebby there'll be a coincidence about twelve layin' all at once, but there won't be no thirteenth on th' job. Mebby yer thinkin' th' Sultan will nest down alongside them to set them a good example? Six boxes will be a-plenty, Tommy, my lad."

Tommy tilted his sombrero to scratch his head. "Well, if you reckon there won't be no stampedin', mebby six will be enough, 'though I'd hate to think of 'em milling frantic for their turn on th' nests. An' while we're speakin' of calamities, I'm sayin' good chickens will fly over th' fence you fellers aim to build. Six feet ain't high enough, nohow."

"We clip their wings, Tommy," enlightened Tex.

"We clip one wing close up," corrected Murphy. "That lifts 'em on one side an' flops 'em around in a circle. I can easy see you ain't no *hen puncher*."

"Th' principle is sound in theory an' proved by practice," said Tex. "Just like when you saw off th' laigs on one side of a steer. That allus keeps 'em from jumpin' fences."

"Too cussed bad you stopped that miner," growled Watkins. "I'd 'a' been a whole lot better off dead."

"We're sorry, too," retorted Murphy. "Now, then; we got a four-sided fence to build, three posts to a side. That's a dozen holes to dig."

"Tell you what," suggested Tommy, winking at Tex. "You can handle a spade all around us, one Irish section-boss bein' worth two punchers. Besides we only got one spade for th' three of us. You dig th' north an' south sides while me an' Tex start on nests an' put up th' roosts. Then we'll dig th' east an' west sides while yo're settin' yore posts an' tampin' 'em."

"An I'll have mine set while you fellers git ready to start on yer roosts," boasted Murphy, grabbing the spade and starting to work. Jane Saunders, who had come up unobserved, suddenly stuffed her handkerchief in her mouth and fled back to the house.

There ensued great hammering and frantic dirt throwing. Tex and his companion were hampered by mirth and were only building the last nest when Murphy stuck his head in the door.

"Ye wouldn't last in no gang av mine!" he jeered. "I got me holes dug an' th' posts set. Set 'em single-handed an' they're true as a plumb line."

"All right, Murphy," said Tommy without looking up. "Run along an' do th' other two while we're finishin' up. It's gettin' late."

"Tryin' to lay it onto me, eh?" demanded Murphy. "You an' yer two post holes! Ye must think—" he stopped short, thought a moment, and then slyly glanced out at the unfinished sides of the enclosure. "Hivin save us!" he muttered and slipped out without another word.

Tommy wiped his eyes and leaned against the wall for support. "Four sides," he babbled. "Three to a side: that's a dozen holes to dig! He will make smart remarks about my thirteen nests, will he?"

"Figures don't lie, an' logic is logic," laughed Tex. "Reckon we can't finish th' fence today; but it don't make no difference, anyhow. Them chickens are as safe in th' toolshed as they'd be up here. Did you close th' doors when you left?" he demanded anxiously.

"Yes; too many hungry, stray dogs around. I'd like to 'a' gone to th' finish with you boys, but I got to get back to th' ranch. Climb up behind me an' I'll let you off at th' hotel."

"I'll wait for Murphy," replied Tex. "He'll mebby need help about somethin'. I'm cussed glad to know you, Watkins; an' I've shore had a circus today."

"You pulled me out of a bad hole, Tex; an' you shore as shootin' dug one for yoreself. This town's run by th' miners, a lot of hoof-poundin' grubs, with pack mules for pardners. There's been feelin's between us an' them walkin' fools," here he voiced the riders' contempt for men who walked, "for a long time. Yo're a puncher, an' you shore come out flat an' took sides today. Tell you what—either you come out to th' ranch with me, or I'll stay here in town with you. Come along: we'll find you a good cayuse, an' not rob you, neither."

"Can't do it, Tommy," replied Tex, warming to his

new acquaintance. "I got my eye on a roan beauty an' I'm goin' to own him by tomorrow. He won't cost me a red cent. So far's danger is concerned, I ain't in none that my tongue or my six-gun can't get me out of. But I'll ride out an' pay yore outfit a visit after I get th' roan."

"That's th' third best cayuse in this section," replied Tommy. "Williams owns all three of 'em, too. There ain't nothin' on th' ranch that can touch any of 'em." He paused and looked closely at his companion. "You heard any war-talk ag'in' th' agent?"

"Only a rumblin', far off," answered Tex. "Th' dust ain't plain yet, so I can't tell how it's headin'. What do you know about it?"

"Not half as much as Murphy, I bet," replied Watkins. "You ask him. It's a cussed shame for a man to be hounded by a pack of dogs. Well, I'm off. Remember that you got friends on th' C Bar when you need 'em, which you shore as shootin' will. We'll come a-runnin'." He shook hands and went out, Tex loafing after him as far as the door. "Tim, I reckon you an' Tex can manage to get along without me now, so I'll drift along. I'm due at th' ranch."

"Whose?" asked Murphy carelessly, trying a post to see if it was well set.

"Julius Caesar Curtis: Judy, for short," answered Watkins, holding out his hand. "You can leave th' other four posts for me to set when I come in again," he grinned.

"For a bye's-sized chew av tobaccy I'd skin ye," chuckled Tim, shaking the hand heartily. "Much obliged, Thomas, me son. Come in an' see us when ye can. There's so few decent men in this part av th' country that ye'll be welcome as th' flowers av spring."

Tommy swung into the saddle, raised his hat to the woman who appeared in the kitchen door, and whirled around to leave.

"Mr. Watkins!" called Jane, running toward the little

group. "You are not going to leave without your supper? Your place is set and Jerry is pouring the coffee."

Tommy Watkins flushed, swallowed his Adam's apple, looked blankly at Tex and Tim, stammered gibberish, and managed to convey the impression that the salvation of the ranch and its outfit depended on his immediate departure. His mute appeal for moral support was coldly received by his fellow-builders.

"I do not wish to be rude, Mr. Watkins," smiled Jane, "and I would not wish to turn you from your duty. But I shall be a little disappointed if you won't allow me to show my poor appreciation of what you have done for us. But I will not press you: if not tonight, then some other time?"

The savior of the C Bar flushed deeper, received scowling looks from his late bosom companions, who knew a liar when they heard one, and he ducked his head quickly. "Yes, ma'am," he blurted eagerly. "I'd admire to stay, but Curtis shore is dependin' on me to git back. If you'll excuse me, ma'am—I—so—by," and he was whirling away in a cloud of dust, his sombrero held out at arm's length.

Murphy looked gravely at Tex and flushed slightly. "He has an important job, miss," he said.

Tex looked gravely at Murphy and did not flush. "A great weight for shoulders so young," he lied, suspecting, however, that Tommy might have acquired, during the course of the day, a very great weight, indeed. He had observed his glances at Jane.

She smiled inscrutably and turned to look at the coop, clapping her hands in delight. "Isn't it fine, and new, and piney!" she exclaimed, sniffing the tangy odor. "And it looks so strong—I must peek in for a moment."

There was not much room to spare when they all had entered, a fact which Tex easily explained.

"You see, Miss Saunders," he said, waving his hands,

"it is to serve only as a nesting place and a shelter from predatory animals. During the day your flock will roam about the enclosure outside; but at twilight, without fail, it must be confined securely in this coop. No self-respecting coyote will be restrained for five minutes by the wire—he either will force himself between the strands, or dig under; and there are any number of those thieves around this town. They cannot be trapped or baffled—they will outwait or outwit any watcher. The only thing that will stop them is something physically impregnable.

"Tim and I intend to weave slats and laths between the lower strands of wire, running them vertically up from the ground, in which their lower ends will be driven. They will offer some protection, but their chief value will be to keep the chickens from getting outside. No coyote will be bothered by them for very long, and in order to save yourself the labor of filling up the tunnels they surely will dig if they can get in in no other way, I'd advise you to leave the fence gate wide open every night.

"We lay this floor for that reason. No matter what they are able to do, they can't get into the coop. I'll wager that you will find tunnels running under it before long. Don't fail to close this building before nightfall, and your flock will be safe."

"Amen," said Murphy. "They're cunnin' divvils, coyotes are!"

"I don't know how to thank you," said Jane, impulsively putting her hands on the arms of her companions. "Think what it will mean to Jerry—a dozen fresh eggs a day!"

Murphy chuckled. "Four a day will be doin' good, an' not that many for awhile. I'll get ye some grit, an' make a batch av whitewash."

"Hey!" called a voice. "Everything's getting cold!"

"There's Jerry, playing domestic tyrant," laughed

Jane. "Isn't it remarkable what a difference it makes to the cook? He thinks nothing of making me wait. Come on—you can tell me all about chicken raising after supper." She cast a furtive glance at Tex, and past him at the twilight-softened range beyond, where Tommy Watkins somewhere rode to save his ranch and outfit.

CHAPTER V

A Trimmer Trimmed

About ten o'clock that night Murphy and Tex neared the station and stopped short at the former's sudden ejaculation.

"Th' switch is open," he said. "Not that anythin' serious might happen, unless th' engineer went blind; but either av them would have plenty to say about it. Trust 'em for that. An' tomorrow is Overton's trick eastbound. He's worse than Casey. Wait here a bit," and the section-boss went over, threw the switch, and returned.

Soon they stopped again at the station to say good night to each other. Murphy seemed a little constrained and worried and soon gave the reason for it.

"Tex," he said in a low voice, "yer takin' sides with th' weakest party, an' yer takin' 'em fast an' open. Right now yer bein' weighed an' discussed, an' to no profit to yerself. I can see that yer a man that will go his own way—but if th' hotel gets unpleasant an' tirin', yer more than welcome in my shanty. 'Tis only an old box car off its wheels, but there's a bunk in it for ye any time ye want to use it. Tread easy now, an' keep yer two eyes open; an' while I'm willin' to back ye up, I daren't do it unless it's a matter av life an' death. I'm Irish, an' so is Costigan. There's a strong feelin' out here ag'in' us—an' when a mob starts not even wimmin an' childer are safe. Costigan has both, an' there's th' lass, as well. I've urged Mike to send his family back along th' line somewhere, but his wife says *no*. She's foolish, no doubt, but I say, God bless such wimmin."

"She's not foolish," replied Tex with conviction. "She's wise, riskin' herself mebby, on a long chance. While she stays here Costigan will use a lot of discretion—if she goes, he might air his opinions too much, or get drunk and leave her a widow. I'll do what I can to stave off trouble, even to eatin' a little dirt; but, Tim, I'd like nothing better than to send for a few friends an' let things take their natural course. Every time I look at that nephew I fair itch to strangle him. It can't be possible that Miss Saunders gives him any encouragement? I'm much obliged about yore offer. I'd take it up right now except that it would cause a lot of talk an' thinkin'. Here, you better hand me two dollars for my day's work—there ain't no use lyin' about anythin' if th' truth will serve. I'll return it th' next time I see you."

"Th' lass won't look at that scut. He follers her around like a dog," Murphy growled, and then a grin came to his face as he dug into his pocket. "Here. Yer overpaid, but I should 'a' dickered with ye before I let ye go to work."

"Thanks, boss," chuckled Tex. "You'll need me to-morrow, for th' wire stringin'?"

"Yer fired!" answered Murphy, his voice rising and changing in timbre. "Yer a loafin', windy, clumsy, bunglin' no-account. By rights that ought to make ye mad. Does it?"

Tex could not fail to read the answer he was expected to make, for it lay in the section-boss' tones; and he thought that he had seen something move around the corner of the station. He stepped on the toe of one of his companion's boots to acknowledge the warning.

"Am I?" he demanded, angrily. "Yo're so d—d used to bossin' Irish loafers that you don't know a good man when you see one. You don't have to fire me, you Mick! I'm quittin', an' you can go to h—l!"

Murphy's arm stopped in mid-air as Tex's gun leaped from its sheath.

"You checked it just in time," snapped Tex. "Any more of that an' I'll blow you wide open. Turn around an' hoof it to yore sty!"

Murphy, strangling a chuckle, backed warily away. "If ye was as handy with tools as ye are with that d—d gun—" he growled. " 'Tis lucky for ye that ye have it!"

"This *is* my tool," retorted Tex. "Shut up an' get out before you make me use it. Fire me, hey? You got one — — gall!"

He stood staring after the shuffling Irishman, muttering savagely to himself, until the section-boss had been swallowed up by the darkness. Then he turned, slammed the gun back into its holster and stamped toward the hotel; but he stopped in the nearest saloon to give the eavesdropper, if there had been one, a chance to get to the hotel before him.

The bar was deserted, but half a dozen prospectors were seated at the tables, and they greeted his entrance with scowls. The two cavalrymen present glanced at him in disinterested, momentary curiosity and resumed their maudlin conversation. Some shavetail's ears must have been burning out at their post.

Tex stormed up to the bar and slammed two silver dollars on it. "Take this dirty money an' give th' boys cigars for it," he growled. "Me, I'm not smokin' any of 'em. Fire me, huh? I'd like to see th' section-boss that fires me! 'Overpaid,' he says, an' me workin' like a dog! 'I don't need ye tomorry,' he says: I cussed soon told him what he needed, but he didn't wait for it. Fire me?" he sneered. "Like h—l!"

The cavalrymen grinned sympathetically and nodded their thanks for the cigars, which they had no little difficulty in lighting. The other men in the room took their gifts silently, two of them abruptly pushing them across the table, away from them.

"There'll be others that'll mebby git what they're needin'," said a rasping, unsteady voice from a corner table. " 'Specially if he sticks his nose in where it ain't wanted."

Tex casually turned and nodded innocently. "My sentiments exactly," he agreed, waiting to receive unequivocal notification that it was he for whom the warning was meant. A little stupidity was often a useful thing.

"Nobody asked you for yore sentiments," retorted the prospector. "Strangers can't come into this town an' carry things with a high hand. Next time, Jake will kill you."

Tex looked surprised and then his eyes glinted. "That bein' a little job he can start 'most any time," he retorted. "When a man fights worse'n a dog he makes me mad; an' he fought like a cur. I'd do it ag'in. He got what he was needin', that's all."

The miner glowered at him. "An' he's got friends, Jake has," he asserted.

"Tell him that he'll need 'em—all of 'em," sneered Tex. "Our little session was plumb personal, but I'll let in his friends. Th' gate's wide open. They don't have to dig in under th' fence, or sit on their haunches outside an' howl. An' let me tell you somethin' for yore personal benefit—I've swallered all I aim to swaller tonight. I'm peaceable an' not lookin' for no trouble—you hold yore yap till I get through talkin'—but I ain't dodgin' none. Somehow I seem to be out of step in this town; but I'm whistlin' that I'm cussed particular about who sets me right. I ain't got no grudges ag'in' nobody; I'm tryin' to act accordin' to my lights, but I ain't apologizin' to nobody for them lights. Anybody objectin'?"

"Fair enough," said one of the cavalrymen. "I like his frank ways."

"That rides for me, too," endorsed his companion, aggressively.

"Shut up, you!" cried the bartender.

"For two bits—" pugnaciously began a miner, but he was cut short.

"An' you, too!" barked the man behind the counter, a gun magically appearing over the edge of the bar. "This has gone far enough! Stranger, you spoke yore piece fair. Tom," he said, looking at the angry miner, "you got nothin' more to say: yo're all through. If you think you has, then go outside an' shout it there. Th' subject is closed. What'll you-all have?"

Tex tarried after the round had been drunk but he did not order one on his own account, feeling that it would be a mistake under the circumstances. It might be regarded as a sign of weakness, and was almost certain to cause trouble. Turning his back on the sullen miner he talked casually with the bartender and the cavalrymen, and then one of the miners cleared his throat and spoke.

"Did you have a run-in with th' big Irishman?" he asked.

Tex leaned carelessly against the bar, grinned and frankly recounted the affair, and before he had finished the narrative, answering grins appeared here and there among his audience. The sputter of a sulphur match caught his eyes as his late adversary slowly reached for and lit the cigar he had pushed from him a few minutes earlier, but Tex did not immediately glance that way. When he had finished the story he looked around the room, noticed that all were smoking and he nodded slightly in friendly understanding. A little later he said good night, smiled pleasantly at the once sullen prospector, and went carelessly out into the night. The buzz of comment following his departure was not unfavorable to him.

When he entered the hotel barroom all eyes turned to him, and he noticed a grim smile on Williams' face and that the evil countenance of the nephew was aquiver with suspicion. Walking over, he stepped close to the table, watching the play, and from where he could keep tabs on Bud Haines' every move. During the new deal Williams leaned back, stretched, and glanced up.

"Had yore supper?" he carelessly asked.

Tex nodded. "Shore: reg'lar home-cooked feed. It went good for a change. I reckon I shore earned it, too." He drew out a sack of tobacco, filled a cigarette paper and held the sack in his teeth while he rolled himself a smoke. "What's paid around here for a good, half-day's work?" he mumbled between his teeth.

"What kind of work?" judicially asked Williams.

Tex removed the sack, moistened the cigarette and held it unlighted while he answered "Freightin' on foot, carpenterin', diggin', an' doin' what I was told to do."

"Dollar to a dollar four bits," replied Williams. "What you doin'? Hirin' out?"

"I was; but I ain't no more," replied Tex, lighting up. He exhaled a lungful of smoke and dragged up a chair. "I asked two dollars, an' there was an argument. That's all."

The hands lay where they had been dealt, Williams having let his own lay, and the players were idly listening until he should pick it up.

"What's it all about?" asked Williams. "You talk like a dish of hash."

The eager nephew squirmed closer to the table and his assumed look of indifference was a heavy failure.

Tex laughed, leaned back, and with humorous verbal pigments painted a rapidly changing picture to the best of his by no means poor ability. He took them up to the digging of the post holes, and then leaned forward. "Murphy said we'd build a four-sided fence, three posts to th' side, makin twelve in all. That suited us, an' as there was only one spade, we told him to go ahead an' dig his holes while we worked on th' nest boxes. He was to do th' north an' th' south sides, which he said was fair." The speaker paused a moment, leaning back in his chair, his eyelids nearly closed. Between their narrowed openings he looked swiftly around. The card players grinned in expectation of some joke about to appear, Williams looked suspicious and puzzled, but the bartender's eyes popped open and he choked back a sudden burst of laughter. Tex drew in a long breath, pushed back into his chair and glanced around at the players. "I was honest an' fair enough to say th' diggin' wasn't evenly divided, us bein' two and' him only one. What do you boys say?"

"What's it all amount to anyhow?" snarled the nephew. "Who cares if it was or not? What did you think of th' gal?" he demanded.

Tex breathed deeply, relaxed, and gravely considered his boots. "Well, if I was aimin' to start a kindergarten I might have took more notice of her—an' you, too, bub. Can't you do yore own lookin'?" he plaintively demanded. "Anyhow, I was warned fair, wasn't I? Huh! When you get to be my age an' have had my experience with this fool world you won't be takin' no more interest in 'em than I do. Beggin' yore pardon for interruptin' th' previous conversation we was holdin'. I'll perceed from where I was." He looked back at the card players. "We was debatin' th' fairness of th' offer to dig them holes. What you boys say?"

The man nearest to him pursed his lips and cogitated. The subject was no more frivolous than the majority of subjects which had furnished bones of contention many a night. Most barroom arguments start on even less. "I reckon it was, him bein' more used to diggin'."

His partner leaned forward. "What did *he* say about it, at first?"

"He was shore satisfied," answered Tex as the bartender, turning his back on the room, shook with the ague.

The last questioner bobbed his head decisively. "Then it shore was fair."

Williams nodded slowly, for his opinions were not lightly given. "I'd say it was. What about it?"

"Oh, nothin' much," growled Tex. "I reckon he changed his mind later on." He looked over at the gambler leaning against the wall, the same gambler he had seen on the train. At this notice Denver Jim, sensing possible bets, straightened up, winked, and made a sign which among his class was a notification that he had declared himself in for half the winnings of a game. Tex shook his head slightly and frowned, as if deeply puzzled over Murphy's conduct. The gambler repeated the sign and moved forward.

Tex did some quick thinking. He could not afford to be linked to a tin-horn and he did not intend to make any money out of his joke. Whatever he won in this town he would win at cards, and win it alone. His second signal of refusal was backed up by his hand dropping carelessly and resting on the butt of his gun. The gambler scowled, barely nodded his acquiescence and went to the bar for a drink. Bud Haines glanced up from the weekly paper he was reading, saw nothing to hold his interest, and returned to his reading.

Tex went on with his story, telling about the supper and his scene with Murphy at the station, repeating the latter word for word as nearly as he could from the time when he detected the approach of the eavesdropper. From the constantly repeated looks of satisfaction on Williams' face he knew that the local boss had been given a detailed account of the incident, and that he was checking it up, step by step. Briefly sketching his trouble in the saloon, Tex threw the cigarette butt at a distant box cuspidor and stretched. "An' here I am," he finished.

Williams picked up his hand, glancing absent-mindedly at the cards. "Yes," he grunted, "here you are." Putting the cards back on the table he carelessly pushed them from him, squaring the edges with zealous care. "You come near not bein' here, though," he said, his level look steady and accusing. "Whatever made you jump on Jake that way?" he demanded coldly.

"Shucks! Here it comes again!"said Tex. He looked suspicious and defiant. "I did it to stop a murder, an' a lynchin'," he answered shortly.

"Very fine!" muttered Williams. "You was a little mite overanxious—there wouldn't 'a' been no lynchin' of Jake; but there might 'a' been one, just th' same. I had to do some real talkin' to stop it. It ain't wise for strangers to act sudden in a frontier town—'specially in this town. That's somethin' you hadn't ought to forget, Mr. Jones."

"If I get yore meanin' plain, yo're intendin' me to think I was in danger of bein' lynched?"

"You shore was."

"Then yo're admittin' that this town of Windsor will lynch a man because he keeps a murder from bein' committed, by lickin' th' man who tried to do it?"

"Exactly. Jake has lots of friends."

"He's plumb welcome to 'em, an' I reckon, if he's that kind of a man, he shore needs 'em bad. But from what I saw of Jake he ain't that kind of a man. I'm a friend of his'n, too. I'm so much a friend of Jake's that if he treads on my toes I'll save him from facin' th' trials an' hardships that come with old age. His existence is precarious, anyhow. He's allus just one step ahead of poverty an' grub stakes. Life for Jake is just one placer disappointment after another. He allus has to figger on a hard winter. Then he has to dodge sickness an' saddles, wrestlin' tricks, boxin' tricks, an' fast gunplay. But Jake is th' kind of a man that does his own fightin' for hisself. Yo're plumb mistaken about him."

"Mebby I am," admitted Williams. "I didn't know you

was acquainted with anybody around here, 'specially th' C Bar outfit."

"I wasn't," replied Tex. "It ain't my nature to be distant an' disdainful, however." He grinned. "I get acquainted fast."

"You acted prompt in helpin' that Watkins," accused Williams.

"I shore had to, or he'd 'a' quit bein' Watkins," retorted Tex. "You look here: We'll be savin' a lot of time if we come right down to cases. I saw a big man tryin' to kick th' head off another man, a smaller one, that was down. I stopped him from doin' it without hurtin' him serious. If it'd been th' other way 'round I'd done th' same thing. As it stands, it's between Jake an' me. We'll let it stay that way until th' lynchin' party starts out. Then anybody will be plumb welcome to cut in an' stop it. Excuse me for interferin' with yore game— but th' fault ain't mine. Talkin' is dry work—bartender, set 'em up for all hands. Who's winnin'?"

Williams picked up his cards again, looked at them, puckered his lips and glanced around at his companions. He cleared his throat and looked back at Tex. "I reckon I was, a little. Want to sit in? After all, Jake's troubles are his own: we got enough without 'em."

Tex looked at the table and the players, shrugged his shoulders and answered carelessly. "Don't feel like playin' very much—ate too much supper, I reckon. Later on, when I ain't so heavy with grub, mebby I'll take cards. I'd rather play ag'in' fewer hands, tonight, anyhow."

Williams looked up and sneered. "Think you got a better chance, that way?"

"I get sort of confused when there's so many playin'," confessed Tex; "but I shore can beat th' man that invented th' game, playin' it two-handed. I used to play for hosses, two-handed. Allus had luck, somehow, playin' for them. Why, once I owned six cayuses at one time, that I'd won."

"That so? You like that gray: how much will you put up ag'in' him?"

"I wouldn't play for no gray hoss—they're plumb unlucky with me. I ain't superstitious, but I shore don't like gray hosses."

"Got anythin' ag'in' sorrels?" Williams asked with deep sarcasm.

"Nothin' much; but I'm shore stuck on blacks an roans. I call *them* hosses!" Tex grinned at the crowd and looked back at Williams. "Yes, sir; I shore do."

"How much will you put up ag'in' a good roan, then?"

"Ain't got much money," evaded Tex, backing away.

"Got two hundred dollars?"

"Not for no cayuse. Besides, I don't know th' hoss yo're meanin'."

"That roan you saw today," replied Williams. "John said you liked him a lot. I'll play you one hand, th' roan ag'in' two hundred."

Tex glanced furtively at the front door and then at the stairway. "Let it go till tomorrow night," he mumbled.

"Yo're a great talker, ain't you?" sneered Williams. "I'll put up th' roan ag'in' a hundred an' fifty. One hand, just me an' you."

"Well, mebby," replied Tex. "Better make her th' best two out of three. I might have bad luck th' first hand."

Williams' disgust was obvious and a snicker ran through the room. "I wouldn't play that long for a miserable sum like that ag'in' a stranger. One hand, draw poker, my roan ag'in' yore one-fifty. Put up, or shut up!"

"All right," reluctantly acquiesced Tex. "We allus used to make it two out of three up my way; but I may be lucky. After you get through—I ain't in no hurry."

Williams laughed contemptuously: "You shore don't have to say so!" He smiled at his grinning companions and resumed his play.

Tex dropped into the seat next to the sneering nephew, from where he could watch the gun-fighter.

Bud's expression duplicated that of his boss and he paid but little attention to the wordy fool who was timid about playing poker for a horse.

"Hot, ain't it?" said Tex pleasantly. "Hot, an' close."

"Some folks find it so; reckon mebby it is," answered the nephew. "What did you people talk about at supper?" he asked.

"Hens," answered Tex, grinning. "She's got a dozen. You'd think they was rubies, she's that stuck up about 'em. Kind of high-toned, ain't she?"

The nephew laughed sneeringly. "She'll lose that," he promised. "I don't aim to be put off much longer."

"Mebby yo're callin' too steady," suggested Tex. "Sometimes that gives 'em th' idea they own a man. You don't want to let 'em feel too shore of you."

Henry Williams shifted a little. "No," he replied; "I ain't callin' too often. In fact, I ain't done no callin' at all, yet. I've sort of run acrost her on th' right-of-way, an' watched her a little. I get a little bit scary, somehow— just can't explain it. But I aim to call at th' house, for I'm shore gettin' tired of ridin' wide."

"Ain't they smart, though?" chuckled Tex; "holdin' back an' actin' skittish. I cured a gal of that, once; but I don't reckon you can do it. It takes a lot of nerve an' will-power. You feel like playin' show-downs, two-bits a game?"

"Make it a dollar, an' I will. How'd you cure that one of yourn?"

"Dollar's purty steep," objected Tex. "Make it a half." He leaned back and laughed reminiscently. "I worked a system on her. Lemme deal first?"

"Suit yourself. Turn 'em face up—it'll save time. What did you do?"

"Made her think I didn't care a snap about her. Want to cut? Well, I didn't know—some don't want to," he explained. "Saves time, that's all. Reckon it's yore pot on that queen. Deal 'em up."

"How'd you do it? snub her?"

"Gosh, no! Don't you ever do that: it makes 'em mad. Just let 'em alone—sort of look at 'em without seein' 'em real well. You dassn't make 'em mad! You win ag'in. Yo're lucky at this game: want to quit?"

"Give you a chance to get it back," sneered the nephew. "Think it would work with her?"

"Don't know: she got any other beaux?"

"I've seen to that. She ain't. Take th' money an' push over yore cards. Do you think it will work with her?" Henry persisted.

"Gosh, sonny: don't you ask me that! No man knows very much about wimmin', an' me less than most men. It's a gamble. She's got to jump one way or th' other, ain't she? How was you figgerin' to win?"

"Just go get her, that's all. She'll tame down after awhile."

"But you allus can do that, can't you? Now, if it was me I'd try to get her to come of her own accord, for things would be sweeter right at th' very start. But, then, I'm a gambler, allus willin' to run a risk. A man's got to foller his own nature. I got you beat ag'in: this shore is a nice game."

"Too weak," objected the nephew. "Dollar a hand would suit me better. My eights win this. Want to boost her?"

Tex reflected covetously. "Well, I might go high as a dollar, but not no more."

'Dollar it is, then. What's yore opinion of that gal?"'

"Shucks," laughed Tex. "She's nice enough, I reckon; but she ain't my style. Yore uncle's game is bustin' up an' he's lookin' at me. See you later. You win ag'in, but I allus have bad luck doublin' th' stakes, 'though I ain't what you might call superstitious. See you later."

Tex arose and went over to the other table, raked in the cards, squared them to feel if they had been trimmed, thought they had been, and pushed them out for the cut, watching closely to see how the face cards had been shaved. Williams turned the pack, announced that high dealt, grasped the sides of the pack and turned a queen. Tex also grasped the sides of the pack remaining and also turned a queen. He clumsily dropped the deck, growled something and bunched it again, shoving it toward his companion in such a way that Williams would have to show a deliberate preference for the side grip. This he did and Tex followed his lead. The ends of the face cards and aces had been trimmed and the sides of the rest of the deck had been treated the same way. Because of this the sides of the face cards stuck out from the deck and the ends of the spot cards projected. Yet so carefully had it been done that it was not noticeable. Williams cut again, turning another queen. Tex cut a king and picked up the pack. As he shuffled he was careful not to show any of his characteristic motions, for although his opponent had forgotten his face in the score of years behind their former meeting, it might take but very little to start his memory back-tracking.

"My money ag'in' th' roan," said the dealer, pushing out the cards for the cut. "Hundred an' fifty," he explained.

Williams cut deep and nodded. "This one game decides it: a discard, a draw, an' a show-down. Right?"

"Right," grunted Tex, swiftly dropping the cards before them. Williams picked up his hand, but gave no sign of disappointment. There was not a face card in it. He made his selection, discarded, and called for three cards. Tex had discarded two. Williams wanted no face cards on the draw, since he held a pair of nines. One more nine would give him a fair hand, and another would just about win for him. He drew a black queen and a pair of red jacks.

"Well," he said, "ready to show?"

Tex grunted again, glanced at Bud Haines, and lay down three queens, a nine, and a jack. "What you got?" he anxiously asked.

"An empty box stall, I reckon," growled his adversary, spreading his hand. He pushed back without another word to Tex, looked at his stableman and spoke gruffly. "John, give that roan to Mr. Jones when he calls for it. He's to keep it somewhere else. I'm turnin' in. Good night, all."

CHAPTER VI

Friendly Interest

FRESHLY SHAVEN, his boots well rubbed, and his clothes as free from dust as possible, Tex sauntered down the street after breakfast the next morning and stepped into the stable. John Graves met him, nodded, and led the way to the roan's stall.

"You got a fine hoss, Mr. Jones," he said, opening the gate.

"Yes, I have; an' you've taken good care of him. His coat couldn't be better. I like a man that looks after a hoss."

"I ain't sayin' nothin' about nobody, but I'm glad to see him change owners," said Graves, glancing around. "Rub yore hand on his flank. I got th' coat so it hides 'em real well."

Tex stroked the white nose, rubbed the neck and shoulders, and slowly passed his hand over the flank. The scars were easily found. He wheeled and looked at the stableman. "Who in h—l did that, an' why?" he demanded.

"That ain't for me to say, an' sayin' wouldn't do no good; but I'm plumb glad he's in other hands. Just because a hoss fights back when he's bein' abused ain't no reason to cut him to pieces. An' a big man can kick hard when he's mad."

Tex held a lump of sugar to the sensitive, velvety lips before replying. "Yes, he can," he admitted. "Anybody in town that'll treat this hoss right, an' give him a stall?"

"Better see Jim Carney in his saloon. He's a good, reliable man an' likes hosses. He'll take good care of Oh My."

Tex stared at him. "Of what?"

"Oh My," replied the stableman. "Th' rest of th' name is Cayenne."

" 'Suffer little children!' " exclaimed Tex. "Who named him that, an why?"

"I reckon Williams did, because he's peppery an' red."

"Good heavens!" ejaculated Tex. He thought a moment. "Huh! Prophet! Mecca! Mohammed!" he muttered. Suddenly seeing a great light, he flipped his sombrero into the air, caught and balanced it on his nose when it came down, sidestepped, and as it fell, punched it across the stable. Turning gravely he shook hands with the surprised stableman, slapped him on the shoulder and burst out laughing. "Where'n blazes did he dig 'em up? He don't know what one of them names means; *There was the Veil through which I might not see.* Come, John: *Oh, many a Cup of this forbidden Wine must drown the memory of that insolence!* Wait till I get my hat: *Better be jocund with the fruitful Grape than sadden after none, or bitter, Fruit.*"

Carney gave them a nonchalant welcome and displayed little interest in them until Graves told him about the horse.

"Th' roan, eh?" exclaimed the saloonkeeper. "I'll shore find a place for it, but I'm afraid it'll miss th' beatin's.

There's a closet built across one corner of th' stable: I'll give you a key to it, Mr. Jones. It'll be handy for yore trappin's."

After a few rounds Tex went out, mounted bareback and, leaving Graves in front of the stable, rode to the hotel to get his saddle. Soon thereafter he dismounted at the station and smiled at the agent.

" 'Richard is himself again,' " he chuckled, affectionately patting Omar. "An' I still have my kingdom."

"He looks fit for a king to ride," replied Jerry.

"He'd honor a king. How's th' hen ranch comin' along? Got th' fence up yet?"

"Yes; Murphy just finished it. That looks like Williams' roan."

"It was. I won it at poker. I could feel in my fingers that I was goin' to be lucky. Hello!" he exclaimed, looking at a box across the track. On it were painted irregular, concentric circles. "Looks like it might be a target."

Jerry laughed. "It is; and so far, unhit."

Tex glanced at the other's low-hung belt and gun. "Have you shot at it yet?"

Jerry nodded.

"From where?"

"Right here."

"Great mavericks!" said Tex. "Here: let's see how fast you can get that gun out, an' empty it at that box. I got a reason for it."

At the succession of reports the toolshed door flew open and a huge Irishman, rifle in hand, popped into sight. Seeing Tex he grunted and slowly went back again.

Tex looked from the box to the marksman, shook his head, silently unbuckled the belt from its owner's waist, took the empty gun from the agent's hand, and tossed the outfit on a near-by box.

"Don't you carry it, Jerry," he said. "Load it up an' leave it home. Popular feelin', even in this town, frowns at th' shootin' of an unarmed man. It's somethin' that's hard to explain away."

"But then I'll be defenseless!" expostulated Jerry. "It's *some* protection."

"You were defenseless before I took it from you," said Tex.

"But it is some protection," Jerry reiterated.

Tex shook his head. "It's a screaming invitation for a killin', that's what it is. Here: That's you," pointing to the target. "You got somethin' I want plumb bad. You try to stop me from gettin' it, an' I won't listen to you. I force th' hand an' you make a move that I can claim was hostile. Yo're armed, ain't you? I might even slap yore face. Then this happens."

The spurting smoke enveloped them both, the stabs of flame and the sharp reports coming with unbelievable rapidity. Stepping from the gray fog, Tex pointed. The box was split and turned part way around. The inner two circles showed six holes.

"I did it in self-defense. What chance did you have?" demanded the puncher.

"Great guns! What shooting!" marveled Jerry, his mouth open.

"That's good shootin'," admitted Tex. "Better mebby, than most men in this town can do, quite a lot better than th' average. There's plenty of men who can't do as good. Th' draw was more'n fair, too; better than most gun-toters; but I know two men that would 'a' killed me before I jerked loose from th' leather. I wasn't showin' off: I was answerin' yore remark about a gun bein' some protection to you. While we're speakin' about guns, can Miss Saunders use one? Bein' a woman I hardly thought so, unless Hennery has taught her."

"Henry!" growled Jerry. "Why would he teach her?"

"Why a young woman like her would be right popular, out here or anywhere else," replied Tex. "House full of admirers, an' others taggin' along. I reckoned Hennery might have showed her how to shoot."

"The devil had a better chance," retorted Jerry. "If Henry ever calls at our house she'll scald him. She thinks about as little of Henry as she does of a snake."

"I'm admirin' Miss Saunders more every day," said Tex. "Havin' disposed of th' interpolation, we'll get at th' main subject. As I was sayin', bein' a woman, she's not likely to be shot at. But I'm sorry yore Colt is so big: she couldn't drag a gun like that around with her. Besides, th' caliber needn't be so big."

"I got a short-barreled .38 home," said Jerry. He looked a little worried. "What makes you talk like that?"

"Bein' a gunman, I reckon; an' my ornery, suspicious nature," answered Tex. "Bein' a poker player for years, readin' faces is a hobby with me. I've read some in this town that I don't like. 'Taint nothin' to put a finger on, but I'm so cussed suspicious of every male biped of th' genus homo that I allus look for th' worst. Anyhow, it wouldn't be no crime if Miss Saunders knew how to use that snub-nosed .38, would it? Sort of give her a sense of security. Then, if Murphy or our adolescent Watkins took her out ridin' an showed her how to get th' most out of its limited possibilities, it ought to relieve yore mind."

"I don't know of anyone better qualified to get the most out of a gun than yourself," replied Jerry. "If it ain't asking too much," he hastily added.

"Havin' a brand-new, Cayenne pepper cayuse to learn about, an' show off," laughed Tex, "it wouldn't set on me like a calamity. Shall I bring a horse for Miss Saunders, or saddle up her own?"

"She hasn't any; but—"

"—me no buts," interrupted Tex. "I'll now pay my respects to yore sister, with yore permission, an' invite her to ride out with me, tomorrow, an' view th' lovely brown hills an' dusty flats, where every prospect pleases, an' only man is vile. Procrastination never was a sin of mine: it's th' one I overlooked. We'll likely go far enough from town so there won't be no panicky fears of a hostile raid. Does Miss Saunders favor any particular hoss?"

"No, and she can ride, so you won't have to get one that's nearly dead."

Tex laughed. "All right; but when she gets it, it won't be as ornery as it might be. How is it that nobody but Murphy paid any attention to our shootin'?"

"They're used to it by this time."

"Well, so-long," and Tex swung into the saddle and rode off.

Jane showed her pleasure at his visit and smilingly accepted his invitation to go riding. They examined the coop and yard, talked of numerous things and after awhile Tex turned to leave, but stopped and grinned.

"Bring your six-gun, Miss Saunders, and we'll have a match," he said. "The great western target, the ubiquitous tin can, is sure to be plentiful, despite the killing drought."

"My gun?" she laughed. "I have no gun. Do you think that I go around with a gun?"

He tapped his forehead significantly. "I'm so used to carrying one that I forgot. Shucks, that's too bad. Well, if we overtake any wild cans you can use mine, although a smaller gun would be more pleasant for you. Too bad you haven't a short-barreled gun—a .32, for instance. Shooting is really great sport. Then I'm to call at two o'clock?"

"If there was some place where we could enjoy a lunch," she murmured. "We could leave earlier and get back earlier."

"There is sure to be," assured Tex, smiling. "Say ten o'clock, then?"

"That will be much better. I'll have everything ready when you come. Is there anything in the eating line which you particularly fancy?"

Tex fanned himself with the sombrero, a happy expression on his face. "Yes, there is," he admitted. "Mallard duck stuffed with Chesapeake oysters. Plenty of cold, crisp, tender celery, and any really good brand of dry champagne. I'll enjoy anything you prepare, and I'll have a round-up appetite."

"I'll try to give you a change from hotel food," she laughed as he swung into the saddle.

She watched him ride away and walked slowly back to the house. Then her face brightened a little as she thought of the revolver in Jerry's room. Jerry had said it was a .38.

The station agent answered the hail and went out to the edge of the platform.

"All fixed?" he asked.

Tex nodded. "You get her to bring that gun. I paved the way for it, but you know her better than I do, and how to persuade her without making her frightened. What's it shoot: longs, or shorts? That's good; shorts are O.K. Is Murphy in th' toolshed?"

"He's married to it," smiled Jerry.

"If you see him, tell him I'm goin' to call on him late tonight. If his light's *out* I'll know he's home. Any fool would know it if it was lit. Well, so-long."

Jerry looked after him and shook his head, a peculiar, baffled, friendly light in his eyes. "I don't know when you are most serious: when you *are* serious, or when you are joking. Was your warning about my gun just a general one, or did it have a special meaning? And about Jane learning to shoot? What do you know, how much do you know, and why are you bothering about us? The Heathen Chinee was simple beside you, Tex Jones."

He coughed and turned to enter the station, but stopped in his tracks as a possible solution came to him. "I wonder, now," he cogitated, and fell into the vernacular. "She's a fine girl, sis is; but headstrong. Cuss it, if it ain't one thing it's another. I don't even know his name is Jones, or how many wives he may have. Oh, well: I'll have to wait and see how it heads."

Tex rode slowly down the street, very well satisfied with himself. He had warned the agent, owned a fine horse that cost him nothing, and was going riding on the morrow with a very interesting and pretty young woman. Suddenly he took cognizance of a thought which had been trying to get his attention for quite some time: Where was Jake and what was he doing?

"I'm gettin' careless," he reproved himself. "I ain't seen my little playmate since I paralyzed his nerve system. He didn't act like a man who would go into retirement with a thing like that tagged to him. I reckon he's plannin' a comeback: but a man like him usually acts quicker. All right, Jake: you take plenty of time an' work it out well. An' that's shore good advice."

There came a sudden yelping from the other side of a near-by building, so high-pitched, continuous, and full of agony that something moved along his spine. He reacted to the misery in the sound without giving it any thought, and when he turned the corner of the store and saw a chained dog being beaten by one of the town's ne'er-do-wells his hand of its own volition loosened the coiled rope at the saddle and swung it twice around his head. The soft lariat leaped through the air like a striking snake, and as it dropped over its victim, the roan instantly obeyed its training.

Jerked off his feet, his arms imprisoned at his sides, the dog beater slid, rolled, and bumped along the ground, at first too startled to protest. Then his voice arose in a stream of blasphemous inquiry, finishing with a petition.

Tex rode along without a backward glance, deeply engrossed by some interesting problem and nearly had reached Carney's saloon before he became conscious of his surroundings A miner, cursing, leaped to the roan's head and checked her, shouting profanely at the rider.

Tex checked the horse, looked curiously down at the protestor and then, sensing the burden of the other's remarks and becoming aware of the maledictions behind him, turned languidly in the saddle and looked back in time to see a dust-covered figure stagger to its feet and throw off the slackened rope.

"Hey!" shouted Tex indignantly. "What you doin' with my rope? Think it's worth th' price of a few drinks, eh? You drop it, *pronto!* An' as for you, my Christian friend," he said to the man at the roan's head, "if you ever grab my cayuse like that again me an' you are shore goin' to have an impolite little party all to ourselves. Drop that hackamore."

"You was killin' that man!" yelled the miner, loosening his hold and showing fight.

"Well, what of it?" demanded Tex. "Any man that chains up a dog an' then beats it like he was, ain't got no right to live. If I don't kill him, somebody else will. What you raisin' all th' hellabaloo about?"

"I reckon you ain't far from wrong," said the other, by this time fully aware of the identity of the dog beater. "I'm nat'rally for law an' order. Whiskey Jim ain't no good, I'm admittin'!"

"If yo're for law an' order you must be lonesome associatin' all by yoreself in this squaw town," replied Tex, grinning, but not for one moment losing sight of Whiskey Jim, who at that moment was stooping to pick up a stone lying against the corner of a building. Tex sent a shot over his head and the incident was closed. "What do you do for company?"

"I ain't hankerin' for none," answered the miner, smiling grimly. "I only come in for supplies, an' don't stay long. You a stranger here?"

"That's unkind; but, seein' as how I ain't as much a stranger now as I was when I come, I won't hold it ag'in' you. Mebby I am gettin' to look like I belonged here." He laughed. "I don't know very many, but everybody knows me. They point with pride when they see me comin'; an' cock their guns behind their backs with their other hand. Where you located, friend?"

"Second fork on Buffaler Crick, th' first crick west of

town. Quickest way is to foller th' track. Be glad to see you any time. Mine's th' shack above Jake's."

"I envy you," replied Tex. "See much of our mutual friend?"

"Only when he wants to borry somethin'," grinned the other. "I see you got th' pick of Williams' animals under yore saddle."

"I *was* lucky pickin', I admits," beamed Tex. "Nice feller, Williams."

"For them as likes him. Well, friend, I'm mushin' on. Name's Blascom."

"Tex Jones is my *nom du guerre*," replied Tex. "Th' north is a better country than this for minin'. How'd you ever come to leave it?"

Blascom looked at him questioningly. "Yes, reckon it is; but how'd you know I come from there?"

"They don't *mush* nowhere else that I know of," chuckled Tex. He coiled the dusty lariat, shook it, and brushed his chaps where it had touched, waved his farewell; and went on to Carney's, where he dismounted and went in.

"Just met Whiskey Jim," he said across the bar.

"I congratulate you."

"Who's he livin' on?"

"Th' whole town," answered Carney. "He used to hang around here, seein' what he could steal, but I kicked his pants around his neckband an' he ain't favorin' me no more. Reckon he belongs to Williams."

"Then he must do somethin' for his keep," suggested Tex. "Our friend Gustavus Adolphus ain't no philanthropist, I'm bettin'."

"No; Gus is a Republican," replied Carney. "Whiskey Jim used to ride for him, an' mebby Gus is scared not to look after him a little."

Tex nodded. "Good reason; good, plain, practical, common-sense reason. Now, Carney—I want a good hoss for a lady, an' I'll have a little ride on it before I turn it over. Want it tomorrow mornin' at eight o'clock."

"Miss Saunders won't thank you much for tirin' it out."

"You couldn't help guessin' right th' first time," accused Tex. "There ain't no other ladies that I've seen or heard about. What th' lady don't know won't hurt her pride or spoil her appetite. Cuss it, man; I ain't aimin' to kill th' beast!"

"I reckon you know what yo're goin' to do with th' hoss," replied Carney, thoughtfully; "but I wonder do you know what yo're doin', goin' ridin' with that little lady?"

Tex regarded him with level gaze. "Meanin'?" he coldly demanded.

"Meanin' that claim is staked, th' notices posted, an' trespassers warned off; which is a d—d shame!"

"Hearsay ain't no good. I ain't been formally notified in writin'," replied Tex. "Until I am, I act natural; an' after I am, twice as natural, bein' mean by nature an' disposition. All of which reminds me that this is a re-markable town, an' that there's a re-markable man in it."

His companion studied him for a moment. "You should keep yore hat on when yo're ridin' around in th' sun. Th' only remarkable thing about this town is that it's still alive. Th' only remarkable man in it has been buried these last twenty years, up yonder on Boot Hill."

"I'm joinin' issue with you on that," replied Tex. "Th' sense of loyalty an' affection of this town for its leadin' citizen is a great an' beautiful thing for these degenerate, money-mad days. Parenthetically, I wonder if there was ever a time when th' days were anythin' else? Why, everybody is his friend! There's Jake, an' th' nephew, Whiskey Jim, Tim Murphy, Jerry Saunders, John Graves, Blascom, you, an' me. I don't know any more at this writin'. An' that leadin' citizen, a man of culture, wealth, and discernment, is our most esteemed Mr. Gus Williams. Hear! Hear!"

"There's some names you can scratch, Carney

among 'em," growled the saloonkeeper, spitting in violent disgust. "Yore touchin' paregoric near makes me weep, an' I'm hard-shelled, like a clam. Two-thirds of th' people here do what he says, because he either scares or fools 'em. Th' rest dassn't lynch him because they ain't strong enough. Wealth? Shore. He got most of it when th' trail was in full swing. His brands, an' he had a-plenty, were copied from some on th' south ranges near th' old trail. A herd comin' up, grazin' wide, or passin' through that scrub an' hill country would near certain pick up a few local head on th' way, cattle bein' gregarious. Whiskey Jim was th' local herd trimmer. He'd throw up a herd, claim any of th' stray brands as belongin' around here. He had th' authority an' th' drawin's of them brands. If it was a herd of Horseshoe an' Circle Dots he claimed every other brand with them that was found this side of th' Cimarron. You know th' rules. He got 'em. Then there was stampedes, an' cattle run off at night. One time it got so bad that there was talk of a third Texan Expedition to clean it up. Only this one would 'a' been for a different purpose than th' other two."

"You better keep off th' Texas Expedition," said Tex. "That was a covered invasion for th' freedom of th' pore, robbed, browbeaten New Mexicans; an' it come to a terrible end."

"Not th' one I'm referrin' to," retorted Carney, his face set and determined. "Th' second one—that plundered caravans on th' old Santa Fe. I called this other one th' third only because of th' number of men who would have been in it, an' because it was a Texas idea. But we'll not quarrel. I had a good friend in th' second, avengin' th' first."

"I won't quarrel about Texas," said Tex. "Not bein' a Texan, my withers are unwrung. What did Williams do in th' face of that threat?"

"Drifted his herds off before snow flew, to a distant winter range an' let th' trail herds alone."

"That story ain't unusual," observed Tex. "He's a strange man. Picks queer names for his hosses. I never heard such names. Take my roan, now: his name is Oh My Cayenne. That's a devil of a name for anythin', let alone a hoss. Where'd he ever git it?"

Carney laughed. "I'm agreein' with you, but he didn't name th' roan. That hoss was named by Windy Barrett, when he was blind drunk. Windy was a peculiar cuss; allus spoutin' poetry an' such nonsense. Read books while he was line ridin'. Well, he woke up one mornin' after a spree in Williams' stable. As he turned his head to see where he was, th' roan, then a colt, poked its nose over th' stall an' nuzzled him. One of th' boys was just goin' in th' stable an' saw th' whole thing. Windy pushes th' hoss away an' says, sadlike: 'Yo're dead wrong, Oh My Cayenne; it don't banish th' sorrers with its whirlwind sword.' Th' boys thought it was such a good joke they let th' name stick."

Tex looked dubious. "Mebby they thought so, but I'm not admittin' that I do; an' it's no joke for any cayuse to have a name like that. There goes Bud Haines, ridin' out of town: he ain't earnin' his pay. Well, reckon I'll drift up an' see Williams. I allus like to be sociable. So-long."

CHAPTER VII

Weights and Measures

THE PROPRIETOR of the general store glanced out of the window as the roan stopped before his door and he frankly frowned at Tex's entry.

"Ain't no letters come for no Joneses," he said brusquely.

"Hope springs eternal," replied Tex. He sauntered up to the counter and was about to turn and lean against it when his roving glance passed along a line of widenecked bottles. They looked strangely familiar and he glanced at them again. A label caught his eye. "Chloral Hydrate" he read silently. He looked at Williams and chuckled. "I don't claim to be no Injun, but just th' same I got a lot of patience when it comes to waitin'. Looks like I'm goin' to need it, far as that letter is concerned." He looked along the walls of the store. "You shore carry a big stock for a town like this, Mr. Williams," he complimented, his eyes again viewing the line of bottles with a sweeping glance. "Strychnine," he read to himself, nodding with understanding.

"Shore, for wolves an' coyotes. Quinine, Aloes, Capsicum, Laudanum—quite a collection for a general store. Takes me back a good many years." Aloud he said. "I was admirin' that there pipe, an' I've got to have it; but that ain't what I'm lookin' so hard for." Again he searched shelves, up and down, left and right, and shook his head. "Don't see 'em," he complained. His mind flashed back to one word, and his medical training prompted him. "Chloral hydrate—safe in the right hands and very efficient. Ought to be tasteless in the vile whiskey they sell out here. You never can tell, an' I might need every aid." He shook his head again, and again spoke aloud. "Too bad, cuss it."

"If you wasn't so cussed secret about it I might be able to help you find what yo're lookin' for," growled Williams. "Bein' th' proprietor I know a couple of things that are in this store. Yore article might be among 'em."

"I'm loco," admitted Tex. "What I want is some center-fire .38 shorts. Couple of boxes will be enough."

Williams flashed a look at the walnut handle of the heavy Colt at his customer's thigh. He could see that it was no .38. Suspicion prompted him and he wondered if his companion was a two-gun man, with only one of them being openly worn. Such a combination was not a rarity. A gun in a shoulder holster or a derringer on an elastic up a sleeve might well use such a cartridge. This would be well to speak to Bud Haines about.

"You would 'a' saved yore valuable time, an' mine, if you'd said so when you first come in," ironically replied Williams. "Got plenty of .45's, quite some .44's, less .41's, and a few .38's in th' long cat'ridges. I ain't got no .38 shorts, nor .32's, nor .22's, nor no putty for putty blowers. Folks around these diggin's as totes guns mostly wants 'em man-size."

"I reckon so," agreed Tex pleasantly. "Don't blame 'em. Failin' in th' other qualifications they'd naturally do th' best they could to make up for them they lacked. I'm shore sorry you ain't got 'em because my rifle cat'ridges are runnin' low. That's what comes of havin' to buy a gun that don't eat regulation food. It was th' only one he had, an' I had to take it quick, bein' pressed hard at th' time. Time, tide, an' posses wait for no man. Yo're dead shore you ain't got 'em, huh?"

"Well, lemme see," cogitated the proprietor, scratching his head. "I did have some—they sent me some shorts by mistake an' I never took th' time to send 'em back. You wait till I look."

"Then you've got 'em now," said Tex. "You never could sell 'em in these diggin's, where folks as totes guns mostly wants 'em man-size. I'll wait till you see." He idly watched the scowling proprietor as he went behind the counter and dropped to one knee, his back to his customer. As he started to pull boxes from against the wall Tex silently sat on the counter as if better to watch him.

Williams was talking more to himself than to Tex, intent on trying to remember what he had done with the shorts, and save himself a protracted search. "Kept 'em with th' rest of th' cat'ridges till I got mad from nearly allus takin' 'em down for longs. I think mebby I put 'em about here."

Tex leaned swiftly backward, his hand leaping to one of the wide-mouthed bottles on the shelf. "They shore are a nuisance," he said in deep sympathy. "I allus have more or less trouble gettin' 'em," he admitted, his hands working silently and swiftly with the cork. "Didn't hardly hope to get 'em here," he confessed as he swung back and replaced the depleted bottle. He assumed an erect position again, one hand resting in a coat pocket. "Shore sorry to put you to all this trouble," he apologized; "but if you got 'em you are lucky to git rid of 'em, in this town."

Williams turned his head, saw his customer perilously balanced on the edge of the counter, and watching him with great interest. "I can find 'em if they're here, Mr. Jones," he growled. "You might strain yore back, leanin' that way—yep, here they are, four boxes of 'em. Only want two?"

"Reckon I better take all I can git my han's on," answered Tex. "No tellin' where I can git any more, they're that scarce."

"Yore rifle looks purty big an' heavy for these," observed Williams, craning his neck in vain to catch a glimpse of it. It lay on the other side of the horse.

"Yes, it's one of them *sängerbund*, or shootin'-fest guns," replied Tex. "Made for German target clubs, back in th' East. Got fine sights, an' is heavy so it won't tremble none. Two triggers, one settin' th' other for hair-trigger pullin'. Cost me fifty-odd. Don't bother to tie 'em up; they carry easier if they ain't all in one pocket. Don't forget that pipe."

Williams did some laborious figuring. "I see yo're gettin' acquainted fast," he remarked, pushing the change across the counter. "Them Saunders are real interestin'."

"Oh, so-so," grunted Tex. "Tenderfeet allus are. But I reckon she'll make yore nepphey a good wife.

"Hennery is a fortunate boy," replied Williams complacently, so complacently that Tex itched to punch him. "He'll make her a good husban', bein' nat'rally domestic an' affectionate. An' he's so sot on it that I'm near as much interested in their courtship as they are. I shore would send anybody to dance in h—l as interfered with it. Gettin' cooler out?"

"Warmer out, an' in," answered Tex. "Well, they ought to be real happy, bein' young an' both near th' same age. I'm sayin' age is more important than most folks admit. Me an' you, now, would be makin' a terrible mistake if *we* married a woman as young as she is. We got too much sense. An' I'm free to admit that I'm rope shy—don't like hobbles of any kind, a-tall. I'm a maverick, an' aim to stay so. When is th' weddin' comin' off?"

"Purty soon, I reckon," replied Williams, his voice

pleasanter than it had been since Tex had appeared in town. "She's nat'rally a little skittish, an' Hennery is sort of shy. Young folks usually are. He was tellin' me you gave him some good advice."

Tex laughed and shrugged his shoulders. "Don't know how good it is," he replied. "An' it wasn't no advice. I just sort of mentioned to him somethin' I found worked real well; but what works with one woman ain't got no call to get stuck on itself—th' odds ain't in favor of its repeatin'. If it was me, howsomever, I'd shore try it a whirl. It can't do no harm that I can see."

"He's goin' to back it a little," responded Williams, "till he sees how it goes."

"A little ain't no good, a-tall," replied Tex. "It might not show any results for awhile, an' then work fast an' sudden. Well, see you later mebby. This cayuse of mine needs some exercise. So-long."

Williams followed him to the door, hoping for a glimpse of the German shooting-club rifle, but Tex mounted and rode away without turning that side of the horse toward the store.

His next stop was the hotel, where he had a few sandwiches put up for him and then he left town, heading for Buffalo Creek. He had no particular object in choosing that direction, the main thing being to get out of town and to stay out of sight until after dark. As he rode he cogitated:

"Chloral hydrate. Twenty to thirty grains is the dose soporific. Yes; that's right. In a hydrous crystal of this nature that would just about fill—what?" He rode on, oblivious to his surroundings, trying to picture the size of a container that would hold the required weight of crystals. "In our rough-and-ready weights a silver half-dime was twenty grains; a three-cent piece was forty grains, and I think my three-cent silver piece of '51 weighed ten grains. But not havin' any of 'em now, all that does me no good. Shucks—there's plenty of miners' scales in this country. Bet Blascom has one that'll

help me out: an' a grain is a grain, all th' way through."
He hitched up his heavily loaded belt and as his hand
came into contact with the ends of the cartridges he
chuckled and slapped the horse in congratulation.

"Omar, we're gettin' close. Bet a .45 shell will hold
the dose. However, not wantin' to kill nobody, we'd
better make shore. Yo're a willin' cayuse, an' I like yore
gait: suppose you let it out a little? We got business
ahead."

When he came to the dried bed of a creek he followed it at a distance and had not gone far before he es-
pied the first fork. On the north side of the gully was a
miserable hut. "That must be Jake's: we'll detour so he
won't see us." Twenty minutes later he came to the second fork and a second hut, not much better than the
first. A familiar figure was just emerging from it, and
soon Tex rode down the steep bank and hailed.

The prospector looked up and waved, turning to
face his visitor. "Glad to see you," he called. "Hope
Whiskey Jim ain't run you out of town."

"He might if he kept close to me, up wind," laughed
Tex. "Busy doin' nothin?"

"Busy as a hibernatin' bear. Git off an' come in th'
house, where th' sun ain't so hot. An' I reckon yo're
thirsty."

Tex accepted the invitation and found a box to sit
on. The interior of the shack was not out of keeping
with the exterior, and it was none too clean. His roving
glances saw and passed the gold scales, two metal cups
hanging by three threads each from a slender, double-
taper bar. Beside it was a tin box which he guessed
contained weights.

"Washin' out lots of gold, Blascom?" asked Tex,
smiling.

"Can't even wash my face without totin' water, or
goin' up to th' sump. Th' crick's like it is out there for
as far up as I've been. If it wasn't for a sump I've dug in
a sandy place in its bed I'd had no water at all." He

reached into his pocket and produced several bits of gold, none of them much larger than a grain of wheat. "Found these when I was gettin' water just now. That sump's goin' to go deeper right quick, 'though I'm scared I'll lose my water."

"What'll they weigh?" asked Tex curiously, handing them back.

"About a pennyweight, I reckon," replied Blascom.

Tex shook his head. "Not them. You've got too trustin' a nature. Yo're too hopeful: but I reckon that's what makes miners."

Blascom arose, dropped the flecks into a scale pan and dug around in the tin box. There was a metallic clink and the two pans slowly sought the same level. "Couple of grains under," he announced. "About twenty-two, I'd say. That's close figgerin', close enough for a guess."

"Cussed good," complimented Tex as the prospector put back the weights and dumped the gold out into his hand. "I ain't never dug out no hunks of gold an' I'm curious. If you aim to put that sump down farther I'm just itchin' to give you a hand. Come on—what you say?"

"You'd be a mess, sloppin' around with me," laughed Blascom. He shook his head. "Better set down an' watch me, lendin' yore valuable advice; or stay here an' keep out of th' sun."

"I can do that in town."

Blascom considered, looking dubiously at his guest's clothes. "Here," he said, finally. "You can help me more by carryin' water an' fillin' up everythin' in here that'll hold it. After I get through wrastlin' with a pan in that sump th' water won't be fit to drink before mornin'. That suit you?"

"Good enough," declared Tex, arising and picking up the buckets. "Come on: reveal yore gold mine. I'm a first-class claim jumper. You had yore dinner yet?"

Blascom shook his head, picked up a shovel and his

gold pan and led the way. "That can wait. It ain't often I have any free help forced on me an' I'd be a sucker to let an empty belly cut in."

"I can cook, too," said Tex. "After I fill th' hut with water I'll get you a meal that'll make you glad yo're livin'; but you got to come after it to eat it; an' when I yell, you come a-runnin'. If you don't I'll eat it myself."

The sump lay about a hundred yards up the creek bed, around a bend which was covered with a thin growth of sickly willows and box elders. It was a hole about two feet square, the sandy sides held up by a cribwork of sticks, pieces of boxes, and barrel staves. Blascom dipped both pails in and started back with them.

"Wait a minute," objected Tex, reaching for them. "Thought you was goin' after nuggets while I toted th' water?"

"I thought so, too," answered Blascom, "till I had sense enough to think that I couldn't go rammin' around in there with my shovel until after th' water was saved. You can carry 'em th' next trip. Sit down an' do th' gruntin' for me, this time. A dozen buckets will empty her, almost."

Tex shrugged his shoulders and obeyed, rolled a cigarette, and then plucked a .45 from its belt loop. Wiping off the grease, he placed his thumb against the lead and pushed, turning the cartridge slowly as he worked. When he heard Blascom's heavy, careless tread nearing the bend he slipped the loosened cartridge into his vest pocket and lazily arose.

"There ain't nothin' else to fill but these here buckets," said the prospector as he appeared. Filling them again he passed them to Tex and reached for the shovel and the gold pan. "There's beans you can warm up, an' some bacon. There's also some sour-doughs. Make a good pot of coffee an' yell when yo're ready. I'm surprised at th' way this hole's fillin' up, but I ain't mindin' that. As long as I dump it close by it's bound to get back again."

Tex picked up the buckets and departed clumsily, his high-heeled boots not aiding his progress. Reaching the house he set down his load and wheeled swiftly toward the swaying balance. The pennyweight disk slid into one pan as his other hand brought from his pocket a generous quantity of the whitish, translucent crystals. Sniffing them, he smiled grimly and then nodded as the biting odor gripped his nostrils. He let them drop slowly into the other pan and when the balance was struck he added one more crystal and put the rest back into his pocket. Glancing around the hut he saw a torn, discarded pamphlet in a corner and he removed some of the inner sheets. When he had finished weighing and wrapping he had a dozen little packages of more than twenty-four, and less than thirty, grains. Wiping out the little tray he replaced the weight, drank deeply from a bucket and then started a fire in the home-made rock-and-clay stove. While it caught he went out, picked up some clean pebbles and returned to the scales, soon selecting the pebble that weighed the same as his powders. He might have use for it sometime in the future. Taking another piece of paper he emptied into it the rest of the crystals from his pocket and, sorting out pieces of thickened lint and bits of tobacco, wrapped the chloral up securely. Then he got busy with the meal and when the coffee was ready he went to the door and shouted the old bunkhouse classic: "Come an' get it!"

Blascom soon appeared, his clothing wet and sandy, and in his hand were several rice grains of gold with quite some dust. "Looks fair to me," he said. "I can't hardly tell what I'm doin', th' sump fills up so fast, an' th' sand is washed in with th' water, fillin' it up from th' bottom as fast as I can dig it out an' pan it. I can't understand where all that water comes from. I know there's cussed little of it further down th' crick bed. When she dried up I nat'rally wanted a sump nearer th' hut, but I couldn't get one nearer than I have. Must be a spring somewhere under it." He sniffed cheerfully. "That coffee shore smells good," he declared, going out to wash his hands.

The meal was eaten rapidly, without much talking, but when it was finished Blascom packed his pipe and passed the pouch to his companion. "New pipe?" he asked. "Then wet yore finger an' rub it around in th' bowl before you light her. You don't want a job cookin', do you? I never drunk better coffee."

The new pipe going well, Tex leaned back and smiled. "I'll cook th' supper if you want. I ain't anxious to get back to town before dark. An' I'll put on them old clothes over there an' help you at th' sump th' rest of th' day. Let's get goin'."

"All right; it's a two-man job with that water comin' in so fast," answered the prospector. "We'll not do any pannin'—just get th' sand out an' dump it up on th' bank, out of th' way of high water. I can pan it any time. You see, this dry spell is due to end 'most any time, an' when it does it'll be a reg'lar cloud-burst. That'll mean no more placerin' near th' sump. Ever see these creek beds after a cloud-burst? They're full from bank to bank an' runnin' like bullets."

Tex nodded and looked steadily out of the door, his mind going back some years and vividly presenting an arroyo and the great, sheer wall of water which swept down it on the day when he and his then enemy, Hopalong Cassidy, were fighting it out in the brush. His eyes glowed as the details returned to him and went past in orderly array. From that sudden and unexpected danger, and the impulsive chivalry of the man who had had him at the mercy of an inspired six-gun, had come his redemption.

"Yes," he said slowly. "I've seen 'em. They're deadly when they catch a man unawares." He drew a deep breath and returned to the main subject. "Why don't you hire somebody, Jake for instance, an' clean up that sump as quick as you can?"

"An' have a knife in my back?" exclaimed Blascom, "or be killed in my sleep? I don't know much about Jake, but what little I do know about him, th' less he, or any of th' fellers in town know about that sump, th' better I'll like it. There ain't one I'd trust, an' most of 'em are busted an' plumb desperate. I've been pannin' a lot better than fair day's wages out here, but I'm doin' without everythin' that I can because I dassn't look so prosperous. Let me show much dust in town an' I'd be raided an' jumped th' same night. They're like a pack of starvin' coyotes. I don't even keep my dust in this shack. I cache it outside at night."

"Suppose you was to buy things in town with coin or bills, lettin' on that it is yore bedrock reserve that yo're livin' on," suggested Tex. "That ought to help some."

"But I ain't got 'em," objected Blascom. "Got nothin' but raw gold."

Tex laughed and dug down into his pocket. "That's easy solved. Here," he said, bringing up a handful of double eagles. "Gold weighs as much in one shape as it does in another—even less, bulk for bulk, without th' alloy. I'll change with you if you want." Then he drew back his hand and grinned quizzically. "It's allus well to think of th' little things. It might be better if we didn't swap. You fellers ain't likely to have a currency reserve: more likely to have it just as you dug it out. That right?"

Blascom nodded. "Yes; though I knowed a feller that allus carried big bills in place of gold when he could get 'em, an' when he wasn't broke. They weighed a lot less. Raw gold would be better, out here."

"All right; how'd you like to drop into th' hotel about eleven tonight an' win heavy from me in a two-hand game of draw? Say as much as we can fix up? How much you want to change? Couple of hundred?" He chuckled. "We can fix it either way: raw gold or currency."

"Make it raw gold, then; better yet, mix it," said Blascom, arising, his face wrinkled with pleasure. He nodded swiftly. "Be back in a minute," and he went out. When he returned he went into a corner where he could not be seen by anyone passing the hut and took several sacks from his pocket. It did not take him long to verify the weights and the cleanness of the gold, he put the odd gold back into a sack and handed the other to his companion.

"Two hundred even," he said. "Keep yore money till I take it away from you tonight. Much obliged to you, Jones."

"How do you know I'll be there?" asked Tex, smiling. "I got th' gold an' a cussed good cayuse. With such a good start it'll be easy."

Blascom chuckled and shrugged his shoulders. "Yore little game with Whiskey Jim an' your soiree with Jake tell me different," he answered. "I've rubbed elbows with all sorts of men for forty-odd years—ever since I was a boy of sixteen. A man's got to back his best judgment: an' I'm backin' mine. If I wasn't shore about you do you reckon I'd be tellin' you anythin' about that sump? Now then: what you say about settin' here an' takin' things easy for th' rest of th' day? I don't want you to get all mucked up."

Tex arose, took the boxes of .38 shorts out of his pockets and lay them on a shelf. He put the heavy little sacks in their places and turned. "It'll do me good; an' I might learn somethin' useful," he said. "A man can't never learn too much. Come on; we'll tackle that sump." As he changed his clothes for those of his host the latter's words of confidence in him set him thinking. To his mind came scenes of long ago. "Deacon" Rankin, "Slippery" Trendley, "Slim" Travennes, and others of that savage, murderous, vulture class returned on his mental canvas. Of the worst class in the great West they had stood in the first rank; and at one time he had stood with them, shoulder to shoulder, had deliberately chosen them for his friends and companions, and in many of their villainies he had played his minor parts. He stirred into renewed activity and dressed rapidly. Changing the gold sacks into the clothes he now wore and putting on his host's extra pair of boots, he stepped toward the door and then thought of Jake, who reminded him somewhat of his former friends, lacking only their intelligence. He turned and swept up his gun and belt, buckling it around him as he left the shack to help his new friend.

CHAPTER VIII

After Dark

MURPHY S BLOCKED-UP box car was dark and showed no signs of life, making only a blacker spot in the night. To any prowler who might have investigated its externals, the raised shades and the closed doors would have left him undecided as to whether or not its tenant was within; but the closed windows on such a night as this would have suggested that he was not, for the baked earth radiated heat and the walls of the modest habitation were still warm to the touch. Inside the closed car the heat must have been well-nigh intolerable.

The silence was natural and unbroken. The brilliant stars seemed rather to accentuate the darkness than to relieve it. An occasional breath of heated air furtively rustled the tufts of drought-killed grass, but brought no relief to man or beast; but somewhere along the branch line a stronger wind was blowing, if the humming of the telegraph wires meant anything. In the west gleamed a single glowing eye of yellow-white, where the switch light told that the line was open. To the right of it blotches of more diffused and weaker radiance outlined the windows and doors of the straggling buildings facing the right-of-way. An occasional burst of laughter or a snatch of riotous song came from them, mercifully tempered and mellowed by the distance. From the east arose the long-drawn vocal atrocity of some mournful coyote who could not wait for the rising of the crescent moon to give him his cue. Infrequent metallic complaints told of the contradiction of the heat-stretched rails.

In the south appeared a swaying thickening of the darkness, an elongated concentration of black opacity. Gradually it took on a more definite outline as its upper parts more and more became silhouetted against a sky of slightly different tone and intensity. First a moving cone, then a saucer-like rim, followed slowly by a sudden contraction and a further widening. Hat, head, and shoulders loomed up vaguely, followed by the longer bulkiness of the body.

This apparition moved slowly and silently toward the rectangular blot at the edge of the right-of-way, advancing in a manner suggesting questionable motives, and it paused frequently to peer into the surrounding void, and to listen. After several of these cautious waits it reached the old car, against whose side it stood out a little more distinctly by contrast. The gently rolling tattoo of finger nails on wood could scarcely be heard a dozen feet away and ceased before critical analysis would be able to classify it. Half a minute passed and it rolled out again, a little louder and more imperative. Another wait, and then came a flat *clack* as a tossed pebble bounced from the wall at the waiter's side. Its effect was magical. The figure wheeled, crouched, and a hand spasmodically leaped hip high, a soft, dull gleam tipping it. While one might slowly count ten its rigid posture was maintained and then a rustling not far from the door drew its instant attention.

"What ye want?" demanded a low, curious voice. "If it's Murphy, he's sleepin' out, this night av h—l."

The figure at the door relaxed, grew instantly taller and thinner and a chuckle answered the query of the section-boss. "Don't blame you," it softly said, and moved quietly toward the owner of the car.

"To yer left," corrected the Irishman. "Who's wantin' Murphy at this time av night, an' for what?"

"Yore fellow-conspirator," answered Tex, sinking down on the blanket of his companion. "Didn't Jerry tell you to expect me?"

"Yes, he did; but I wasn't shore it was you," replied Murphy. "So I acted natural. Th' house is past endurin' with th' winders an' door closed; an' not knowin' what ye might have to talk about I naturally distrusted th' walls. This whole town has ears. Out here in th' open a man will have more trouble fillin' his ear with other people's business. How are ye?"

"Hot, an' close," chuckled Tex. "Also curious an' lonesome." He crossed his legs tailor fashion, and then seemed to weigh something in his mind, for after a moment he changed and lay on his stomach and elbows. "I don't stick up so plain, this way," he explained.

"I hear ye trimmed old Frowsyhead at poker," said Murphy, "an' won a good hoss. Beats all how a man wants to smoke when he shouldn't. Have a chew?"

"I'll own to that vice in a limited degree and under certain conditions," admitted Tex, taking the huge plug. "An' I'll confess that to my way of thinkin' it's th' only way to get th' full flavor of th' leaf; but I ain't sayin' it's th' neatest."

" 'Tis fine trainin' for th' eye," replied Murphy, the twinkle in his own hidden by the night.

"An' develops amazin' judgment of distance," supplemented Tex, chuckling. "There's some I'd like to try it on—Hennery Williams, for instance."

"Aye," growled Murphy in hearty accord. "He'll be

lucky if he ain't hit by somethin' solider than tobaccy juice. I fair itch to twist his skinny neck."

"A most praiseworthy longing," rejoined Tex, a sudden sharpness in his voice. "How long has he been deservin' such a reward?"

"Since *she* first came here," growled his companion. "That was why I wanted Mike Costigan to get his family out av th' way, for I'm tellin' ye flat, Costigans or no Costigans, that little miss will be a widder on her weddin' day, if it gets that far. Th' d—d blackguard! I've kept me hand hid, for 'tis a true sayin' that forewarned is forearmed. They'll have no reason to watch me close, an' then it'll be too late. Call it murder if ye will, but I'll be proud av it."

"Hardly murder," murmured Tex. "Not even homicide, which is a combination of Latin words meanin' th' killin' of a human bein'. To flatter th' noble Hennery a little, I'd go as far as to admit it might reach th' dignity of vermicide. An' no honest man should find fault with th' killin' of a worm. Th' Costigans should be persuaded to move."

"Ye try it," grunted Murphy sententiously. "Can ye dodge quick?"

"Nobody ever justly accused me of tryin' to dodge a woman," said Tex. "There must be a way to get around her determination."

"Yes?" queried Murphy, the inflection of the monosyllables leaving nothing to be learned but the harrowing details.

"Coax her to go to Willow," persisted Tex.

"She don't like th' town."

"Yore inference is shore misleadin'," commented Tex. "I'd take it from that that she does like Windsor."

"Divvil a bit; but she stays where Mike is."

"Then you've got to shift Mike. There's not enough work here for a good man like Costigan," suggested Tex.

"Yer like a dog chasin' his tail. Costigan stays where th' lass an' her brother are."

"Huh! Damon an' Pythias was only a dual combination," muttered the puncher. "Cussed if there ain't somethin' in th' world, after all, that justifies Nature's labors."

"An'," went on Murphy as though he had not been interrupted, "th' lass sticks to her brother, an' he stays where he's put. He's not strong an' he has a livin' to make for two. Ye can take yer change out av that, Mr. Tex Jones."

Tex grunted pessimistically. "Well, anyhow," he said, brightening a little, "mebby Miss Saunders won't be pestered for a little while by Hennery—an' then we'll see what we see. I'm unlucky these days: I'm allus with th' under dog," and he went on to tell his companion of his suggestions to the nephew.

" 'Tis proud av ye I am," responded Murphy. "May th' saints be praised for th' rest she'll be gettin'. We can all av us breathe deep for a little while; an' meanwhile I'll be tryin' my strength with Lefferts, th' boss at th' Junction. I've hated to leave town even that long, but now I can make th' run; 'though I know it will do no good. Ye'll be stayin' in town tomorry?"

"Why, no; I'm goin' ridin' with Miss Saunders," and Tex explained that, to his companion's admiration and delight.

"It'll be a pleasure for her to be able to leave th' house without bein' tagged after by that scut," said the section-boss. "Yer a bye with a head. An' I see where ye not only get th' suspicions av that Tommy lad, but run afoul of that Henry an' his precious uncle. Haven't ye been warned yet?" The gleam of hope in his eyes was hidden by the darkness. "Ye'll mebby have trouble with th' last two—an' if ye do, keep an eye on Bud Haines. Ye'll do well to watch him, anyhow. Why don't ye slip out quiet-like, straight southwest from her house? Less chance av bein' seen; but a mighty slim one. They've eyes all over town."

"We are shore to be seen," quietly responded Tex. "If we sneak out it will justify their suspicions. I don't want to do that. I'm aimin' to ride plumb down th' main street, through th' middle of town, an' pay Tommy a little visit out at his ranch. *There is no shuffling, there th' action lies in his true nature.* Like Caesar's wife, you know. An', by th' way, Tim: we have some friends in town, an' I'm addin' an ally from Buffalo Crick. Time works for us." He paused and then asked, curiously: "Who is our friend Bud Haines, an' what does he do for a livin'? I've my suspicions, but I'd rather be shore."

Murphy swore softly under his breath. "He used to ride for Williams till he earned a reputation as a first-class gunman; but now he follows old Frowsyhead around like a shadder. Cold blooded, like th' rattlesnake he is; a natural-born killer. They say he's chain lightnin' on th' draw."

"I've heard that said of better men than him; some of them now dead," said Tex. "Must be a pleasant sort of a chap." He cogitated a bit. "An' how long has he been playin' shadow to friend Williams? Since I come to town, or before?" he asked as casually as he could, but tensely awaited the answer.

"Couple av years," answered Murphy; "an' mebby longer." He tried to peer through the darkness. "Was ye thinkin' ye made th' job for him?"

"Well, hardly," replied Tex. "I'm naturally conceited, suspicious, and allus lookin' out for myself. Th' thought just happened to hit me."

Their conversation began to ramble to subjects foreign to Windsor and its inhabitants, and after a little while Tex arose to leave. He melted out of sight into the night and half an hour later rode into town from the west, along the railroad, and soon stopped before the hotel.

The customary poker game was in full swing and he

nodded to the players, received a civil greeting from Gus Williams, and after a short, polite pause at the table, wandered over to the bar, where Blascom leaned in black despondency.

"How'd'y," said Tex affably. "Fine night, but hot, an' close."

"Fine, h—l!" growled Blascom, sullenly looking up. "Not meanin' you no offense, stranger," he hastily added. "I'm grouchy tonight," he explained.

"Why, what's th' trouble?" asked Tex after swift scrutiny of the other's countenance. "Barkeep, give us two drinks, over yonder," and he led his companion to the table. "No luck?"

Blascom growled an oath. "None at all. My stake's run out, all but this last bag," and he slammed it viciously onto the table. "Th' claim's showin' nothin'." He scowled at the bag and then, avarice in his eyes and desperation in his voice, he looked up into the face opposite him. "This is next to no good: I'll double it, or lose it. What you say to a two-hand game?"

Tex looked a little suspicious. "I don't usually play for that much, rightaway, ag'in' strangers." He looked around the room and flushed slightly at the knowing smiles and sarcastic grins. "Oh, I don't care," he asserted, swaggering a little. "Come on; I'll go you. Deck of cards, friend," he called to the dispenser of drinks, and almost at the words they were sailing through the air toward his hands. "You've got as much chance as I have; an' if I don't win it, somebody else will. Draw, I reckon?" he asked nervously. "All right; low deals," and the game was on.

Blascom won the first hand, Tex the second. For the better part of an hour it was an up-and-down affair, the ups for Tex not enough to offset the downs. Finally, with a big pot at stake he pressed the betting on the theory that his opponent was bluffing. Suddenly becoming doubtful, he let a palpable fear master him, refused to see the raise, and slammed his hand down on the table with a curse. Blascom laughed, grandiloquently spread a four-card flush under his adversary's nose, and raked in his winnings.

"Shuffle 'em up," chuckled the prospector. "Things are lookin' better."

Glancing from the worthless hand into Blascom's exultant face Tex kicked the chair in under him, arose and went to the bar where he gulped his drink, glanced sullenly around the room, and strode angrily to the stairs to go to his room. Wide and mocking grins followed him until he was hidden from sight, the expressions on the faces of Williams and his nephew transcending the others.

The prospector gleefully pocketed the money and dust, sighed with relief and swaggered over to the other table, one thumb hooked in an armhole of his vest. He stopped near Williams and beamed at the players, patting his pocket, but saying nothing until the hand had been played and the cards were being scooped up for a new deal.

"Williams," he said, laughing, "my supplies are cussed low, but now that I can pay for what I want I'm comin' in tomorrow mornin' an' carry off 'most all yore grub."

The storekeeper had glanced meaningly at one of the players and now he lazily looked up, his face trying to express pleasure and congratulation. The man he had glanced at arose, yawned and stretched, mumbled something about being tired and out of luck and pushed back his chair. As he slouched away from the table he turned the chair invitingly and nodded to Blascom.

"Take my place; I'm goin' to turn in soon," he said.

"Why, shore," endorsed Williams. "Set in for a hand or two, Blascom. It's early yet, too early to head for yore cabin. This game's been draggin' all evenin'; mebby it'll move faster if a new man sets in." Waiting a moment for an answer and none being forthcoming, he leaned back and stretched his arms. "How you makin' out on th' crick—bad?"

"Couldn't be much worse," answered the prospector, his face becoming grave. "I can't do much without water, an' th' only water I got is a sump for drinkin' an' cookin' purposes. You know that I ain't th' one to put up no holler as long as I'm gettin' day wages out of it; but when I can't make enough to pay my way, then I can't help gettin' a little mite blue."

"We all have our trials," replied Williams. He waved his hand toward the vacant chair. "Better set in for a little while. You've had good luck tonight: give it its head while it's runnin' yore way. Besides, a little fun an' company will shore cheer you up. You ain't got no reason to be hot-footin' off to yore cabin so early in th' evenin'."

The prospector smilingly shook his head. "I ain't needin' no cheerin' now," he asserted, again slapping the pocket. "I got a little stake that'll let me stick it out till we get rain. I got too much faith in that claim to clear out an' leave it; but now I got still more faith in my luck. It broke for me tonight an' I'm bettin' it's th' turnin' point; an' if a man ain't willin' to meet a turn of good luck at sunrise, with a smile, he shore don't deserve it. At sunup I'll be in that crick bed with a shovel in my hand, ready to go to work. I've been busted before; more'n once; but I don't seem to get used to it, at all. Well, good luck, everybody, an' good night," and he turned and strode briskly toward the door and disappeared into the darkness.

Williams looked disappointed and cautiously pushed the substitute deck farther back in its little slot under the table. Looking around, he beckoned to the unselfish player and motioned for him to resume his seat. The lamb having departed, the regular friendly game for small stakes would now go on again.

"You fellers heard what I said about sand, th' very first night that Jones feller showed up," remarked Williams, chuckling. "I'm sayin' it ag'in: he figgered Blascom was bluffin', played that way until th' stakes got high an' then got scared out an' quit. Quit cold without even feedin' in a few more dollars to see th' hand. Left th' table in a rage just because he lost a hundred or two. I was watchin' him as much as I could, an' I could see he was gettin' madder an' madder, nervouser an' nervouser all th' time; an' when a man gets like that he can't play poker good enough to keep warm in h—l. He ain't no poker player; an' as soon as I can buffalo him into a good, stiff game, I'll show you he ain't!"

He paused and looked around knowingly. "He didn't win that roan. I just sorta loaned it to him. Might have to bait him ag'in, too; but before he leaves this town I'll git it back, with all he's got to-boot. There ain't no call for nobody to start yappin' around about what I'm sayin'," he warned.

"I was a-wonderin' about him winnin' that hoss," said the unselfish player as he resumed his seat and drew up to the table. A broad grin spread itself across his face. "Prod him sharp, Gus: we'll get him playin' ag'in th' gang, some night, an' win him naked."

The subject of their conversation was upstairs behind his closed door. He had taken off his coat and vest and was seated facing the washstand, from which he had removed the basin and pitcher. On the bench was a pile of .45s, their bullets greaseless, and he was working assiduously at the slug of another cartridge, his thumb pressing this way and that, and from time to time he turned the shell for assaults on the other side. It was hard on the thumb, but no other way would do, for no other way that he could take advantage of would leave the soft lead entirely free from telltale marks.

Time passed, but still he labored, changing thumbs at intervals. At last, all the leads removed and each one standing against its own shell, he emptied the powder from the brass containers and made a little paper package of it. Going to his coat and taking out the packets of chloral, he put the powder package in their place and returned with them to the bench.

The translucent crystals were of all sizes, some of them too large to be economically contained by the shells, which he had cleaned of powder marks. These crystals were larger only in two dimensions, for in thickness they were practically the same as the others. Doubtful whether the shells would hold a full dose and permit the leads to be replaced, he felt some anxiety as he placed the chloral in the folds of a clean kerchief and began crushing them by the steady pressure of the butt of his Colt. This was slower than pounding, but the latter was too noisy a process under present conditions. Dumping the reduced crystals into a shell lined with paper against possible chemical action on the brass, he gently tapped the outside of the container and watched the granules settle until there was room for the lead. He did not dare tamp it for fear it would not easily empty when inverted. Pushing home the bullet he up-ended the cartridge and tapped it again to loosen the contents. Shaking it close to his ear, he smiled grimly. The dose was loose enough to fall out readily, large enough to insure its proper effect, and the granules of a size small enough to dissolve quickly. When he had filled and reloaded the last shell he chuckled as he made a slight notch on the rim of each, for they would bear close inspection by weight, sight, and sound, and it was necessary that he mark them to keep from fooling himself.

He put them back into the pocket of the coat and grinned. "As I remember the action of chloral hydrate somebody may lose consciousness and muscular power and sensibility. Their expanding pupils as they wake up will expand under sore and inflamed eyelids. They'll sleep tight and not be worth very much for an hour or two after they do awaken. And these men gulp their whiskey without waiting to taste it, and it is so vile that they'll never suspect an alien flavor, 'specially if it's not too strong. Gentlemen, I bid you all good night: and may you sleep well and soundly."

CHAPTER IX

A Pleasant Excursion

AFTER AN early breakfast, early for him these days, Tex went down the street toward Carney's. As he passed Williams' stable he heard hammering, and paused to glance in at the door to see what his friend, Graves, was doing.

The stableman looked up and turned halfway around at the hail. "Hello!" he mumbled through a mouthful of nails. Removing them he nodded at the door. "Tryin' to fasten that lock so it'll do some good. It must 'a' been forced off more'n once, judgin' by th' split wood, which is so old that it ain't much good, anyhow. Th' nails sink into it like it was putty."

Tex was about to suggest the sawing out of the poorest part of the plank and the in-letting of a new piece in its place, but some subconscious warning bade him hold his peace.

"Much ado about nothin', Graves," he said, smiling ironically. "Hoss stealin' is a bigger risk in these parts than it is a profit; an' anyhow, th' slightest noise will wake you up, sleepin' like you do right next to th' door." He examined the wood. "Huh; them splits were made when th' wood was tough—it wouldn't split as dead as it is now: th' nails would just pull out. So you see it was done years ago. Hoss stealin' has gone out of style since then. All you want is a catch to hold it shut ag'in' th' wind." He winced suddenly and held a hand gently against his jaw. "That's all it wants."

"Reckon yo're right," agreed the stableman, glancing curiously at his companion's hand. "What's th' matter? Toothache?"

Tex growled a profane malediction and nodded. "Reckon I'll have to go around an' see th' doc, an' get some laudanum."

"An' pay that thief three prices!" expostulated Graves indignantly. "Chances are he's so drunk he'll give you strychnine instead. Why don't you go up to Williams' store? He's got th' laudanum, an' knows how to fix it up for toothaches an' earaches, I reckon."

"Williams?" queried Tex in moderate surprise. "What you talkin' about? He ain't runnin' no drugstore! What's he doin' with drugs an' such stuff?"

Graves laughed and contemplated the lock with strong disapproval. "No, it ain't no drug-store," he replied. "But th' doc drinks so hard he ain't got no money left to carry a full line of drugs, so Williams carries 'em for him, an' sells him stuff as he needs it. Besides, he allus did sell strychnine to th' ranchers, for coyotes an' wolves—though I ain't never heard it said that any wolves was ever poisoned. Sometimes they do get a coyote—but not no wolves. They've been hunted so hard they just about know as much as th' hunters." He stepped forward and felt of the wood around the lock. "I reckon yo're right," he admitted; "though while I ain't nat'rally a sound sleeper, it would take quite some racket to wake me up if I'd had a couple of drinks before goin' to bed, which I generally do have. I'll just let her stay like she is."

Tex looked at the lock and at the bolt receptacle on the door jamb. The lock was fastened securely for most people, seeing that the pressure from being pushed inward would not work against it very much; but the receptacle, the keystone of the door's defense, was nailed to even poorer wood than the lock itself and he saw at once that any real strain would force it loose.

"Shore; good enough," he said. "Have an eyeopener?"

Graves accepted with alacrity and in a moment they were smiling across Carney's bar at the good-natured proprietor.

"That hoss ready?" asked Tex when the conversation lulled.

"In th' stall next to th' roan," answered Carney. "Th' stable boys went to Europe last night an' won't be back till tomorrow; but I reckon you can saddle her yoreself."

"I'd rather do it myself," replied Tex.

"Labor of love?" queried Carney, grinning.

"Measure of precaution," retorted Tex, a slight frown on his face.

Carney nodded endorsement. "Can't take too much," he rejoined. "That goes for every kind, too. Nice gal, she is—though a little mite stuck up. I reckon she—"

"Nice day," interrupted Tex, looking straight into the eyes of the proprietor; "though it's hot, an' close," he added slowly.

"It is that," muttered Carney. "As I was sayin', you'll find both hosses ready for saddles," he vouchsafed with slight confusion.

"Much obliged," answered Tex with a smile, turning toward the rear door. "See you boys later," he said, going out. In a few minutes they saw him ride past on a nettlesome black which put down its white feet as though spurning contact with the earth.

"Whitefoot shore glistens," observed Graves.

"She ought to," replied Carney. He mopped off the bar and looked up. "Beats all how them fellers ride," he observed. "They sit a saddle like they'd growed there.

An'," he cogitated, "beats all how touchy some of 'em are. I can't figger him, a-tall," whereupon ensued an exhaustive critique of cowpunchers, their manners, and dispositions.

Meanwhile the particular cowpuncher who had started the discussion was riding briskly northeastward along the trail which he knew led to the C Bar, and after he had put a few miles behind him he took a package from his pocket and sowed black powder along the edge of the trail. After a short while he turned and rode back again.

Jane Saunders answered the knock and smiled at the self-possessed puncher who faced her, hat in hand. "Come in a moment," she invited, stepping aside. "This coffee is hardly cool enough to be put into the bottles, but it won't be long before it is. I am so glad you have brought Whitefoot. I have ridden her before."

"She's quite a horse," he replied. "Gaited as easy as any I ever rode."

She flashed him a suspicious glance. "Then you've ridden her? When, and what for?"

"I thought it would do no harm to learn her disposition," he answered carelessly. "She hasn't been out of the stable for two weeks. We had a nice five-mile ride, and she took it with plenty of spirit. She's a good hoss."

After awhile Jane filled two bottles with coffee and placed them with the lunch on the table. Tex took down a blackened tin pail from a hook over the stove and, picking up the bottles and the lunch, went out to his horse, followed by Jane, who had at the last moment buckled on a cartridge belt and the .38 Colt.

Tex looked at them and cogitated. "That'll be quite heavy and annoying, bobbing up and down at every step," he observed. "Why not leave the belt behind and let me slip the gun into my pocket?"

"But I should get accustomed to it," she protested.

"Intend to wear it steadily?"

"No; hardly that," she laughed.

"Then there's no reason to get accustomed to it," he replied. "Surprise is a great factor, because what is known can be guarded against. Will you allow me to advise you in a matter of this kind?"

"Jerry says I couldn't have a better adviser," she replied. She regarded him with level gaze. "Of course, Mr. Jones; but I want to carry it: you have too much without taking it. Frankly, I'm amused by your suggestion that I learn to use it, by Jerry's earnestness that I do learn, and by Tim's fear that I will not. Let us start out by being frank: Why do you think it necessary that I do?"

"Necessary?" asked Tex. "Why, I am not claiming that it is necessary; but I do know that it is a very pleasant diversion. Miss Saunders, there is a great deal said and written about the chivalry of western men. I won't say that most of it, or even nearly all of it is not deserved, for I believe that it is; but I will say that there are men who have no idea of chivalry, honesty, or even decency. You find them wherever men are, be it any point of the compass, or in any stratum of society. The West has some of them, even if less than its proportionate share; and this town of Windsor was not overlooked in their distribution. I know of no particular reason why you should learn the use of a revolver; but we are dealing with generalities. They suffice. With the odds a hundred to one that you never will have need to call upon knowledge of firearms, why refuse that knowledge when it is so easily acquired; and when the acquirement not only will be a pleasure but will lead to further pleasures? Shooting calls for that coordination of nerves and muscles which make all sports sport. And let me say, further, that the feeling of confidence, of security, which comes from the proper handling of a six-shooter is well worth what little effort has been expended to learn its use. Later I hope you will make use of my rifle—after I reduce the powder charges a little— but the short gun should come first. And I would much prefer that you carry it yourself, and make its carrying a habit rather than an exception."

"You are a very difficult man to argue against successfully, Mr. Jones," she said smiling. "I believe, quite the hardest I ever have met."

She took off the belt, slipped the gun inside her waist and hung the belt on a branch of a small tree beside her.

Tex dismounted, took the belt and carried it into the house and, returning, lifted her into the saddle, which she wisely sat astride. Swinging onto the roan he led the way toward town. She was about to speak of the direction when she decided to keep silent, and, glancing sidewise at him, smiled to herself at his easy assurance and rather liked his open defiance of the townspeople. She had no illusions as to what effect their ride together might have in certain minds, and she allowed her feelings, if not her thoughts, to choose her words.

"What a relief it is to have a day's freedom," she exulted, patting the black.

Tex nodded understandingly. "Yes," he said. "Being cooped up and hedged around does get tiresome, I suspect. Well," he laughed, "the fences are all down today. We ride where we listeth and let no man say us nay."

She looked at him smilingly. "Do you know that you are something of an enigma? I'm curious to know what's going on in your head," she daringly declared. "You just said the fences are all down, you know."

He laughed and glanced down the main street, into which they at that moment turned, and a certain grimness came to his face, which she did not miss. "Why allow yourself to be disappointed?" he asked. "Illusions have their worth; and a mystery solved loses its interest. As a matter of fact, the less that is known of what goes on in my head, the better for my reputation for wisdom and common sense. It reminds me of the mouse in the cave."

"Yes?"

"Yes. It was such a big cave and such a little mouse," he explained. "And except for the little mouse the cave was empty."

"I admire your humility; it is refreshing, especially in this country; but I fear it is a very great illusion. Like the other illusions to which you just referred, has it its worth?"

"Confession is good for the soul, and always has worth."

While he spoke he saw a lounger before the hotel come to startled life and hurry inside. Down the street three conversing miners stopped their words to stare open-mouthed at the two riders nonchalantly jogging their way. The door of the hotel became jammed and curious, surprised faces peered from its dirty windows, among them the angry countenance of Henry Williams.

The ordeal of proceeding naturally and carelessly down that street under such frank scrutiny would have tried the balance of any poise, and Jane, flushing and trying to ignore the stares, flashed a searching glance at her companion and felt a quick admiration for him. She could imagine Tommy under these conditions. For all she could detect, her companion might have been riding across the uninhabited plains with no observing eyes within a day's ride of him. Swaying rhythmically to the motion of his horse, relaxed, unconcerned, and natural, he talked with ease and smoothness; and unknowingly made an impression on her which time never would efface.

"That simile of the mouse in the cave," he was saying, "naturally sets up a train of thought—all thought being an unbroken, closely connected, although not necessarily manifest to us, concatenation—and leads to the ass in the lion's skin, being helped materially by the great number of asses in sight, despite the scarcity of even the skins of the nobler beasts. The dual combination does not end there, however; there are jackals in lobos' hides, and vultures posing as eagles. Even the lowly skunk has found a braver skin and bids for a reputation sweeter to bear than the one earned by his own striking peculiarity. For such a one there is nothing so disconcerting as a six-gun appearing from a place where no six-gun should be—and it loses none of its potency even if the bore be small and the charge light. Have you ever had the opportunity to study animals at close range, Miss Saunders?"

His companion, bent over the saddle horn in her mirth, gasped that she never had enjoyed such an opportunity, especially before today, whereupon he continued.

"The ass in the lion's skin was all right and got along famously until he brayed," he explained; "but the skunk fools no one for one instant, not even himself. He can't even fool Oh My, here," and he slapped the glossy neck of the roan.

"Who?" demanded Jane, her face red from laughter.

"Oh My; my horse," he answered. "He was named by one Windy Barrett, when that person awakened from a stupor acquired by pouring libations to Bacchus. The rest of the name is Cayenne."

"Why, that's an exclamation, not a name—Oh!" Jane went off into another fit of laughter. "*Omar Khayyam!* Isn't that rich! Whatever did you do when you heard it?"

"I led Graves to the tavern door agape," answered Tex, grinning.

By this time they had swung into the trail leading to the C Bar and the miles rolled swiftly behind them. Suddenly Tex touched his companion's arm, both reining in abruptly. Squarely in the middle of the trail was a rattlesnake, huge for the prairie, and it coiled swiftly, the triangular head erect and the tail whirring.

"Ugh!" exclaimed Jane, a wave of revulsion sweeping over her. "What a monster! Can you shoot it from here?"

Tex nodded. "Yes, but while I usually do, I rather dis-

like the job. He's a snake all right, man's hereditary
enemy since the world was young, and the hatred for
him comes to us naturally. Sinister, repellant, and all
that, that chap is as square as any enemy in the wild,
and he is coolly business-like. He hasn't a friend outside his own species, and even in that is to be found
one of his chief enemies. There he lies, for all to see, his
gauntlet thrown, whirring his determination to defend
himself, and to depart if given a chance. Look at those
coils, their grace and power, not an ungainly movement the whole length of him. Look at his markings—
from the freshness of his skin and its vivid coloration
I'd say he has very recently parted with his old skin,
and the parasites which infected it. You shed your skin
in vain, OldTimer—you'll not enjoy it long," and his
hand dropped to the holster. A flash and a roar, a rolling burst of smoke, and the defiant head jerked sidewise, hanging by a few shreds of muscle to the writhing
coils. " 'Dead for a ducat, dead!' " quoted Tex, leading
the way past his victim.

A little farther on he pointed to a track along the side
of the trail.

"Dog or wolf," he said. "They're identical except for
directness. A dog's track wavers, a wolf's does not.
From the fact that it follows the trail I'd say that was a
dog; but it may puzzle us before we lose it. He was a big
animal, though, and if a wolf he's a lobo, the gray buffalo wolf, cunning as Satan and brave as Hector. And
what a killer! No carrion for him, no meat killed by anyone but himself, and usually he's shy about returning
to that. He creates havoc on a cattle range. Poison he
sneers at, and it takes mighty shrewd trapping to catch
him. To avoid the scent of man is his leading maxim.
Before the snow comes he is safe—afterwards his troubles begin if a tracer crosses his trail."

"Why I thought he was a big coyote," said Jane. "You
make him out to be quite a remarkable animal."

"And justly," responded her companion. "Coyote?

They shouldn't be mentioned together in the same breath. The buffalo gray is a king—the coyote a crawling scavenger, with wits in place of courage. The difference in the natures is indicated graphically by the way they hold their tails. The coyote's droops at a sharp angle, but the lobo's is held straight out. A single wolf is more expensive to ranchers now than he once was, because he has been hunted so hard with traps and poison that he now has learned not to eat dead animals, and in some cases even to ignore his own kill after once he has left it. I've heard of several wolves, each of which have been blamed for the killing of sixty cows in a year, and their score might have run quite some higher. Have you been watching this track? I'd say it's wolf—and as direct as an arrow. And there is the great western target—tomato, from the color of it. Suppose you try your hand at it?"

Jane produced the pistol and listened intelligently (and how rare a gift that is!) to all her companion had to tell her. When the pistol was emptied the can was still untouched. Laughing, Tex dismounted, and drew a long rectangle in the sand, with the can in the median line and to one end.

"The ground laying flat instead of standing up like a man," he explained, "I had to figure on your line of vision. If the upper half of a man's body were placed on the line nearer you, his head would just about intercept your view of the farther line. Now your third and sixth shots, having struck inside the four lines, would have hit a man at that distance. I'd say you hit his stomach with the third shot, and his right shoulder with the other. The can is of no moment, for cans are not dangerous; but when I show you how to reload, I want you to aim at the can, as if it were the buckle of a belt. You take to that Colt like a duck takes to water—and by the way, Miss Saunders, if I were you, carrying that gun as you must carry it, I'd leave one cartridge out, and let the hammer rest on the empty chamber."

The lesson went on, his pupil slowly becoming enthused and finding that it truly was a sport. When she had made four out of five in the marked-off space she was greatly elated and would have continued shooting after she was tired, but her tutor refused to let her.

"That is enough for now," he laughed. "On our way back you may try a few more rounds if you wish. No use to tire yourself, especially after such a creditable showing. In these few minutes you graduated out of the defenseless-woman class, and may God help anybody who discounts your defense. You see, the main thing is not the shooting, but the freedom from fear of weapons and knowing how to use them. There is nothing mysterious about a Colt—it won't blow up, or shoot behind. Whatever timidity you may have had about handling one has been overcome, and in a few minutes you have learned to hold it right and to shoot it. The bare threat of a gun held in capable hands is in most cases enough. Now, if you please, I'll try my left hand at the can. I wear only one gun, but it may be necessary to wear two—and while my left hand has been trained to shoot well, this is a good opportunity to exercise it."

Filling the can with sand and dirt to weigh it against rolling, he stepped back twenty paces, tossed his own Colt into his left hand, dropped the butt to his hip and sent six shots at the crimson target. Stepping from the smoke cloud he advanced and examined the can. One bullet had clipped its upper edge, another had grazed one side, while the other four were grouped in the sand within a radius only a little larger than that of the target.

"That wouldn't do for two of my friends," he laughed, "but it's good enough for me. Not a shot would have missed the target I had in mind. Had I shot as quickly as I could, I might have missed the target altogether, but close enough for practical purposes. On the other hand, had I taken a little more time, the score would be better."

Jane's mouth still was open in delighted surprise. "Do you mean to tell me that anyone can do better than that, from the hip, without sighting at all?" she demanded incredulously.

"Oh, yes," he replied, reloading the weapon. "Quite some few, notably those two friends of whom I spoke. You see I am satisfied in attaining practical perfection in my left hand, knowing that my other is skilled to a higher degree; but my friends must spend their time and cartridges painting the lily. Either Johnny or Hopalong would feel quite chagrined if at least five hadn't cut into the can. You should see them shooting against each other, breaking matches to get the exact measurements and arguing as if a fortune depended on it. Why, Miss Saunders, either of them could walk into Williams' hotel on a busy night, give warning, and empty two guns in less than ten seconds, every shot hitting a man. They have faced greater odds than that, both of them."

"You mean that one man could defeat a crowd like that?"

"Exactly; but they would not have to fire a shot," he said, smiling. "You see, such a man would only have to throw down on the crowd to hold them in check, if they know he will go through with his play. It isn't unlike an arch. The keystone in this case is the fear of certain death to the man who leads. The first man in the crowd to make a play would die. To some people martyrdom has a morbidly pleasant appeal as an abstract proposition; but in a concrete state, where the suffering is not vicarious, it really has few devotees. And here is a psychological fact: every man in the front rank of such a crowd is fully convinced that he has been selected for the target if the rush starts. Hopalong and Johnny would go through with their play if their hand was forced, and they are the kind of men whose expressions assure that they will. It is a great comfort to have them with you if you must enter a hostile town. It's a gift, like the gift of keener, swifter reflexes."

"It seems so impossible," commented Jane. "Won't you please try your other hand at a can? Somehow I felt that the snake was killed by accident more than skill. It seemed absurd, the offhand way you did it."

"This really is no test," he responded, filling another can and stepping back as he shifted the weapon to the right hand. "There is not the tenseness which a great stake causes; but, on the other hand, there is not the high-tension signals to the muscles. Watch closely," and the jarring crashes sounded like a loud ripping. One hole through the picture of a perfect tomato, two just above it, two lower down, and the sixth on the upper edge of the can gave mute testimony that he shot well.

She fairly squealed with delight and clapped her hands in spontaneous enthusiasm. "Wonderful! Wonderful! Oh, if I ever could shoot like that! I don't believe those friends can even equal it, and I don't care how good they are." Her face beamed. "But that must have taken a great deal of practice."

"Years of it," he replied, "coupled to a natural aptitude. While the accuracy is good enough, that is of secondary consideration. Had only one bullet struck the target, or grazed it, the other five would not have been necessary. The speed of the draw is the great thing. Any man used to shooting a revolver can hit that mark once in six—but he is far from a real gunman if he can't beat ninety-nine men out of a hundred in firing the first shot. That is what counts with a gun-fighter. His target is almost any place between the belt and the shoulders. If he strikes there and does not kill his man he will have time for a second shot if it is needed. My left hand is as deadly as my right against a living target so far as accuracy is concerned; but pit it against my right and it would be hopelessly lost, dead before it could get the gun out of the holster. And Hopalong Cassidy twice gave me lessons in the fine art of drawing—once in an exhibition and the second time in what would have been mortal combat if he had not allowed his heart to guide his head. I did not in the least merit his mercy. I had lived a wild, careless life, Miss Saunders; but it changed from that day."

"Jerry told me why you made him give up wearing his revolver," she said, thoughtfully. "I did not fully appreciate his words; but the graphic exposition lacks nothing to be convincing. Was your interest in his welfare another of your generalities?"

Her companion laughed. "Jerry is a very likable chap, Miss Saunders. Knowing that some feeling against him existed, and not knowing into what it might develop, I only followed the promptings of caution. He is a gentleman and a man infinitely finer grained than the rest of the inhabitants of Windsor. He is honorable and he lacks insight into the common motives which impel many men to perform acts he would not countenance. I have knocked about the West for twenty years, seeing it at its best and at its worst—and you simply cannot conceive what that worst is. I have met many Gus Williamses and Jakes and Bud Haineses and Henry Williamses. They are almost a distinct variation of the human species; they are a recognized and classified type. I knew them all as soon as I saw them. Bud Haines is a natural killer. He'd kill a man at a nod from the man who hired him. Gus Williams hires him, knowing that. Henry, the nephew, is foul, a sneak, and a coward. I'd rather see a sister of mine in her grave than married to him. But he is Gus Williams' nephew, the second power in town and must not be overlooked; and he never will know how close to death he has been these last few days. It fairly has breathed in his face. But we've had enough of this: not far ahead is a fairly good place for our lunch, unless you would prefer to go on to the C Bar."

"Why have you mentioned the nephew to me?" demanded Jane, her cheeks flushed and a fear in her eyes.

"Did I single him out?" asked Tex in surprise. "Why, I only mentioned him, along with the others, while giving examples of a detestable type and to explain why Jerry should not go about armed. I hope I have not frightened you, Miss Saunders?"

"You have not frightened me," she answered. "I have been frightened for a long time. We are so helpless! Things which bother me, I dare not speak to him about them, for he only would get into trouble and to no avail. He cannot pick and choose; and I must stand by him, no matter where he goes, or what he does. Is there mercy in heaven, is there justice in God, that we should be so circumscribed, forced by ills hard enough in themselves to bear, into still greater ills? Jerry's lungs would be tragedy enough for us to bear; but when I look around at times and see—do you believe in God, Mr. Jones?"

"What I may or may not believe in is no aid to you, Miss Saunders," replied Tex, amazed at his reaction to her distress. It was all he could do to keep from taking her in his arms. It was a lucky thing for Henry Williams that he finally abandoned the idea of following them. "If you have been taught to believe in a Divine Power, then don't you turn away from it. To say there is no God is to be as dogmatic as to say there is; for every reasoning being must admit a First Cause. It is only when we characterize it, and attempt to give It attributes that differences of opinions arise. I am not going to enter into any discussion with you on subjects of this nature, Miss Saunders. Nor am I going to tell you what my convictions are. They do not concern us. If you have any religious belief, cling to it: this is when it should begin paying dividends."

"Have you read Kant?"

"Yes; and Spencer tears him apart."

"You are familiar with Spencer?"

"As I am with my own name. To my way of thinking his is the greatest mind humanity ever produced—but, with your permission, we will change the subject."

"Not just yet, please," she said. "You admire his logical reasoning?"

"I refuse to answer," he smiled. "Here, let me give you an example of logical reasoning, Miss Saunders. Here are two coins," he said, digging two double eagles out of his pocket, "which, along with thousands of others, we will say, were struck from one die. You and I would say that they are identical, especially after the most thorough and minute examination failed to disclose any differences. I hardly believe that any man, no matter how much he may be aided by instruments of precision, can take two freshly minted coins from the same die and find any difference. But what does pure logic say?"

"Certainly not that there is any difference?" she challenged in frank surprise.

He chuckled. "That is just what it claims, and here is the reasoning: No one will deny that the die wears out with use, which is the same as saying that the impressions change it. To deny that they do is to say that it does not wear out, which is absurd. Therefore each impression, being a part of the total impressions, must have done its share in the changing. And each impression, having changed it, must be different from those preceeding and following it. Now, if the die changes, as we have just proved that it does, so must the coins struck off from it, for to say otherwise is to claim that effects are not produced by causes, and that a changed die will not make changed coins. Therefore, there are no two coins absolutely alike, never have been, and never can be, even at the moment they leave the die. Put them into circulation and the hypothetical differences rapidly increase, since no two of the coins can possibly receive the same treatment in their travelings. There you have it, in pure logic: but does it get you any place? On the strength of it, would you persist in denying that these coins are dissimilar? Are they so practically? And it is from practical logic that we draw the deductions by which we think and move and live. So you take my word that it will be better for you to cling to whatever faith you may have. If it is not practical enough for you, I'll look after that end for you; and between your faith and the cunning of my gun-hand I'll warrant that your brother will come to no harm. Shall we lunch at the C Bar, or in that little clump of burned and sickly timber on the bank of that dried-up creek?"

"I'm really too hungry to postpone the lunch," she said, smiling; "besides I want to watch you in camp, and to listen to you. It seems to me that you have too keen a brain to be spending your life where it all is wasted."

"Your compliment is disposed of by the fact that I am what I am," he responded. "The return compliment of not being able to be in a better place, under present conditions, is so obvious that I'll not spoil its effect by saying it. Anyhow, a fair vocabulary and a veneer of knowledge are not the measures of wisdom, but rather a disguising coat. To come right down to elementals, I heartily agree with you about the lunch. I'll be better company after the inner man has been properly attended to, for food always leavens my cynicism. Did I hear you ask why I do not eat continually?"

The clump of browned trees reached, it took but little time to unpack the lunch and start a cunningly built fire of twigs and broken branches, over which the coffee quickly heated. Depressing as the surroundings were, barren and sun-baked as far as eye could see, the bed of the creek dried and cracked and curling, this scene was destined to live long in the memory of Tex Ewalt. The food, better cooked and far more daintily prepared than any he could recall, tasted doubly good in the presence of his intelligent, good-looking companion. The subjects of their interested discussions were wide in range and neither very long maintained a certain restraint which had characterized their earlier conversations. She led him to talk of the West as it was, as he had seen it, and as he hoped it would become; a skillful question starting him off anew, and her intelligent comments keeping him at his best. So absorbed were they that even he failed to hear the step of a horse and did not know of its presence until an eager, if timid, hail stopped him short.

"Gosh, you people look cheerful," called Tommy Watkins, gazing at Jane with his heart in his eyes.

"Sorry I can't say the same about your looks," chuckled Tex, his quick glance noting the boyishness of their visitor, his youthful freshness and the rebellious admiration in his unblinking eyes. Tex took himself in hand and crushed the feeling of jealousy which tingled in him and threatened to show itself in words, looks, and actions. He looked inquiringly at his companion and at her slight nod, he beckoned to the youth. "Come over here an' make it three-handed, cowboy," he called. "We'll salvage what we can of th' lunch an' feed it to you. Did you find the ranch there, when you got home th' other night?"

Tommy rode up and gravely dismounted. "Yes, it was there. They said you hadn't been around so far as they knew, so I had my hasty ride for nothin'. How'd'y do, ma'am?" he asked, his hat going under his arm.

"Very well, indeed," replied Jane, smiling and fixing a place for him at her other side. "I'm sorry you did not come while there was more to eat, although I'll confess that I am not apologizing for my share of the havoc. It has been a long time since I have enjoyed a meal as I have this lunch. Sit here, Mr. Watkins—I am glad that there is some coffee left."

"That's what I get for being thrifty and thinking of the future," laughed Tex. "It's like the men who work hard and save all their lives, so that someone else can spend for them. Here you go, Thomas: look out—it's still hot."

"Thank you ma'am," said Tommy, flushing and embarrassed, as he dropped onto the spot indicated. "I ain't a bit hungry, though."

"You will be after the first bite," assured Tex. "The cups have been used, and there's no water for washing them. That's excuse enough for any man to drink out of the pail, and I envy you there, Tommy Watkins. Cattle gettin' along all right in spite of the drought? Expect to have a big gain this round-up? They ought to bring top-notch prices if they're in good shape."

Steered easily into familiar channels of conversation, Tommy got on well, so well that his embarrassment gradually disappeared and he was nearly his natural self; but he did envy his friend's ability to think coherently and to talk with fluent ease on any subject mentioned. Jane Saunders learned more about cows, cattle, steers, calves, cows, cattle, riding, roping, round-ups, branding, cows, calves, horses, cattle, and other ranch subjects than she thought existed to be learned. And she shot a glance of grateful appreciation at Tex Jones for the way in which he put their guest on his feet and kept him there through several vocal flounderings. It was so tactfully done that Tommy did not realize it.

Gradually Tex worked out of the conversation and studied his companions. He saw clean youth entertaining clean youth; a bubbling mirth free from suspicion or irony; an absence of cynicism, and an unbounding faith in the future. He hid his smile at how Tommy was led to talk of himself and of his ambitions. They looked to be about the same age, Tommy perhaps a few years her senior; and when she looked at Tommy there was friendliness in her eyes; and when Tommy looked at her there was a great deal more in his.

The keen, but apparently careless, observer silently and fairly reviewed the years that had passed since he had been at Tommy's age; the lack of illusions, the cold, cynical practicality of his thoughts and actions; the laws, both civil and moral, which he contemptuously had shattered. He could not remember the time when he had had Tommy's faith in men, nor his enthusiasm. Tommy was looking forward to a life of clean, hard work, and actually with a fierce eagerness. Never had such a thing been an impelling motive in the life of Tex Ewalt. Instead he had planned shrewdly and consistently how to avoid working for a living, and when it was solved, then how to live higher and higher with the least additional effort. And he now admitted that if he had the chance to live that period over again, under the same circumstances, he would repeat his course in the major things. He felt neither regret nor remorse at the contrast—he had lived as it pleased him, and the Tex Ewalt of today had no censure for the Tex Ewalt of yesterday. But he was fair, at all events; and to draw true deductions from accepted facts was an art not to be perverted because expediency might beckon. After all, he did not try to fool himself; and he was no hypocritical whiner. Being fair, he calmly realized that he was the unfitting unit of this triangle, that he did not belong there. But there would be time enough for such cogitation later on.

"Shore," Tommy was dogmatically asserting. "Th' rattler gets all cramped up an' tired, an' there is an instant when he can't turn fast enough to keep his nasty little eyes on th' other, that's racin' around him like a flash. That's th' end of th' rattler. Th' kingsnake darts in, grabs th' rattler behind th' head, an' after a great thrashin' around, kills him dead. *Ain't* that so, Mr. Jones?"

Tex lazily turned his head and looked at the doubting auditor and then at the anxious Tommy. He gravely nodded. "Yes that's th' end. That's the enemy within the snake's own species which I mentioned back on the trail, Miss Saunders."

The look of doubt faded from her face and a nebulous smile transformed it. She was certain of it now.

Tex flamed at what that change told him, tingling to his finger tips with a surging elation. He felt that he had but to speak three words to put her vague feelings into a coherent wonder of wonders; but to crystallize them into an everlasting passion by the alchemy of his avowal, or the touch of his lips. The lulled storm within him broke out anew and blazed fiercely. He arose, kicked an inoffensive tin can over the bed of the creek and spun it in mid-air by a vicious, eye-baffling shot from his Colt. Realizing how he had forgotten himself, and his resolutions, he, the cool, imperturbable Tex Ewalt, he recovered his poise and bowed, smilingly, to the surprised pair.

"That's shootin', Tex!" cried Tommy.

"It's more than that," smiled Tex. "It's notice that it's time to try that .38, Miss Saunders," he announced. "She is learning to use a gun, Tommy—I've been telling her how much fun it is. I'll call th' shots while you stand by her to answer questions. Suppose we have a more suitable target, this time. What can we use?"

Tommy grinned expansively. "Who's goin' to do th' shootin'?" he demanded.

"Miss Saunders," answered Tex. "Why?"

"Oh; all right then—here, prop up my hat," offered Tommy; "But not too all-fired close!" he warned.

"There's chivalry for you, Mr. Jones!" triumphantly exclaimed Jane, her eyes dancing.

"Think so?" queried Tex, grinning. "Huh!" He shook his head. "I'd say he is not paying you any compliment. Just for that I hope you shoot it to pieces."

He took the sombrero from Tommy's extended hand, went down and crossed the creek bed, and placed the hat against the opposite bank. Stepping off twenty paces he drew a line on the earth with the side of his boot sole and beckoned to the flushed markswoman.

"That hat is a pressing danger," he warned. "You've got to get it, or it'll get you. Don't be careless, and don't waste any sympathy on the grinning wretch who owns it."

"But I don't want to ruin it," she protested. "Surely something else will answer?"

"You go ahead an' ruin it, if you can," chuckled Tommy. "Don't *you* worry none—I ain't!"

"I do believe it wasn't a compliment, or chivalry, at all," she laughed. "All right, Mr. Watkins: here goes for a new hat!" Slowly, deliberately, holding her arm as she had been instructed, she aimed and fired until the weapon was empty. The hat had a hole near one edge of the crown and another near the edge of the brim.

"Glory be!" exclaimed Tommy. "I'm votin' for a new target! Why that's plumb fine, Miss Saunders—if it ain't an accident!"

"Let's see if it was," suggested Tex, handing her another round of cartridges. "Here!" he exclaimed, glancing at Tommy. "Where you goin' so fast?"

"To collect th' ruins," retorted the puncher over his shoulder. "*You* got a hat, ain't you?"

"I have, and I'm keeping it right where it belongs," rejoined Tex. "I didn't suggest that it was any accident, did I?"

CHAPTER X

Speed and Guile

TEX AND Tommy said their adieus, watched Jane enter the house, and then rode slowly toward the station where, after a few words with Jerry Saunders, Tommy went on alone, leaving Tex talking with the agent.

The C Bar puncher rode down the main street full of more kinds of emotion than he ever had known before, and among them was a strong feeling of his inability to gain Jane's attention while Tex Jones was around. Jealousy was working in the yeasty turbulence of his heart and mind. Taking off his perforated sombrero he gazed at it as though it were something sacred. There they were, two of them, made by her blessed bullets! Reverently pushing the ragged felt of their rims back into place, he patted the nearly closed holes and put the sombrero on his head again. There would be no new hat for Tommy Watkins, as she had laughingly said. No, sir! No, sir-e-e!

Opposite the hotel he became aware of his surroundings and suddenly decided that he needed a drink to steady himself, to shock himself into a more natural condition of mind. As he made the decision, he idly observed Bud Haines emerge from the door of the general store and start toward him on the peculiar, bow-legged, choppy stride he so much affected. And as Tommy swung off the horse and carelessly tossed the reins across the tie-rail he caught sight of Tex Jones waving to the agent and slowly wheeling the roan.

Tommy made his way through the card-table end of the room, noticing without giving any particular weight to the fact, that he was the cynosure of all eyes. Still strange to himself and very much occupied by his thoughts, he did not note whether there were six or two dozen men in the room; nor that their eager and low-voiced conversation abruptly ceased upon his entry, and that there was an air of expectancy which seemed to fill the room. He passed Henry Williams, who was seated at a small table, with a nod and rested his elbows on the bar. Silently a bottle and glass were placed before him, silently he poured out a drink and downed it mechanically. Then Henry spoke, his ratlike eyes for a moment not shifting.

"That's a fenced range," he said in a low, tense voice. "You keep off it!"

Tommy, not realizing that the words were intended for him, still rested his elbows on the bar, his back to the speaker and the rest of the room, buried in his abstractions. He neither saw nor heard the quiet, quick entry of Bud Haines through the front door, nor knew that the gunman stopped suddenly and leaned against the jamb. Neither he, nor anyone else, caught the quiet step nearing that same door from the street.

Henry Williams, finding his warning totally ignored, let his anger leap to rage.

"You!" he snarled. "I'm talking to *you*, Watkins!"

Tommy started and swung around, momentarily out of touch with his surroundings. The meanness in the voice, the deadly timbre of it, warned him subconsciously rather than acutely, and he stared at the speaker.

"What you say, Williams?" he asked, rapidly sensing the hostility in the air. "I was thinkin' of something'," he explained.

"I'm givin' you somethin' to think about!" retorted Henry, slowly arising and slowly leaning forward on the table. "You don't want to stop thinkin' about it, neither—unless you want to join th' dead uns on Boot Hill. I said that range is fenced—*you keep off!*"

Tommy, alert as a coiled snake now, watched the angry man while he considered. A fenced range. He was to keep off. "I ain't gettin' th' drift of that," he said, slowly. "Any reason why you shouldn't talk so I'll know what yo're meanin'?"

"Yo're dumb as h—l, ain't you?" sneered Henry, his voice rising shrilly and the little, close-set eyes beginning to flame. "I wouldn't have nobody say you wasn't warned plain. I'm tellin' you for th' last time, to do yore courtin' somewhere else! I'm claimin' that Saunder gal. Keep away, that's all!"

Tommy went a little white around his stiffening lips. When his words came they sounded the spirit of the C Bar, but where they came from he did not know; perhaps he had heard them or read them somewhere. Certainly they did not by right belong to his direct method of conveying thought. He knew Henry Williams, his baseness, his petty villainies, his bestial nature. The picture of Jane, innocent and sweet, came to him and made a contrast which sickened him. Looking straight into Henry's eyes his voice rasped its insulting, deadly reply.

"It's bad enough for a coyote like me to admire a rose; but I'm d—d if any polecat's goin' to pluck it!"

Before the words were all spoken and before either of the disputants could move they heard the startling crash of a gun and instinctively glanced toward the sound. They saw Bud Haines, his smoking revolver forced slowly up behind his back, higher and higher, the gun wrist gripped in the sinewy fingers of Tex Jones, whose right hand held his own Colt at his hip, the deadly muzzle covering the two in front of the bar, without a tremble of its steely barrel. His gripping fingers kept on twisting, while one knee held the killer from writhing sidewise to escape the grip of the punishing bending of the imprisoned arm. Slowly the tortured muscles grew numb, slowly beads of perspiration stood out on the killer's forehead, and as his throbbing elbow neared the snapping point, he gasped, released his hold on the Colt and then went spinning across the room from the power of his captor's whirling shove. When he stopped he froze in his tracks, for Tex carelessly held two guns now, the captured weapon covering its owner.

"Phew!" sighed Tex, a grin slowly spreading across his red face. "That was close, *that* was! Reckon I done saved quite a mess in here." He glared at Tommy. "You get th' h—l out of here an' don't come back till you know how to act! Runnin' around like a mad dog, tryin' to kill men that never done you no harm! G'wan, or I'll let Hennery loose at you! I heard what you said, an' I wouldn't blame him if he blowed you wide open! G'wan! Shove that gun back where it belongs, an' git: *Pronto!* You've gone an' got Bud an' me bad friends, I reckon, an' I can't hardly blame him, neither."

Henry's eyes were riveted on the menacing Colt, his hand frozen where it had stopped, a few inches above the butt of his own. Bud Haines leaned forward, balanced on the balls of his feet, but not daring to leap. The spectators were staring, open-mouthed, quite content to let things take their course without any impetus from them.

Tommy sullenly slid the gun back into its holster and walked toward the door, too angry to speak. Glaring at Tex he went out, mounted and rode toward the ranch; and it was half an hour later before he came to the realization that his life had been saved from a shot from the side, and by the time he had reached the ranchhouse he was grinning.

Tex flipped the captured gun into the air, caught it by the barrel, and tossed it, butt first, to the killer. "I shore am apologizin' to you, Bud," he said, "for cuttin' in that way—but I had to act sudden, an' rough."

As the weapon settled into its owner's hand it roared and leaped, the bullet cutting Tex's vest under the armpit. Before a second shot could follow from it Bud twisted sidewise and plunged face down on the floor.

Tensed like a panther about to spring, Tex peered through the thinning cloud of smoke rising from his hip, his attention on the others in the room. "Sorry," he said. "You saw it all. I gave him his gun, butt first, an' he shot at me with it. Clipped my vest under my left shoulder. I couldn't do nothin' else. I'm sayin' that doin' favors for strangers is risky business—but is anybody findin' any fault with this shootin'?" He glanced quickly from face to face and then nodded slightly. "It was plain self-defense. If I'd 'a' thought he was a-goin' to shoot I shore wouldn't 'a' chucked him his loaded gun. Reckon I'm a plain d—d fool!"

There were no replies to him. The tense faces stared at the man who had killed Bud Haines in a fight after the killer had shot first. While there were no accusations in their expressions, neither was there any friendliness. The killing had been justified. This seemed to be the collective opinion, for in no way could the facts be changed. Bud had been man-handled in a manner which to him had been an unbearable insult, the fight could be considered as of his adversary's starting, but the actual shooting was as the victor claimed; and it was the shooting which they were to judge.

Tex, feeling ruefully of the bullet-torn vest, shoved his gun into its sheath and went over to Henry's table. The nephew hardly had moved since the first shot.

"I got somethin' to talk to you about, Henry," said

Tex in a low, confidential voice. " 'Tain't for everybody's ears, neither; so sit down a minute. That fool Watkins came cuttin' in as we was ridin' back, or I might have more news."

Henry slowly followed his companion's movements and straddled his chair. He motioned to the bartender for drinks and then let his suspicious eyes wander over his companion's face. He had a vast respect for Tex Jones.

"I reckon he's been cured of cuttin' in," he growled, a momentary gleam showing. "That's a habit of yourn, too," he said. "An' it's a cussed bad one, here in Windsor."

Tex spread his hands in helpless resignation. "I know it. Ever since I've been in this town I been puttin' my worst foot forward. I'm allus bunglin' things; an' just when I was beginnin' to make a few friends, Bud had to go an' git blind mad an' spoil everythin'. I didn't have nothin' ag'in' Bud; but I reckon mebby I was a little mite rough."

"Oh, Bud be d—d!" coldly retorted Henry. "He had th' edge, an' lost. That's between him an' you. What I'm objectin' to, Jones, is th' way you spoiled my plans. Don't you never cut into my affairs like you did just now. I'm tellin' you fair. I'm admittin' yo're a prize-winnin' gun-thrower; but there's other ways in this town. Savvy?"

Tex shook his head apologetically and nodded. "You an' me ain't goin' to have no trouble, Hennery," he declared earnestly. "If you want that C Bar fool, go git him. It ain't none of my business. But I'm worryin' about what yore uncle's goin' to say about me shootin' Bud," he confessed with plain anxiety. "He's a big man, Williams is; an' me, shucks: I ain't nothin' a-tall."

"He'll take my say-so," assured Henry, "after he cools down. Now what you got to tell me?"

"It's about that Saunders gal," answered Tex. He hitched his chair a little nearer to the table. "You remember what I told you, couple of nights ago? Well, I got to thinkin' about it when I was near th' station yesterday, so I went in an' got friendly with her brother." He rubbed his chin and grinned reminiscently. "There was a box across th' track that he had been using for a target. I asked him what it was an' he told me, an' he said he couldn't hit it. I sort of egged him on, not believin' him; an' shore enough he couldn't—an', Hennery, it was near as big as a house! I cut loose an' made a sieve of it—you must 'a' heard th' shootin'? His eyes plumb stuck out, an' we got to talkin' shootin'. Finally he ups an' asks me can I show his sister how to throw a gun an', seein' my chance to learn somethin' about her, I said I shore could show anybody that wasn't scared to death of one, an' that had any sense. 'How much will you charge for th' lessons?' says he. I had a good chance to pick up some easy money, but that wasn't what I was playin' for. I just wanted to get sort of friendly with her, an' him, too. I says, 'Nothin'.' Well, we fixed it up, an' today we goes off practicin'—you should 'a' seen that lunch, Hennery! I'm cussed near envyin' you!" He laughed contentedly, leaned back, and rubbed his stomach.

"Well?" demanded Henry, grinning ruefully.

"Well," echoed Tex. "You know that sewin' an' crochetin' is a whole lot different from shootin' a .45; an' so does she, now. I reckon a .22 would 'most scare her to death. Did you ever shoot with yore eyes shut? You don't have to try: it can't be done, an' hit nothin'. Sixguns an' wimmin wasn't never made to mix; an' they shore don't. We ate up th' lunch an' started back ag'in, an' I was just gettin' set to swing th' conversation in yore direction, carelesslike, but real careful, an' see what I could find out for you, when cussed if that C Bar coyote didn't come dustin' up, an' I don't know any more than I did before. But I'm riskin' one thing, Hennery: I'm near shore she ain't got nothin' ag'in' you; an' on th' way out, when I refers to you she speaks up quicklike, with her nose turned up a little, an' says:

'Henry Williams? Why, he'll be a rich man some day, when his uncle dies. Ain't some folks born lucky, Mr. Jones?' Hennery, there ain't none of 'em that are over-lookin' th' good old pesos, U. S. You keep right on like you are; an' save me a front seat at th' weddin'.'"

Henry sat back, buried in thought. He glanced at the huddled figure near the door and then looked quickly into his companion's bland eyes. "Her brother's dead set ag'in' it. He knows he done me a dirty trick, stealin' my job, an' like lots of folks, instead of hatin' hisself, he hates me. Human nature's funny that way. So he can't hit a box, hey?"

Tex chuckled and nodded. "He up an' says he's so plumb disgusted with hisself that he ain't never goin' to tote a gun again, not never. Seems to me yo're doin' a lot of foolish worryin' about losin' that job. That ain't no job to worry about. If I was Gus Williams' only rela-tion, you wouldn't see me lookin' for no jobs! You shore got th' wrong idea, Hennery. What do *you* want to work for, anyhow?"

"Well," considered the nephew of the uncle who some day would die, "that *is* one way of lookin' at it; but, Tex, he did me out of it. That's what's rilin' me!"

Tex leaned back and laughed heartily. "Hennery, you make me laugh! If I got mad an' riled at every dog that barked at me I'd be plumb soured for life by this time. A man like you should be above holdin' grudges ag'in' fellers like Saunders. It ain't worth th' risk of spoilin' yore disposition. Let him have his dried-out bone: you would 'a' dropped it quick enough, anyhow. An' if it wasn't for him gettin' that two-by-nothin' old job you wouldn't never 'a' seen his sister, would you? Ever think about it like that? Well, what you think? Had I bet-ter try to go ridin' with her ag'in an' git her to talkin'? Or shall I set back an' only keep my eyes an' ears open?"

"What's interestin' you so much in this here affair?"

questioned Henry, his glance resting for a moment on the face of his companion.

"Well, I ain't got that letter," confessed Tex, slyly; "an' what's more, I'm afraid I ain't goin' to get it, neither, th' coyote. He lets me come out here, near th' end of th' track, an' then lets me hold th' sack. Time's comin' when I'll be needin' a job; an' yo're aces-up with yore uncle." He grinned engagingly. "My cards is face up. I got to look out for myself."

Henry laughed softly. "You shore had me puzzled," he replied. "Well, we'll see what we see. I don't hardly know, yet, what kind of a job you ought to have. There's good jobs, an' poor jobs. An' while I think of it, Tex, you'd mebby better go ridin' with her ag'in. But don't you forget what I was sayin' about there bein' other ways than gun-throwin' in Windsor. I——"

The low hum of conversation about them ceased as abruptly as did Henry's words. He was looking at the door, and sensing danger, Tex pushed back quietly and followed his companion's gaze. Jake, under the influence of liquor, stood in the doorway, a gun in his upraised hand, staring with unbelieving eyes at the body of Bud Haines.

"Stop that fool!" whispered Tex. "I've done too much killin' today: an' he's drunk!"

Henry arose and walked quietly, swiftly toward the vengeful miner, who now turned and looked about the room. A spasm of rage shot through him and his hand chopped down, but Henry knocked it aside and the heavy bullet scored the wall. Two men near the door leaped forward at the nephew's call and after a short struggle, Jake was disarmed, pacified, and sent on his way again.

Tex dropped his gun back into the holster and went up to the nephew. "Much obliged, Hennery," he said. "I've been expectin' him most every minute an' I'm glad you handled it so good. Where's he been keepin' hisself, anyhow?"

"Out in his cabin, nursin' his grudge," answered Henry. "He's one of them kind. He's got it chalked up ag'in' you, Tex, an' it'll smolder an' smolder, no tellin' how long. Then it'll bust out ag'in, like it did just now. Keep out of his way—he's a good man, Jake is. He's a friend of mine."

"That's good enough for me," Tex assured him. "I ain't got no grudge ag'in' Jake. It's th' other way 'round. Reckon I'll put up my cayuse. See you later."

CHAPTER XI

Empty Honors

THE DRAMATIC death of Bud Haines created a ripple of excitement in Windsor which ran a notch higher than any killing of recent years. The late gunman posed as a gunman, swaggeringly, exultantly. Himself a contributor of victims to Boot Hill, his going there aroused a great deal more satisfaction than resentment. He was unmourned, but not unsung, and the question raised by his passing concerned the living more than the dead. How would his conqueror behave?

Bud was an out-and-out killer, cold, dispassionate, calculating; one whose gun was for hire and salary. He had no sympathy, no softer side to his nature, if his fellow-townsmen knew him right. The crooked mouth, grown into a lop-sided sneer, had been a danger signal to everyone who saw him, and through his up-to-then invincible gun Williams had passed his days in confidence, his nights in sleep. He had been taciturn, unsmiling, grim, and the few words he occasionally uttered were never cryptic. On the other hand Tex Jones was voluble, talked loosely and foolishly and had shown signs at poker that his courage was not what it should be to wrap the mantle of the fallen man about him and play his part; but had it been truly shown? Was his poker playing a true index to his whole nature? There was his brief, high-speed, complete mastery over Jake, himself a man bad enough to merit wholesome respect; there was the cool killing of Bud, and the nonchalant actions of the victor after the tragedy. He scarcely had given his victim a second look.

This question, as all questions do, provided argument. Gus Williams, sullen and morose at losing a valuable man in whose fidelity he could place full trust, and on whose prowess his own power largely rested, maintained that Tex Jones had pulled the trigger mechanically, and that it had been for him a lucky accident. His nephew took issue with him and paid his new companion full credit. The miners were about evenly divided, while Carney openly exulted and made the victory his principal topic of conversation. It helped him in another way, for there are some who blindly follow a champion, and the Windsor champion kept his horse and spent many of his spare hours at Carney's. John Graves sighed with relief at Bud's passing, due to an old score he had feared would be reopened, and he urged the appointment of Tex Jones for city marshal, a position hitherto unfilled in Windsor. Carney was for this heart and soul, and offered a marshal's office rent free. It was a lean-to adjoining his saloon.

The railroad element breathed easier now. Tim Murphy wanted to bet on the new man against anyone, at any style, and he glowed with pride as he realized that he, perhaps, was nearer to Tex Jones than any man in town. He had no trouble in persuading Costigan to look with warm favor on the successor to Bud Haines. Jerry Saunders, remembering a bit of gun practice, said he was not surprised and he exulted secretly. Tex Jones had been the first man outside of the railroad circle to give him a kind word and to show friendship; but he had little to say about it after the door of his home closed upon him.

Jerry's sister puzzled him. He saw traces of tears, strange moods came over her which swept her from gaiety to black despondency in the course of an hour or two, and no matter how he figured, he could not understand her. The story of how the affair had started and of Tommy Watkins' part in it made her moods more complex and unfathomable. Jane, he decided, was not only peculiar, but downright foolish. Bud Haines, being but a free member of Williams' own body, executing his wishes and the wishes of the detestable nephew, had been an evil whose potentiality could only be conjectured. He had been swept off the board and his conqueror was at heart very friendly to the Saunders family. They no longer were the most helpless people in town.

When Jerry had gone home on the day of the tragedy he had been full of the exploit, for Murphy and he had discussed it from every angle, and he had absorbed a great deal of the big Irishman's open delight.

Stunned at first, Jane flatly refused to talk about it, and had fled from the supper table to her room. Later on when he had cautiously broached the subject again, quoting the enthusiastic Murphy almost entirely, to show that his own opinions were well founded, she had listened to all he had to say, but had remained dumb. The evening was anything but pleasant and he had gone to bed in an unconcealed huff. She gave credit to Watkins but withheld it from Jones, who had earned it all. "D—n women, anyhow," had been his summing up.

The following morning he ate a silent breakfast and hurried to the station as he would flee to an oasis from the open desert. He found Tim waiting for him, eager to talk it all over again.

Hardly had the station been opened when Tex rode up, leaped from the magnificent roan, and sauntered to the door. His face was grave, his manner dignified and calm. "How'd'y, boys," he said in greeting.

"Proud I am this mornin'," beamed Murphy, his thick, huge hand closing over the lean, sinewy one of the gunman. " 'Twas a fine job ye done, Tex, my boy; an' a fine way ye did it! Gave th' beast th' first shot! There's not another man could do it."

"There's plenty could," answered Tex. "I can name two, an' there's many more. I'm no gunman, understand: I'm just plain Tex Jones. But I didn't come here to hold any pow-pow—I'm wonderin' if you'd let me look in th' toolhouse—I might 'a' left it there when we loaded th' hand car."

"An' what's 'it'?" asked Murphy.

"My knife."

"Come along then," said the section-boss, swinging his keys and leading the way. They found no knife, but Murphy was given some information which he considered worth while. As they reached the station door again Tex burst out laughing.

"I know where it is! Cuss me for a fool, I left it in Carney's stable, stickin' in th' side of th' harness closet. Oh, well; there's no harm done." He turned to Jerry. "I wonder if Miss Saunders would like another bit of practice today?"

Jerry's face clouded. No matter how much he might admire Bud Haines' master in the late Bud's profession of gun-throwing, and no matter how much he might admire him for sundry other matters, nevertheless none of them qualified the new-found friend as an aspirant for his sister's hand. He did not wish to offend Tex, and certainly he did not want his enmity. To him came Jane's inexplicable behavior and in coming it brought an inspiration. Jane, he thought, could handle this matter far better than he could.

"She didn't seem to be feeling well this morning," he answered. "Still, I never guess right about her. If you feel like riding again, go up and ask her."

"I hear there's some talk about them makin' you marshal of this town," said Tim. "Don't you shelve it. This town needs a fair man in that job. It's been quiet of late, but ye can't allus tell. Wait till th' rains come an' start th' placerin' a-goin'. They'll have money to spend, then, an' trouble is shore to follow that. You take that job, Tex."

Jerry nodded eagerly, pointed to some bullet holes in the frame of one of the windows of the office and, grasping Tex by the arm, led him closer to the window. "See that bullet hole in there, just over the table an' below the calendar? The first shot startled me and made me drop my pen—I stooped to pick it up. When I sat up again there was a hole in the glass and under the calendar. When I stooped I saved my life. Just a drunken joke, a miner feeling his oats. One dead man a week was under the average. This town, under normal conditions, is a little bit out of h—l. Take that job, Jones: the town needs you."

Tex laughed. "You better wait till it's offered to me, Jerry. There's quite some people in this town that don't want any marshal. Gus Williams is the man to start it."

"He will," declared Tim. "Bud was his bodyguard, but he was more. Williams has a lot of property to be protected, an' now Bud is gone, th' saints be praised. He'll start it."

While they spoke, a miner was seen striding toward the station and soon joined them. "How'd'y," he said, carelessly, glancing coldly at Tim and Jerry. His eyes rested on Tex and glowed a little. "Th' boss wants to talk with you, Jones. Come a-runnin'."

"Come a-runnin'," rang in Tex's ears and it did not please him. If he was going to be the city marshal it would be well to start off right.

"Th' boss?" he asked nonplused.

"Shore; Gus—Gus Williams," rejoined the messenger crisply and with a little irritation. "You know who I mean. Git a move on."

"Mr. Jones' compliments to Mr. Williams," replied Tex with exaggerated formality, "an' say that Mr. Jones will call on him at Mr. Jones' convenience. Just at present I'm very busy—good day to you, sir."

The miner stood stock-still while he reviewed the surprising words.

Tex ignored him. "No," he said, "I ain't lookin' for no change in th' weather till th' moon changes," he explained to the two railroad men. "But, of course, you know th' old sayin': 'In times of drought all signs fail.' An' there never was a truer one. I wouldn't be surprised if it rained any day; an' when it comes it's goin' to rain hard. Still, I ain't exactly lookin' for it, barrin' the sayin', till th' moon changes. That's my prophecy, gents; you wait an' see if I ain't right. Well, I reckon I'll be amblin'. Good day."

They watched him walk to the roan, throw the reins over an arm, and lead it slowly down the street, followed by the conjecturing messenger. Tex Jones evidently was in no hurry, for he stopped in two places before entering the hotel, and in there he remained for a quarter of an hour. When premature congratulations were offered him he accepted them with becoming modesty and explained that he was not yet appointed.

Gus Williams looked up with some irritation when the door opened and admitted Tex into the store. The newcomer leaned against the counter, nodded to Gus and grinned at Henry. "Hear you want to see me about somethin'," he said, flickering dust from his boots with a softly snapping handkerchief.

"What made you shoot Bud Haines?" growled the proprietor, turning on the stepladder against the shelves.

Tex shook his head in befitting sorrow. "I shore didn't want to shoot Bud," he answered slowly. "Bud hadn't never done nothin' to me; but," he explained, wearily, "he just made me do it. I dassn't let him shoot twice, dast I?"

Williams growled something and replaced several articles of merchandise.

"Hennery says you had to do it," he grudgingly admitted. "I reckon mebby you did—*but*, I don't see why you went at Bud like that, in th' first place."

"I aimed to stop a killin'," muttered Tex, contritely; "an', instead of doin' it, I went an' made one. I ain't none surprised," he said, sighing resignedly, "for I generally play in bad luck. Ever since I shot that black cat, up at Laramie, I've had bad luck—not that I'm what you might call superstitious," he quickly and defiantly explained.

"Well, a man can't allus help things like that," admitted Williams. "I had streaks of luck that looked like they never would peter out." He shifted several articles, leaned back to study their arrangement, and slowly continued. "You see, Bud had a job that ain't very common; an' men like Bud ain't very common, neither. He allus was plumb grateful because I saved his life once in a—stampede," he naively finished. "I got a lot of valuable property in this here town, and Windsor gets quite lively when th' placerin' is going good. I shore feel sort of lost without Bud." He wiped his dusty hands on his trousers and slowly climbed down. "Now, I remembered that Scrub Oak an' Willow both has peace officers, an' Windsor shore ain't taking a back seat from towns like them. Hennery was sayin' that folks here sort of been talkin' about a city marshal, an' mentionin' you for th' office. We ought to have our valuable property pertected, an' me, bein' the owner of most of th' valuable property here an' here-abouts, nat'rally leans to that idea; but, bein' th' biggest owner of valuable property, I sort of got to look the man over purty well before I appoint him. I got to have a good man, a man that'll pertect th' most property first. What you think about it?"

Tex removed his sombrero, turned it over slowly in his hands and stared at its dents. Punching them out and punching in new ones, he gravely considered them. "Well," he drawled, "you see, if that letter comes—I don't know how long I'm goin' to stay in town; but if I *did* stay, I'd shore do my damndest to pertect property, an' you havin' the most of it, you'd nat'rally be pertected more'n others that had less."

Williams glanced swiftly at his nephew. "You still expectin' that letter, Jones?" he slyly demanded.

Tex hesitated and turned the hat over again. "Can't hardly say I am," he admitted, frowning at Henry. "But there's a sayin' that hope springs infernal—an' I reckon that's th' h—l of it; a man never knows when to quit waitin' for it to spring. Meanwhile I got to eat—an' I like a game of poker once in awhile. Here, tell you what—I'll take the job as long as I can hold it, if the pay is right. What you reckon the job's worth, in a lawless, desperate town like this, where no man's life or property is worth very much?"

Williams scowled. "This here town ain't lawless an' desperate," he denied. "There ain't a more peaceable town in Kansas!"

"Which same ain't payin' no compliments to Kansas towns, once the rains come," chuckled Tex. "I'm admirin' your humor, Mr. Williams—I ain't never heard dryer," he beamed in frank admiration. "But, wet or dry, there's allus them mean low-down cow-wrastlers comin' to town to likker up—an' them an' miners are as friendly as a badger and a dog. Let's name over them as would want the pertection of a marshal, an' then figger how much they'd sweeten the pot. Take Carney, now—he ought to be willin' to ante up han'some, his business bein' so healthy."

"Carney," sneered Williams in open contempt. "Huh! Here, gimme that pencil an' that old envelope!" He worked laboriously, revised the figures several times and then looked up. "I reckon two hundred a month ought to be enough. Scrub Oak pays that—Willow does likewise. You got your outfit. We furnish th' office, ammernition, an' pay extra expenses. That's th' best Windsor can do. Yore office will be next door to this store."

Tex looked questioningly at Henry, who nodded decisively, and carefully put the hat back on his head. "All right," he said. "When do I start in?"

"Right now," answered Williams, fumbling under the counter. "We ain't got no marshal's badge, but I got a sheriff's star somewhere around. He was killed up on Buffaler Crick last spring. Yep—here it is: this'll do for awhile. Lean over here, Marshal," he chuckled. "There: It ain't every marshal that's a sheriff, too." Smiling at Henry he said, jokingly, "Now let her rain!"

Tex nodded. "Let it come," he said. "Everybody that deserves it will have a slicker ag'in' th' rain. As marshal I'm playin' no favorites—there's no strings to a city marshal. My job's to keep th' peace of Windsor, an' let th' devil whistle." He smiled enigmatically, hitched up his belt, and then looked at Henry. "You know where Bud's belt an' gun are?"

Henry nodded. "Baldy's got 'em, behind th' bar. Want 'em?"

"Yes," answered Tex, slowly turning. "When it starts rainin', two guns will keep me on an even keel. My left hand feels empty-like. Reckon I'll go git Bud's outfit an' have th' harness-maker turn th' holster so it'll set right for th' left side; or mebby he's got a cavalry sheath, which won't need so much changin'."

"But you ought to have a rifle heavier than a .38 short," suggested Gus Williams. "That ain't no gun for this country."

Tex smiled. "For town use that's plenty heavy enough. But we won't argue about that because I ain't got it no more. I swapped with that section-boss, paying him fifteen dollars to-boot. To a thick Mick like him there ain't much difference between a .38 short and a .45-90. He can't use either one worth a cuss, anyhow. I'd say I was lucky stumblin' on him." He turned and walked toward the door, glanced up at the cloudless sky, and chuckled. "No signs of rain, yet. Oh, well; it'll come when it gets here. *Adios*," and the slow steps of the walking roan grew softer down the street.

The harness-maker looked from the belt and holster to an up-ended box and waved at the latter. "Set down, Mr. Jones. 'Twon't take a minute, but you might as well set. Many a one I've turned. A new cut here, a new strap, an' a scallop out of th' top on th' other side so yore fingers'll close on th' butt first thing. Let's see th' other. Yep; deep cut down to th' guard. Now, if I put back on th' belt at th' same place, it'll throw th' buckle around back—all right, then. They won't match each other, but that don't make no difference, I reckon. Ain't there been some talk of appointin' you city marshal?"

Tex nodded. "This star was th' only one they had," he explained.

"Well, you may be workin' both jobs afore long if Gus Williams has th' say-so," commented the harness-maker. "Funny, but I never work on a gun sheath but I think of th' one I made to order for Jack Slade after he got around ag'in from Old Jules' shotgun. Jack blamed it on his holster, an' it shore made him particular. That was back in Old Julesburg when I was a harness-apprentice there. Soon after that he was sent up to take charge of th' Rocky Ridge division of th' stage line, which was th' worst division of th' whole line. Holdups was a reg'lar thing. They soon stopped after he took charge. He was th' best man with a short gun I ever saw. I heard that he wore that holster to th' day th' vigilantes got him, up in Virginia City, Montanny. Now, Mr. Marshal, strap this on you an' see if th' gun comes out right. Sometimes they got to be shaped a little mite—ah, that looks all right. Reckon it'll do?"

With the newly acquired belt hanging over the old one, sloping loosely from the right hip across his body to a point below the left, the marshal went out, mounted the roan, and rode carelessly down to the toolshed, where he told Murphy of his appointment and of the fictitious swapping of rifles, and then went up to the station. As he neared it Jerry came out of the door, caught the flash of the sun on the nickel-plated star and turned, grinning, to await the coming of the new marshal.

"That looks mighty good to the station agent," Jerry laughed. "An' so you're wearin two guns instead of one? Gosh, that looks business-like!"

Tex reined in and grinned down at him. "Any time you feel urged to shoot up th' town, Mr. Agent, you'll find out that it *is* business-like. Better start by gettin' th' marshal first: it'll be a lot safer, that way."

"That's good advice, and I won't forget it," replied Jerry. "I'll notify the company of your appointment. That ought to make it feel good, and it might want to pay its share of your salary. I'm certainly wishing you luck."

"I may be needin' it," responded the marshal. "Reckon I'll go on to th' house an' show off my new bright an' shinin' star." He glanced down at the badge and grinned. "Seein' how you reads 'Sheriff' instead of 'Marshal' she'll mebby wonder what you are. So-long, Jerry!"

Reaching the little house, Tex swung gravely off Omar and proceeded to the door in mock dignity. Knocking heavily, he assumed a stern demeanor and waited. When the door opened he removed his sombrero, bowed, and grinned. "Behold the Law, Miss Saunders, in the person of the marshal of Windsor."

"I congratulate you, Marshal," she coldly replied. "Doubtless you may now take life with legal authority. It is too bad it comes a little late."

"I did not need legal authority, Miss Saunders, if I

rightly interpret your remark," he rejoined. "The authority of Nature ever precedes and transcends it. Self-preservation is the first law. He fired, and I did not dare let him fire again."

"You provoked his attack!" she flashed. "He could do nothing else."

"That was because I preferred to risk his life than the certainty of him taking that of Tommy Watkins, who was being deliberately baited. Bud lost his rights when he drew his gun against an unsuspecting man. I am sorry if you look upon the unfortunate incident in any other light; but I am so sure of my position that I would repeat it today under the same conditions. Besides I am naturally prejudiced against assassins."

"Why did you give him his gun before he had time to master his anger?" she demanded, her eyes flashing.

"Because I wanted to show him how impersonal my interference was, and to help smooth over a tense situation. It was one of those high-tension moments when a false move might easily precipitate a shambles. There were a dozen armed men in the room, a ratio of ten to two. I followed my best judgment. I am not apologizing, Miss Saunders, even to you; I am merely explaining the situation as it existed. When Bud Haines drew his gun from the side to shoot a man who did not know of his danger, he broke our rules. I would have been justified in shooting him down at the move. Instead I tried to stop his shot and give him a way out of it." While he spoke his right hand had risen to his belt and now hung there by a crooked thumb, a position he was in the habit of assuming when he spoke earnestly.

She glanced down at it involuntarily, shuddered, and slowly closed the door.

"I am very sorry, Mr. Jones, but—" the closing of the door ended the conversation for both.

He studied the warped, weather-beaten panel and the white, china knob for a full minute, and then slowly replaced his hat and slowly walked back to his horse. Patting the silky neck he shook his head. "Omar, it's been comin' to me for twenty years—but it might have waited till I really deserved it. Come on—we'll go back to th' herd, where we belong."

Thoughtfully he rode away, his face older and sterner, its lines seemingly a little deeper.

CHAPTER XII

Closer Friendships

IN THE selection of the marshal's office Williams was overruled and rather than make a contest of it, since he could not deny the economy in using a building already erected, and knowing that his store was nearly as well protected, he gave his slow assent to Carney's offer; and soon the lean-to was cleared out, a table, some chairs, and a rough bunk put in it, the latter at the marshal's insistence. Over the door were two words, newly painted: CITY MARSHAL. The question of a jail came next, and was quickly solved by the addition to the lean-to of a room constructed of two-inch planks, walls, floor, and roof. Two pairs of new, shining handcuffs and a new badge, appropriately labeled, completed the civic improvements in the way of law and order. All prisoners guilty of major offenses were to be taken down to Willow and there tried; while minor offenders could sit in the jail until a suitable time had elapsed.

From his chair in the door of his office, Tex could

keep watch of nearly all of the main street, and the trail leading in from the C Bar for half a mile. The end of his first week as peace officer found him in his favorite place, contentedly puffing on his pipe, despite the heat of the day. A few miners straggled past, grinning and exchanging shafts of heavy wit with the smiling officer. Blascom drifted into town a little later, learned of the appointment, and hurried down from the hotel to congratulate his new friend.

Tex reached behind him and pulled a chair outside the door. "Sit down, Blascom," he invited. "How's th' sump comin' along?"

Blascom glanced around before replying. "I'm sorry you ain't sheriff, as well," he replied. "I reckon I'm out of bounds, out there on Buffalo, an' I'm shore to be rushed if I'm figgerin' right on that crick. Anybody in th' new jail?"

"Not yet," smiled Tex. "Talk low an' nobody'll hear you. Strike somethin'?"

"I'll gamble on it. I'm so shore of it, I'm filin' a new claim: th' old one didn't quite cover it. You know where th' sump's located, of course; an' you remember how rapid it filled up with water every time I tried to bail it out?"

Tex nodded and waved carelessly at the C Bar trail as though discussing something far from placering. "Send th' location papers off through Jerry Saunders—tell him they're from me. Ever follow a trail herd day after day?" he asked.

"No; why?"

"Ever do anythin', out here, except minin'?"

"Shore; why?"

"What was it?"

"Freightin' from Atchison to Denver an' back: why?"

"Then yo're tellin' me about it now," prompted Tex, handing him a cleaning rod. "Trace th' old trail in th' sand an' keep referrin' to it while you talk. You don't know me good enough to talk long an' steady an' earnest. Here, gimme that rod—" and the marshal took it and drew a line. "This end is Atchison—from there you went up th' Little Blue, like this. Then, crossin' that divide south of th' Platte, you rolled down to that river near Hook's Station, an' follered it past Ft. Kearney, Plumb Crick, an' O'Fallon's Bluffs, an' so on. Here's Hook's Station, th' Fort, Plumb Crick, an' O'Fallon's—now you go on with it."

Blascom took the rod and finished the great curve. "As I was sayin', th' water in that sump kept me guessin'. I couldn't figger where it all come from. I had tried for sumps nearer to th' shack, of course, but got nothin'. Then I found water a-plenty when I dug *this* one." He jabbed at Ft. Kearney and waved his other arm. "I kept gettin' curiouser all th' time, an' yesterday, when th' idea hit me all of a sudden, I went back down th' crick bed twenty paces an' started diggin'. No water; an' yet, sixty feet up stream was more'n I could handle. I just sat down an' wrastled it out."

Tex leaned over and drew another line, one starting on the great curve. "Th' Salt Lake branch run up here, didn't it, Blascom? Th' ones th' troops used, near Old Julesburg, goin' out to lick th' Mormons?"

"How'd you come to know so much about that old trail?" demanded the miner. "It shore did—an' it was a bad section for stages. Well, I cut me a pinted stick an' after it got dark I went out an' jabbed it inter th' crick bed between th' wet sump an' th' last one I put down. About five feet below th' wet one I hit rock, not more'n six inches under th' sand, an' it sloped sharp, both ways, I'm tellin' you. Sort of a sharp hog-back, it is. Humans are blasted fools, Marshal: we can set right on top of a thing that's fair yellin' to be seen, an' not know it's there till somethin' knocks it inter our fool heads. Do you know what I got up there at that sump?"

Tex shook his head and grabbed the stick, a trace of vexation on his face. "You got it all wrong, Blascom," he declared loudly, drawing another line. "Th' old, original Oregon Trail never went up th' Rocky Ridge a-tall. It followed th' North Fork of th' Platte, all th' way to Ft. Laramie. It crossed th' river at Forty Islands, about twelve miles south of th' Fort. I crossed it there with a herd, myself. If you don't believe me, ask Hawkins—he was apprenticed to th' harness-maker at Old Julesburg, on th' South Fork."

"I got you there," laughed Blascom. "Th' Oregon Trail didn't cross at Forty Islands; but a lot of trail herds did. There was a waggin ferry at th' Fort that th' chuck waggins often used."

"It crossed either at Forty Islands or between 'em an' th' Fort," asserted Tex.

"Well, mebby yo're right, Marshal," admitted Blascom. He took the rod again. "That sump of mine is located in a rocky basin that's full of sand. Th' downstream side is that hog-back. That means that there's a thunderin' big, natural riffle in th' bed of th' crick, an' it's stopped and held th' sand till th' basin was full. Every freshet that comes along riles that sand up, lots of it bein' washed over th' riffle, an' carried along. More sand settles there as th' water quits rushin'; but here's th' pint." He jabbed at Denver and drew a line into the Gilpin County country, stopping at Central City. "Gold is heavy, an' it don't wash over riffles if it can settle down in front of 'em. While th' sand is soft from bein' disturbed by a strong current, it can settle. Ever since that crick has been a crick, gold has been settlin' in front of that riffle, droppin' down through th' sand till it hit th' rock bottom. Great Jehovah, Marshal—can you figger what I got?"

Tex roughly took the cleaning rod, traced a line in sudden vexation, slammed the rod on the floor behind him, and fanned his face with his hat.

"An' how long you been settin' on that?" he asked in weary hopelessness.

Blascom waved his arms and slumped back against the chair. "Three years," he confessed, and went off into a profane description of his intelligence that left nothing to imagination.

Tex laughed heartily. "If you was as bad as you just said I'd shore have to take you in. Cheer up, man: it's there, ain't it? You only have to git it out."

Blascom looked at him reproachfully. "Shore: that's all," he retorted with sarcasm. "Git it out before th' rain starts again, an' do it without Jake catchin' me at it! If he learns what I got, I'm in for no sweet dreams; an' if this starvin' bunch of gold hunters learn about it, I'll be swamped in th' rush! Good Lord, man! It'll take me a week to git th' water out, an' then there's th' sand!"

Tex stretched, caught sight of a rider bobbing along the C Bar trail and looked reflectively at Williams' Mecca. "You got to get some dynamite or blastin' powder. Dynamite's better. Put some sticks on th' downstream side of that rock riffle an' wait till Jake comes into town. You crack that riffle open an' th' water will move out for you. Then you can dig down th' other face of it an' get to th' pocket a lot quicker." He laughed suddenly. "Do that blastin'. Then when Jake gets back to his shack, saunter over with a jug of whiskey an' forget to take it home with you. That'll give you a solid week for yore diggin' without him botherin' you."

"Good idea," said Blascom, arising. "I'll go over an' see if Williams has got any sticks. That's th' way to handle it, Marshal. You ever do any prospectin'?"

Tex pushed him back again. "No, I ain't; but I've been doin' a lot of thinkin' these days. Sit still. What does a miner want explosives for? To get gold, of course. Bein' a placer worker don't make no difference: th' connection is there, just th' same. It'll only make 'em that much more curious. You go buyin' any dynamite an' th' parade will start for yore place before night. I'd get it for you, only me not havin' no reason to buy th' stuff, it would be near as big a mistake as you buyin' it. *I* ain't got no call to want any dynamite. Sit still: you ain't in no hurry!" He leaned over and put his finger on the map in the sand. "They hit Ft. Hall about here," he explained. "We got to get somebody that ain't connected with you, gold diggin', or Buffalo Crick, that won't make no troublesome connections. They usually left their waggins at Ft. Hall an' went up this way. If this feller comin' down th' trail is young Watkins, an' I'm sayin' he is, we got th' way. I reckon he can buy dynamite for th' ranch. That'll be all right, but suppose somebody else from that outfit comes ridin' in an' gets pumped dry? Lean back, stick yore feet on th' Overland, an' don't look so cussed tense. Here: I got it! Th' railroad uses dynamite! I shore got it, Blascom. Tim Murphy can buy it as innocent as you can buy chewin' tobacco!"

"But I don't know him well enough!" expostulated Blascom. "Anyhow, what excuse can I give him?"

"None at all," said Tex. "Wait till yore feet are in th' stirrups before you spur a hoss! You don't have to know him. *I* know him, an' that's a-plenty. Here, you listen close to every word I say, an' act careless-like while yo're doin' it." The explicit directions were rich in details, but Blascom soaked them into his memory like water in a sponge. "Th' whole thing is gettin' to him nat'ral, an' then gettin' th' stuff from him afterward," Tex wound up. Thoughtful for a moment, he nodded in sudden decision. "Got it ag'in! It's near train time. You, bein' restless an' lonesome, hanker to watch it come in. Th' Lord knows nobody in towns like this ever needs any excuse to see a train come in. That's one of th' idle man's inalienable rights—an' it seldom weakens. An' now I know how yo're goin' to git it from him afterwards: you listen ag'in," and further directions came in rapid-fire order.

The rider was near enough now to dispel all doubts as to his identity. Blascom arose, gripped the marshal's hand and faced the Mecca.

"I'm goin' over to git a jug: much obliged, Marshal." He crossed the street diagonally and disappeared in the store.

The rider came nearer and nearer, a great dust cloud rolling behind him not much unlike the smoke of a moving locomotive. When even with Carney's he drew rein suddenly and in another moment had dismounted in front of the lazy Tex.

"I'll be cussed!" he exclaimed, staring from Tex to the sign over the door and then back at the new peace officer, cocking his head as he read the badge.

"Good for you!" he cried. "It's about time this dog's town had a white man to run it; an' they couldn't 'a' picked a better, neither!" His enthusiasm ebbed a little and he looked curiously and thoughtfully into the marshal's eyes. "How'd you come to get th' job?" he demanded.

Tex stuck his thumbs in the armholes of his vest and grinned. He knew the thought that had sobered his companion's face. "Pop'lar clamor, Thomas; 'an all that sort of a thing,' as Whitby used to say. My great popularity an' my pleasin' nature an' disposition, not to mention my good looks an' winnin' ways, seem to have turned th' balance in my favor. But, outside of that I don't know why I got it. Carney thought I'd mebby bring him more trade; Williams mourned th' lack of anybody to give him adequate police protection, an' th' harness-maker mentions Jack Slade. He admires Jack Slade, an' says I remind him of that person by th' way I let him fix up my left-hand holster. That suits me because Slade was lynched."

"Then Williams really made th' play stick?" Tommy asked with poorly concealed suspicion.

"Williams pinned on my nickel-plated authority," said Tex. "Nobody else had one. He reckons I'm wearin' his colors; but, my Christian friend, th' only colors th' new marshal wears are his own. I'm to keep order in 'this dog's town,' as you put it, an' I'm goin' to do it. Miners, railroaders, storekeepers, cattlemen, an' ornery punchers please listen an' be enlightened. Th' badge is only a nickel-plate affair; but there ain't no nickel, nor rust, neither, on my Cyclopean twins. They're my real authority. Now, then, don't walk all over Blascom's Overland Trail, but set down in th' chair he just vacated. Tell me all about yoreself."

"Marshal," began Tommy in some embarrassment, "I didn't get th' hang of that little mix-up in th' hotel till I got quite some distance out of town. My head was whirlin' a little, an' I'm nat'rally stupid, anyhow. I just want to say that yo're wrong about them Colts bein' some kind of twins. Mebby they are durin' these peaceful days; but if things got crowded they'll turn into triplets, th' missin' brother bein' right here on my laig. Besides that, you got a craggy lot of deputies out on th' C Bar any time you need 'em. Don't stop me while I'm runnin' free! I'm saying I never saw a squarer, cleaner piece of shootin' than you showed us all in th' hotel th' other day. An'—you keep off th' trail while I'm comin' strong!—an' I've been somethin' of a fool about us an' that little lady. From now on I'm afoot where she's concerned, an' you know what us punchers amount to, afoot."

"I'm glad you said you was stupid," replied Tex. "It saves me from saying' it, an' comin' from me it might sound sorta official." He glanced up the street and back to his companion. "Yo're not afoot, cowboy; yo're ridin' strong. I'm th' one that's afoot, an' I'll agree with you about a cowpunch amountin' to nothin' off his cayuse. Did you ever have a door slammed plumb in yore face, Tommy?"

Tommy wiped out Denver, Central City, Old Julesburg, and Ft. Kearney with one swing of his foot. "You—I—you *mean* that?"

The marshal nodded. "Every word of it. Outlawed steers should keep to th' draws an' brakes, Tommy. Besides, I'm over forty-five years old, an' I never was any parson. Keep right on ridin', Adolescence; an' I'm hopin' it's a plain, fair trail. Tommy, did you ever shoot a man?"

"Not yet I ain't; but I've come cussed near it. Seein' what's goin' on in this town, I has hopes."

"Don't yield to no temptations, Tommy; an' let yore hopes die," warned the marshal. "If there's any of that to be done, I'll do it. I reckon you'll shore have a easy trail."

"I—will—be—tee-totally—d—d!" said Tommy. He shook his head and leaned back against the front of the office. "Does she know all about it?"

"Everythin'; I owed myself that much," answered Tex, and then he helped to maintain a reflective, intro-spective, and emotional silence.

Blascom emerged from the Mecca with a two-gallon jug, empty from the way it jerked and swung. He looked at the silent pair leaning against the marshal's office, abruptly made up his mind, and strode over to them.

"You shore look sorrerful," he said.

"We've just been to a funeral," said Tex. "Th' corpse looked nat'ral, too."

"Sufferin' wildcats!" ejaculated Tommy in pretended dismay, his chair dropping to all fours. "Whiskey by th' jug! I'm plain shocked, but mighty glad to see you, Mr. Blascom." He turned to the marshal. "Here, Officer! Shake han's with Mr. Blascom, of Buffaler Crick. Give th' gentleman a cordial welcome."

Tex regarded the newcomer and his jug with languid interest. "Huh! I reckoned th' drought would shore end some day, but I figgered on rain. However, facts are facts. Pleased to meet you, sir!" He waved at Tommy. "Pass it to our friend first. It's dry work, settin' here, lis-tenin' to me."

"It's like workin' in pay-dirt," retorted Blascom. He tapped the jug and it rang out hollowly. "I ain't give Baldy a chance at it, yet. Anyhow, a man's got to have some protection ag'in' snakes," he defended.

"A protection ag'in' snakes!" repeated Tex, thought-fully. "Yes; he has."

"I'll perfect you ag'in' 'em as far as th' hotel," offered Tommy, arising and whistling to his horse, "seein' as yo're temporary defenseless. Come on, Blascom. See you later, Marshal," and he grabbed at the jug, missed it, and led the way, Tex smiling after the grinning pair.

Tommy's stride was swift and long for a puncher, due to his agitated frame of mind, and he suddenly slowed it to make an observation to his companion.

"Blascom, th' new marshal is shore quick on th' gun— this town ought to be right proud of him. I'm admittin' that he's a reg'lar he-man."

"He's a cussed sight quicker with his head," replied the miner, "an' that's shore sayin' a large an' bounteous plenty. If he don't play no favorites he's shore as h—l goin' to meet friends, one of these days. I'm admittin' myself to that cat-e-gory: but it'll be my hard luck to be out on th' Buffaler when it starts."

Tommy nodded and spat emphatically. "I'll be a cat, an' gory, too," he affirmed. "Wild as a wildcat, an' gory as all h—l. That's me!" He glanced up quickly. "Talkin' ceases, for here we are." He tossed the reins over his pony's head and followed his companion into the hotel, where half a dozen men lounged dispiritedly.

Baldy grinned and lost no time in filling the jug, his efforts creating pleasant, anticipatory smackings among the dry onlookers, who from their previous unobserving weariness suddenly snapped into Argus-eyed interest. The alluring gurgle of the wicker-covered demijohn, the *slap-slap*, *plop-plop* of the leaping, amber stream, ebbing and flooding spasmodically up and down and around the greenish copper funnel, truly was liquid music to their ears, and the powerful odor of the rye diffused itself throughout the room, penetrated the stale tobacco smoke, and wrought positive reactions upon the olfactory nerves of the staring audience. It was scarce enough by the glass, these days, yet here was a reckless Croesus who was buying it by the gallon!

Blascom, smiling with quiet reserve, leaned against

the bar to the right of the jug; Tommy, grave and forbidding, leaned against the bar to the left of the jug, both making short and humorous replies to the gift-compelling remarks of the erect crowd. The jug at last filled, Blascom pushed the cork in and slammed it home with a quick, disconcertingly forbidding gesture, which was as cruel as it was final. He paid for the liquor with one of the bills he had won from Tex, nodded briskly, and went out, Tommy bringing up the rear.

Reproachful, accusing eyes followed their exit, hoping against hope. A lounger nearest the bar, thirsty as Tantalus, shook his head in sorrowful condemnation.

"A man can be mean an' pe-nurious up to a certain limit," he observed; "but past that it's plumb shameful."

An old man, his greasy, gray beard streaked with tobacco stains, nodded emphatically. "There *is* limits; an' I say that stoppin' before ye begin is shore beyond 'em!"

"Yo're dead right," spoke up a one-eyed tramp who honored himself with the title of prospector. "As for me, I never *did* think much of any man as guzzles it secret. Show me th' man that swizzles in public, an *I'll* show you a man as can be trusted. Two whole gallons of it! A whole, bloomin' jugful, at onct! Where'd he git all that money? I'm asking' you, *where'd* he git it? On Buffaler Crick?" His voice rose and cracked with avarice and suspicion.

"Naw!" growled the man in the far corner, slumping back against his chair. "He won it from that Tex Jones feller—th' new marshal—two hundred or more—playin' poker. Th' same Tex Jones as shot Bud Haines. There ain't more'n day wages on Buffaler Crick. I know, 'cause I been lookin' around out there, quiet-like." He stiffened suddenly and sat up, excitement transforming him. "Boys, this here marshal has got money—I saw his wad when he an' Blascom was a-playin'."

"Yo're shore welcome to it," pessimistically rejoined

the man nearest the bar, his vivid imagination picturing the amazing death of Bud Haines. "Yes, sir; yo're welcome to *all* of it. I don't want none, a-tall!"

The discoverer of the marshal's roll regarded the objector with deep scorn.

"That's you!" he retorted. "Allus goin' off half-cocked, an' yowlin' calamity! This here marshal likes poker, don't he? An' he can't play it, can he? Didn't Blascom clean him? He's scared to bluff, or call one, no matter how brave he is with a gun. Who's got any dust? Dig down deep, an' we'll pool it, lettin' Hank an' Sinful do th' playin' for us. Where's Hennery?" he demanded of the bartender.

Baldy mopped the bar and glanced at the ceiling. "Upstairs, sleepin' off a stem-winder. He got drinkin' to th' mem'ry of th' dead deceased last night—an' his mem'ry is long an' steady. He's too senti-mental, Hennery is, for a man as can't handle his likker good. If you fellers are goin' after th' marshal's pile, I'm recommendin' stud-hoss. He's nat'rally scared of poker, an' stud's so fast he won't have no time to start worryin'. Draw will give him too much time to think. Better try stud-hoss," he reiterated, unwittingly naming the form of poker at which the marshal excelled.

"Stud-hoss she is, then," agreed Sinful, licking his lips. "I like stud-hoss. We'll bait him tonight; an' we'll *all* have jugs of our own by mornin', since Buffaler Crick's settin' th' style."

The meeting forthwith went into executive session, depleted gold sacks slowly appearing.

Outside, Blascom offered the jug to his companion, who pushed it away, and shook his head in sudden panic.

"Don't want to smell like no saloon where I'm goin'," he hastily explained. "Now that yo're safe from snakes I'll be driftin' to my cayuse."

"All right, Watkins; I'll treat next time," and the miner, jug in hand, strode toward the station as Tommy mounted and wheeled to ride in the direction of the Saunders' home.

Blascom had timed his arrival to a nicety, for Murphy was on his way from the toolshed to the station to await the coming of the train, the smoke from which could be seen on the eastern horizon.

Blascom held up the jug invitingly and grinned.

The section-boss came to an abrupt stop, saluted, and stepped on again with the bearing of a well-trained English soldier. "Hah!" he called. " 'Tis better from a jug; an' 'twould be better yet if it had a little breath av th' peat fire in it; but 'tis well to be content with what we have. Thank ye: I'll drink yer health!" Handing the jug back to its owner Murphy wiped his lips with the back of his hand and seated himself on the bench at the prospector's side. "Have ye seen th' new marshal?" he asked, glancing from the distant smudge of smoke to his watch. "I hear he's fixed up in style."

"Yes; an' he gave me a message for you, if you'll lean over a little closer," replied Blascom, and, as Murphy obeyed his suggestion, he said what he had come for.

"It sounds like Tex," grunted Murphy. "All thought out careful. Have ye ever used stick explosive? It's treacherous stuff at any time above freezin', an' more so after this spell av hot weather. Ye have? Then there's no use av me tellin' ye to handle it gintly. If I was knowin' th' job ye have, I might help ye in th' number av sticks. But if yo're used to it, ye'll know. I'll get it after Number Three pulls out; an' after dark tonight ye'll find it where he said—but deal gintly with it, Mr. Blascom. I've seen it exploded by impact—it was a rifle ball fired into it—this kind av weather. Ye might even do better to load th' shots, this kind av weather, after th' sun goes down. Carry it as ye find it, without unpackin' th' box."

Blascom nodded. "If I leave th' jug for you to put away when you go down for th' box, would you mind puttin' it out tonight with th' dynamite? No use of me makin' two trips to my cabin, an' I don't want to tote it around till dark."

"I will that, an' be glad to. There she comes now, leavin' Whiterock Cut. Casey's late ag'in; but that's regular, an' not his fault, as I've told them time an' time ag'in. Th' grades are ag'in' him comin' west, an' with his leaky packin's an' worn cylinders it's a wonder he does as well as he has. 'Economy,' says th' super. 'No money for repairs that are not needed on this jerk-water line.' I wonder does he ever figger th' fuel wasted through them steam leaks? An' poor Casey gets th' blame—though divvil a bit he cares."

Number Three wheezed in, panted a moment, and coughed on again. Murphy took a package consigned to him, picked up the jug and went down the track toward the toolshed, Blascom wandering idly over to the Railroad Saloon to pass some of the time he had on his hands. In a little while the big Irishman, a small wooden box under his arm, sauntered carelessly down the street, nodded politely from a distance to the sleepy marshal and went into the Mecca.

"Good day, Mr. Williams," he said with stiff formality. "I'll be havin' six dynamite sticks if ye have them, with th' same number av three-minute fuses. Handle it gintly, if ye don't mind. Th' weather is aggravatin' to th' stuff, an' it's timpermental enough at best."

Williams glowered at him. "Don't you worry about me handlin' it gentle, because I ain't goin' to handle it at all. If you want any I'll give you th' key to th' powder-house an' wish you good luck. Th' sun beatin' down on that house, day after day, has got me plumb nervous. I wish you'd come for it all!" He shook his head. "I wouldn't let you even open th' door if it wasn't for gettin' that much more of it out of th' way."

"Is it ventilated well?" demanded Murphy, smiling a little.

"As well as it can be," sighed Williams. "You'll never

catch me carryin' anythin' but powder over th' summer any more. I'm afraid a thunderclap will set it off every storm. What you got in that to pack it in?"

"Sawdust. While yo're cuttin' th' fuses I'll be gettin' th' stuff."

"You'll not come back for any fuses! Wait an' take 'em with you! An' when you are through with th' powderhouse, throw th' key close to th' back door: I don't want no man with six sticks of dynamite hangin' around this store today. Want a bill?"

Murphy nodded. "Two av them is th' rule av th' company. You can mark 'em paid an' take it out av this."

The receipted bills in his pocket, he threw the fuses over his shoulder, their wickedly shining copper caps carefully wrapped in a handkerchief, took up the bunch of keys and the box, and grinned. "If ye hear an explosion out back, ye needn't come out to gimme any help. I'm cleanin' up some bad cracked rocks hangin' from a cut west av town, over near Buffalo Crick. I'm tellin' ye th' last so ye won't think it's thunderclaps on their disturbin' way to town. But ye'll sleep through it, no doubt, an' never hear th' shot."

"Blastin' at night?" exclaimed Williams in incredulous surprise.

"I don't like th' sun shinin' on th' darlin's while I'm pokin' 'em in th' hot rocks, so I may load her an' shoot her after dark," replied Murphy. "I've a lot av respect for th' stuff, much as I've handled it. Good day, sir," and he left behind him a man who was nervous and jumpy until after the keys had tinkled on the ground near the rear door; indeed, such an impression had been made on him that he mentioned it, with profane criticisms and observations, at the table that night in the hotel.

The marshal moved his chair farther around in the shade and on his tanned face there crept a warm, rare smile. " 'Lo, I will stand at thy right hand, and keep the bridge with thee!' Well said, Herminius! Yonder you go in spirit: Tim Murphy, you'd make complete any 'dauntless three'!"

The shadows were growing long when Tommy came into sight again, buried in thought as he rode slowly down the street. He stopped and swung to the ground in front of the lazy marshal.

"They shore do beat th' devil," he growled, throwing himself into the vacant chair and lapsing into silence.

Tex nodded understandingly. "They do," he indolently agreed, a smile flickering across his face. "Black is white an' red is green—they're the worst I've ever seen," he extemporized. "They're intuitive critters, son; an' don't you let anybody tell you that intuition hasn't any warrant for existing. It has. It's got more warrant than reason. It was flowering long before reason poked its first shoot out of the ground. Reason only runs back a few thousand generations, but intuition goes back to the first cell of nervous tissue—I might qualify that a bit and say before nervous tissue was structurally apart from the rest. Reason starts anew in every life, usually upon a little better foundation— often a poorer one. It is nursed and trained and cultivated an' when its possessor dies, it dies with him. Not so our venerable friend, intuition. He, or rather she, is cumulative. She is th' sum of all previous individuals in the life chain of th' last. She picks up an' stores away, growing a little each time—an' while she is vague, an' can be classified as a 'because,' or 'I don't know why,' she operates steady. Don't ask me what I know about it, for it has been a long time since I gave any study to things like this. I might guess an' say that it's th' physical changes in th' thought channels due to experience, or in th' structure of th' brain cells or th' quality of their tissues. Anyway, so far as practicability is concerned, you've summed up th' whole thing: 'They shore do beat th' devil'."

Tommy was looking at him, puzzled and intent; but puzzled intelligently. There is a difference.

"With me an' you, two opposites in thought result in th' cancellation of one of them. We don't say of th' same object: 'This is white, this is black,' at th' same time an' believe 'em both. Th' words themselves are intelligible; but th' conception ain't. We can't do it. One is chosen an' th' other dies. But I won't bet you that a woman cancels. She may not get a dirty white or a slate gray, but she gets a combination, all right. That's where intuition's family tree comes in. No matter how absurd its contentions may be they have force because of th' impetus, coming from age. What did she get out th' colors for you?"

"Yo're th' easiest man to talk to that I ever met," said Tommy wonderingly. "I don't know how you do it. Why, she got a bright red with a dull green cast—said you was justified, 'but a life's a life': an' then she cried!"

Over Tex's face came a light which only can be compared to the rising sun seen from some lofty peak, for in the radiance there were shadows.

CHAPTER XIII

Outcheating Cheaters

GUS WILLIAMS left the supper table, where he had held forth volubly upon the subject of dynamite, in his almost lecture to the other diners, some of whom knew more about it than he did, and walked ponderously toward the poker table for his usual evening's game. Seating himself at the place which by tacit consent had become his own, he idly shuffled and reshuffled the cards and finally began a slow and laborious game of solitaire to while away the time until his cronies should join him. This game had become a fixture of the establishment, played for low stakes but with great seriousness, and often ran into the morning hours.

The rest of the diners tarried inexplicably at the plate-littered table, engaged in a discussion of stud poker and of their respective abilities in playing it, and of winnings they had made and seen made. It slowly but surely grew acrimonious, as any such discussion is prone to among idle men who are very much in each other's company.

The new marshal sat a little apart from the eager

disputants, taking no share in the wrangling. Finally Sinful, scorning a shouted ruling on a hypothetical question concerning the law of averages, turned suddenly and appealed to the marshal, whose smiling reply was not a confirmation of the appellant's claim.

Sinful glared at his disappointing umpire. "A lot you know about stud!" he retorted. "Bet you can't even play mumbly-peg!"

"That takes a certain amount of skill," rejoined Tex without heat. "In stud it's how th' cards fall."

Hank laughed sarcastically. "Averages don't count? We'll just start a little game an' I'll show you how easy stud-hoss is. Come on, boys: we'll give th' marshal a lesson. Clear away them dishes."

All but Sinful held back, saying that they had no money for gambling, but they were remarkably eager to watch the game.

Sinful snorted. "Huh! Two-hand is no good. I'm honin' for a little stud-hoss for a change. It's been nothin' but draw in this town. Reckon stud's too lively to suit most folks: takes nerve to ride a fast game. A man can have a-plenty of nerve one way, an' none a-tall another way. Fine bunch of paupers!"

Hank's disgust was as great. "Fine bunch of paupers," he repeated. "An' them as ain't busted is scared. You called th' turn, Sinful: it shore does take nerve—more'n mumbly-peg, anyhow. A three-hand game would move fast—*too* fast for these coyotes."

"Don't you let th' old mosshead git off with that, Marshal!" cried a miner, "Wish *I* had some dust: I'd cussed soon show 'em!"

Tex was amused by the baiting. Hardly an eye had left him while the whole discussion was going on, even the two principals looking at him when they spoke to each other. He looked from one old reprobate to the other, and let his smile become a laugh as he moved up to the table, a motion which was received by the entire group with sighs of relief and satisfaction.

"I reckon it's my luck ag'in' yore skill," he said; "but I can't set back an' be insulted this way. I'm a public character, now, an' has got to uphold th' dignity of th' law. Get a-goin', you fellers."

Sinful and Hank, simultaneously slamming their gold bags on the table, reached for the cards at the same time and a new wrangle threatened.

"Cut for it," drawled Tex, smiling at the expectant, hopeful faces around the table. Williams' irritable, protesting cough was unheeded and, Hank dealing, the game got under way. Tex honorably could have shot both of his opponents in the first five minutes of play, but simply cheated in turn and held his own. At the end of an hour's excitement he was neither winner nor loser, and he shoved back from the table in simulated disgust. He scorned to take money so tragically needed, and he had determined to lose none of his own.

"This game's so plumb fast," he ironically observed, "that I ain't won or lost a dollar. You got my sportin' blood up, an' I ain't goin' to insult it by playin' all night for nothin'. I told you stud was only luck: That skill you was talkin' about ain't showed a-tall. If there's anybody here as wants a *real* game I'm honin' to hear his voice."

"Can you hear mine?" called Williams, glaring at the disappointed stud players and their friends. "There's a real game right here," he declared, pounding the table, "with real money an' real nerve! Besides, I got a hoss to win back, an' I want my revenge."

Tex turned to the group and laughed, playfully poking Sinful in the ribs. "Hear th' cry of th' lobo? He's lookin' for meat. Our friend Williams has been savin' his money for Tex Jones, an' I ain't got th' heart to refuse it. Bring yore community wealth an' set in, you an' Hank. Though if you can't play draw no better'n you play stud you ought to go home."

"I cut my teeth on draw," boasted Sinful. He turned and slapped his partner on the shoulder. "Come on,

Hank!" he cried. "Th' lone wolf is howlin' from th' timber line an' his pelt's worth money. Let's go git it!"

They swept down on the impatient Williams, their silent partners bringing up the rear, and clamored for action. Tex lighting a freshly rolled cigarette, faced the local boss, Hank on his right and Sinful on his left, the eager onlookers settling behind their champions. The thin, worried faces of the miners appealed to the marshal, their obvious need arousing a feeling of pity in him; and then began a game which was as much a credit to Tex as any he ever had played. He rubbed the saliva-soaked end of his cigarette between finger and thumb and gave all his attention to the game.

Williams won on his own deal, cutting down the gold of the two miners. On Hank's deal he won again and the faces of the old prospectors began to tense. Tex dealt in turn and after a few rounds of betting Williams dropped out and the game resolved itself into a simulated fiercely fought duel between the miners, who really cared but little which of them won. Hank finally raked in the stakes. Sinful shuffled and Tex cut. Williams forced the betting but had to drop out, followed by Tex, and the dealer gleefully hauled in his winnings. Again Williams shuffled, his expression vaguely denoting worry. He made a sharp remark about one of the onlookers behind Tex and all eyes turned instinctively. The miner retorted with spirit and Williams suddenly smiled apologetically.

"My mistake, Goldpan," he admitted. "Let's forget it, an' let th' game proceed."

Tex deliberately had allowed his attention to be called from the game and when he picked up his cards he was mildly suspicious, for Williams' remark had been entirely uncalled for. He looked quickly for the nine of clubs or the six of hearts, finding that he had neither. He passed and sat back, smiling at the facial contortions of Hank and the blank immobility of Sinful's leathery countenance. Hank dropped out on the next round and after a little cautious betting Sinful called and threw down his hand. Williams spread his own and smiled. That smile was to cost him heavily, for in his club flush lay the nine spot, guiltless of the tobacco smudge which Tex had rubbed on its face in the first hand he had been dealt.

Tex wiped the tips of his sensitive fingers on his trousers and became voluble and humorous. As he picked up his cards, one by one as they dropped from Hank's swiftly moving hand, he first let his gaze linger a little on their backs, and his fingers slipped across the corners of each. Williams had cheated before with a trimmed deck and now the marshal grimly determined to teach him a lesson, and at the same time not arouse the suspicions of the boss against the new marshal. With the switching of the decks Williams had set a pace which would grow too fast for him. Marked cards suited Tex, especially if they had been marked by an opponent, who would have all the more confidence in them. After a few deals if he wouldn't know each card as well as a man like Williams, whose marking could not be much out of the ordinary, and certainly not very original, then he felt that he deserved to get the worst of the play. He once had played against a deck which had been marked by the engraver who designed the backs, and he had learned it in less than an hour. So now he prepared to enjoy himself and thereafter bet lightly when Williams dealt, but on each set of hands dealt by himself one of the prospectors always won, and with worthy cards. Worthy as were their hands they were only a shade better than those held by the proprietor of the hotel and the general store. One hand alone cost Williams over eighty dollars, three others were above the seventy-dollar mark and he was losing his temper, not only because of his losses, but also because he did not dare to cheat too much on his own deal. Tex's eyes twinkled at him and Tex's rambling words hid any ulterior motive in the keen scrutiny.

Finally, driven by desperation, Williams threw caution to the winds and risked detection. He was clever enough to avoid grounds for open accusation, but both of the miners suddenly looked thoughtful and a moment later they exchanged significant glances. Thereafter no one bet heavily when Williams dealt.

The finish came when Tex had dealt and picked up his hand. Sinful stolidly regarded the cheery faces of three kings—spades, clubs, and hearts. Williams liked the looks of his two pairs, jacks up. Hank rolled his huge cud into the other cheek and tried to appear mournful at the sight of the queen, ten, eight, and five of hearts. Tex laid down his four-card spade straight and picked up the pack.

"Call 'em, boys," he said.

Sinful's two cards, gingerly lifted one at a time from the table, pleased him very much, although from all outward signs they might have been anything in the card line. They were the aces of diamonds and clubs. He sighed, squared the hand, and placed it face down on the table before him. Williams gulped when he added a third jack to his two pairs, and Hank nearly swallowed his tobacco at sight of the prayed-for, but unexpected, appearance of another heart. All eyes were on the dealer. He put down the deck and picked up his hand for another look at it. After a moment he put it down again, sadly shaking his head.

"Good enough as it is," he murmured. "I ain't havin' much luck, one way or th' other; an' I'm gettin' tired of th' cussed game."

"Dealer pat?" sharply inquired Williams, suspicion glinting in his eyes.

"Pat, an' cussed near flat," grunted Tex. "Go on with her. I'll trail along with what I got, an' quit after this hand."

Notwithstanding the dealer's pat hand and his expression of resignation, the betting was sharp and swift. On the first round, being forty-odd dollars ahead,

Tex saw the accumulated raises and had enough left out of his winnings to raise five dollars. He tossed it in and leaned back, watching each face in turn. Sinful was not to be bluffed by any pat hand at this stage of the play, no matter how craftily it was bet. He reflected that straights, flushes, and full houses could be held pat, as well as threes or two pairs, all of which he had beat. A straight flush or fours were the only hands he could lose to, and Williams had not dealt the cards. Pat hands were sometimes pat bluffs, more terrifying to novices than to old players. He saw the raise and shoved out another, growling: "Takes about twenty more to see this circus."

Williams hesitated, looking at the dealer's neat little stack of cards. He was convinced from the way Tex had acted that the pat hand was a bluff, for its owner had not been caught bluffing since the game started, which indicated that he had labored to establish the reputation of playing only intrinsic hands, which would give a later bluff a strong and false value. He saw and raised a dollar, hoping that someone would drop out. Hank disappointed him by staying in and boosting another dollar. They both were feeling their way along. Hank also believed the pat hand to be worthless; and worthless it was, for Tex tossed it from him, face down, and rammed his hands into his pockets.

Sinful heaved a sigh of relief, which was echoed by the others, squinted from his hand to the faces of the two remaining players, and grinned sardonically. "Bluffs are like crows; they live together in flocks. I never quit when she's comin' my way. Grab a good holt for another raise! She's ten higher, now."

With the disturbing pat hand out of it, which was all the more disturbing because it had belonged to the dealer, Williams gave more thought to the players on his left and right. He decided that Hank was the real danger and that Sinful's words were a despairing effort to win by the default of the others. He saw the raise and let it go as it was. Hank rolled the cud nervously and with a sudden, muttered curse, threw down his hand. A flush had no business showing pride and fight in this game, he decided. Sinful grinned at him across the table.

"Terbaccer makin' you sick, Hank?" he jeered. "I'm raisin' ten more, jest to keep th' corpse alive. He-he-he!"

There was now too much in the pot to give it up for ten dollars and Williams met the raise, swore, and called, "What you got, you devil from h—l?"

"I got quite a fambly," chuckled Sinful, laying down a pair of aces. "There's twin brothers," he said, looking up.

Williams snorted at the old man's pleasure in not showing his whole hand at once, and he tossed three jacks on the table. "Triplets in mine," he replied.

Sinful raised his eyebrows and regarded them accusingly. "Three jacks can tote quite some load if it's packed right," he said. "Th' rest of my fambly is three more brothers, an' they bust th' mules' backs. Ain't got th' extry jack, have you?"

Slamming the rest of the cards on the table Williams arose and without a word walked to the bar. Sinful's cackles of joy were added to by his friends and they surrounded the table to help in the division of the spoils, in plain sight of all.

"Win or lose, Marshal?" demanded Sinful shrilly above the hubbub of voices.

"Lost a couple of dollars," bellowed Tex.

"Much obliged for 'em," rejoined Sinful. He looked at Hank, winked and said: "Marshal's been real kind to us, Hank," and Tex never was quite certain of the old man's meaning.

Williams looked around as Tex leaned against the bar. "How'd *you* come out?" he asked, his face showing his anger.

"I lost," answered Tex carelessly. "Not anythin' to

speak of: a few dollars, I reckon. I told 'em two dollars, for they're swelled up with pride as things are. They must 'a' got into you real heavy."

Williams sneered. "Heavy for them, I reckon. I ain't limpin'. They got too cussed much luck."

"Luck?" muttered the marshal, gazing inquiringly at the glass of whiskey he had raised from the bar, as though it might tell him what he wanted to know. "I ain't so shore of that, Williams," he slowly said. "Them old sour-doughs get snowed in near every winter, up in th' hills; an' then they ain't got nothin' to do but eat, sleep, swap lies, an' play cards. Somethin' tells me there wasn't a whole lot of luck in it. I know I had all I could do to stay in th' saddle without pullin' leather— an' I ain't exactly cuttin' my teeth where poker is concerned. Listen to 'em, will you? Squabblin' like a lot of kids. I reckon they had this cooked up in grand style. They're all sharin' in th' winnin's, you'll notice." He paused in surprise as a dull roar faintly shook the room. "What's that?" he demanded sharply. "It can't be thunder!"

His companion shook his head. "No, it ain't; it's that Murphy blowin' up rock, like I was sayin' at supper. Hope he went up with it!" He laughed at a man who was just coming in, and who stopped dead in the door and listened to the rumble. "Yore shack's safe, Jake," he called. "Th' Mick's blastin' over past yore away. You remember what I've told you!" he warned.

Jake looked from the speaker to the careless, but inwardly alert, city marshal, scowled, shuffled over to a table, and called for a drink, thereafter entirely ignoring the peace officer.

Henry came in soon after and joined the two at the bar. "Yes, I'll have th' same. You two goin' ridin' ag'in, Marshal?" he asked.

Tex shrugged his shoulders. "It shore don't look like it. She mebby figgered me out. Anyhow, she slammed th' door plumb in my face." He frowned. "Somehow I don't get used to things like that. She could 'a' treated me like I wasn't no tramp, anyhow, couldn't she?"

Henry smiled maliciously, and felt relieved. "They're shore puzzlin'. I hear that coyote Watkins was out there this afternoon. There wasn't no door slammed in *his* face." His little eyes glinted. "I see where he's goin' to learn a lesson, an' learn it for keeps!"

"Oh, he got throwed, too," chuckled Tex, as if finding some balm in another's woe. "He stopped off on his way home an' told me about it. Got a busted heart, an' belly-achin' like a sick calf. That's what he is; an' it's calf love, as well. Shucks! When I was his age I fell in love with a different gal about every moon. Besides, he ain't got money, nor prospects; an' she knows it."

Henry took him by the arm and led him to a table in a far corner. "I been thinkin' I mebby ought to send her a present, or somethin'," he said, watching his companion's face. "You, havin' more experience with 'em, I figgered mebby you would help me out. *I* don't know what to get her."

"Weakenin' already," muttered the marshal, trying to hide a knowing, irritating smile. "Pullin' leather, an' ain't hardly begun to ride yet!"

"I ain't pullin' no leather!" retorted Henry, coloring. "I reckon a man's got a right to give a present to his gal!"

"Shore!" endorsed Tex heartily. "There ain't no question about it—when she comes right out an' admits that she *is* his gal. This Saunders woman ain't admittin' it, yet; an' if she figgers that yo're weakenin' on yore play of ignorin' her, then she'll just set back an' hold you off so th' presents won't stop comin'. This is a woman's game, an' she can beat a man, hands down an' blindfolded: an' they know it. I tell you, Hennery, a wild cayuse that throws its first rider ain't no deader set on stayin' wild than a woman is set on makin' a man go through his tricks for her if she finds he's performin' for her private amusement, an' payin' for th' privilege, besides. It ain't no laughin' matter for you, Hennery; but I can't hardly keep *from* laughin' when I think of you stayin' away to get her anxious, an' then sendin' her presents! It's yore own private affair, an' yo're runnin' it yore own way—but them's *my* ideas."

Henry stared into space, gravely puffing on a cold cigarette. His low, furrowed brow denoted intense mental concentration, and the scowl which grew deeper did not suggest that his conclusions were pleasant. The simile regarding the wild horse sounded like good logic to him, for he prided himself that he knew horses. Finally he looked anxiously at his deeply thinking companion.

"It sounds right, Marshal," he grudgingly admitted; "but it shore is hard advice to foller. I'm plumb anxious to buy her somethin' nice, somethin' she can't get in this part of th' country, an' somethin' she can wear an' know come from me." He paused in some embarrassment and tried to speak carelessly. "If you was goin' to get a woman like her some present—mind, I'm sayin' *if*—what would you get?"

Tex reflected gravely. "Candy don't mean nothin'," he cogitated, in a low, far-away voice. "Anybody she knew at all could give her candy. It don't mean nothin' special, a-tall." He did not appear to notice how his companion's face fell at the words. "Books are like candy—just common presents. A stranger almost could give 'em. Ridin' gloves is a little nearer—but Tommy, or me, could give them to her. Stockin's? Hum: I don't know. They're sort of informal, at that. 'Tain't everybody, however, could give 'em. Only just one man: get my idea?"

"I shore do, Marshal," beamed Henry. "You see, livin' out here all my life an' not 'sociatin' with wimmin— like her, anyhow—I didn't know hardly what would be th' correct thing. Wonder what color?"

Tex was somewhat aghast at his joke being taken so seriously. "Now, you look here, Hennery!" he said in a warning voice. "You promise me not to send her no stockin's till I says th' word." He had wanted to give Jane more reason to dislike the nephew, but hardly cared to have it go that far. "Stayin' away, are you? You make me plumb sick, you do! Stayin' away, h—l!"

A roar of laughter came from the celebrating miners and all eyes turned their way. Sinful and Hank were dancing to the music of a jew's-harp and the time set by stamping, hob-nailed boots. They parted, bowed, joined again, parted, courtesied and went on, hand in hand, turning and ducking, backing and filing, the dust flying and the perspiration streaming down. It seemed impossible that in these men lurked a bitter race hatred, or that hearts as warm and happy could be incubating the germs of cowardly murder. Not one of them, alone, would be guilty of such a thing; but the spirit of a mob is a remarkable and terrible thing, tearing aside civilization's training and veneer, and in a moment hurling men back thousands of years, back to the days when killing often was its own reward.

CHAPTER XIV

Tact and Courage

THINGS WERE going along smoothly for the new marshal until two of the C Bar punchers, accompanied by two men from a ranch farther from town, rode in to make a night of it. It chanced that the C Bar men had been with a herd some forty miles north of the ranch, where water and grass conditions were much better, and they had become friendly with the outfit of another herd which grazed on the western fringe of the same range. A month of this, days spent in the saddle on the same rounds, and nights spent at the chuck wagon with nothing to vary the monotony of the cycle, had given the men an edge to be blunted at the first opportunity; and their ideas of working off high-pressure energies did not take into consideration any such things as safety valves. Action they craved, action they had ridden in for, and action they would have. The swifter it started, the faster it moved, the better it would suit them. So, with an accumulation of energy, thirst, and money they tore into Windsor one noon at a dead run, whooping like savages, and proclaiming their freedom from restraint and their pride of class by a heavenward bombardment which frightened no one and did no harm.

It so chanced that when they passed the new marshal's office they were going so fast, and were so fully occupied in waking up the town, that the lettering over the door of the lean-to escaped their attention. And they were past, bunched in a compact group, and nearly hidden in dust before the mildly curious officer could get to the door. He watched them whirl up to the hotel, the stronghold and stamping ground of Williams and the miners and, dismounting with shrill yells, pause a moment to reload their empty guns, and then surge toward the door.

Tex rubbed his chin thoughtfully as he considered them. Carney's was the cowman's favorite drinking place, yet these four cheerful riders had not given it a second glance, judging from the way they had gone past it. This was no matter for congratulation, but bespoke rather, a determination to show off where their efforts would create more interest. Who they were, or what they came in for, he neither knew nor cared. They were celebrating punchers from somewhere out on the range and they were going to hold their jamboree in the miners' chosen place of entertainment. A less experienced marshal, filled with zeal and conceit, might forthwith have buckled on his guns, and started for the scene of the festivities, to be on hand as a preventive, rather than a corrective, or punitive, force; and very probably would have hastened the very thing he sought to avoid. Tex hoped to take the edge from the class feeling, and determined to be openly linked with neither one side nor the other. His place was to be that of a neutral buffer and his justice must be impartial and above criticism. So, after turning back to buckle on the left-hand gun, he did not sally forth to blaze the glory of the law and precipitate a riot; he sat down patiently to await the course of events.

Williams poked his head out of the door of his store and looked anxiously down the street at the dismounting four. As they went into the hotel he hurried across to the marshal's office and stopped, panting, in the doorway.

"See 'em?" he asked excitedly. "Hear 'em?"

"What or who?" asked Tex, throwing one leg over the other.

"Them rowdy punchers!" exclaimed the storekeeper. "Nobody's safe! Go up an' take 'em in, quick!"

"What they do?" interestedly asked the marshal.

"Didn't you *see* an' *hear*?" demanded Williams incredulously.

"I saw 'em ride past, an' I heard 'em shootin' in th' air; but what did they do so I can arrest 'em?"

"Ain't that enough? That, an' th' yellin', an' everythin'?"

"Sinful and his friends made more noise th' other night when they left town," replied the marshal. "I didn't arrest them. Hank was of a mind to see if it was true that a bullet only punches a little, thin-edged hole in a pane of glass an' don't smash it all to pieces. Bein' wobbly, he picked out yore winder, seein' they was th' biggest in town; but Sinful held him back, an' they had a scufflin' match an' made more noise than sixteen mournful coyotes. There bein' no pane smashed I didn't cut in. A man is only a growed-up boy, anyhow."

Williams looked at him in frank amazement. "But these here fellers are punchers!" he exploded.

"I shore could see that, even with th' dust," confessed the marshal. "That ain't no crime as I knows of."

"It ain't th' four to one that's holdin' you back, is it?" demanded Williams insinuatingly. "They're punchers, too: bad as h—l."

Tex languidly arose and removed the pair of guns

and the belts, laying them gently on the floor. He pitched his sombrero on the bunk and faced his caller.

"Mebby I didn't understand you," he coldly suggested. "What was it you said?"

Williams raised both hands in quick protest, one foot fishing desperately behind him for the ground below the sill. "Nothin' to make you go on th' prod," he hastily explained.

"Listen to me, Williams," said the cool peace officer, his voice level and unemotional. "Anybody callin' me a coward wants to go into action fast, an' keep on goin' fast. That includes everybody from King Solomon right down to date. I'm responsible for th' peace in this town, an' when *anybody* starts smashin' it I'll go 'em a whirl. Yellin', ridin' fast, an' shootin' in th' air, 'specially by sober men, ain't smashin' nothin' in a town like this. I don't aim to run no nursery, nor even a kindergarden. I ain't makin' a fool out of myself an' turnin' th' law into a joke. Once let ridicule start an' h—l's pleasant by contrast. They ain't shootin' now. Th' first shot fired inside any buildin', or dangerously low, an' I inject myself an' my two guns. I can't make no arrests on a blind guess, mine nor yourn. You better go back to th' store an' keep th' vinegar from sourin' on its mother."

Williams' jaw dropped. This was not Tex Jones at all, at least it didn't sound like him. "As th' owner of th' most valuable property in town I want them coyotes stopped from ruinin' it. I——"

"When they show any signs of ruinin' *any* property I'll step in an' stop 'em," the marshal assured him. "I got my ears open, an' had my authority buckled on—which I'll now resume wearin'." He picked up a heavy belt and slung it around him, deftly catching the free end as it slapped against him. "We'll have law an' order, Williams—even if I have to fill some fool as full of holes as a prairie-dog town; but I ain't goin' out an' trample on a man's pride an' make him get killed defendin' it, unless I got good reason to. This is a long speech, but I'm goin' to make it longer so I can impress somethin' on yore mind. Bein' a busy merchant you've mebby never had time to think about it much; but me, bein' a marshal, I *got* to think of everythin' like that. This is one of 'em: When bad feelin's exist between two classes, helpin' one ag'in' th' other, without honest reasons, is only goin' to make more bitterness. It can be held down only by impersonal justice. That's me. I don't give a d—n what a man is as long as he behaves hisself." Picking up the second belt he slung it around him the other way and buckled it behind him. As he shook them both to a more comfortable fit a yell rang out up near the hotel, followed by a shot. Grabbing his hat from the bunk he pushed Williams out of his way and dashed through the door, flinging over his shoulder: "I'm injectin' myself *now*! You'd better go look to th' vinegar!"

He saw Whiskey Jim, the man whom he had caught beating the dog, in his blind terror run against the side of the harness-shop, recover from the impact and, stupefied by fear, frantically claw at the bleached boards. A spurt of dust almost under one of his feet made him claw more frantically. The hilarious puncher walked slowly toward him, raising the Colt for another shot. Behind him, laughing uproariously, stood his three friends, solidly blocking the hotel door.

"Hold that gun where it is!" shouted the marshal, dropping into a catlike stride. He was coming down the middle of the street, not more than forty paces, now, from the performing puncher.

The gun arm stiffened in air as the whiplike, authoritative phrase reached its possessor and, grinning exultantly, the puncher wheeled to get a good look at his next victim. He saw a grave-faced man of forty-odd years walking toward him, a bright star pinned to the open vest, two guns hanging low down on the swaying hips, the swinging hands brushing the walnut grips at every lithe, steady step.

"See what we got to play with!" exulted the surprised puncher, calling to his friends. "I want his badge: you can have th' rest!" His hand chopped down and a spurt of dust leaped from the ground at the marshal's side.

Disregarding it, the peace officer maintained his steady, swinging stride, his eyes fixed on those of the other, intently watching for a change in their playful expression. Another shot and the dust spurted close to his left foot. The hilarious laughter of the three in the doorway died out, and their friend in the street stood stock still, trying to figure out what he had better do next. The deliberate marshal was now only five paces away and at the puncher's indecision, plain to be seen in the eyes, he leaped forward, wrested the gun from the feebly resisting fingers, whirled the nonplussed man around and then kicked him his own length on the ground.

Ignoring the three men in the doorway, thereby tacitly admitting their squareness, the marshal calmly ejected the cartridges from the captured weapon and, as the angry and astonished puncher arose, handed it to him.

"It's empty," he said in a matter-of-fact voice. "Keep it that way till you leave town; an' when you come in again, intendin' to likker up an' raise h—l, either unload it or leave it with me, unless you promise to behave yoreself." He turned to Whiskey Jim, who appeared to be frozen into a statue. "Come over here, Jim," he commanded, and again turned to the puncher, who did not know whether to laugh or to curse. "I reckon Jim's th' only injured party. His feelin's has been trampled on to th' tune of about five dollars. Pay him before he takes it out of yore hide. He's a desperate bad·man, Jim is!"

The three men in the door, who were nowhere near

drunk yet, knew sparkling courage when they saw it, and they shouted with laughter at their crestfallen friend, who grudgingly was counting the fine into the eager hand of the aggrieved citizen.

"Hey, Walt!" burbled one of them, a beardless youth on one end of the line. "Still want to play with that badge?"

"If you do," jeered the man in the middle, laughing again, "better rustle, *pronto,* 'cause I'm buyin' its boss a drink."

Walt grinned expansively, shoved the money into Whiskey Jim's clutching fingers, took hold of the quiet marshal, and turned toward the hotel. "You come along with me, officer," he said. "I'll pertect you. That fool says he's buyin' you a drink—mebby he *is,* but I'm payin' for th' first one. Yo're about th' best he-man I've seen since I looked into a lookin'-glass. I'm obliged to you for not losin' yore valuable temper." He waved a hand at the unbelieving Jim, who doubted his reeling senses. Five whole dollars, all at once! Gosh, but the new marshal was a hummer. "Now don't you lay for me, Jim," laughed the puncher. "We're square, all 'round, ain't we?"

The cheerful three in the door grabbed the marshal of Windsor and hauled him in to the bar, where he pushed free and surveyed them.

"Four cheerful imbeciles," he murmured sadly. "Don't you reckon you better quit drinkin', or else empty them guns?"

"Now don't you be too hard on us, Marshal," chuckled the eldest. "We're so dry we rattles, an' th' dust, risin' out of our throats gets plumb into our eyes. Here," he said, dragging out his gun and gravely emptying it, "these are shore heavy. I'll carry 'em in my pocket for a change," and he made good his words. The others laughingly followed his example, Tex's smile growing broader all the time.

"This ain't nothin' personal, boys," he said. "It's only

that th' law has come to town. Knowin' you'll leave 'em empty till after you get out, I'll have one drink an' go about my business." He made no threats and his voice was friendly and pleasant; and it did not have to be otherwise. He had made four friends, and they knew that he would go through with any play he started. "Know Tommy Watkins?" he asked as he put down his glass.

"Shore!" answered Walt. "He's workin' with my outfit—C Bar. Ain't seen him for a month, him bein' off somewhere when we rode in for our pay. Marshal, shake hands with another C Bar rider—Wyatt Holmes. These two tramps is Double S punchers—Lefty Rowe, an' Luke Perkins. My name's Butler—Walt Butler. What's Tommy up an' done?" he finished somewhat anxiously.

"Glad to see you, boys," said Tex, heartily shaking hands all around. "My name's Tex Jones. Come in ag'in," he invited. "Oh," he said in answer to Walt's question, "Tommy ain't done nothin', yet. I was just wonderin'. Good boy, Tommy is. Sort of wild, I reckon, bein' young. Busy after th' gals. Most young fellers are hellers anyhow, or think they are. But he's a likable pup."

Walt laughed and the others grinned broadly. "You've shore figgered him wrong, Marshal. He's scairt of th' gals—won't have nothin' to do with 'em; an' I ain't never seen him nowhere near drunk; but" he hastily defended in loyalty to his absent friend, "he's all right, other ways. Yes, sir—barrin' them things, Tommy Watkins is a good man, an' I can lick any feller that says he ain't."

"Which won't be me," replied Tex, smiling. "I like him, first-rate. We been gettin' acquainted fast. Well, boys," he said, turning toward the door, "have a good time an' come in often. I like a little company from th' outside. It relieves th' monotony. So-long."

"You shore had th' monotony busted wide open today," chuckled Walt. "But Tommy's a good boy—

whatever th' h—l he's been doin' since I saw him last."
Watching the marshal until out of sight past the door
he turned and regarded his companions. "I'm tellin' you
calves there's a man who'd spit in th' devil's eye," he
said. "We was playin' with giant powder like four fools.
Here's to Tex Jones, Marshal of Windsor!"

Lefty, tenderly putting the glass on the bar, looked
thoughtfully around the room and then at the partially
stunned barkeep. "How's friend Bud takin' th' new
marshal? Bud an' him shore will have an' interestin'
Colt fandango some of these fine days."

Baldy sighed, wiped off the bar, and looked sorrowfully at the group. "Bud's planted on Boot Hill. They
done had th' fandango, an' he did th' dancin'. My
G—d, I can see it yet! It was like this—"and he left the
bar, walked to the door, and painstakingly enacted the
fight. When it was finished, he mopped his head and
slowly returned to his accustomed place.

Wyatt Holmes reached out and gravely shook hands
with his friends and finished by shaking his own. "You
allus was a fool for luck, Walt," he said thoughtfully.
"Giant powder?" he muttered piously. "Giant h—l! It
was dynamite with th' fuse lit. Here," he demanded,
wheeling on the startled Baldy. "I *need* this drink! Set
'em up!"

Walt shook his head. "Now, what th' devil has
Tommy done?" he growled.

Baldy, remembering Tommy's share in the altera-
tion, maintained a discreet silence.

CHAPTER XV

A Good Samaritan

Out on **Buffalo Creek, Blascom**, haggard, drawn, gaunt, and throbbing with an excitement which was slowly mastering him, scorning time to properly prepare and eat his food, drove himself like a madman. The creek bed at the old sump showed a huge, sloping-sided ditch from bank to bank, the upper side treacherous dry sand, the lower side a great, slanting ridge of rock, riven through in one place by the force of the dynamite, which had blown a great crater on the down-stream side of the natural riffle. In the bottom of the ditch a few inches of water lay, all that had saved him from fleeing from the claim because of thirst.

For year after weary year the miner had labored over the gold-bearing regions of the West, South, and North, beginning each period full of that abiding faith which clings so tenaciously to the gold-hunter and refuses to accept facts in any but an optimistic manner. A small stake here, day wages there, grubstakes, and hiring out, he had persistently, stubbornly pursued the will-o'-the-wisp and tracked down many a rainbow of hope, only to find the old disappointment. From laughing, hope-filled youth he had run the gauntlet of the years, through the sobered but still hopeful middle age, scorning thought of the twilight of life when he should be broken in strength and bitter in mind. Teeming, mushroom mining camps, frantic gold rushes, the majestic calm of cool canyons, and the punishing silences of almost unbearable desert wastes had found him an unquestioning worshiper, a trusting devotee of his goddess of gold. It was in his blood, it was woven into every fiber of his body, and he could no more cease his pursuit than he could stop the beating of his heart, or at least he could not cease while the goal remained unattained. Now, after all these years, he had won. He had proved that his quest had not been in vain.

Before the sun came up, even before dawn streaked the eastern sky, his meager, ill-cooked breakfast was bolted, and his morning scouting begun. First of all he slipped with coyote cunning down to the lower fork to see if Jake still kept his drunken stupor. The cold chimney of the miserable hut was the first eagerly sought-for sign, and every furtive visit awakened dread that a ribbon of smoke would meet his eye. A nearer approach made with the wariness of some hunted creature of the wild, let him sense the unnatural quiet of the little shack. A stealthy glance through a glassless opening, called a window, after the light made it possible, showed him morning after morning that his jug had not failed him. The unshaven, matted, unclean face of the stupefied man lay sometimes in a bunk, sometimes on the floor, and once the huge bulk was sprawled out inertly across the rough table amid a disarray of cracked, broken, and unwashed dishes. On the fifth morning the anxious prowler, fearing the lowered contents of the jug, had left a full bottle against the door of the hut and, slinking into the scanty cover, had run like a hunted thing back to the riven riffle and its unsightly ditch and crater.

Feverishly he worked, scorning food, unconscious of the glare of a molten sun rising to the zenith of its scorching heat. Shovel and bucket, trips without end from the ditch to a place above the steep bank where the carried sand grew rapidly higher and higher; panting, straining, frantic, worked Blascom. Foot by foot the ditch widened, foot by foot it lengthened, inch by inch it deepened, slide after sandy slide slipping to its bottom to be furiously, madly cursed by the prospector.

Then at last came the instant when the treasure was momentarily uncovered. Dropping the blunted, ragged-edged shovel, he plunged to all fours and thrust eager, avaricious fingers, bent like the talons of some bird of prey, into the storehouse of gold. Noiselessly responding to the jar and the impact of the groveling body, the great bank of sand had collapsed and slid down upon him, burying him without warning. The mass split and heaved, and the imprisoned miner, wild-eyed, sobbing for breath after his spasmodic exertions, burst through it and, raising quivering fists, cursed it and creation.

Hope had driven him remorselessly, but now that he had seen and felt the treasure, his efforts became those of a madman. More buckets of sand, jealous of each spilled handful, more punishing trips at a dog-trot, more frantic digging, and again he stared wildly at the pocket under his knees. Suddenly leaping erect, he cast anxious glances around him and a panicky fear gripped him and turned him into a wild beast. Yanking his coat from the rock riffle he spread it over the treasure and then, running low and swiftly, gun in hand, he scouted through the brush on both sides of the creek, and then bounded toward the lower fork. Approaching the hut on hands and knees, cruelly cut by rock and thorn, he studied the door and the open window. The bottle was where he had left it, the snores arose regularly, and once more he was reassured. Had there been signs of active life he would have murdered with the exultant zeal of a religious fanatic.

The day waned and passed. Night drew its curtains closer and closer, and yet Blascom labored, the treacherous sand turning him into a raving, frenzied fury. Higher and higher grew the sand pile on the bank, a monument to his mad avarice. With gold in lumps massed at the foot of that rock ridge, yet he must save the sand for its paltry yield in dust, pouring out his waning strength in a labor which, to save pence, might cost him pounds. At last he stumbled more and more, staggering this way and that, his tortured body all but asleep, forced on and on by his fevered mind, flogged by a stubborn will. Then came a heavier stumble, following a more unbalanced stagger and his numbed and vague protests did not suffice to get him back on his feet. When he awakened, the glaring sun shocked him by its nearness to the meridian, and the shock brought a momentary sanity; if he scorned the warning he would be lost—and another shadowy prompting of his subconscious mind was at last allowed to direct him. Calmly, but shakily, he weakly crawled and staggered toward his shack, from which came a thin streamer of smoke, climbing arrow-like into the quiet, heated air.

He stopped and stared at it in amazement, doubting his senses. Had he seen it the day before it would have enraged him to a blind, killing madness; but now, suspicious as he was, and deadly determined to protect his secret, the reaction of the high tension of the last six days made him momentarily apathetic. The abused body, the starved tissues and dulled nerves, now took possession of him and forced him, even though it was with gun in his hand, to approach the door of his squalid, disordered habitation erect and without hesitation. At the sound of his slowly dragging steps a well-known, friendly voice called out and a well-known, friendly face appeared at a window.

The marshal was nearly stunned by what he saw and then, surging into action, leaped through the door and caught his staggering friend.

The well-cooked, wholesome breakfast out of the way, a breakfast made possible only by the marshal's forethought in bringing supplies with him from town, he refused Blascom's request for a third cup of coffee and smilingly offered a glass of whiskey, over which he had made a few mysterious passes.

"Don't want none," objected the weary miner.

"But yo're goin' to overcome yore sudden temperance scruples an' drink it, for me," persuaded Tex. "A good shock will do you a lot of good—an' put new life into you. As you are you ain't worth a cuss."

The prospector held out his hand, smilingly obedient, and downed the fiery draught at a gulp. "Tastes funny," he observed, and then laughed. "Wonder I can taste it at all, after th' nightmare I've had since th' smoke of that blast rolled away. Where'd you think I was when you came?"

Tex chuckled and stretched. "I didn't know, but from th' glimpse I got of th' crick bed I was shore I wasn't goin' huntin' you, an' mebby get shot accidental. Did you find it, Blascom?"

"My G—d, yes!" came the explosive answer. "There's piles of it, all shapes an' sizes, layin' on a smooth rock floor. When that sand stops slidin' I can scoop it up with a shovel, like coal out of a bin. Half of it belongs to you, Jones: go look at it!"

"I don't want any of it," replied Tex with quiet, but unshakable, determination. "If you divide it, no matter how much there is, by th' number of years you've sweat an' slaved and starved, it won't be too much to pay you. You set here a little while an' I'll go on a scout in th' brush an' watch it till you come out. Better lay down a few minutes, say half an hour, an' give that grub a chance to put some life into you. I'll shake you if you fall asleep."

"Feel sleepy now," confessed the prospector, yawning and moving sluggishly toward his bunk. "Seein' as how yo're here, I'll just take a few winks—don't know when I'll get another chance. That sand shore is gallin' an' ornery as th' devil. Go up an' take a look at it—I'll foller in a little while."

Tex, closing the door behind him, slipped into the brush, where he made more than a usual amount of noise for Blascom's benefit, and as he worked up toward the ditch he chuckled to himself. There had been no need for a full dose, he reflected, and he was glad that he had not given one. Blascom's drink of whiskey had just enough chloral in it to deaden him and give his worn-out body the chance it sought; besides, he was not too certain of the effect of a full dose on a constitution as undermined as that of his friend.

The ditch, again slowly filling with sand, showed him nothing, and he stood debating whether he should disturb it for a look at the treasure, when he suddenly thought of Jake and the whiskey jug. He remembered that Jake had been almost senselessly drunk when he had left the hotel on the night of the blast and that he had not been seen by anyone since. It would do no harm to go down to the lower fork and see what there was to be seen. The thought became action, and he was on his way, down the middle of the creek bed, where the footing was a little more to his liking.

The hut appeared to be deserted and the bottle of whiskey outside the door brought a frown to his face, which deepened as nearer approach showed him that the door was fastened shut by rope and wire on the outside, and that the snoring inmate virtually was a prisoner. There was a note in the snores that disturbed him and aroused his vague, half-forgotten professional knowledge. Hastening forward he pushed the bottle aside with an impatient foot and worked rapidly with the fastenings on the door. At last it opened, and gun in hand against any possible contingency, he entered the hovel and looked at its tenant, sprawled face down near the jumbled bunk. A touch of the drunken man's cheek, a tense counting of his pulse, sent Tex to his feet as though a shot had nicked him. Running back to Blascom's hut, where he had left his horse, he leaped into the saddle and sent Omar at top speed toward town.

His thundering knock on the doctor's door brought no response and, not daring to pause on the dictates of custom, he threw his shoulder against the flimsy barrier and went in on top of it. Scrambling to his feet, he dashed into the rear one of the two rooms and swore in sudden rage and disgust.

Doctor Horn lay on his back on a miserable cot and his appearance brought a vivid recollection to his tumultuous caller. Tex turned up a sleeve and nodded grimly at the tiny puncture marks and, with an oath, faced around and swept the room with a searching glance. It stopped and rested on a heavy volume on a shelf and in a moment he was hastily turning the pages. Finding what he sought he read avidly, closed the book, and hunted among the bottles in a shallow closet. Taking what he needed, he ran out, leaped into the saddle and loped south to mislead any curious observer, only turning west when hidden from sight of the town.

When night fell it found a weak and raving patient in the little hovel on the lower fork, roped in his bunk, and watched anxiously by the two-gun man at his side. The long dark hours dragged, but dawn found a battle won. Noon came and passed and then Tex, looking critically at his patient, felt he could safely leave him for a few minutes. Glimpsing the filled bottle of liquor at the door of the hut he grabbed it and hurled it against a rock.

Blascom was up and around when Tex reached the upper fork, dragging heavy feet by strangely dulled legs.

"Just in time to feed," he drawled. "Didn't sleep as long as I thought," he said dully, glancing at the sun patch on the floor. "Must be near two o'clock—an' I felt like I could sleep th' sun around."

Tex would not correct the mistake and nodded. "You must 'a' slept some last night," he suggested. "Looked like you had when I saw you from th' window this mornin'."

Blascom nodded heavily. "Near sixteen hours. I feel dead all over."

"A long sleep like that often makes a man feel that way," responded Tex. "Th' muscles are stubborn an' th' eyes get a little touchy, too," he added.

They ate the poorly cooked dinner and leaned back for a smoke, Blascom allowing himself to lose the time because he felt so inert.

"Have any visits from friend Jake?" carelessly asked the marshal.

Blascom laughed. "Not one. You see, Jake come home that night about as drunk as a man can get an' walk at all. I planted th' jug, a full bottle of gin, an' near half a quart of brandy in his cabin where he'd shore see it. He's been petrified for a week steady. To make shore I put another bottle of whiskey ag'in' his door."

Tex nodded. "I busted that, just now. You come near killin' him. I just about got him through. Don't give him no more. I sat up all last night with him, draggin' him back from th' Divide, an' only left him a little while ago. Get yore gold out quick an' you don't have no call to want him drunk. Cache it, an' then spend a week takin' things easy. You wasn't far behind Jake when I saw you."

Blascom was staring at him in vast surprise. "I never thought good likker would hurt an animal like him!"

"I didn't say it was good likker," rejoined Tex. "Even good likker will do it when drunk by th' barrel; an' there's no good likker in Windsor, if I'm any judge.

Well," he said, arising and taking up his hat, "I'll drift along for another look at Jake an' then head for town. Seein' as how you got him that way, through my suggestion; I'll admit, you better look in at him once in awhile an' see he has what he needs. Take some of yore water with you: his stinks."

CHAPTER XVI

Buffalo Creek in the Spotlight

WHAT INSTINCT it is and how it operates, that leads vultures from over the horizon to a dying animal, has never been satisfactorily explained to a lot of people; no more than the instinct which led Sinful and Hank to go prowling around Buffalo Creek when by all rights they should have been hanging around their own camp or loafing in the hotel; but prowl they did, their cunning old eyes missing nothing, certainly nothing so new and shining and high as the sand heap above the creek bank.

Sinful saw it first and he nudged his companion, whose cud nearly choked him before he could cough it back where it belonged.

"Glory!" he choked. "Jest look at it! Come on, Sinful: we got to inwestigate. Nobody's diggin' all that out an' totin' it up there for th' fun of it. But why's he luggin' it so far?"

Sinful snorted scornfully. "Too busy totin' to pan it,"

he snapped. "Rain's due 'most any time an' he's workin' to beat it. I don't have to inwestigate it—anybody that's workin' like that knows what he's doin'; an' I ain't never heard it said that Blascom's any fool. If he didn't know it was rich, he wouldn't be workin' so hard in th' sun."

"Well, mebby," doubted Hank, always a cold blanket in regard to his companion's contentions. "Looks like he ain't got no water for pannin', like everybody else. He ain't lazy like you, an' instead of wastin' his time around th' hotel like us he's totin' sand so he can work while th' crick's floodin'. When th' floodin' comes everybody else'll have to set down an' watch it till it gets low enough. Me an' you would be doin' somethin' if we follered his example. Where you goin'?" he demanded as his sneering companion walked away.

Sinful flashed a pitying glance over his shoulder. "To git a handful of that sand an' prove you ain't got no sense, that's where. You keep yore eye open for Blascom while I raid his sand pile. Here's a can," he said, stooping to pick it up. "It'll mebby tell us somethin' when we gits it to some water. If you see him a-comin' out, throw a pebble at me. 'Twon't take me long, once I git my boots off."

Hank obeyed and scouted toward the hut, finally stopping when he could see its door. Watching it a few minutes he saw Blascom pass the opening, and after another few minutes, the watcher slipped away, hastening toward the sand pile. Reaching it, he saw no signs of his partner and backed into the brush to await developments. He no sooner had stopped behind a patch of scrub oak than he caught sight of Sinful carefully picking his way across the stony ground in his socks, one hand carrying the can, the other a pair of boots. On his leathery face was an expression of vast surprise and pious awe. He seemed almost stunned, but he was not so lost to his surroundings that he ignored a bounding, clicking pebble which passed across his path. Clutching can and boots in a firmer grip, he sprinted with praiseworthy speed and agility toward the somewhat distant railroad track. In his wake sped Hank, an unholy grin wreathing his face at the goatlike progress of his old friend over the rocky ground. To Sinful's ears the sound of those clattering boots spelled a determined pursuit and urged him to better efforts. At last, winded, a cramp in his side and his feet so tender and bruised that he preferred to fight rather than go any farther in his socks, he dropped the boots, drew his gun, and wheeled. At sight of Hank's well-known and inelegant figure a look of relief flashed over his face, swiftly followed by a frown of deep and palpitant suspicion.

"What you mean, chasin' me like that?" he shouted.

"Gosh!" panted Hank as he drew near. "That was shore close! An' for an old man yo're a runnin' fool. Jack rabbits an' coyotes can cover ground, but they can't stack up ag'in' you. Did you see him?"

Sinful, one boot on and the other balanced in his hand, looked up. "No, I didn't; did *you*?" he demanded, suspicion burning in his old eyes.

"Shore," answered Hank, lying with a facile ease due to much practice. "He suddenly busted out of th' door with a rifle in his hands an' headed for his sand pile. I dusted lively, heaved th' pebble; an' here we are." He cast an apprehensive glance behind him and then sharply admonished his friend. "Hustle, you! Yo're settin' there like there ain't no mad miner projectin' around in th' brush with a Winchester! Think I want to git shot?"

"I reckon mebby you ought to," retorted Sinful, struggling erect and trying each tender foot in turn. "Stone bruises, cuts, an' stickers, an' all because you git in a panic!" he growled. "Come on, you old fool: there's a pool of water in th' crick, t'other side of th' railroad bridge. Yo're too smart, you are. Mebby yore eyes'll pop out when you see what's in this here can. Great guns, what a sight I've seen!"

Panning gold in a tomato can might be difficult for a novice, but Sinful's cunning old hands did the work speedily and well. After repeated refillings and mystic gyrations he carefully poured out the last of the water and peered eagerly into the can, bumping his head solidly against his companion's, for Hank was as eagerly curious.

Sinful placed it reverently on the creek bank and looked at his staring friend.

"An' only a canful," he muttered in awe.

"Glory!" breathed Hank, and looked again to make sure. "Nothin' but dust—but Good Lord!" He packed a vile pipe with viler tobacco, lit it, and arose. "No wonder he grabbed his gun an' dusted for his sand pile! Come on, Sinful: we got a long walk ahead of us, some quick packin' to do, an' a long walk back ag'in. If we only could get a couple of mules, we'd load 'em with three-hundred pounds apiece an' go down th' crick a day's journey. It'd be worth it."

Sinful looked scornfully at his worrying companion and slowly arose. "No day's journey for me, mules or no mules," he declared, spitting emphatically. "I ain't shore it would be worth it, considerin' th' time an' th' trouble; but it's worth pannin' right where it is. I've jumped claims before in my life an' I ain't too old to jump another. When I looked over that bank an' saw that wallopin' big rock a-stickin' up in th' crick bed, from bank to bank; an' th' ditch he's put down on th' upstream side, I purty near knew what th' sand pile would show. I'm bettin' he's got *bushels* of gold at th' foot of that riffle. If his location don't run up that far, an' mebby it don't, we got somethin' to keep us busy. An' if it does, we've mebby got more to keep us busy. Come on, you wall-eyed ijut: we got to be gittin' back to camp. Great Jerus'lam!"

The marshal of Windsor, riding slowly toward town south of the railroad track after a long detour to mask his trail, saw two scarecrows bumping along the ties, bobbing up and down jerkily as they tried to stretch their stride to cover two ties and repeatedly fell back to one. They were well to the northeast of him and to his left, but he thought they looked familiar and he pushed more to the south to remain hidden from them while he rode ahead. When he finally had reached a point south of the station he turned and rode toward it, timing his arrival to coincide with theirs.

Sinful grinned up at the smiling rider, his missing teeth only making more prominent the few brown fangs he had left. Two dribbles of tobacco juice had dried at each corner of his mouth and reached downward across his chin, giving him an appearance somewhat striking. He mopped the perspiration from his face by a vigorous wipe of his soiled shirt sleeve and lifted each palpitating foot in turn.

"Been ridin' far?" he asked in idle curiosity and in great good humor, considering the aches in his body and the soreness of his feet.

"Oh, just around exercisin' Oh My," answered Tex. "I thought you two was located out on Antelope, west of town?"

"We are," replied Hank, ignoring his partner's furtive elbow. "Been gettin' sorta tired of it, though, not havin' nothin' to do but set around an' look at th' same things. Thought we'd take a look at th' Buffaler, south of th' track; but it ain't much better, though there is some water in th' pools. Anyhow, Antelope's kinda crowded. We may shift our camp. Jake's out on Buffaler som'er's, ain't he?"

Tex nodded and glanced at the can. "Been fishin'?"

"If we had enough bait to fill that can we'd 'a' ate it ourselves," chuckled Hank.

"Naw, there ain't no fish left now," said Sinful.

"Hard-luck coffeepot, that's all it is. Good as anythin' else, an' shore plentiful. Punch a hole in each side of it an' shove in a piece of wire, an' she'll cook anythin' small. Ain't it hot?"

"Hot, an' close," replied the marshal. "Well, I reckon I'll be gettin' along. Feels like rain is due 'most any time, though I don't reckon we'll get any before th' moon changes. Still, you can't allus tell."

"Can't tell nothin' about it at all, this kind of weather," observed Hank, the can now against the other side of his body. "But one thing's shore—it's gettin' closer every day. So-long," and the grotesque couple went bobbing down the track toward their own camp.

Tex looked after them, humorously shaking his head. " 'It's gettin' closer every day,' " he mimicked. "Shore it is. Pair of cunning old coyotes, an' entirely too frank about Buffalo Creek." Just then Sinful leaped into the air, cracked his sore heels together and struck his companion across the shoulders. This display of exuberance awakened a strong suspicion in the marshal. "I'll keep my eye on you two old codgers," he soliloquized, thoughtfully feeling of the handcuffs in his pocket. Wheeling abruptly he rode up to the station, where Jerry grinningly awaited him. "Let me know when those mossbacks go west, Jerry, if you see them," he requested. "They're too cussed innocent an' happy to suit me. How are things?"

Jerry shook his head. "I'll be cussed if I know. But I know one thing, and that is that I'm apologizing to you for the way Jane shut the door in your face. I don't know what's the matter with her lately."

"There's never any tellin' about wimmin," said Tex, smiling. "An' don't you ever apologize to anybody for anythin' she does. Wimmin see things from a different angle, an' they ain't got a man's defenses. A difference in structure is likely to be accompanied by differences in nature, in this case notably in the more delicate balance of th' nervous system. Their reactions are both more subtle an' more extreme. I wasn't insulted, but just folded my tents like th' Arabs, an' as silently stole away. Which I'm now goin' to repeat. See you later, mebby."

Jerry watched his visitor ride off and a puzzled frown crept over his face.

"Wish I knew more about you, Mr. Tex Jones," he muttered. "You're either as fine a human as I have seen, or the smoothest rascal: and I'm d—d if I can tell which."

The marshal rode to his office and sought the chair outside the door, his thoughts running back over recent events. Blascom's find and the physical condition of the man naturally brought to mind Jake's narrow escape. The latter bothered him, notwithstanding the certainty that Blascom would keep a good watch over the sick man. While he anxiously ran over his scant knowledge of Jake's illness and the remedies he had employed, he glanced up to see Doctor Horn nervously hurrying toward him. The doctor, in view of what he now knew of him, became a very interesting study for the marshal.

"Marshal!" cried the physician while yet a score of paces away, "somebody burst down my door during my absence and took some drugs which by their nature are not common out here and, consequently, hard to obtain. I am formally reporting it, sir."

"Doctor," replied Tex, "when a patient comes to you for help you naturally expect him to be frank and truthful. It is the same with a peace officer, who endeavors to cure not the ills of a single unit of society, but the ills of society as a whole. Here, as in your own field, a refractory or diseased unit may, and generally does, affect the body of which he is a part. So, as a social physician, I must ask of you that frankness so valuable to a medico. First, what drugs did you miss?"

"Your analogy, while clever, is sophistical and is entirely unwarranted," retorted the physician, taken somewhat aback by the words and attitude of a "cowhand," as he contemptuously characterized punchers. "Leaving it out of the argument, except to say, in passing, that your 'social physician' does not exercise a corrective influence, but rather a punitive one, I hardly see how the naming of the missing drugs will give any enlightenment to a layman. There still exists the forcible breaking into, and the unlawful entry of, my residence."

"For purposes of identification it might be well to know the drugs that were stolen; but I'll waive that. What time would you say this occurred?" asked Tex with professional interest.

"Some time yesterday," answered the physician.

"You certainly are not very specific, Doctor," commented Tex. "I'm afraid we must come closer to it than that. You say you were away at the time?"

"Yes: I did not return until quite late."

"In body or in spirit, Doctor Horn?"

"Sir, I do not understand you!" retorted the complainant, flushing slightly and gazing with great intensity into the marshal's eyes.

"There have been many others who did not understand me," replied Tex, calmly rolling and lighting a cigarette. "I'm mentioning that so you won't think you are an exotic variation of our large and interesting species. The study of man is the greatest of all, Doctor. The words were more of a joke than anything else. Have you ever suffered from hallucinations, Doctor? I've heard it said that too close confinement, too close an application to study, and too intimate relations with chemicals, volatile and otherwise, operate that way in these altitudes. Hothouse gardeners, for instance, notably those engaged in raising poppies, have slight touches of mental aberration. You are certain that your house was entered while you were away?"

The doctor, arms akimbo, was staring at this calm mind-reader as though in a trance, too stunned to be insulted.

Tex continued: "The value of the missing drugs and the damage to the door undoubtedly will be paid to you, Doctor, in a few days. In fact, I am so confident of that that I will pay you just damages now, taking your receipt in return. Do you agree with a great many people that a physician to the body has much the same high obligations as those belonging to a minister or a priest, who are physicians to the soul? That his work is of a humanitarian nature before it is a matter of remuneration; that he should hold himself fit and ready to answer calls of distress without regard to his own bodily comfort?"

Doctor Horn still stared at him, rallying his thoughts. He nodded assent as he groped.

"There are professional secrets, Doctor, which need not be divulged," continued Tex. "I understand that you have a horse?"

The physician nodded again.

"Then use it. I have reason to believe that a man named Jake, a miner, who is located on the first fork of Buffalo Creek, west of town, urgently needs your professional services. I understand that he has been brought back from death from alcoholic poisoning, but will be much safer if you look at him. Did you say you are going now? And by the way, before you start, let me say that the old idea of peace officers being corrective forces, in a punitive sense only, is rapidly becoming obsolete among the more intelligent and broader-minded men of that class. While punishment is undoubtedly needed as a warning to others, the cure's the thing, to paraphrase an old friend of mine. Is there any connection between the natures of the missing drugs and alcoholic poisoning, Doctor? But we are wasting time. This little problem can wait. Just now speed's the thing. Drop around again soon, Doctor: I always enjoy the companionship of an educated man," and the marshal, slowly arising, bowed and entered his little office, the door softly closing behind him.

CHAPTER XVII

The Rush

THE MARSHAL was leaving the hotel after breakfast the following morning when he saw Jerry walking briskly toward him from the station and he waited for the agent to come up.

"Those two old prospectors just passed the station, going west along the track," Jerry informed him. "From the way they were loaded down it looked as though they are moving their camp. And how men as old as they are can carry such packs is beyond my understanding."

"Thanks, Jerry," said the marshal. "Go back to th' station. I've got to take a ride. Trouble's brewin', I reckon."

Passing the hotel on his way to Carney's stable, Tex saw a running miner hurrying into it and in a moment an excited half-score of armed prospectors poured into the street, shouting and gesticulating. The little crowd picked up additions as it passed along the street and headed westward to strike the railroad at an angle. Some of them had partners with them and, when the tracks had been reached, quite a number turned and ran eastward toward their camps to pack up belongings and supplies.

"Mental telepathy?" murmured Tex, watching them in some surprise. "Hank and Sinful are too clever rascals to tell anybody anything of value that they might know. Huh! That's only a name, I guess, for subconscious weighing of facts subconsciously received: instinctive deductions from observations too vague to be definitely recognized. Instinct, I'm afraid you have more names than most people recognize. But it does beat the devil, at that! An animal does seemingly wonderful and impossible things because of the keenness of its scent, which passes our understanding; birds of prey have eyes nearly telescopic in power—but how the knowledge of this gold strike has spread about so quickly when everyone concerned in it naturally would be secretive, is too much for me. One thing is certain, however: it is known, and I have work to do, and quickly!"

Omar welcomed him and soon was stringing the miles out behind him as smoothly almost as running water. There was no need to urge the animal at its best speed, for it was doing two miles to the miners' one and easily would beat them to the scene of action.

When he reached the second fork, Blascom was not at the hut and, leading the roan into a brush-filled hollow, the marshal took his rifle from its scabbard and went up to the scene of the miner's operations. His hail was followed by a startled crouching on the prospector's part and a rifle barrel leaped up to the top of the ditch.

"Don't shoot: It's Jones," called the marshal, slowly emerging from his cover. "I come up to warn you that th' rush has started. Hank an' Sinful ought to get here in about half an hour, th' others a little behind them. I'm aimin' to be referee: th' kind of a referee I once saw

at a turf prize fight: he had to jump in an' thrash both of
th' principals—an' he did it, too. Get that bonanza
cleaned out and cached yet?"

Blascom swore as he stood up again. "Yes: but nobody's goin' to git *this* without a fight! How th' devil
did they find out I'd struck it rich?"

"Shore this claim is staked an' located?" demanded
Tex.

"Yes; an' there's work enough done on it to make it
stick. But how did they find out I'd struck it?"

"Don't know," answered the marshal. "You better
climb out an' go off an' hide somewhere in th' brush
from where yore rifle will cover th' cache. They're
keen as hounds an' there's no use takin' chances of
losin' th' greater to save th' less. I'll handle this end of
it. If you hear a shot you better slip back an' look things
over. Get a rustle on you—time's flyin'."

In a few minutes the creek bed and the little hut appeared to be deserted. Blascom lay on his stomach at a
point from which he could see his cache and the ditch
as well. After a short silence there came the sound of a
snapping twig and a few minutes later Sinful's greedy
eyes peered over the creek bank down at the big ditch.
He slid a rifle over the edge and looked around eagerly.
To his side crept Hank, who added his scrutiny to that
of his partner. Sinful spoke out of one corner of his
mouth as he gazed intently down the creek bed, where
one corner of Blascom's hut could be seen through the
scrawny timber on the little point. Hank nodded,
crawled to the edge of the bank and was about to slip
over it when a low warning from the brush at their side
froze them both.

"Stay where you are," said a well-known voice, cold
and unfriendly. "That claim's got one owner now, an'
he ain't lookin' for no partners, a-tall. Better shove up
yore hands an' face th' crick. You know me—an' so far
you ain't seen me miss, yet."

Tex emerged from his cover, a Colt in one hand, a pair of shining handcuffs clinking from their short chains as they swung from the other. Snapping one over Sinful's wrist he curtly ordered Hank to his partner's side and linked the two together. Disarming them he unloaded the weapons, appropriated the cartridges, and searched them both to make certain they could do him no injury.

"Sit down," he said, "an' keep quiet. Th' real show is about to start. Who all did you chumps tell about this strike?"

Hank glared at Sinful, Sinful glared at Hank, and then both glared at their captor. "Nobody, so strike me blind!" snapped Sinful. "Hank ain't been out of my sight since we left here yesterday. Think we're fools?"

"Anything but that," grimly rejoined Tex. "Shut up, now: I want to listen. Any play you make that don't suit me will call for a gun butt bein' bent over yore heads. If I need you, I'll call: an' you come a-runnin'. Hear me?"

"We could come faster if we was loose from each other," whispered Sinful in bland innocence. "*Couldn't* we, Hank?"

"Can't come fast, a-tall, hooked up this way," said Hank earnestly.

"Shut up!" snapped the marshal in a low voice.

A winged grasshopper rasped up over the bank and rasped back again instantly. A few birds chirped and sang across the creek bed and chickadees flashed and darted in an endless search for food. Several birds shot suddenly into the air from the fringe of timber and brush on the farther bank halfway between the ditch and the cabin, quickly followed by vague movements along the ground. Then more than a half-score of men popped into sight and, leaping from the steep bank, landed in the bed of the creek and scurried to different points, fooled by the numerous sumps which Blascom had dug in his quest for water. None of them had the knowledge possessed by Hank and Sinful, and the weather conditions had been such that the ages of the various sumps could not be quickly determined. Each man, eager to grab a hole while there was one left to grab, and to become established chose a mark and appropriated it without loss of time. No sooner had the scurrying crowd selected their grounds than the marshal, who had crept along the top of the high bank, jumped over it and held two guns on them, guns which they had good reason to respect.

"Han's up!" he roared. "*Pronto* an' high! You-all know me—don't gamble! I drop th' first man that makes a gunplay. *Hank! Sinful!*" he shouted. "Come a-runnin'!" Crouched, he faced the scowling crowd, his steady hands before his hips, his steady guns ready to prove his mastery. The handcuffed pair, squabbling as they came, shuffled up to him.

"You yank me any more an' I'll bust yore fool head!" growled Sinful to his bosom friend. "Just because yore laigs is longer is no reason for playin' kite with me! Knock-kneed old fool! Here we are, Marshal: what you want?"

"Hold yore han's close," ordered Tex, his left gun slipping into its sheath, his right becoming even more menacing. With the free hand he fished out the key, handed it to Hank and waited until he had made use of it. It went swiftly back into the pocket and the left hand again held a gun. "Slip around an' take their weapons!" he snapped. "Don't get between them an' me. Lively!"

"We ain't goin' to spoil yore aim, Marshal," Hank assured him with great fervor. "Come on, you baldheaded old buzzard—git them guns for th' marshal!" He gave his companion a shove forward. "He done us a good turn—an' one good turn deserves another. Come on!"

"Who you shovin'?" blazed Sinful, starting away.

"You ain't got no right, cuttin' in here!" shouted a red-faced, angry miner, his companions growling and cursing their hearty endorsements. "Yo're a town marshal, not a county sheriff! Turn them guns off us!"

"I got a wider range than marshal," rejoined Tex grimly and not for an instant relaxing his alertness. "Gus Williams said so when he 'pinted me; an', besides, I got th' very same authority out here as I have in town: twelve sections of th' Colt statutes as made an' pervided. Blascom has legally established his claim, drove his stakes, and done his work on it. When he comes he'll p'int out his boundaries. Hold still, you two! Git 'em all, Sinful; don't overlook nothin', Hank! No use turnin' this crick into a slaughter-pen."

"I ain't likely to overlook nothin'," replied Sinful, moving more rapidly, "though I'm shore bothered by these here cussed contraptions on my wrist. You'll notice Hank unlocked *his* end of 'em! D—d claim jumpers! A man's rights ain't safe no more these days. Hank an' me shore would 'a' planted some of this passel if they'd bothered us. How th' devil did they find out about it, *I* want to know?"

"What you reckon yo're goin' to do with us all?" sneered a wrathy prospector, his hands slowly coming down toward a harmless belt.

"I'll tell you that after I see Blascom," answered the marshal, firing a shot into the ground. He ordered Sinful and Hank to pile the weapons at his feet, locked them together again and ordered them to get closer to the rest of the miners. The shot brought Blascom as rapidly as he could get there with a due regard to caution. Obeying Tex's terse command he slid down the bank and went to him.

"Shore yore claim takes in th' ditch an' th' riffle?" asked Tex in a whisper.

"Th' new one does," answered Blascom. "I sent off th' papers with Jerry, like you said, th' day I got th' dynamite."

"Th' old one any good?"

"Not much; not much better'n day wages. 'Tain't no good without water; but neither is th' other, now."

"This crowd is fooled by yore old sumps," explained Tex hurriedly. "If we drive 'em off they'll be back ag'in, an' mebby add yore murder to th' rest of their crimes. I can't stay here day an' night; an' if I could, they'd get us both after dark, or at long range in daylight. You got to let 'em stay. By tomorrow there'll be twice as many. I'm scared some'll come slippin' up any minute an' turn th' tables on us. You let Sinful an' Hank divide a quarter of th' sand pannin' between 'em—they'll commit murder for half that, an' you've got to have partners in case of a rush. Besides, rain's due any day now, an' you need 'em to beat it."

"I hate like—" began Blascom stubbornly.

"We all has to do things we hate!" cut in his companion. "You can't do anythin' else. If you can, tell me quick!"

Blascom shook his head. He could do nothing else. He turned and faced the crowd, telling it to go ahead and stake out claims where each man had started to, on condition that there was to be no more jumping and that they join him in putting up a solid front against any newcomers other than partners. The scowls died out, heads nodded, and the hustle and bustle began again from where it had left off.

Tex called the Siamesed pair to him and they listened, with their eyes glowing, to Blascom's offer of limited partnership, Hank nearly swallowing his cud when asked if he was satisfied with the terms. Sinful smelled a rat and looked properly suspicious, his keen old mind racing along on the theory that no one ever gave away anything valuable. Suddenly he grinned so expansively that a generous stream of tobacco juice rolled down his sharp chin.

"Us three ag'in' that gang," he mused. "Huh! Fair enough, *I* says. Hank an' *me* can lick 'em by ourselves. *Can't* we, Hank?"

"Shore!" promptly answered the other weather-beaten old rascal. "We shore kin, Sinful!"

Tex smiled at the cheerful old reprobates, bound closer together now than ever they had been before. "I ought to dump th' pair of you in th' new jail," he said, "though it shore wouldn't get no benefit from it. Yo're a pair of land pirates an' you both ought to be hung from th' yardarm of some cottonwood tree. Hold out yore hands till I turn you loose. You two youngsters want to keep th' bargain, or I *will* hang you!"

"Glad to git shet of them cuffs," growled Sinful. "Hank takes sich long steps an' walks sideways, th' old fool. We'll play square, *won't* we, Hank? There; he said so, too. We allus has felt kind of friendly to Blascom, *ain't* we, Hank? Shore we has. An' he needs us to keep our eyes on them blasted claim jumpers. 'Sides, he's a friend of yourn, Marshal: an' we ain't forgettin' them few dollars we won from you t'other night—*are* we, Hank?" His shrewd old eyes baffled Tex's attempt to read just what he thought about the poker game.

"We ain't!" emphatically replied Hank, spitting copiously and vehemently. "We'll make these claim jumpers herd close to home; yes, sir, by glory!" He paused a moment and leaned nearer to his companion's ear. "*Won't* we, Sinful?" he suddenly shouted.

"Who you yowlin' at that way?" blazed Sinful, and then his eyes popped wide open in frank surprise. "Cussed if th' doc ain't got th' fever, too!" he ejaculated. "Here he comes up th' crick! Beats all how news does spread! An', great Jerus'lam: if he ain't as sober as a watched Puritan!"

Nodding right and left Doctor Horn rode slowly among the busy claim jumpers and drew rein in front of Tex and his companions.

"How do you do, gentlemen?" he said, smiling. "I see you're quite busy, Marshal, which seems to be a habit of yours. I happened to have a patient out this way, down on the lower fork, and while I was in his vicinity I thought I would drop in and compliment Blascom for his care of Jake. While the efficient treatment he first received undoubtedly saved his life, Blascom's nursing comes in for well-earned praise. He is still a sick man, although out of danger. I hope you will disregard our former conversation, so far as my part of it is concerned, Marshal. Good day to you all," and wheeling, he rode up a break in the creek bank and slowly became lost to sight among the bowlders and timber.

Sinful had watched both men carefully while the doctor spoke, and now he covertly glanced at the marshal, who was gazing after the departing physician. Then he looked at Blascom, and from him to his own, disreputable partner.

"Come on, Hank," he said. "If any of these gold thieves start swappin' claims, we'll play 'em a smart tune for 'em to dance to. There's shore been a-plenty of lives saved on this crick plumb recent—our own, mebby, among 'em. An' who do you reckon yo're a-starin' at?"

"You, you pore ol' fool!" retorted Hank. He blew out a bleached cud, rammed in a fresh one, nodded at Blascom and the contemplative marshal, and followed his impatient partner toward their packs and guns.

Tex slowly turned and looked after them. "Hey, Sinful!" he called. "You still makin' coffee in old tin cans? If you are, you want to watch 'em close on account of sand gettin' in 'em!"

Sinful nudged his companion, stopped, scratched his head, and then grinned.

"Don't have to use 'em *now*. We got all our traps along, an' th' old coffeepot is with 'em, kivver an' all. Anyways, *we* don't mind a little sand once in awhile— *do* we, Hank?"

"No, sir, by glory!" cried Hank. "Not no more, we don't, a-tall!"

CHAPTER XVIII

"Here Lies the Road to Rome!"

A FEW nights later Tex awakened to feel his little lean-to shaking until he feared it would collapse. A deafening roar on the roof made an inferno of noise, the great hailstones crashing and rolling. Flash after flash of vivid lightning seemed wrapped in the volleying crashes of the thunder. A sudden shift in the hurricane-like wind drove a white broadside against his front windows, both panes of glass seeming spontaneously to disintegrate. Another gust overturned a freight wagon in the road before the office and tore its tarpaulin cover from it as though it were tied on with strings, whisking it out of sight through the incessant lightning flashes like the instant passing of some huge ghost. The teamster, who saw no reason to pay for hotel beds while he had the wagon to sleep in, went rolling up the slatted framework and down again, bounced to his knees, and crawled frantically free, beaten by the streaking hail and buffeted by the shrieking wind. He was blown solidly against the lean-to, almost constantly in the marshal's sight because of the continuous illumination. Groping along the wall, he reached the shattered window and, desperate for shelter, promptly dived through it and rolled across the room.

Tex laughed, the sound of it lost to his own ears. "Yo're welcome, stranger!" he yelled. "But I'm sayin' yo're some precipitate! Better gimme a hand to stop up' that window, or she'll blow out th' walls and lift off th' roof. Grab this table an' we'll up-end it ag'in th' openin'. I'll prop it with th' benches from th' jail. That's right. Ready? Up she goes."

After no mean struggle the window was closed enough to give protection against the raging wind, the two benches holding it securely. Then Tex struck a match and lit both of his lamps.

"We don't hardly need any light, but this is a lot steadier," he shouted, turning to look at his guest. His eyes opened wide and he stared unbelievingly. "Good Lord, man! You look like a slaughter-house! Here, lemme look you over!"

The teamster, cut, bruised, and streaked with blood, held up his hand in quick protest, shouting his reply. " 'Taint nothin' but th' wallerin' I did when th' wagon turned over, an' th' beatin' from th' hail. I've seen it worse than this, friend. These stones are only big as hens' aigs, but I've seen 'em large as goose aigs, an' lost three yoke of oxen from 'em. I was freightin' in a load of supplies for a surveyin' party, down on th' old Dry Route, southwest of th' Caches. One ox was killed, his yokemate pounded senseless, an' th' others couldn't stand th' strain an' lit out. I never saw 'em again. I was under th' wagon when they left, which didn't turn over till th' hail changed into rain, an' I wouldn't 'a' poked out my head for all th' oxen in th' country. This here's a little better than a fair prairie hail storm. Gosh," he said, grinning, as he glanced at the badge on his companion's vest. "I got plenty of nerve, all right, bustin' into th' marshal's office! Ain't got any likker, have you?"

Tex handed him a full bottle and packed his pipe. The deafening crashing of the hailstones grew less and less, a softer roar taking its place as the rain poured down in seemingly solid sheets. The great violence of the wind was gone and the lightning flashed farther and farther away.

"Feel better now," said the teamster, passing the bottle to his host and taking out his pipe. He accepted the marshal's sack of tobacco and leaned back, puffing contentedly. "Sounds a lot better, now. I'd rather drowned than be beat to death, any time. There won't be a trail left tomorrow an' not a crick, ravine, or ditch fordable. Some of 'em with sand bottoms will be dangerous for three or four days. I once saw th' Pawnee rise so quick that it was fetlock deep when I started in, an' wagon-box deep before I could get across—an' a hull lot wider, too, I'm tellin' you. An' yet some fools still camp in dried crick beds!"

"That's just what I been thinkin' about," said the marshal, a look of worry on his face. "Out on Buffalo Crick there's near two dozen miners with claims staked out on th' dried bed. It shore would be terrible if this caught 'em asleep!"

"Don't you worry, Marshal," reassured his guest, laughingly. "Them fellers may have claims in a crick bed, but they don't sleep on 'em. They know too much!"

Tex related what a hail storm had done to a trail herd one night years before, and so they talked, reminiscence following reminiscence, until dawn broke, dull and watery, and they started for the hotel, to rout out the cook for hot coffee and an early breakfast.

All day it rained, but with none of the fury of the darker hours, and for the next ten days it continued intermittently. There was no special news from Buffalo Creek except that it had changed its bed in several places, and that two miners had been forced to swim for their lives. It was noteworthy, however, that the prospectors of the country roundabout began to spend dust with reckless carelessness. The hotel was well patronized during the day, and the nights were times of great hilarity. Drink flowed like water and old quarrels, fed by fresh fuel, added their share of turbulence to the new ones.

Sleeping late in the mornings, the marshal was on his feet until nearly every dawn, stopping brawls, deciding dangerous contentions, and once or twice resorting to stern measures. The little jail at one time was too full for further prisoners and had forced him to resort to fines, which brought his impartiality and honesty into question. He had been forced to wound two men and had been shot at from cover, all on one night. He grew more taciturn, grimmer, colder, wishing to avoid a killing, but fearing that it must come or the town would turn into a drunken riot. Then came the climax to the constantly growing lawlessness.

Busy in repairing washouts along the railroad and strengthening the three little bridges across the creeks of his section of track, Murphy and Costigan, reinforced by half a dozen other section-hands from points east, who had rolled into town on their own hand car, had scarcely seen the town for more than a week when they came in, late one Saturday afternoon. The extra hands were bedded at the toolshed and at Murphy's box car, and took their meals at Costigan's, whose thrifty wife was glad of the extra work for the little money it would bring her. Well knowing the feeling of the Middle West of that time against his race, the section-boss cautioned his crew to avoid the town as much as they could; but rough men are rough men, and wild blades are wild. Knowing the wisdom in the warning did not make it sit any easier on them, added to which was the chafing under the restraint and the galling sense of injustice.

Sunday morning found them quiet; but Sunday noon

found them restless and resentful. The lively noise of the town called invitingly across the right-of-way and one of them, despite orders, departed to get a bottle of liquor. He drew hostile glances as he made his way to the bar in the saloon facing the station, but bought what he wanted and went out with it entirely unmolested. The news he brought back was pleasing and reassuring and discounted the weight of the section-boss' admonitions, and later, when the bottle had been tipped in vain and thirsts had only been encouraged by the sops given them, some wilder soul among the crowd arose and announced that he was going to paint the town. There was no argument, no holding back, and the half-dozen, laughing and singing, sallied forth to frolic or fight as Fate decreed.

The first saloon they entered served them and let them depart unharmed and without insult, raising their spirits and edging their determination to enjoy what pleasures the town might have for them. They were as good as any men in town, and they knew it, which was right and proper; but soon it did not satisfy them to know it: they must tell everyone they met. This, also, was right and proper, although hardly wise; but in the telling there swiftly crept a fighting tone, a fighting mood, a fighting look, and fighting words; yet they were behaving not one whit different from the way gangs of miners had behaved since the town was built. The difference was sharp and sufficient: The miners had been in the town of their friends; the section-gang was in the town of its enemies.

The half-dozen entered the hotel barroom, jostled and elbowed, jostling and elbowing in return, their tempers smoldering and ready to burst into flames. Calling for whiskey at the bar they drank it avidly and turned to look over the room, where all sorts and conditions of rough men and ready fighters were frowningly watching them. The frowns grew deeper, and here and there a gibe or veiled insult arose above the general noise. The gibes became more bitter, the insults less veiled, and finally a huge miner, belted and armed, stood up and shouted for silence. Sensing trouble the crowd obeyed him, waiting with savage eagerness to hear what he would say, to see what he would do.

"I'm goin' to tell you a story," he cried, and forthwith made good his promise. It was not a parlor story by any stretch of imagination, and it ended with St. Peter slamming shut the gates of heaven as he repeated one of the then popular slogans of the country along the roadbeds, "No Irish need apply." It was not couched in language that St. Peter would use, and suitable epithets of the teller's own gave added weight to the insult of the tale. Still swearing the miner sat down, an ugly leer on his face, while shouts, laughter, catcalls, and curses answered from every part of the room.

"Run 'em out of town!" came a shout, which swiftly became a universal demand.

The track-layer nearest the door, a burly, red-haired, red-faced fighting man, leaped swiftly to the miner's table, kicked the half-drawn gun from his hand, and went to the floor with him. "St. Peter will open no doors to th' like av ye!" he shouted. "I'm sendin' ye to h—l, instead!"

The bartender, fearing pistol work, whipped his own over the counter and yelled his warning and his demand for fair play. "I'll drop th' man that draws! Let 'em have it out, man to man!"

This suited the crowd as an appetizer for what was to follow, and chairs and tables crashed as it surged forward to better see the fight, the five section-hands their broad backs against the bar, forming one side of the pushing, heaving ring, their faces set, their huge fists clenched, in spirit taking and giving the flailing blows of the rolling combatants, so intent, so lost in the struggle that consciousness of their own danger gradually faded from their minds. They had faith in their champion and were with him, heart and soul.

The miner could fight like the graduate he was of the merciless, ultra-brutal rough-and-tumble of the long frontier, biting, kneeing, gouging, throttling as opportunity offered, and he was rapidly gaining the advantage over his cleaner-fighting opponent until, breaking a throat hold, barely escaping the fingers thrust at his eyes and a wolflike snap of murderous jaws, the Irishman broke free, and staggered to his feet to make a fight which best suited him. Great gasps of relief broke from his tense friends, their low words of advice and encouragement coming from between set teeth.

"Steady, Mac, an' time 'em!" whispered his nearest friend. "He fights like a beast—lick him like th' man ye are. He's as open as a book!"

Panting, his breath whistling through his teeth, the miner scrambled to his feet, needlessly fearing a kick as he arose, and rushed, his great arms flaying before him as he tore in. Met by a straight left that caught him on the jaw a little wide of the point aimed at, he rocked back on his heels, his knees buckling, and his arms wildly waving to keep his balance. Before he could recover and set himself, a right flashed in against his chest and drove him back against the ring of men behind him. Gasping, he bent over and threw himself at his enemy's thighs, missing the hold by a hair. The Irishman retreated two swift steps and waited until his opponent had leaped up and then, feinting with his left at the swelling jaw, he swung his right shoulder behind a stiffening right arm and landed clean and squarely above the brass buckle of the cartridge belt. The crash shook the building, for the miner's feet came up as he was hurled backward and he struck the floor in a bunched heap.

The bruised and bleeding victor, filling his lungs with great gulps of foul air, started backing toward the bar to regain his breath among his friends, but he staggered sidewise on his course, coming too close to the first line of the aroused crowd and one of them leaped on him, the impact toppling him over, just as the five friends charged. Chaos reigned. Shouts, curses, the stamping of feet, bellows of rage and pain filled the dusty air with clamor as the crowd surged backward and forward, the storm center ever nearing the door. The valiant half-dozen, profiting by experience, resisted all efforts to separate them, keeping in a compact group, shoulder to shoulder, with their rapidly recovering champion in their middle. They had passed the end of the bar, which had been a sturdy bulwark against their complete encircling, and the crowd was pouring in to attack from that once-protected side when a hatless figure leaped through the deserted rear door, bounded onto the long bar without changing his stride, dashed along it and jumped, feet first straight at the heads bobbing nearest to the stout-hearted six. It was Costigan who, not finding Murphy, was acting on his own initiative and according to his lights. In his hand was a broken mattock handle and under its raining blows an opening rapidly grew in the crowd. Had he been given arm room, where his full strength could have been used, Boot Hill would have reaped a harvest. Audacity, that Audacity which is the fairest child of Courage, the total unexpectedness of his hurtling, spectacular attack won more for him and his friends than the deadly effectiveness of the hickory handle. The astonished crowd drew back in momentary confusion and Costigan, cursing at the top of his panting lungs, shoved the nearly exhausted handful through the door and into the street. As the last man staggered through and pitched to the ground, the club wielder leaped to the door, barring it with his body. He was about to tell the crowd what he thought of it when the situation changed again.

A hand clutched his shirt collar and yanked him back and he went striking with the club as he sprawled beside a battered friend. The change had been so sudden and the crowd just recovering from its surprise at

Costigan's flaying attack that it looked like magic. One instant a red-shirted Irishman, his clothing torn into shreds, lovingly balancing his favorite weapon; the next, a calm, cold-faced, blue-shirted, leather-chapped gunman, bending eagerly forward behind the pair of out-thrust Colts, his thumbs holding back swift death in each hand.

"The devil!" growled a miner.

"Aye!" snapped Tex. "An' I'll find work for idle hands to do! *Why do you stop and turn away? Here lies th' road to Rome!*" he laughed, exultantly, sneeringly, insultingly; and never had they heard a laugh so deadly. It chilled where words might have inflamed. There was not a man who did not shrink instinctively, for before him stood a killer if ever he had seen one.

"I only got twelve handy—which dozen of you want to open th' way for th' rest?" asked the marshal. His quick eye caught a furtive movement in the crowd and the roar of his flaming Colt jarred the room. The offender pitched forward before the paralyzed front line, rocking to and fro in his pain. "Th' next man dies!" snapped the marshal, his deadly intent fully revealed by his face.

The crowd gazed at impersonal Death, balanced in the two firm hands. They saw no hesitancy reflected between the narrowed lids of those calculating eyes, no qualifying expression on that granite face; and they were standing where Bud Haines had stood, facing the man he had faced. A restless surge set the mass milling, those behind pushing those in front, those in front frantically pushing back those behind. Tense and dangerous as the situation was, a verse of an immortal fighting poem leaped to the marshal's mind and a sneering smile flashed over his face. *Was none who would be foremost to lead such dire attack; but those behind cried "Forward!" And those before cried "Back!"* He seemed to tense even more, like some huge, deadly spider about to spring, and his clearly enunciated warning, low as it was spoken, reached the ears of every man in the room. "Go back to yore tables, like you was before."

The surge grew and spread, split following split, until the dragging rearguard sullenly followed its companions. The dynamic figure in the door slowly forsook its crouch, arising to full height. The left-hand gun grudgingly slid into its sheath, reluctantly followed by its more deadly mate. Casting a final, contemptuous look at the embarrassed crowd, each unit of it singled out in turn and silently challenged, the marshal shoved his hands into his pockets, turned his back on them with insolent deliberation and stepped to the street, where a bloody, battered group of seven had waited to back him up if it should be needed.

"Yer a man after me own—" began Costigan thickly between swollen lips, but he was cut short.

"That'll keep. Take these fellers back where they belong, an' *keep* 'em there," snapped Tex, the fighting fire still blazing in his soul. He watched them depart, proud of every one of them; and when they had reached the station he wheeled and went back into the hotel, had a slowly sipped drink, nodded to his acquaintances as though nothing out of the ordinary had occurred, and then sauntered out again without a backward glance, turning to go to the station.

When he reached the building he stopped and looked toward the toolshed where Murphy, just back from a run of inspection up the line, and Costigan, had turned the corner of the shed and stopped to renew their argument, which must have been warm and personal, judging from their motions. Finally Costigan, looking for all the world like a scarecrow, hitched up what remained of his trousers, squared his shoulders, and limped determinedly toward his little cottage, glancing neither to the right nor to the left. Murphy, hands on hips, gazed after him, nodded his head sharply, and was about to enter the shed when he caught sight of the motionless two-gun man. Snapping his fingers in sudden decision, he started toward his capable friend, his frame of mind plainly shown by the way his stride easily took two ties at once.

"God loves th' Irish, or 'twould be diggin' graves we'd now be doin'," he said. "An' me away! But they'll be mindin' their P's an' Q's after this. I was goin' to skin Costigan, but how could I after I learned what he did? It ain't th' first time he's tied my hands by th' quality av his fightin'. But 'twas well ye took cards, an' 'twas well ye played 'em, Tex."

"I have due respect for Costigan, but if he leaves th' railroad property he'll lose it quick," replied the marshal. "I turned that mob into a mop, but there's no tellin' what might happen one of these nights. Tim, I wish his family was out of town. It's no place for wimmin an' children these days, not with ten marshals. I can't be everywhere at once, an' I'm watchin' one house now more than I ought to."

"They're leavin' on tomorry's train east," said Murphy, breathing a sigh of relief. "I've Mike's word for it, an' if he can't get 'em to go without him, then he's goin' with 'em, superintendent or no superintendent! I'm sorry that it's my fault that ye had th' trouble, Tex; I should 'a' stayed close to them d—d fools."

"There's no harm done, Tim, as it turned out. It was comin' to a show-down, gettin' nearer an' nearer every day. Now that it's over th' town will be quiet for a day or two. I know of marshals who were paid from eight hundred to a thousand dollars a month—I'm admittin' that I've earned my hundred in just about five minutes today. For about fifteen seconds th' job was worth a hundred dollars a second—it was a close call."

"But look at th' honor av it," chuckled Murphy. "It's marshal av Windsor ye are, Tex—an' ye have yer Tower, as well!"

Tex laughed, glanced over the straggling town from

Costigan's cottage to another at the other end of the street. "I'm not complainin'. I'm only contrastin' and showin' that Williams didn't pull any wool over my eyes when he offered me my princely salary. I agreed to it, and I'm paid enough, under th' circumstances."

"Aye," said Murphy, following his friend's glance, a sudden smile banishing his anxious frown. "Money ain't everythin'. Perhaps yo're not paid much now, Tex—but later, who can tell?"

CHAPTER XIX

A Lecture Wasted

THAT EVENING Tex had a caller in the person of Henry Williams, who seemed to be carrying quite a load of suspicion and responsibility. He nodded sourly, and nonchalantly seated himself on a chair at the other side of the door. His troubled mind was not hidden from the marshal, who could read surface indications of a psychological nature as well as any man in the West. No small part of his poker skill was built upon that ability. Should he lead his visitor by easy and natural stages to unburden himself; make a hearty, blunt opening, or make him blurt out his thoughts and go on the defensive at once? Having anything but respect and liking for the vicious nephew, he determined to make him as uncomfortable as possible. So he paid him the courtesy of a glance and resumed his apparently deep cogitations.

Henry waited for a few minutes, studying the ground and the front of his uncle's store and then coughed impatiently.

" 'Tis that," responded Tex abstractedly; "but hot, an' close. I was thinkin'," he said, definitely.

Henry looked up inquiringly: "Yes?"

"Yes," said the marshal gravely. "I was." His tone repulsed any comment and he kept on thinking from where he had left off.

Henry shifted on the chair and recrossed his legs, one foot starting to swing gently to and fro. To put himself *en rapport* with his forbidding companion, he too, began thinking; or at least he simulated a thinker. The swinging foot stopped, jiggled up and down a few times, and began swinging more energetically. Soon he began drumming on the chair with the fingers of one hand. Presently he shifted his position again, recrossed his legs, grunted, and drummed alternately with the fingers of both hands. Then they drummed in unison, the nails of one set clicking with the rolling of the pads of the fingers of the other hand. Then he puckered his lips and began to whistle.

"Don't do that!" snapped Tex, and returned to his cogitations.

"What? Which?" asked Henry, starting.

"That!" exploded the marshal savagely and lapsed into intense concentration.

Henry's lips straightened and he looked down at the drumming fingers, and stopped them. Squirming on the chair, he uncrossed his legs and pushed them out before him, intently regarding the two rounded groves in the dust made by his high heels. Then he glanced covertly at his frowning companion, cleared his throat tentatively, and became quiet as the frown changed into a scowl.

The marshal thought that his visitor must have something important on his mind, something needing tact and velvety handling. Otherwise he would have become discouraged by this time and left. Was it about Jane? That would be the natural supposition, but he slowly abandoned it. Henry never had shown any timidity when speaking about her. It must be something concerning the riot in the hotel.

"I say it can't be nothin' else!" fiercely muttered the marshal, his chair dropping solidly to all fours as he rammed a fist into an open palm. "No, sir! It *can't*!" He glared at his companion. "What did you say?"

"Huh?" demanded Henry, his chair also dropping to all fours because of the impetus it had received from his sudden start. "What for?" he asked inanely.

"What for what?" growled Tex accusingly. "Who said: 'What for'?"

"I did: I just wanted to know," hastily explained Henry in frank amity.

"That's what you said!" retorted Tex, leaning tensely toward him; "but what did you *mean*?" he demanded.

"What you talkin' about?" queried Henry, truly and sincerely wondering.

"Don't you try to fool me!" warned Tex. "Don't pretend you don't know! An' let me tell you this. You are wrong, like th' ministers an' all th' rest of th' theologians. That's th' truest hypothesis man ever postulated. It proves itself, I tell you! From th' diffused, homogeneous, gaseous state, whirlin' because of molecular attraction, into a constantly more compact, matter state, constantly becomin' more heterogeneous as pressure varies an' causes a variable temperature of th' mass. Integration an' heterogeneity! From th' cold of th' diffused gases to th' terrific heat generated by their pressure toward th' common center of attraction. Can't you see it, man?"

Henry's mouth remained open and inarticulate.

"You won't answer, like all th' rest!" accused Tex. "An' what heat! One huge molten ball, changing th' force of th' planets nearest, shifting th' universal balance to new adjustments. 'Equilibrium!' demands Nature. An' so th' struggle goes on, ever tryin' to gain it, an' allus makin' new equilibriums necessary, like a dog chasin' a flea on th' end of his spine. Six days an' a breathin' space!" he jeered. "Six trillion years, more likely, an' no time for breathin' spaces! What you got to say to that, hey? Answer me this: What form of force does th' integration postulate? Centrifugal? Hah!" he cried. "You thought you had me there, didn't you? No, sir; not centrifugal—centripetal! Integration—centripetal! Gravity proves it. Centrifugal is th' destroyer, th' maker of satellites—not th' builder! Bah!" he grunted. "You can't disprove a word of it! Try it—just try it!"

Henry shook his head slowly, drew a deep breath and sought a more comfortable position. "These here chairs are hard, ain't they?" he remarked, feeling that he had to say something. Surely it was safe to say that.

Tex leaped to his feet and scowled down at him. "Evadin', are you?" he demanded. Then his voice changed and he placed a kindly hand on his companion's shoulder. "There ain't no use tryin' to refute it, Hennery," he said. "It can't be done—no, sir—it can't be done. Don't you ever argue with me again about this, Hennery—it only leads us nowhere. Was it Archimedes who said he could move th' earth if he only had some place to stand? He wasn't goin' to try to lift himself by his boot straps, was he, th' old fox? That's th' trouble, Hennery: after all is said we still got to find some place to stand." He glanced over Henry's head to see Doctor Horn smiling at him and he wondered how much of his heavy lecture the physician had heard. Had he expected an educated man to be an auditor he would have been more careful. "That was th' greatest hypothesis of all—the hypothesis of Laplace—it answered th' supposedly unanswerable. Science was no longer on th' defensive, Hennery," he summed up for the newcomer's benefit.

"Truly said!" beamed the doctor, getting a little excited. "In proof of its mechanical possibility Doctor Plateau demonstrated, with whirling water, that it was not a possibility, but a fact. The nebular hypothesis is more and more accepted as time goes on, by all thinking men who have no personal reasons strong enough to make them oppose it." He clapped the stunned Henry on the back. "Trot out your refutations and the marshal and I will knock them off their pins! Bring on your theologians, your special-creation adherents, and we'll pulverize them under the pestle of cold reason in the mortar of truth! But I never thought you were interested in such beautiful abstractions, Henry; I never dreamed that inductive and deductive reasoning, confined to purely scientific questions appealed to you. What needless loneliness I have suffered; what opportunities I have missed; what a dearth of intellectual exercise, and all because I took for granted that no one in this town was competent to discuss either side of such subjects. But he's got you with Laplace, Henry; got you hard and fast, if you hold to the tenets of special creation. Now that there are two of us against you, I'll warrant you a rough passage, my friend. 'Come, let's e'en at it!' We'll give you the floor, Henry—and here's where I really enjoy myself for the first time in three weary, dreary years. We'll rout your generalities with specific facts; we'll refute your ambiguities with precisions; we'll destroy your mythological conceptions with rational conceptions; your symbolical conceptions with actual conceptions; your foundation of faith by showing the genesis of that faith—couch your lance, but look to yourself, for you see before your ill-sorted array a Roman legion—short swords and a flexible line. Its centurions are geology, physics, chemistry, biology, astronomy, and mathematics. Nothing taken for granted there! No pious hopes, but solid facts, proved and reproved. Come on, Henry—proceed to your Waterloo! Special creation indeed! Comparative anatomy, single-handed, will prove it false!"

"My G—d!" muttered Henry, forgetting his mission entirely. His head whirled, his feet were slipping so rapidly that he did not know where he was going. He stared, open-mouthed at Doctor Horn, dumbly at the marshal, got up, sat down, and then slumped back against his chair, helpless, hopeless, fearing the worst. Over his head hurled words he thought to be foreign, as his companions, having annihilated him, were performing evolutions and exercises of their verbal arms for the sheer joy of it. Finally, despairing of the lecture ever ending, he arose to escape, but was pushed back again by the excited, exultant doctor. Daylight faded, twilight passed, and it was not until darkness descended that the doctor, finding no opposition, but hearty accord instead, tired of the sound of his own voice and that of the marshal, and after profuse expressions of friendship and pleasure, departed, his head high, his shoulders squared, and his tread firm and militant.

Henry's sigh of relief sounded like the exhaust of an engine and he shifted again on the chair and tried to collect his scattered senses. Before he could get started the marshal sent him off on a new track, and his unspoken queries remained unspoken for another period.

"Seen Miss Saunders yet?" asked Tex, struggling hard to conceal his laughter.

Henry shook his head. "No; but I ain't goin' to wait much longer. I don't see no signs of her weakenin', an' that C Bar puncher is gittin' too cussed common around her house. For a peso I'd toss him in th' discard. I reckon yore way ain't no good with her, Marshal. I got to do somethin'—got to get some action."

"I know about how you feel," sympathized Tex. "I know how hard it is to set quiet an' wait in a thing like this, Hennery, even if action does lose th' game. Who was it you aimed to have perform th' ceremony?"

"Oh, there's a pilot down to Willow—one of them roamin' preachers that reckons he's found a place where he can stick. He'll come up here if th' pay's big enough, an' if I want any preacher. He'll only have to stay over one night to git a train back ag'in. Anyhow, if

we has to wait a day or two it won't make much difference, as long as we're goin' to git hitched afterward."

Tex closed his eyes and waited to get a good hold on
himself before replying. "He'll come for Gus, all right,"
he said. "Think you can hold out a few days more—just
to see if my way will work? It'll be better, all around, if
you do. Where was you aimin' to buy them presents
for her?"

"Kansas City or St. Louie—reckon St. Louie will be
better. Gus gets most of his supplies from there. You
still thinkin' stockin's is th' proper idea?"

Tex cogitated a moment. "No; they're a little embar-
rassin': better try gloves. I'll find out th' size from her
brother. Nice, long white gloves for th' weddin'—an'
mebby a nice shawl to go with 'em—Cashmere, with a
long fringe. They're better than stockin's. You send for
'em an' wait till they come before you go around. You
shouldn't go empty-handed on a visit like that. An' you
want th' minister with you when you go after her—
you can leave him outside till he's needed. Folks'll talk,
an' make trouble for you later. There's tight rules for
weddin's; very tight rules. You don't want nobody pokin'
their fingers at yore wife, Hennery. It'll shore mean a
killin', some day."

"I ain't so cussed anxious to git married," growled
Henry. "It's hard to git loose ag'in—but I reckon mebby
I better go through with it."

"I—reckon—you—had," whispered Tex, his vision
clouding for a moment. He grew strangely quiet, as
though he had been mesmerized.

"A man can allus light out if he gits tired of it," reflected Henry complacently.

The marshal arose and paced up and down, thankful
for the darkness, which hid the look of murder graven
on his face. "Yes," he acquiesced; "a man—allus—
can—do—that." This conversation was torturing him.
Anything would be a relief, and he threw away the

results of all his former talking. "What was on your mind when you come down to see me today?"

"Oh!" exclaimed his companion a little nervously. "I plumb forgot all about it. You see," he hesitated, shifting again on the chair, "well, it's like this. Us boys admires th' way you handled things in th' hotel this afternoon, but somebody might 'a' been killed. 'Tain't fair to let a passel of Irish run this town—an' they started th' fight, anyhow. Th' big Mick kicked Jordan's gun out of his hand an' jumped on him. Then th' others piled in, an' th' show begun. We sort of been thinkin' that th' marshal ought to back up his town ag'in' them foreigners. Gus is mad about it—an' he's bad when he gits his back up. He thinks we ought to go down to th' railroad an' run them Micks out of town on some sharp rails, beatin' 'em up first so they won't come back. Th' boys kinda cotton to that idea. They're gettin' restless an' hard to hold. I thought I'd find out what side yo're on."

Tex stopped his pacing, alert as a panther. "I ain't on no side but law an' order," he slowly replied. "I told that section-gang to stay on th' right-of-way. They're leavin' town early tomorrow mornin', an' may not come back. A mob's a bad thing, Hennery: there's no tellin' where it'll stop. Most of 'em will be full of likker, an' a drunken mob likes bright fires. Let 'em fire one shack an' th' whole town will go: hotel, Mecca, an' all. It's yore best play to hold 'em down, or you an' yore uncle will shore lose a lot of money. Th' right-of-way is th' dead line: I'll hold it ag'in' either side as long as I can pull a trigger. You hold 'em back, Hennery; an' if you can't, don't you get out in th' front line—stay well behind!"

"Mob's do get excited," conceded Henry, thoughtfully. "Reckon I'll go see what Gus thinks about it. See you later."

Tex watched him walk away, silhouetted against the faintly illuminated store windows, and as the door slammed behind him the marshal shifted his heavy belts and went slowly up the street and into the hotel, where he received a cold welcome. Seeing that the room was fairly well crowded, accounting for most of the men in town and all of the afternoon crowd, he sat in a corner from where he could see both doors and everything going on.

In a few minutes Gus Williams and Henry entered and began mixing with the crowd, which steadily grew more quiet, but more sullen, like some wild beast held back from its prey. Henry sat at one table, surrounded by his closest friends, while his uncle held court at another. The nephew was drinking steadily and his glances at the quiet marshal became more and more suspicious. Around midnight, the temper of the crowd suiting him, Tex arose and went down the street toward his office, passed around it and circled back over the uneven plain, silently reaching the railroad near the box car.

Murphy quietly crept out of his bunk, gun in hand, and slipped to the door, pressing his ear against it. Again the drumming of the fingers sounded, but after what had occurred earlier in the day he wanted more than a tapping before he opened the door or betrayed his presence in the car. Soon he heard his name softly called and recognized the voice. As quietly as he could, he slid back the door and peered into the caller's face from behind a leveled gun.

"Don't let that go off," chuckled Tex, stepping inside. "Close th' door, Tim."

Murphy obeyed and felt his way to his visitor and they held a conversation which lasted for an hour. Tex's plans of action in certain contingencies were more than acceptable to the section-boss and he went over them until he was letter-perfect. To every question he gave an answer pleasing to the marshal and when the latter left to go up and guard the toolshed and its inmates he felt more genuine relief than he had known since he had become actively engaged in the town's activities. Things were rapidly approaching a crisis and the knowledge had filled him with dread; now let it come—he was ready to meet it.

Silently he chose a position against the railroad embankment close to the toolshed and here he remained until dawn. Murphy and Costigan passed him in the darkness on a nearly silent hand car, going west, but did not see him; and he did not know that they had returned until the sky paled. For some time he had heard a bustling in the building, and just as he was ready to leave he saw the section-gang roll out their own hand car and go rumbling up the line toward Scrub Oak.

CHAPTER XX

Plans Awry

FOR THE next few days a tense equilibrium was maintained in the town, the marshal, grim, alert, and practically ostracized by nine-tenths of the population. He could feel the veiled hostility whenever he went up and down the street, and silence fell abruptly on groups of men conversing here and there whenever he was seen approaching. Hostile glances, sullen faces, shrugging shoulders greeted him on every side, and he felt more relieved than ever when he reviewed his arrangements with the section-boss.

Henry Williams was growing openly suspicious of him, impatiently awaiting the arrival of the presents from St. Louis, which he had ordered through Jerry's telegraph key, and he was drinking more and more and keeping more and more to himself, his only company being two men whom Tex had been watching since the death of Bud Haines. The marshal felt that with the coming of the presents trouble would begin, and he had asked Jerry to keep a watch for them, and let him know the moment they arrived. Fate tricked him here, for when they did come they were packed in a large consignment of goods for Gus Williams, and since he regularly was receiving shipments there was nothing to indicate to the station agent that Henry's gifts had passed through his hands.

Henry's suspicions of the marshal were cumulative rather than sudden. Never very confident about what Tex really thought and what he might do, certain vague memories of looks and of ambiguous words and actions recurred to the nephew. He was beginning to believe that the marshal would shoot him down like a dog if he pressed the issue as he intended to press it in regard to Jane Saunders, and he was determined that Tex should have no opportunity to go to her defense. Several methods of eliminating the disturbing marshal presented themselves to the coyote-cunning mind of the would-be lover. He could be shot from cover as he moved about in his flimsy office, or as he slept. He could walk into a rifle bullet as he opened his door some morning, or he could be decoyed up to Blascom's while Henry's plans went through. This last would taste sweeter in the public mouth than a coldly planned murder, but on the other hand the return of the marshal might end in cyclonic action. There was no doubt about Tex's feelings in regard to killing when he felt it to be necessary or justified. He would kill with no more compunction than a wolf would show. Then from the mutterings of rebellion and the sullen looks of discontent among the hotel habitues a plan leaped into the nephew's mind. It solved every objectionable feature of the other schemes; and Henry forthwith went to work.

The nephew was no occult mystery to a man like the marshal, who almost could see the mental wheels turning in any man like him. Tex was preparing for eventualities and part of the preparation was the buying of a pint flask of whiskey from Carney—a bottle locally regarded as pocket-size. When night fell he emptied into the liquor a carefully computed amount of chloral hydrate, recorked it, shook it well, and placed it among sundry odds and ends in a corner of the office, where it would be overlooked by any thirsty caller, whose glance was certain to notice the bottle of whiskey in plain sight on a shelf. Against the consciousness of sixteen men that innocent-looking flask would tip the scales to its own side with an emphasis; and the marshal not only knew the proper dose for horses but also how to shove it down their throats with practiced ease and swiftness. Buck Peters had paid him no mean compliment when he had said that Tex could dose a horse more expertly than any man he ever had known. Having put all of his weapons in order he marked time, awaiting the pleasure of the enemy.

He did not have long to wait. To be specific he waited two days more, which interval brought time around to the last day on the calendar for that month, the day which railroad regulations proclaimed to be the occasion for making out sundry and numerous reports, a job that kept many a station agent writing and figuring most of the night. Having sense and imagination, the agent at Windsor did what he could of this work from day to day and as a consequence saved himself from a long, high-tension job at the last minute; but he did not have imagination enough to know that a packing-case of formidable dimensions which he had received that noon from the west-bound train and later saw hauled to the Mecca, held the watched-for gifts that Henry Williams would eagerly present to Jane.

Contemptuous of any interference that Jerry might make in a physical sense, Henry nevertheless preferred to have him absent when he made his determined attempt. The brother doubtless would have great influence on Jane by his protests, and that would necessitate drastic measures which only would make the matter worse. If Jerry were detained by force, injured, or killed to keep him from the house it would cause a great deal of unpleasantness, from a domestic standpoint, to run through the years to come. There was only one night a month when the agent remained away from his house for any length of time, and this must be the night for the action to be carried through.

The mob was being slowly, but surely, inflamed by the nephew and his two friends, its anger directed against Murphy and Costigan since the section-gang had not returned to town. The section-boss and his friend came in every night while they worked along Buffalo Creek, and were careful not to give any excuse for a hostile demonstration against them. They were even less comspicuous because they walked in instead of rolling home on the hand car. But on this last night of the month the whole crew, rebelliously disobeying orders, came in on their crowded hand car, much to Henry's poorly concealed delight, and to Tex's rage. Murphy had promised otherwise.

Here was oil for the flames Henry had set burning! Here was success with a capital letter! The mob now would surely attack, divert Jerry's attention, and perhaps rid the town of its official nuisance. He would act on the marshal's kindly warning, for he would not be in the front rank of the mob; in fact, he would not be with the mob at all. He had other work to do.

The sudden look of joyous expectation, so poorly disguised, on Henry's face acted on Tex like the warning whirr of an angry rattlesnake and he quietly cleaned and oiled his guns, broke out a fresh box of cartridges, and dumped them into his right-hand pocket. The remaining chloral-filled shells he slipped in the pocket of his chaps. Shaking up the flask of whiskey to make certain of the crystals being dissolved and the drug evenly distributed throughout the fluid, he hid it again and, seating himself in his favorite place, awaited the opening number.

Darkness had just closed down when Tommy loped in from the ranch and stopped to say a few careless, friendly words, but he never uttered them, for the marshal's instructions were snapping forth before the C Bar rider could open his mouth.

"This is no time for pleasantries!" said Tex in a voice low and tense. "Turn around, ride back a way, circle around th' town an' leave yore cayuse a couple of hundred yards from Murphy's box car. Tell him trouble's brewin' an' to look sharp. Then you head for her house, actin' as cautious, an' go up to it on foot, an' as secretly as you know how. Lay low, outside. Don't show yourself at all—a man in th' dark will be worth five in th' light tonight. Stay there no matter what you hear in town. If she should see you, on yore life don't let her think there's any danger—on yore life, Tommy! Mebby there ain't, but there's no tellin' what drunken beast will remember that there's a woman close at hand. You stay there till daylight, or till I relieve you. Get-a-goin'—an' good luck!"

Tommy carried out his orders, gave Murphy the warning, and was gone again before the big Irishman, seething with rage at his crew's disobedience, could say more than a few words. Murphy had been forced to construct a plan of his own, and he wished to get word of it to the marshal's ears. Tommy having left so quickly, he could not send it. Convincing himself that it was not really necessary for the marshal to be told of it, and savagely pleased by the surprise in store for him and every man in town, the section-boss went ahead on his own initiative. Going to the toolshed he went in, frowning at the thoroughly cowed and humbled crew, blew out the lamps and with hearty curses ordered the gang to put their car on the rails and to start east for the next town.

"Roll her softly, by hand, till ye get out av th' hearin' av this hell-town, an' then board her, an' put yore weight on th' handles," he commanded. "An' don't ye come back till I send for ye. Costigan an' me are plannin' work for ourselves an' will not go with ye. Lively, now—an' no back talk. A lot depends on yer doin' as yer told. One more order disobeyed an' I'll brain th' pack av ye with a crowbar. Ye've raised h—l enough this night. Now git out av here, an' mind what I've told ye!"

The orders quickly obeyed and the car quietly placed on the rails, the gang went into the night as silently as bootless feet would take them, pushing the well-greased car ahead of them, and as gently as though it were loaded with nitro-glycerin. When far enough away not to be heard by anyone in town, they put on their boots, climbed aboard, and sent their conveyance along at an ordinary rate of speed. They hated to desert their two countrymen, and began to talk about it. Finally they made up their minds that Murphy's orders, in view of their recent disobedience, were to be followed, and with hearty accord they sent the car rolling on again, the greater part of the grades in their favor, toward the next town. The distance was nothing to become excited about with six husky men at the handles to pump off the miles.

Up at the station a single light burned in the little office where Jerry worked at his reports. Outside the building in the darkness Murphy lay on his stomach in a tuft of weeds, a rifle in his hand, and a Colt beside him on the ground. Within easy reach of his right hand lay a coatful of rocks culled from the roadbed, no mean weapons against figures silhouetted by the lamp-lighted windows of the buildings facing the right-of-way; and close to them were half a dozen dynamite cartridges, their wicked black fuses capped and inserted. Tim Murphy, like Napoleon, put his trust in heavy artillery.

Costigan was nowhere to be seen. Down the track

lights shone under the cracks of the doors of the tool-shed and the box-car habitation of the section-boss, and one curtained window of Costigan's rented cottage glowed dully against the night. Crickets shrilled and locusts fiddled, and there were no signs of impending danger.

In the hotel the tables were filled with lowly conversing miners in groups, each man leaning far forward, elbows on the table, his shoulders nearly touching those on either side. Gus Williams and his closest friends had pulled two tables together and made a group larger than the others. Henry and his two now inseparable companions were at a table near the back door, talking earnestly with Jake, who by this time had recovered from his recent sickness. The Buffalo Creek miner was quieter and more thoughtful than he had been before Blascom had nearly killed him, and his mind for several days had been the battle ground of a fiercely fought struggle between contending emotions, which still raged, but in a lesser intensity. He listened without comment to what was being said to him, swayed first one way and then another. His last glass of liquor was untasted, which was something of no moment to Henry's whiskey-dulled mind. Finally Jake nodded, tossed off the drink with a gesture of quick determination, hitched up his cartridge belt and, forgetting his sombrero on the floor, arose and slipped quietly out of the door. As he left, another man, peremptorily waved into the vacated chair, also listened to instructions and also slipped out through the rear door. He set his course toward the right-of-way, whereas Jake had gone in the other direction, toward Carney's saloon and the marshal's office.

The last man stopped when even with the line of shacks facing the railroad, noted the dully glowing shade in Costigan's house, the yellow strips of light around the rough board shutters of the box car, and the broader yellow band under the toolshed door. Satisfied by his inspection he slipped back the way he had come and made his report to Henry.

Jake crept with infinite caution toward the marshal's office, but when nearly to it he paused as the battle in his mind raged with a sudden burst of fury. The marshal had humbled him in sight of his friends and acquaintances and had boasted of worse to follow if his victim forced the issue; the marshal had saved his life in the little hut on the lower fork, laboring all night with him. Doctor Horn had said so, and Blascom, playing nurse at the marshal's request, had endorsed the doctor.

Ahead of him, plain to his sight, was the marshal's side window, its flimsy curtain tightly drawn; and silhouetted against it were the hatted head and the shoulders of the man he had been sent to kill. Again he crept forward, the Colt gripped tightly in his right hand. Foot by foot he advanced, but stopping more frequently to argue with himself. A few yards more and the mark could not be missed. He, himself, was safe from any answering fire. A heavy curse rumbled in his throat and he stopped again. He fought fair, as far as he knew the meaning of the term in its generally accepted definition among men of his kind. He never had knifed or shot a man from behind, and he was not going to do it now, especially a man who had no reason to save his sotted life, but who had done so without pausing. Jake arose, jammed the gun back into its holster and walked briskly to the door of the flimsy little office, which he found locked against him. He knocked and listened, but heard nothing. Again he knocked and listened and still there was no answer.

"Marshal!" he called in a rasping, loud whisper. "Marshal! Git away from that d—d window: th' next man won't be one that owes you for his life. I'm goin' back to Buffaler Crick. Look out for yoreself!" and he made good his words, striding off into the dark.

Back of the hotel, lying prone behind a pile of bleached and warped lumber, the marshal watched the rear door. He saw Jake leave, recognizing the man in the light of the opening door by certain peculiarities of carriage and manner. He smiled grimly when the man turned toward the north, and he waited for the sound of the shot which would drill the window, the shade, and the old shirt hanging on the back of a chair. He wondered if the rolled-up blanket, fastened to the broken broom handle, which made the head and held Carney's old sombrero, would fall with the impact. Then the door opened again and the second man hurried out, turning to the south. He came back shortly, left the door open behind him and with his return Henry's voice rang out in an impassioned harangue. The hotel was coming to life. The stamp of heavy boots grew more continuous; loud voices became louder and more numerous, and shouts arose above the babel. The protesting voice of Gus Williams was heard less and less, finally drowned completely in the vengeful roar. Sudden noises in the street told of angry men pouring out of the front door, simultaneously with the exodus through the rear door. Oaths, curses, threats, and explosive bursts of laughter arose. One leathern-lunged miner was drunkenly singing at the top of his voice, to the air of *John Brown's Body*, a paraphrase worded to suit the present situation.

The marshal leaped to his feet, secure against discovery in the darkness, and sprinted on a parallel course for an opening between the row of buildings facing the right-of-way. His sober-minded directness and his lightness of foot let him easily outstrip the more aimless, leisurely progress of the maudlin gang, which preferred to hold to a common front instead of stringing out. Drunk as they were, they were sober enough to realize, if only vaguely, that a two-gun sharpshooter by all odds would be waiting for the advance guard. In fact, their enthusiasm was largely imitation. Henry's mind had not been keen enough to take into consideration such a thing as anticlimax; he had not realized that the psychological moment had passed and that in the interval of the several days, while the once white-hot iron of vengeful purpose still was hot, it had cooled to a point where its heat was hardly more than superficial. The once deadly purpose of the mob was gone, thanks to Gus Williams' efforts, the ensuing arguments, and the wholesome respect for the marshal's courage and the speed and accuracy of his two guns. Instead of a destroying flood, contemptuous of all else but the destruction of its victims, the mob had degenerated into a body of devilish mischief-makers, terrible if aroused by the taste of blood, but harmless and hesitant if the taste were denied it.

Tex, sensing something of this feeling, darted through the alleyway between the two buildings he had in mind, dashed across the open space paralleling the right-of-way, crossed the tracks, and slipped behind the toolshed to be better hidden from sight. Its silence surprised him, but one glance through a knot hole showed the lighted interior to be innocent of inmates. He forthwith sprinted to the box car and a warped crack in one of the barn-door shutters told him the same tale. A sudden grin came to his face: Murphy had done what he could to offset the return of his section-gang. He glanced at Costigan's house and its one lighted curtain, and at that instant he remembered that he had not noticed the gang's hand car in the toolshed. He brought the picture of its interior to his mind again and grunted with satisfaction. Its disappearance accounted for the disappearance of the gang.

The mob would now become a burlesque, having nothing upon which to act. Chuckling over the fiasco, he trotted toward the station to see that Jerry got away before the crowd discovered its impotence to commit murder as planned, and to stay on the west side of the main street in case the baffled units of the mob should head for Jerry's house. There was no longer any shouting or noise. He knew that it meant that the advance guard of rioters was cautiously scouting and approaching the lighted buildings with due regard to its own safety; and he reached the station platform before he saw the sudden flare of light on the ground before the toolshed which told of its doors being yanked open. Figures tumbled into the lighted patch and then milled for a moment before hurrying off to join their fellows on the way to attack the other two buildings.

"That you, Tex?" said a low voice close to him. "This is Murphy."

"Good!" exclaimed the marshal. "You've beat 'em, Tim. They're like dogs chasin' their tails; an' from th' beginnin' they didn't sound very business-like. But there's no tellin' what some of them may do, so you go up an' join Costigan while I take a look around Jerry's house. Where is he? His light's out."

"He went home when he heard th' yellin'," answered Murphy, "to git th' lass out av th' house an' to Costigan in case th' mob started that way. 'Tis lucky for them they didn't, an' pass within throwin' distance av me! 'Tis dynamite I'd 'a' fed 'em, with proper short fuses. Look out ye don't push that lighted cigar too close to th' darlin's!"

Tex stepped back as though he had been stung. "I'm half sorry they didn't give you a chance to use th' stuff," he growled. "Well, I reckon mobs will be out of style in Windsor by mornin'. This ain't no wolf-pack, runnin' bare-fanged to a kill, but a bunch of coyotes usin' coyote caution. We'll let Costigan stay where he is, just th' same. You better join him as soon as these fools go back to get drunker. Th' woman in this makes us play dead safe. I'll head up that way an' look things over. If I hear a blast I'll get back fast enough. Don't forget to throw 'em quick after you touch 'em to that cigar!"

"I'll count five an' let 'em go," chuckled Murphy. "I got 'em figgered close."

"Too close for me!" rejoined the marshal, moving off toward the Saunders' home.

"I'd like to stick one in Henry's pocket," said the Irishman, growling.

"D—n me for a fool!" snapped Tex, leaping into the darkness.

CHAPTER XXI

An Equal Guilt

TOMMY WATKINS, after delivering his message to Tim Murphy, hastened to the Saunders' home, where he carried out his orders, with but one exception; but the exception nullified all his efforts for a stealthy approach and a secret watch. The best cover he could find around the house was a little building near the back door in which firewood, kerosene, and odds and ends were kept. Despite the kindling and the darkness his entrance had been noiseless and he was paying himself hearty compliments upon the exploit when his head collided with a basket of clothespins which hung from a peg in the wall, and sent the basket and its contents clattering down on the kerosene can and a tin pan. He started back involuntarily and his spurred heels struck the side of a washtub which was nearly full of water, kept so against drying out and falling apart. Into this he sat with a promptness and abandon which would have filled the heart of any healthy small boy with ecstasies. Bounding out of the tub, he fell over the pile of kindling and from this instant his rage spared nothing in his way. Had he deliberately started out with the firm intention of arousing that part of Kansas he scarcely could have made a better job of it. While he cursed like a drunken sailor, and burned with rage and shame, the door was suddenly flung open and Jane, lamp in hand, stared at him in fright and determination, over the trembling muzzle of a short-barreled .38.

"Oh!" she exclaimed, the hand holding the gun now pressing against her breast. "Oh!" she repeated, and the lamp wobbled so that she tremblingly blew it out. For some moments she struggled to get back to normal, Tommy thankful that the lamp no longer revealed him in his present water-soaked condition. He felt that his flaming face would give light enough without any further aid.

He sidled out of the door, tongue-tied, crestfallen, miserable, and placed his back against the shed, intending to slip along it, and dash around the corner into the kindly oblivion of the black night.

"Wait!" she begged, sensing his intention. "Oh, my; how you frightened me! Whatever made you get into this shed, anyway? What were you trying to do?"

Here it was, right in his teeth. Tex fairly had hammered into him the warning not to frighten her—on his life he was to keep from her any thought of danger if she should see him. She had seen him, all right. She had seen entirely too much of him—and he was not to frighten her! Holy Moses! He was not to frighten her! He resolved that plenty of time should elapse before he allowed Tex Jones to see him. Not to frighten her—it was a wonder she had not died of fright.

"What on earth ever made you go in there?" she demanded, a little acerbity in her voice.

"Why, ma'am, I was hidin' from you," said the culprit. "Let me light th' lamp, ma'am, an' straighten things out in there. Everythin' slid that wasn't nailed fast. That tub, now: was you savin' th' water for anythin', ma'am? If you was I plumb spoiled it."

"No; it was only to keep the staves swelled tight—for heaven's sake, do you mean that you fell in it?" She reached out and grasped his coat, and suddenly collapsed against the building, shrieking with laughter. When she could speak she ordered him to feel for and pick up the lamp, and to lead the way into the house. "Go right into Jerry's room and change your clothes—I hope you can get his things on. But whatever made you go in there, anyway? What was it?"

"Like I done said, ma'am," he reiterated, flushing in the dark. "I was goin' to play a joke on Jerry when he came home—but I didn't aim to do no damage, ma'am, or scare you!" he earnestly assured her.

"Oh, but you were willing to scare Jerry!" she retorted.

"I don't reckon he'd 'a' been scared," he mumbled. "Here's th' lamp, ma'am, on th' step; I'll see Jerry at th' station. I'm fadin', now," and before she could utter a protest he had put down the lamp and disappeared around the house. But he did not go far. Wet clothes meant nothing to him, nothing at all in his present state of mind, and he intended to stay, and to keep his watch faithfully. And it was to his present flurried state of mind that he owed his more serious misadventure of the night, for he blundered around the second corner squarely into two figures hugging the wall and a descending gun butt filled his mental firmament with stars. He sagged to the ground without even a sigh and was quickly disarmed and bound. A soiled handkerchief was forced into his mouth and he was rolled against the wall, where he would be out of the way.

One of the two hirelings nudged the other as they stood up, putting his mouth close to his companions ear. "Hey, Ike!" he whispered. "This fool is wet as a drownded pup—wears a gun an' cowpunch clothes. He ain't the agent!"

"H—l, no!" responded Ike; "but he meant us no good, bein' here. We'll git th' agent, too. He'll be comin' soon, an' fast. Git over by th' path he uses."

Jane, somewhat vexed, had picked up the lamp and entered the house. The constantly repeated "ma'am" and the stammering explanations, which she put but little stock in, made her suddenly contrast this big, overgrown boy with a man she knew, and to Tommy's vast discredit. She had hit it: one was no more than an overgrown boy, coarse, unlearned, clumsy, embarrassed; the other, a grown man, cool, educated, masterful, unabashed. One was in his own way; the other, unobtrusive in manner but persistently haunting in his personality. She might not be able for good reasons to see Tex Jones in a room filled with people, but she could not fail to sense his presence. But the marshal was no longer to be thought of; he had taken a human life and was forever beyond the pale of her interest and affections. He had blood on his hands.

Suddenly she started and cast an apprehensive glance toward the window which faced the town. A low, chaotic roaring, indistinct in its blurred entirety, but fear impelling because of its timbre, came from the main street. A shot or two sounded flatly and the roaring rose and fell in queer, spasmodic bursts. Before she could move, a knock sounded on the door and, fearing bad news about her brother, she took a tight grip on herself and walked swiftly toward the summons, flinging the door wide open.

Henry Williams, a smirk on his face, bowed and entered, not waiting for an invitation. He forgot to remove his hat in his eagerness to place his packages on the table where she plainly could see them. Selecting the easiest chair, he seated himself on the edge of it, and tossed his sombrero against the wall.

"Nice evenin', ma'am," he said, flushing a little. "I was hopin' for more rain but don't reckon we'll git none for a spell. What we had has helped wonderful. You an' Jerry feelin' well?"

"It doesn't feel like rain, Mr. Williams," she replied, torn between her fear and mirth at the presence of this unwelcome visitor. "Both my brother and myself are as well as we can expect to be. If you'll go to the station you'll find him there—this is report night and he may not be home until quite late."

"I ain't waitin' for Jerry," explained Henry, leering. "It's just as well if he is a little late. My call is shore personal, ma'am; personal between me an' you."

She was staring at him through eyes which were beginning to sparkle with vexation. She was now beginning to accept her first, intuitive warning.

"I am not aware that there is anything of a personal nature which concerns us both," she rejoined. "I believe you must be mistaken, Mr. Williams. If you will close the door behind you on your way out I will be duly grateful. Jerry is at the station." She stepped back to let him pass, but he ignored the hints.

There came an increase in the roaring from the direction of town and she started, casting an inquiring and appealing glance at her visitor.

"Th' boys are a little wild tonight," he said, smiling evilly. "They've got so much dust that they're bustin' loose to paint th' old town proper. There ain't nothin' to be scared about."

"But Jerry: my brother!" she exclaimed fearfully. "He's alone in the office!"

"No, he ain't ma'am," replied Henry with an air meant to reassure her. "I got four good boys, deputized by th' marshal, watchin' the station in case some fool gets notions. Jones, hisself, is settin' on a bench outside, an' you know what *that* means. I allus look after my friends, ma'am." He smiled again. " 'Specially them that are goin' to be real close to me. That's why I'm here—to look after you now—now, an' all th' time, now an' forever. Just see what I brought you—sent all th' way to St. Louis for 'em, an' shore got th' very best there was. Why," he chuckled, going to the table, and so engrossed in his packages that he did not see the look of revulsion on her face, a look rapidly turning to a burning shame and anger.

"These here gloves, now—they cost me six dollars. An' lookit this Cashmere shawl—you'd think I was lyin' if I told you what *that* cost. I told th' boys you'd show 'em off handsome an' proper. Put 'em on and let's see how they look on you." He held the gifts out, looking up at her, surprised by her silence, her lack of pleased exclamations, and paused, dumbfounded at her expression.

Mortification yielded place to shame and fear; shame and fear to anger with only a trace of fear, and then rage swept all else before it. The colors playing in her cheeks fled and left them white, her lips were thin as knife blades and her eyes blazed like crucibles of molten metal. She struck wildly at the presents, sending them across the room and raised her hand to strike him. Never in all her life had she been so furious.

"Why—what's th' matter?" he asked, not believing his senses. He put out a hand to pacify her. It touched her arm and turned her into a fury, her nails scoring it deeply as she struck it away.

"What's th' matter with you?" he demanded angrily, looking up from his bleeding hand. "Oh!" he sneered, his face working with anger. "That's it, huh? All right, d—n you! I'll cussed soon show you who's boss!" he gritted, moving slowly forward. "If you won't come willin'ly, you'll come unwillin'ly! Puttin' on airs like you was too good for me, huh? I'll bust yore spirit like you was a hoss!"

She flung a quivering arm toward the door, but he pressed forward and backed her into a corner, from where she struck at him again and again, and then felt his arms about her as he wrestled with her. Her strength amazed him and he broke loose to get a more punishing hold. "Ike!" he shouted. "George! Hurry up: she's worse'n a wildcat!"

Ike's head popped in through a window, George dashing through the door, and with them at his side Henry leaped for her. She clutched at her breast and crouched, as savage and desperate as any animal of the wild. He shouted something as he closed with her and then there came a muffled roar, a flash, and a cloud of smoke spurted from between them. Henry, his glazing eyes fixing their look of fear, amazement, and chagrin, spun around against his companions, his clutching hands dragging down their arms, and slid between them. For him the mob had been incited in vain.

His two friends, stupefied for an instant, gazed unbelievingly from Jane to Henry and back again, vaguely noticing that her horror and revulsion were unnerving her and that the short-barreled Colt in her hand was wobbling in ever-widening circles. Ike recovered his self-possession first and, reaching out swiftly, knocked the wavering weapon from her hand. Shouting savagely he leaped for her as a streak of flame stabbed in through the window he had entered by, the deafening roar filling the room. He stiffened convulsively, whirled halfway around and pitched headlong under the table, dead before he touched the floor. His companion's arms jerked upward with spasmodic speed.

"Keep 'em there! Sit down, Miss Saunders," came an even, unflurried voice from the window as the marshal, hatless and coatless, hoping that George would draw, crawled into the house behind a steady gun. "Good Lord!" he muttered, glancing over the room, his eye passing the fallen .38 without betraying any recognition. "Steady!" he cried as Jane's knees buckled and she slid down the wall. "Keep 'em up!" he snarled at George as he swiftly disarmed him. "Face th' door!" As the frightened man obeyed, the marshal stepped quickly to a shelf on which stood a bottle of brandy and some glasses. He changed his gun to his left hand, snatched a cartridge from his chaps' pocket and, yanking out the lead with his teeth, emptied the shell into a glass. Quickly filling this and another he wheeled and thrust one out at the rigid prisoner. "Drink this," he ordered. "You shore need it; an' if you don't I'll blow you apart." George's stare of amazed incredulity changed to one of hope and relief and he downed the drink at a gulp. Tex slipped a pair of handcuffs over his wrists and ordered him to sit down. "Sit down in that big chair, an' close yore eyes. I got somethin' for you to do—relax!"

As he bent over Jane she stirred, opened her eyes, glanced at him, and then fixed them on the men on the floor, shuddering and shrinking from the sight; but she could not look away. "I killed him! I killed him!" she sobbed hysterically, over and over again.

"Drink this," ordered the marshal, forcing the glass between her lips. He nodded with quiet satisfaction. "Shore," he replied in an assumed matter-of-fact voice, as though it were an everyday occurrence. "Good job, too. I should have done it, myself, days ago." He held up the glass again. "Can you drink a little more of this, Miss Saunders? There are times when a little brandy is very useful." His low, even, unemotional tones were almost caressing, and she thankfully put herself in his capable hands. Slowly growing calmer she began to see things with a less blurred vision and the slow slumping of the sleepy man in the chair took her wondering attention.

"Why, is he—killed—too?" she asked shuddering.

"Oh, no; he's only half asleep," replied Tex, smiling. "Three more minutes an' he'll be sound asleep, for a dozen hours or more. Brandy has an hypnotic effect on some people, Miss Saunders, while it stimulates others. Will you please collect a small valise of your most valuable and indispensable possessions, all the money in the house, a good wrap of some kind, and allow me to escort you to Murphy and Costigan? You are leaving town, you know, never to return."

"But I've killed a man, and you are an officer of the law! Do you mean—" she paused unbelievingly.

"You shot a mad skunk in plain self-defense," he replied. "He has powerful friends and influence to avenge him. The jury would be packed and justice scorned. I'm marshal no longer, Miss Saunders. I accepted the appointment on the definite understanding that I would be marshal only as long as I could. The term has automatically come to an end. So far as this town is concerned I'm a rabid outlaw." He tore the badge from his vest and threw it on the table. "Ah! George is sleeping more soundly than he ever slept before. There's no need of gagging him, for he'll give no alarm. Please fill that satchel, Miss Saunders—time presses."

"You are a good friend, Mr. Jones; and I have wronged you," she said, her words barely audible. "My hands are as bloody as yours—and I scorned you for taking life! Take me away from here—please—please!"

"As fast as I can," replied Tex, soothingly. "You help me by filling a satchel and getting your wrap. Put your mind on your possessions, please; think what you wish to take with you, and then get them. Money? Jewels? Miscellaneous valuables, intrinsic or sentimental? Documents? Apparel? Please—you must aid me all you can if I'm to aid you. We have no time to lose!"

"But my brother—he is safe?"

"Waiting outside, tied, and gagged. I couldn't stop to free him," Tex answered. "Watkins, likewise. They laid their plans well, but the mob was a misfire and didn't keep me as busy as they counted on. Will you obey me, Miss Saunders, or must we leave bare-handed? I'll give you just three minutes by that clock—then we go."

A pious, shocked exclamation came from the window where Murphy stared suddenly into a magic gun before he was recognized. "Holy Mother!" he whispered, and then: "I found Tommy—where is Jerry?"

"Don't you ever do that again!" snapped Tex, a little

white showing in his face. "I don't know how I kept th' hammer up! You look around by that clump of scrub oak, where the path goes around the big bowlder. I nearly fell over him. Take them both with you—we'll follow close. Any signs of anyone coming from town?"

"Not yet—but ye needn't stay here all night! Hurry, miss, or there'll be a slaughter that'll shake this country!"

As Jane obeyed, Tex walked over, drew up one of George's eyelids and smiled grimly. Then he placed a hand on each of the figures on the floor and nodded, a sneer flickering over his face. In a moment Jane, still a little unsteady, returned and found the ex-marshal pinning the nickeled badge on the lapel of Henry's coat, and while it meant nothing to her then in her agitated state of mind its significance came to her later. When that badge was found she would be freed of blame for Henry's death. Opening the door Tex blew out the light and led the way. They hurried over the uneven, hard ground and soon reached the railroad, where a hand car, with Murphy, Costigan, and Tommy at the handles, waited to run them over a trail where no tracks would tell any tales.

"Head for Scrub Oak, an' stop outside th' town till Jerry's party gets away," ordered Tex. "Th' grades are mostly against you an' all of you came from th' east, where Mike's family went. They'll figger you went th' same way, if they think of th' hand car at all. It ain't likely they will, because I'm aimin' to give them something plain to read, when they're *able* to read it. Got money? Got enough to buy three good cayuses with saddles, grub, an' everythin' you need? Good! Tommy, when you get to town, go in alone, get three outfits, an' take Miss Saunders an' Jerry to Gunsight as fast as they can travel. When you get there, ask for Nelson, an' tell him Tex Ewalt says to hold off h—l an' high water before givin' up these two. I'll join you there as soon as I can. Here, listen close," and he gave a description of Gunsight's location sufficient for a rider of the plains.

"Off with you, now—let her roll gently near Buffalo Crick—she'll rumble deep crossin' that bridge an' Jake *may* be at home. So-long—get a-goin'!"

"But you?" cried Jane. "Where are you going? Surely not back into that town!" The distress and anxiety brought a smile to the ex-marshal's lips. "You must come with us! You must! You must!" she insisted almost hysterically. "You can't fight the whole town!"

"I'm bettin' he can," growled Murphy. "Here, Tex! Better take a couple av these little firecrackers! Count five an' let 'em go; but *you* better count sorta fast."

"No, thanks, Tim," laughed Tex. "I can't go with you, Miss Saunders. I've got a pack of coyotes to make fools of—see you at th' SV in four or five days. Don't you worry—it was clean self-defense. He brought it on himself. All right, Tim: get a-goin'!"

He listened to the sounds of the cautiously propelled car, the clicks of the rail joints growing softer and softer. When they had died out, he walked swiftly back to the house, where he got his hat and coat and then went on to town. Going to where the roan patiently waited for him he led it to John Graves' stable and reconnoitered the building. John was not at home on this night of excitement.

Tex forced the door, and quietly saddled the sorrel and the gray, threw a sack of corn across the latter and, leading them forth, led the three animals back of a deserted building and then went toward the hotel.

CHAPTER XXII

The False Trail and the True

THE MAUDLIN crowd was ugly and did not accept the marshal's appearance with any enthusiasm. While he had not opposed them he had warned and sent away their hoped-for victims. Frank scowls met him wherever he looked. He stopped at the table where Gus Williams and a dozen cronies, the bolder men of the town, were drinking and arguing.

"Blascom's cussed sick," he announced. "Sick as a dog. I rode out to spend th' night with him, knowin' that when that coyote section-boss sent his pack out of town there wouldn't be no reason for me to stay here an' make myself unpopular. I got a good job in this town, an' I've got a right to have friends here. Anyhow, I told Murphy that if his men came back they'd have to do their own fightin'. Reckon that's why he sent 'em along. Him an' Costigan follered 'em on th' other hand car." He glanced over the room. "Where's Hennery?" he asked. "I heard he wanted to see me."

Williams roused himself and looked up through bloodshot eyes. "Th' fool's gone courtin', I reckon; an' on a night like this, when I needed him. Don't know when he'll git back. He mus' be enjoyin' hisself, anyhow."

John Graves chuckled and endorsed the sentiment.

Tex nodded. "I reckon mebby he is, his star bein' bright tonight. Much excitement in town after I left? Station agent make any trouble?"

"A lot of chances he'd 'a' had to make any of us any trouble," sneered a miner. "I reckon he cut an' run right quick. We've been figgerin' he's better off in some other town. Been thinkin' of chasin' him out. Any objections from th' marshal of Windsor?"

"Not a cussed one," answered Tex. "He's a trouble-maker, stayin' here. Chuck him on th' train tomorrow an' send him back East, where he comes from. An' his sister, too, if you want."

William shook his head. "Not her," he said. "Henry'll never let her git away from him. He's aimin' to take care of her; an' he shore can handle her, *he* can."

"I reckon he can," agreed Tex. "I just come in to get th' doc to go out an' look at Blascom. Since he's struck it rich he's been feedin' like a fool. Them as live by canned grub, dies by canned grub, says I; an' he's close to doin' it. I got a bottle of whiskey for him, but I reckon gin will be better for his stummick. Yes, a lot better. Hey, Baldy!" he shouted. "Put me out a bottle of gin an' set up th' drinks for all hands. We'll drink to a better understandin' an' to Hennery an' his bride." He pulled the pint flask from his pocket and winked at his companions. "I got a little somethin' extra, here. Th' smoke of Scotch fires is in it. Might as well use it up," and he quickly filled the glasses on the table, discovering when too late that he had none left for himself. "Oh, well; whiskey is whiskey, to me. I'll take some of Baldy's with th' boys," and he swaggered over to the bar, tossing a gold piece on the counter.

"Where's yore badge, Marshal?" asked Baldy, curiously.

Tex quickly felt of his coat lapel and then of his vest. "Cuss it!" he growled. "I knowed I'd lose that star—th' pin was a little short to go far enough in th' socket. Oh, well," he laughed, holding up his glass, "everyone knows me now; an' they'll know me better as time goes on. Here's to Hennery!" he shouted. "Drink her standin'!"

The toast drunk to roaring jests, he took the gin and went back to Williams. "Goin' after th' doc," he remarked. "Lost my badge, too; but lemme say that anybody found wearin' it shore will have bad luck. See you all tomorrow. He's sick as a pup, Blascom is. Good night, an' sleep tight, as th' sayin' is!" he shouted laughingly and nodding at the crowd he wheeled and went out.

Once secure from observation of any curious inhabitants of the town, he ran to the horses, mounted, and rode up to the Saunders' house, a home no longer. Entering it he quickly collected a bag of provisions and then, milling the horses before the door to start a plain trail, he cantered toward the station, where he crossed the tracks and struck south for the old cattle trail.

All night he rode hard, sitting the sorrel to keep his own horse fresh, and at dawn, giving them a ration of corn each, he ate a cold and hurried breakfast and soon was on his way again. During the forenoon he let the sorrel go, riding the gray with the depleted corn sack tied to the pommel. Several hours later he threw the still further depleted sack on the roan, changed horses again and turned the gray loose. After nightfall he came within sight of the lights of a small town and, waiting until the hour was quite late, rode through it casually to lose the tracks of his horse among the countless prints on its streets. He left it along a well-traveled trail leading westward, one which would take him, eventually, to Rawlins.

In the town of Gunsight, Dave Green was polishing glasses behind his bar when a dusty, but smiling, stranger rode up to the door and called out. Grumbling, Dave waddled forth to answer the summons.

"Which way to th' SV?" asked the stranger. "I'm lookin' for my friend Nelson."

"What is it—a house-raisin' or a christenin'?" asked Dave, grinning broadly. "Th' SV's gettin right pop'lar these days—as it ought to be." Dave cogitated a moment. This man said Nelson was a friend of his; but if not, there would be no harm done to anyone on the SV. Dave was quite certain of that, with Hopalong, Red, and the outfit at Johnny's back. Still, his curiosity was aroused. "Yore name Jones, or Ewalt?" he asked.

"Ewalt," replied Tex, grinning.

Dave left the door and gravely held out his hand. "Heard tell about you, long ago," he said. "We're good friends till you horn into a poker game that I'm settin' in. Heard about you this mornin', too. A tenderfoot, a cowpunch, an' a reg'lar picture in skirts stopped an' asked me what you did. Also wanted to know if I had seen Jones or Ewalt. You just foller that Juniper trail," and he gave a description tiresome, and needlessly detailed, to a man to whom compass points would have sufficed. "Jones comin', too? Don't know I ever heard of him."

"Jones is dead," said Tex with touching sorrow. "Th' pore ol' soul, we'll never see him more. He had buttons runnin' up his back, an' buttons down before."

"Too bad," replied Dave, but he was suspicious of the other's grief. He shook his head. "Life shore is uncertain. You tell Johnny if he's havin' a party that I ain't too fat to ride that far, not if I'm invited. I ain't much on dancin', but I'll do my best."

Tex nodded, thanked him for his information and went on, gradually becoming lost in introspective musings.

"Omar," he muttered, shaking his head sadly, "I ain't got no right. I'm hard-boiled, an' I've reached purty low levels th' last twenty years. There ain't no human meanness, no human weaknesses, hardly, that I ain't seen. My view of life is so cynical that it near scares me, now. I lost my illusions years ago, an' I'm allus lookin' for th' basest motives for a man's actions. Besides, I'm forty-odd years old—an' that's *too* old.

"Now you take Tommy Watkins. He's fresh, young, chock-a-block with illusions; trustin', ambitious, steady. He's clean, body an' mind. When he grows up, ten years from now, he'll be a purty fair sort of a young man. It shore does beat all, Omar."

A little farther along he drew a deep breath and patted the roan. "Omar, I've made up my mind: Youth should be for youth; illusions, for illusions; freshness, for freshness; innocence, for innocence. Her purity deserves better than my mildewed soul—if a man's got one." After a moment's silence he patted the horse again. "Omar, yore name brings somethin' back to me:

Ah Love! could you and I with Him conspire
To grasp this sorry Scheme of Things entire,
*   Would not we shatter it to bits—and then*
*   Remould it nearer to the Heart's Desire!*

Raising his head he saw a rattlesnake sunning itself on a rocky patch of ground near the trail and his gun leaped into crashing life. The snake writhed, trying in vain to coil. A second shot stretched it lifeless.

"There, d—n you!" shouted Tex, shaking his fist at the quivering body, "that's how I feel!" and, the burst of passion gone as quickly as it had come, he shook his head and rode on again, calm and determined. At last he came to the top of the last hill hiding the ranchhouse and drew rein as he looked down into the north branch of the SV valley. A boy was riding along the bottom of the slope and Tex hailed him.

"Hey, sonny!" shouted the ex-marshal. "I'm lookin' for Hopalong Cassidy. Know where he is?"

"He's at th' house!" replied the boy. "Yo're Tex Ewalt! Foller me, an' I'll beat you to him!"

"Bet yo're Charley!" responded Tex. "Yo're shore goin' to ride some, cowboy, if you aim to beat me!" and a race was on.

There came a flurry of movement at the ranchhouse door and three men ran to their saddled horses. A sudden cloud of dust rolled up and the three, bunched leg to leg, raced toward the galloping newcomer. Heedless of Charley's vexatious appeal they shot past him and kept on while he swung his pony around and saw them sweep up to the slowing roan and surround him and his rider. More soberly, after a hilarious welcome, the four, with Charley endeavoring to wedge into shifting openings not half large enough for his pony, they rode up to the ranchhouse, where Jerry had run out to meet them, Margaret Nelson at his heels. As soon as he could Tex asked for Jane and learned that she was resting.

"She has been under a very heavy strain, Mr. Ewalt," Margaret told him. "She asked that you see her as soon as you came; but she is sleeping, now, and it will be better for her if you wait. Her remorse is as great as her horror and fatigue."

"I suppose so," replied Tex. "That's the woman of it. She shot a beast in plain self-defense and now she's remorseful. Shucks—it's all my fault. I should have done it, myself, days before."

"I didn't say just what I think is causing her remorse," replied Margaret, smiling enigmatically; "but that is something a man should find out for himself," and, turning quickly, she entered the house.

Tex stared after her and then around the circle of happy, grinning faces. An answering smile crept to his own, a smile wistful, but shaded with pain.

The next few days were busy ones from a conversational standpoint, for there was a great deal to talk about. Tex learned the history of the SV's rejuvenation, and his friends eagerly listened to the news he brought from Montana, and to the messages he brought from their friends; while Jane, much better because of the rest she had had, sat by the cheerful group, smiling at the perfect accord between its units and rapidly changing her ideas of western men. Here she saw friendships which seemed to be founded on the eternal rock, unshakable, unquestioning. She found it almost impossible to believe that these thin-lipped, yet kindly and smiling men, whose trick of looking out through narrowed lids at first made her wonder, each had killed again and again, as Margaret had told her. To her they were gravely kind, courteous, and deferential, accepting her without question, their manner a soothing assurance as to her safety. Jerry and Tommy were unquestionably accepted and made part of the happy circle—they were friends of Tex Ewalt, whom she now knew by his right name. Johnny's boyish enthusiasm and mischievous smile made it hard for her to believe that he, single-handed, had overcome the odds against him and cleared this range of its undesirable inhabitants. Margaret's proud account of his deeds rang true, and Jane knew that they were true.

There they all sat on the front porch, telling anecdotes on each other which amazed Jane, speaking of remarkable exploits in matter-of-fact voices. She learned of Tex's part in the saving of Buck Peter's ranch, and gradually pieced together the story of his activities in Windsor. Prodded by Tex, at last Johnny and Hopalong gave a grudging exhibition of revolver shooting which made her catch her breath. Tex Ewalt had been right: these two cheerful men could ride into Windsor and wipe it from the map; and she no longer feared the appearance of any of the Williams' friends. If they could find and follow the trail, let them!

Tex was the quietest man in the party, and she was pleased because he spoke only in the vernacular. She had not heard him deviate from it for one instant. He had no wish to "show off" at the expense of his roughly speaking friends. Tommy's garrulity, considering how little he really had to say, sounded like the prattle of a child among grown-ups; but he was a good, well-meaning boy. Daily he spoke of getting work on the Double X, where Lin Sherwood could use another rider; but he had made no attempt to go, preferring to stay where *she* was and to follow her about at every opportunity.

Then came the afternoon when Johnny volunteered to show his guests about the ranch and they had set out, Tex remaining behind. Jane had felt a restraint at the thought of how close she and the ex-marshal would be thrown together on this ranch, but soon found it to be groundless. Deferential, reserved, friendly, he had not obtruded, and apparently had not noticed Tommy's attentions. They rode off, Jerry with their host, Tommy at the side of Jane. When down in the main valley Johnny had turned off to look at the fenced-in quicksands, Jerry going with him to see the now harmless death trap, and Tommy remained behind with her; and when they returned they found a flushed Jane and a despondent Tommy. The following morning when she sat down to a late breakfast with Mr. Arnold, Johnny's father-in-law, she learned quite casually that Tommy had gone to the Double X and that the rest of the men, her brother included, had ridden up to the north wire to make some repairs. Arnold explained about the difficulty of keeping the posts up along the bottom of the ravine where he had suffered his broken leg, and he told her of the fondness of the cattle for the wilderness of brush and of the difficult task of running a round-up on that part of the ranch.

"Let me throw a saddle on yore horse, Miss Saunders," he suggested. "It will make a pleasant ride for you; an' you can take 'em up some lunch if you like.

They've got a bigger task than they think, for th' ravine floor is solid rock. I'll send Charley with you—he's on th' rampage because he overslept and I wouldn't let him go up and bother them. But he might as well go."

She thought for a moment, and then turned a grave and pitiful face to him.

"I feel that I can ask you anything, Mr. Arnold; and I'm so upset."

"You certainly can, Miss Saunders," he replied, abandoning the vernacular in response to her way of speaking.

She hurriedly told him of the killing of Henry Williams, of the blood on her hands, but avoided the real appeal, the question she must find her own answer to. He heard her through, and, arising, placed a fatherly hand on her shoulder.

"Jane," he said, slowly shaking his head. "Environment, circumstances, change all things. There's not a man on this ranch that doesn't feel proud of what he knows about you. A woman has as much right, and often a greater need, to defend herself, as a man has. Don't you worry about that beast; and don't you worry about anyone coming down here after you. We can muster forty fighting men, if we need them, purely on Johnny's say-so. We're all proud of you. Now I'll saddle your horse while Peggy puts up the lunch. You and Charley can easily carry it between you. There's no place down here where you can't safely go; but please keep in the saddle while you're on the range. These cattle are dangerous to anyone afoot."

While the simple preparations were being made she heard Charley's exultant whoops and soon she rode with him toward the upper end of the small valley, listening to his worshiping chatter about his heroes. Now he had a new one, the man who could pull poker hands out of a fellow's nose, eyes, and ears.

"He'd 'a' got that Hennery feller, too," he averred, "only you beat him out. Gee, Miss Saunders! Wish I'd 'a' been there! I ain't never shot nobody yet—but you just wait, that's all! I heard Tex say he'd 'a' shot up th' whole d—d town if they'd tried to bother you—an' Hoppy said he could 'a' done it, *easy*! Hoppy knows, too. Why don't you like Tex, Miss Saunders? I think he's aces-up!"

"Why, I do, Charley. Whatever made you ask me that?"

"Well, if you do, Tex don't think so," he grumbled. "You know that pile of rock, up on th' hill where th' Gunsight trail winds like a letter S?"

She nodded. She could see it plainly from her window.

"Well, I was layin' up there, keepin' watch for that Williams' gang, an' he never even reckoned anybody was near him!" he boasted. "Takes a good man to find me when I don't want him to, I tell you. Injuns can't, an' they're cussed cute, Hoppy says."

"Who was it who didn't see you?"

"Tex," chuckled the boy. "He come walkin' along like there wasn't nobody around, an' he sorta slammed hisself down on th' rock next to th' top one. You an' Tommy an' Jerry was ridin' back from th' main valley. We could just see you, me an' him, only he didn't know *I* was there. After awhile we could see plain. Jerry rode off to look at somethin', an kinda fell back, leavin' you an' Tommy goin' on without him. I was watchin' Tex, because he had a funny look on his face. He just looked steady, an' when he saw you two ridin' along together, he threw out his arms an' said somethin' about bein' like Jerry. Somethin' about falling back an' seein' you an' Tommy ridin' through life together—as if anybody would ride as long as that! Tell you what: These grown-ups say some cussed foolish things. There was tears in his eyes—him, a grown-up, gun-fightin' son-of-a-gun! Huh! An' they used to tease *me* when *I* cried! What you think about that?" He looked eagerly at her for the answer and then snorted in frank disgust. "Cuss it—an' yo're snifflin', too! I'll be a son-of-a-gun!"

"You mustn't tell anyone about it, Charley!" she pleaded. "They won't understand!"

"I won't," he promised. "Don't blame you for bein' ashamed. Tex would 'a' been, too, if he knowed I saw him. Then mebby he wouldn't go up there every night an' watch yore window till the light goes out, an' I wouldn't have nobody to trail. Reckon he's scared that Williams gang will trail you down here? Huh! With him settin' up there, me roamin' loose, an' with Johnny, Hoppy, an' Red in th' house, I shore wish they *would* come a-pokin' their noses around here! I tell you, things'd shore pop. If Tex could clean out their whole town all alone, they'd shore have a pleasant time down here ag'in' him an' his friends! Gee!"

After supper the nightly gathering on the porch passed a pleasant hour or two and then dwindled as its members retired, the two women and Charley going first. Jerry followed soon afterward and not much later Red and Hopalong left to go to the bunkhouse, where they now were berthed. Arnold soon went into the house, to the room which Tex stubbornly had refused to occupy, the latter preferring the bunkhouse with his old friends. After a cigarette or two Johnny said good night and left his companion alone. Tex arose, paced restlessly to and fro across the yard and, wheeling abruptly, went toward the corral. He had not been gone very long when Charley, noiselessly crawling out of the window of the room he shared with his father, froze in his tracks as he heard a noise beyond the summer kitchen. He had Red's Winchester, which he had taken from the gun rack in the dining-room, and he scouted cautiously toward the suspicious sounds. The moonlight let him see plainly, and he drew back behind the corner of the building as Jane rode away, leaving the light burning brightly in her room.

Charley frankly was puzzled. "Somethin's goin' on," he cogitated. "I was goin' to stalk Tex—now I dunno. Shucks! He can look out for hisself, but she might get lost. Reckon I'll foller her." He suited action to the words and soon was riding after her, keeping out of her sight with a woodcraft worthy of his elders.

She led him along the Gunsight trail, closer and closer to the S it made up the rocky hill, and because of the view commanded by the rocky pile on the summit, he had to dismount, picket his horse, and proceed on foot, working from cover to cover, often on hands and knees.

Tex had taken his time, buried in thought, oblivious to everything outside of himself. He followed the well-marked trail instinctively and soon reached the top of the hill, where he sat quietly in the saddle for a few minutes. Finally, shaking his head, he dismounted and listlessly walked to the place of his nightly vigil. Seating himself on the top-most bowlder he gazed steadily at the yellow light of the distant window and, like many men of his class, given to solitude, he argued his problem aloud. It seemed that often he could think more clearly that way.

This could not go on. Tomorrow he would start back to Montana, and he soon arose to return to the SV, to spend his last night there. As he went back to his horse another verse came to his mind, a verse of finality, and one fitting the present situation. He laughed bitterly and flung out his arms:

And when like her, O Sákí, you shall pass
Among the Guests Star-scatter'd on the Grass,
And in your blissful errand reach the spot
Where I made One—turn down an empty Glass!

Suddenly he stiffened, his hands leaping instinctively to his guns. Then he let them fall to his sides and stared unbelievingly: "Miss Saunders!" he exclaimed in amazement. "Why—what are you—?" and ceased, tongue-tied.

"You are—going away?" she asked, her voice break-ing, speaking so low he barely could hear her words.

"Tomorrow."

She hung her head for a moment and then turned a wistful, anxious face up to him. "I—I heard what you have been saying. O Tex—I—I am going with you!"

TOR BOOKS

 Check out these titles from
CLARENCE MULFORD

Westerns available from

TRAPPER'S MOON • Jory Sherman
"Jory Sherman takes us on an exhilarating journey of discovery with a colorful group of trappers and Indians. It is quite a ride."—Elmer Kelton

CASHBOX • Richard S. Wheeler
"A vivid portrait of the life and death of a frontier town."—*Kirkus Reviews*

SHORTGRASS SONG • Mike Blakely
"*Shortgrass Song* leaves me a bit stunned by its epic scope and the power of the writing. Excellent!"—Elmer Kelton

CITY OF WIDOWS • Loren Estleman
"Prose as picturesque as the painted desert..."—*The New York Times*

BIG HORN LEGACY • W. Michael Gear
Abriel Catton receives the last will and testament of his father, Web, and must reassemble his family to search for his father's legacy, all the while pursued by the murdering Braxton Bragg and desire for revenge and gold.

SAVAGE WHISPER • Earl Murray
When Austin Well's raid is foiled by beautiful Indian warrior Eagle's Shadow Woman, he cannot forget the beauty and ferocity of the woman who almost killed him or figure out a way to see her again.